The PRINCE'S BRIDE

*Also by Victoria Alexander
in Large Print:*

The Marriage Lesson
The Husband List

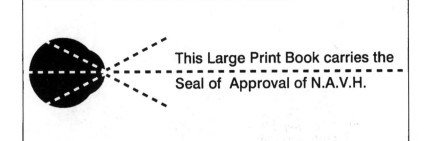

This Large Print Book carries the
Seal of Approval of N.A.V.H.

WITHDRAWN

**Large Print Ale
Alexander, Victoria, 1965-
The prince's bride**

NEWARK PUBLIC LIBRARY
NEWARK, OHIO

GAYLORD M

The PRINCE'S BRIDE

VICTORIA ALEXANDER

WHEELER
PUBLISHING

Published in 2002 by arrangement with Avon Books, an imprint of HarperCollins Publishers.

Wheeler Romance Series.

The text of this Large Print edition is unabridged. Other aspects of the book may vary from the original edition.

Cover design by Thorndike Press Staff.

Set in 16 pt. Plantin by Elena Picard.

Printed in the United States on permanent paper.

Library of Congress Control Number: 2002105934
ISBN 1-58724-267-2 (lg. print : hc : alk. paper)

This book is dedicated to
Lucia Macro,
with affection and thanks
for your wisdom,
your guidance and your great laugh.

Prologue

Autumn, 1811

The chill wind blew through the trees, plucking dried leaves from their rest to dance unfettered beneath the harvest moon. It was a night fraught with the promise, the threat, of ghosts and goblins and other creatures that lingered in bad dreams and menacing shadows. A less determined child would have turned back at the first odd sound, if indeed he or she had had the courage to brave the dark in the first place. Ten-year-old Jocelyn Shelton was made of sterner stuff.

If you bury your wish beneath the light of the full moon it will come true.

Jocelyn knelt on the hard ground and tilted the paper in her hand under the moonlight in an effort to once again read the lines she'd labored over in recent days. Not that she didn't already know every word by heart. Still, when one's future was at stake, one shouldn't leave any detail to chance. If she'd come to a single conclusion

7

in her young life, that was certainly it.

She nodded with satisfaction, carefully re-folded the paper and tucked it under her knee to keep it from blowing away. It wouldn't do to have to chase it with nothing to see by but the light of the moon. Besides, day or night, she'd scarcely be able to see it at all past a stone's throw, which, until recently, she'd always thought perfectly normal. Who would have ever suspected other people could see much farther than she? Imagine.

This was as good a spot as any. Jocelyn had taken a large, battered spoon from the kitchen. She'd need it now to dig.

Molly, their one remaining house servant and more a family member than anything else, had told her if she buried a wish, forest fairies, wood nymphs, and all manner of magical folk would help make it come true.

Since then, she and her younger sister, Becky, had buried any number of wishes. In truth the grounds of Shelbrooke Manor were littered with tiny burial spots planted with dreams. It was one of many secrets the girls shared. Their older sisters, Emma, who was ten-and-four, and Marianne, a year younger than Emma, probably wouldn't understand and might well discourage the sowing of wishes in the night. Even if some of those wishes had been for fine husbands with great fortunes for all four of them someday.

Jocelyn and Becky were not so silly as to

believe they could wish for everything. Even Molly's magic couldn't return their mother to this life. Still it would be pleasant to at least remember her. Jocelyn had been only three when Mama had died, Becky a year younger, and they had nothing to recall of her save a vague scent, faint in the air when old clothes were shaken out in the rooms she'd once occupied.

No, they'd wished for things that they hoped could come true. They'd wished that Papa would stay at home at Shelbrooke Manor instead of spending his days gaming in London. Privately, Jocelyn had wished, at the very least, he could win now and again. But neither of those wishes had come true. Whenever their father did make an appearance it was brief and more often than not to strip the walls of a painting or divest the rooms of yet another valuable piece he could sell.

They'd wished their older brother, Richard, would come home as well. On those rare visits when he did appear he seemed nice enough, but Aunt Louella said he was little better than Papa and was heading down the very same path to ruin. Aunt Louella said the Shelton men were all alike and not to be trusted. Shelton women had to depend upon themselves.

Precisely what Jocelyn was doing.

The hole was deep enough to fit her hand in, and while that was the standard size she and Becky had agreed on for previous wishes, Jocelyn kept working at the ground with her spoon, ignoring the knowledge that it would be easier with Becky's help. This was not something she wished to share, even with Becky, and it was far too important to waste on a shallow hole.

This was no mere wish. It was, in fact, a plan for her life carefully considered and laid out on paper. Hopes and dreams mingled with rules and regulations but it was far more than that. Jocelyn called it a *treatise*, which seemed terribly important. She had no idea what a *treatise* was, but the word did have a grand sound to it.

She'd tried to use as many big words as possible, not all of which she understood but all of which sounded as delightful as *treatise*. She'd picked them up mostly from Marianne, who usually had her nose in a book, fancied herself quite literary, and used big words all the time.

Jocelyn rather liked the sound of words, the way they filled her mouth and slipped off her tongue even though it scarcely mattered. She was destined to be the prettiest one of the family. Everybody said so, and as such, she would never have to worry about silly things like words.

Still, words were very important when it came to wishes or treatises. She'd considered every one with a great deal of care. She'd left nothing out, nothing to chance.

Jocelyn Shelton wanted a prince, and more, she wanted to be a princess.

The hole was deep enough now for her fist and halfway up her elbow. She nodded with satisfaction. This would do.

She pulled the paper from beneath her knee, held it with both hands against her heart, squeezed her eyes closed tight, and sent a quick prayer heavenward — all the while ignoring a tiny twinge of guilt. It was one thing to ask magical creatures for help for the family, but the vicar frowned on prayer for selfish gain, droning on and on about rewards not in this world but the next. Still, she'd prefer to get hers while still alive, thank you. Besides, if fairies and nymphs couldn't make her dreams come true, did it really hurt to put in a word with the Almighty?

Jocelyn placed the paper gently in the bottom of the hole and pushed the loose dirt over it, packing down the earth firmly. She sat back on her heels and considered her work. There really wasn't much more she could do. She'd written down everything she could think of about princes as well as everything that came to mind about the behavior and deportment of princesses. Jocelyn knew full well that was crucial to success.

After all, one couldn't possibly marry a prince unless one was a true princess. It would certainly be easier to be a princess as the daughter of a king instead of the daughter of a mere earl, but being a real princess had nothing to do with the circumstances of birth. Jocelyn wasn't sure exactly when she had decided that but the conviction had taken root a long time ago, fueled by her sisters' books and Molly's stories and Becky's dreams.

Jocelyn knew, somewhere deep inside where such things were measured and determined, that she was indeed a princess. A true princess. She was as certain of that as she was of the morning sunrise. She simply had to convince the rest of the world. And grow up, of course. Then someday when a prince happened along she'd be ready. He'd recognize a true princess and they'd be married at once and live in a palace with lots of money and lots of servants and very, very good sweets. And her aunt and sisters would never have to worry about leaky roofs or mending well-worn clothes or making do.

The face of the man in the moon grinned down at her as if amused by her thoughts. She smiled back with confidence.

"I will find a prince and I will be a princess someday," she said in a firm whisper. "Just you wait. Someday."

It was entirely possible. No, it was inevitable. It was her fate. She knew it with every fiber of her being.

Lady Jocelyn Shelton was destined to be a prince's bride.

A Treatise on Princes and Princesses and Other Related Matters
by Lady Jocelyn Shelton, age 10

Part One: On Princes

In order to marry a prince, one first needs to find a prince. Storybooks are filled with all kinds of princes but it does seem to me, in real life, they are extraordinarily difficult to find. Therefore, one should probably travel to other countries where castles with towers and lovely colored flags sit on the tops of tall mountains. Such countries are surely overrun with princes. There are English princes but they do not seem nearly as interesting as foreign princes nor as handsome.

If one can't travel far, the best place in England to find a prince is London as it is the grandest city in the whole world according to Aunt Louella. London attracts a lot of princes.

A prince should be handsome and have a great fortune and a wonderful castle. He should be kind to the peasants and give them festivals once a year. He should be willing to give his wife's sisters very big dowries just to make his

13

wife happy. And he should be able to laugh and tell a good joke.

A prince should rule gently but firmly and only put people in dungeons who really, really deserve it. And even then not for very long. He should take away all their money instead. That would serve them right. Bad people do not deserve money.

A prince should always have new clothes, a sound roof, and very good sweets.

And he should be willing to slay dragons for his princess.

Chapter 1

Late Spring, 1819

It was generally acknowledged, in the circles of polite society, that staring was not permissible — *never* permissible, regardless of the circumstances. Yet each and every guest in the too crowded ballroom — from jaded rakes to overdressed matrons, from sweet young things in the first flower of youth to elderly lords on their last legs, from the envious to the curious to the vastly amused — did indeed stare . . . or at least observed carefully, which was much the very same thing.

Oh, discretion was in order, of course. There were no open mouths or overly wide eyes. No pointed fingers or upraised brows. Besides, regardless of the rules of proper behavior, no one who was anyone would ever admit he was not already privy to the liaison unveiling itself before the very eyes of the ton. And everyone in attendance at the gala reception given by the Marquess of

Throubridge for the crown prince of Avalonia was indeed someone, or at least believed himself to be someone, which was nearly as important.

Still, even the illusion of good breeding and fine manners could not prevent a fair amount of discreet tittering behind fans, an inordinate number of speculative smiles, and more than a little nudging of elbows.

And why not? It wasn't every day London had a foreign prince in its midst. That he was handsome and wealthy and unmarried made his every move of utmost interest to the mothers of eligible daughters as well as to the daughters themselves. That he was showing particular attention to one young lady made him the subject of intense curiosity for everyone else. And that the young woman in question was the incomparable Lady Jocelyn Shelton made him the envy of the majority of men, married or otherwise.

Whatever their circumstances, each and every guest in the room watched Prince Alexei Frederick Berthold Ruprecht Pruzinsky escort the lady from the dance floor. Jocelyn herself was well aware of the scrutiny. Indeed, she could feel it almost as if the gazes directed toward her had a physical presence: long, probing fingers of curiosity. She lifted her chin the tiniest notch and tried to maintain as natural a smile as possible.

Not that she was uncomfortable at the at-

16

tention. On the contrary. She reveled in it. She simply didn't want to appear too smug, too satisfied, and too, too triumphant.

At this particular moment, Lady Jocelyn Shelton, sister of the Earl of Shelbrooke and relation by marriage to the Duke of Roxborough and the wealthy Effington family, believed, regardless of the differences in their stations, that she would soon be the bride of the heir of the House of Pruzinsky, the crown prince of the Kingdom of Greater Avalonia.

The prince bent closer to speak low into her ear. "I had quite forgotten the English tendency to stare."

"Had you, Your Highness?" Jocelyn said lightly. "I was under the impression that you rarely forgot anything. Or that you were especially bothered by being the subject of observation."

"Quite right." He smiled that particular smile worn only by men who have no question as to their standing in the world. "When one knows one's own worth, one expects such attention. But then I need not tell you that." He studied her in a satisfied manner. "You are as aware of your worth as I am of mine."

She ignored his comment as she could not deny it and raised a brow. "Are all royal princes as arrogant as you, Your Highness?"

His eyes widened with surprise and she feared she'd gone too far. Then he laughed, the kind of unfettered, rather personal laugh that ensured the continued attention of on-lookers and upped the stakes of any number of wagers made in recent days in the betting books of London.

"Indeed we are, my dear. Arrogance is a privilege of rank and the higher the station, the easier it is accepted. Besides, I see no need for false humility." He shrugged. "Surely my attitude does not surprise you?"

"Not at all. Since our first meeting, nearly everyone of my acquaintance has made it a point to tell me all they know of you. About your arrogance and your reputation and" — she paused for effect — "your women."

"You are extremely impertinent, my lady." A wicked gleam danced in his eye. "I have always enjoyed impertinence."

"I have heard that as well, Your Highness."

He laughed again, the intimate nature of the sound increasing her confidence. They reached the edge of the dance floor and he turned toward her. "You have not told me if you liked the flowers I sent today."

"Haven't I? Do forgive me. They were lovely." She tilted her head to gaze up at him, allowing the slight enigmatic smile men had likened to those seen on Renaissance portraits to graze her lips. A smile well practiced and always well received. "As were those delivered yesterday and the day before and the day before that. In truth though, we

18

are inundated in blossoms. Your generosity is appreciated yet it seems a bit excessive."

"Only a bit? I shall have to do better then." He caught her hand and raised it to his lips.

"Better, Your Highness?"

"Alexei. Perhaps it is too soon for such familiarity but . . ." His gaze never left hers. "I am an impatient man, my dear. And my position permits me to be. I feel no need for subtlety when I see something I want."

Anticipation shivered in her blood. "And what is that?"

"I want precisely what I wanted when I first danced with you last week. And again each and every time I have seen you since then. And now." He brushed his lips across the back of her gloved hand. "You, my dear Jocelyn, are what I want."

A wave of triumph swept through her. It was all she could do to keep from grinning like a lunatic. A genuine, wealthy, handsome prince wanted to marry her. Prince Alexei Frederick Berthold and so forth and so on wanted her to be his bride. His princess. And one day . . . his queen.

"Am I?" she murmured with a collected air she didn't feel but which suited a future princess nonetheless. Would he ask her here? Now? In front of everyone? It would be scandalous, yet also terribly romantic and wonderfully satisfying.

"You are indeed." He lowered her hand yet did not release it. "But this is far too public a place to discuss such matters."

She brushed aside a stab of disappointment. He was right, of course; this was not the place for a proposal. By rights, the prince — no, Alexei. She should start thinking of him now as Alexei if she was to marry him. *Alexei* should ask her brother for her hand.

But Richard was still in America with his pregnant wife and her parents, the Duke and Duchess of Roxborough. This left only her Aunt Louella to grant permission for her to wed — or perhaps Thomas Effington, the Marquess of Helmsley and son of the duke and duchess, could officially approve of the match.

Jocelyn and her sisters were staying at Effington House for the season and Thomas was to wed her sister Marianne next week at his family's country estate. Of course, at eighteen, Jocelyn was of age and well able to make such decisions on her own. After all, hadn't she already refused two proposals thus far this season without anyone's opinion but her own? Besides, Alexei was a prince and ordinary rules really didn't apply to him.

Alexei leaned closer. "There is a music room here. Far enough from the crowd for private discussion of . . . delicate matters. I shall be there, alone, in an hour. Join me."

"Without a chaperone?" She cast him a

teasing smile. "Surely you don't wish me to indulge in something so improper?"

"There is no need for chaperones between us. Between Alexei and Jocelyn." His tone was light but his brown eyes simmered. His fingers tightened around hers. "An hour then."

She gently pulled her hand away. It would not do to seem too eager. "We shall see, Your Highness. Alexei."

"Will we?" His eyes narrowed slightly. "I warn you, I am not accustomed to refusal."

Jocelyn met his gaze firmly. "And I am not accustomed to orders."

He considered her for a long moment, and again she wondered if she'd pushed him too far. Still, prince or not, if he was to be her husband he should understand she would not be treated as a mere servant subject to his demands. She would certainly do her duty as a wife, and a princess, but she was neither wife nor princess yet. At last he smiled and nodded with approval. "You shall do, my dear. You shall do very well."

He escorted her to the spot where Marianne stood with Thomas and her younger sister, Becky, bowed slightly, and took his leave. But not before his gaze met hers, and she knew he had no doubt that she would indeed meet him.

If Aunt Louella were here it would be impossible to slip away but she had fallen earlier in the day, injuring her ankle, and was forced to stay at home tonight. Jocelyn watched Alexei's tall figure stride off into the crowd that parted at his passage, and realized he was right. She would keep their appointment.

"Well, that was certainly interesting," Marianne murmured.

"To nearly everyone in the room," Becky said dryly.

Marianne studied Jocelyn carefully. "What on earth did he say to you?"

"Oh, nothing of any significance." Jocelyn lifted a shoulder in a casual shrug.

Becky snorted in a most unladylike way. "Not one of us believes that. Tell us —"

"I don't like him," Thomas cut in. He took a sip from the glass in his hand, his gaze fixed firmly on the prince.

"You're being overprotective again, Thomas," Marianne chided. "The man is really charming."

"And he's a prince. A real prince with his own country and castle and . . . and a crown I would imagine." Becky directed her question to Jocelyn. "Does he have a crown? With jewels and gold and whatever else?"

"I have no idea," Jocelyn said loftily. "I would think so."

"I would hope so. It would scarcely be worth the effort of being a prince without a crown." Becky's gaze shifted back to Alexei.

"Of course, even without a crown he is rather dashing."

"Quite handsome really." Marianne too studied the prince.

"And very wealthy," Jocelyn said softly. He was, in fact, all she had ever wanted.

"I don't like him," Thomas repeated.

"Thomas, we heard you the first time." Marianne's tone was gentle. "And as much as I hate to point this out to you, *you* don't have to like him."

"Good." Thomas huffed. "Because I don't and I am an excellent judge of character."

The sister exchanged long-suffering glances. It was not necessary to mention it aloud. Even Marianne, who loved Thomas with all her heart, was well aware that his assessment of the character of other men, particularly when it came to those men who showed any interest in the Shelton sisters, was scarcely accurate.

"I don't trust him either." Thomas's eyes narrowed. "All those flowers. A man who goes to such extremes is up to no good."

"Come now. You've been known to go to extremes on occasion." Marianne paused thoughtfully. "However, I can certainly see your point."

"You can?" Suspicion sounded in his voice.

"Most definitely." A teasing spark showed in Marianne's eye. "I know from personal experience that a man willing to go to such lengths is usually up to no good."

Thomas stared at Marianne for a moment, then a grin spread across his face. "That was entirely different, my love. My intentions have always been honorable."

Jocelyn coughed. Becky choked. Marianne laughed. It was amusing to hear Thomas's declaration of his honorable intentions, given the merry chase Marianne had led him on before agreeing to marriage. A chase where *farcical* might well be a more appropriate term than *honorable*.

Thomas cast the sisters a quelling glance. "Say what you will, you cannot deny my interest has always been in marriage."

He took Marianne's hand and drew it to his lips. Only a fool would fail to see the love they shared. Jocelyn's heart tightened at the sight and she pushed away the disturbing thought that the gleam in Alexei's eye when he looked at her bore little resemblance to the look in Thomas's. But love was not what she was seeking.

Marianne turned her attention back to her younger sister. "Come now, Jocelyn. We are all dying to know. What did he say to you?"

"Not a thing." Jocelyn struggled to maintain her reserved composure. "Really."

"Do tell, Jocelyn," Becky said impatiently. "Does he wish to marry you?"

The grin Jocelyn could no longer contain broke on her face.

Becky's eyes widened. "He does, doesn't he? Has he asked you yet?"

"I'm the one he should ask," Thomas said firmly. The sisters ignored him.

"We cannot bear this another moment." Marianne took Jocelyn's hands. "Has he asked you to marry him?"

"Not yet." Jocelyn shook her head. "But he has indicated he will." Tonight.

"Are you certain?" Marianne's voice was cautious. "Don't princes tend to marry, well, princesses?"

"I *will* be a princess when we marry." Jocelyn couldn't help sounding a bit smug. "And it's precisely because he is a prince that he can marry whomever he chooses."

"How wonderful." Excitement rang in Becky's voice. "Do I get to be a princess too?"

"No," Thomas said wryly.

Becky wrinkled her nose.

"Is this truly what you want?" Marianne stared at her sister. "Do you love him then?"

"It's what I've always wanted," Jocelyn said firmly, ignoring the second question. "And now I shall have it."

Marianne's gaze searched her face. Her voice was soft. "And is it worth what you won't have? What you might never have?"

Without warning the years of their impoverished childhood flashed through her head. Of making do with little. Of overly mended clothes and frugal meals and leaking roofs. Of dreams of wealth and position and, yes, a prince. And any doubts in the back of her mind vanished.

"It's what I've always wanted," she said again and favored her sister with a reassuring smile. "I shall be very happy."

"Then that's all that matters." Marianne returned her smile, squeezed her hands and released them.

"I should think there are all kinds of plans to be made." Becky chattered on and Jocelyn nodded at appropriate moments but her mind wandered.

Alexei was not in her sight and the gathering had turned its collective attention elsewhere. Still, speculation hovered in the air. Jocelyn and the prince had already given gossips a great deal to fuel their talk. She was confident tomorrow the curious would have a royal announcement to discuss and consider and dissect. It would be the talk of London. And why not? It would be the match of the season. Maybe of any season.

In something less than an hour, all her dreams would come true.

Jocelyn pushed open the door. "Your Highness?"

Jocelyn thought it was a very good sign that it had been remarkably easy to slip away from the reception and find the music room.

But the chamber was empty.

She couldn't possibly be early. If anything she was a bit tardy. Perhaps he had already come and been too impatient to wait for her, though more likely, he was making *her* wait for *him*. She wouldn't, of course. Not for longer than a minute or two at any rate.

She glanced around and stepped farther into the room, closing the door behind her. It was impressively large, a space eminently suited for the musicales the ton was so fond of publicly but privately and individually abhorred. There were sofas scattered here and there. A large shape, probably a pianoforte, stood near the far wall, which she assumed, from the glittering reflections, was lined with windows or possibly French doors. She was quite good at interpreting her surroundings, but then she'd had her entire life to practice.

She heaved a resigned sigh. Maybe she should give serious consideration to her sister's continuing suggestion that she at least try donning spectacles. It did get wearing to live one's life within a small circle of clarity bounded by a large fuzzy, indistinct world. Jocelyn freely admitted that nothing more than vanity kept her vision impaired, and acknowledged it might not make one whit of difference. After all, Marianne wore glasses and she was about to marry the son of a duke. Jocelyn could surely do as well with spectacles.

But Jocelyn was to marry a prince. A smug sense of victory washed through her. She stepped away from the door. She had no doubt what he wanted to discuss. No doubt why he wished to see her in private. He would declare his intentions to her before formally asking for her hand. It would be the height of romance. The thrill of a lifetime. The ultimate social triumph. And what she had always wanted.

Still, he should be here by now. Absently she wondered if life with Alexei would be a series of little games like this with each of them striving to get the upper hand. She had to acknowledge that he was a prince and would no doubt win the majority of the time. And she could accept that. Well, she would have to work on accepting that. It would be well worth it. She would be a princess and live in a castle with servants to attend to her every whim. Her life would be a series of royal balls and state events, and people would seek to curry her favor. And if she never had what her sister and Thomas shared, well, that was the price one paid for achieving one's dreams. Besides, there was no reason why love couldn't follow marriage. She did *like* the man after all.

Her toe caught the edge of the carpet and she stumbled, dropping her fan, which skittered across the floor to disappear beneath a sofa. Annoyed, she bent to retrieve it and dimly heard a door open on the far side of the room. Damnation. She certainly didn't want the prince to find her crouching on the floor. It was not at all the way a future princess would behave.

"Is it wise to meet like this?" a male voice asked.

Another man chuckled. "There is no better place to be alone than in a crowd."

Relief coursed through her. It obviously wasn't Alexei. Simply two guests seeking a place for a private conversation.

"Do you think he suspects?" the first man said.

"Not at all. As long as we are discreet, neither he nor anyone else can put the two of us together. At the moment, nothing connects us. We simply have to make certain nothing ever does."

Private but definitely unusual. Not that it was any of her business. Her fingers closed around the fan and she started to rise.

"He has far more interesting things on his mind this evening."

The men shared a licentious laugh and Jocelyn paused. There was something about their laugh and their tone that was distinctly unnerving. She brushed aside the uneasy feeling, attributing it to the discomfort anyone would have when caught, however innocently, eavesdropping.

She pulled a deep breath, stood, and cast

them her most charming smile. "Do forgive the intrusion. I had no idea anyone —"

"You! What are you doing here?" the one on the right snapped although it could have been the one on the left. They were little more than dark-clad, blurry figures.

Indignation lifted her chin. "There is no need to be rude, particularly since I believe I was here first. I simply came in —"

"She's seen us." The low voice of the second man carried a note of menace, and a curious tremor of fear fluttered through her. "Take care of it."

"I scarcely think you need to *take care* of anything." She backed toward the door. "Given your attitude, I am more than happy to take my leave, although I daresay those who have something of a serious nature to discuss can find better locations than —"

Beside her, the door creaked in advance of opening. The prince? She moved toward it. A twang sounded near her ear.

She turned and her heart plunged to her knees.

A knife quivered in the door frame beside her.

lips closer to his, she absolutely would not kiss him back.

After a very long, rather delightful moment, he raised his head from hers. Eyes dark as a winter's night stared down at her from a face too sinfully handsome to trust. "Are you going to scream now?"

Her gaze slipped from his eyes to his lips. Full and finely sculptured and . . . inviting. She raised her gaze to his, to the amused light dancing there. At once any sense of temptation vanished.

"You kissed me," she said in the haughtiest manner she could muster. "The moment you release me, I shall slap your face. You had no right to accost me like that."

"I had to shut you up." His voice was somber but his eyes smiled. It was most annoying. "It would not do to attract a crowd."

"You couldn't simply have clapped a hand over my mouth? Isn't that what one does to keep someone from screaming?"

"I could have, I suppose, but it wouldn't have been nearly as —"

"Effective?"

"Enjoyable." He grinned.

He was outrageous and, well, a touch amusing. Not to mention his good looks and the fact that he certainly was an outstanding kisser. Still, it would never do to let him, whoever he was, know, although she suspected he already did.

"Are you all right then?" he asked.

"I daresay I will be when you release me."

"I would like nothing better but wisdom dictates otherwise." He shook his head in mock reluctance. "You have vowed to hit me and I suspect you are far stronger than you appear. Or at least far more determined, which can lend a great deal of power to even the weakest —"

"Very well." She huffed a short sigh. "I will not slap you although it will take a great deal of self-control on my part."

"Excellent." He released his grip on her shoulders and stepped back, studying her curiously. "You're not scared?"

"Why should I be?" she said blithely. "I have been kissed a time or two before. It's not always as pleasant as one would hope but it's scarcely frightening."

"Actually," he said, the twinkle once again in his dark eyes. "I wasn't referring to the kiss." He reached out and she wondered if he was about to pull her back into his arms. "I was talking about this."

He jerked the knife from the wall and held it out to her. It was long and decidedly wicked, and her stomach lurched at the sight.

She stared at the weapon with growing horror. It was easy to ignore, in fact to forget, with his lips on hers. But now . . . Her head spun. The room seemed to narrow and she felt the wall moving behind her. Or was she slipping down the wall?

"Now, now, we'll have none of that," he said in a no-nonsense tone.

He tossed the knife aside and caught her up in arms strong and hard and carried her to a nearby sofa. For a moment a lovely sense of warmth and safety filled her.

"Put me down," she murmured and nestled against him in spite of herself.

"You were about to faint."

"Nonsense. I have never fainted. Shelton women do not faint."

"Apparently they do when their lives are in danger." Abruptly he deposited her on a sofa and pushed her head down to dangle over her knees.

"Whatever are you doing?" She could barely gasp out the words in the awkward position. Jocelyn tried to lift her head but he held it firmly.

"Keep your head down," he ordered. "It will help."

"What will help is finding those men. There were two, you know. Or perhaps you don't." It was rather confusing. All of it. She raised her head. "Aren't you going to go after them?"

"No." He pushed her head down again and kept his hand lightly on the back of her neck. It was an oddly comforting feeling. "I have my men searching now but I suspect they will be unsuccessful. One of the rascals is familiar to me. I was keeping an eye on him tonight. He is no doubt the one who threw the knife."

"Apparently you weren't keeping a very good eye on him," she muttered.

He ignored her. "I have yet to discover the identity of his accomplice and they obviously wanted to prevent you from identifying him. I doubt that I will learn anything further this evening. It's far too easy to fade unnoticed into a crowd of this size." He paused, the muscles of his hand tensing slightly on her neck. "Would you know him again if you saw him?"

"Not really," she lied. In truth, not at all. They were nothing more to her than blurry figures and dimly remembered voices. "He could be anyone then, couldn't he?"

"Indeed he could."

It was a most disquieting thought. Well matched to her most discomforting position. "I feel ridiculous like this."

"Quiet."

It was no use arguing with the man. Whoever he was he obviously knew what he was doing. She was already feeling better. Even though someone had just tried to kill her.

"Am I in danger?" she said in a meek voice that didn't sound like herself at all.

He took a moment to answer. "Probably not."

His hesitation was not reassuring. Still, this

had to be a mistake. Why would anyone want to do away with her? Oh, certainly there were more than a few of this year's debutantes who were green with envy at Jocelyn's triumphant season but surely none would resort to violence. Even a few of their more over-zealous mothers would never go so far. Perhaps those two vile men had confused her for another lady here tonight?

"Do you think this was a mistake then? They thought I was someone else?"

Again he took his time in answering. It was an annoying habit that did not bode well. "Possibly."

She ignored his hesitation and clung to the single word. Of course, that was the answer. Tonight's gala was rampant with political rivals and foreign dignitaries and who knew what else. Intrigue was probably seething in every shadow. Still, it was not a pleasant thought. The very idea that someone would wish to harm anyone, let alone her, here, at a reception for the —

"Good Lord! Al— the prince!" She jerked upright, shoving his restraining hand away.

"What about the prince?" The man's eyes narrowed.

"He was supposed to meet —" She bit back her words. What was she thinking? She certainly couldn't tell this man, this stranger, that she was about to meet the prince. Privately. In a secluded setting. With no chaperones whatsoever. Aside from his rescue of her she really had no reason to trust him. Her reputation would be ruined if word got out, and Alexei would never marry a woman touched by scandal. Oh, certainly it was worth the risk initially because he was going to ask for her hand and that would put their meeting in the realm of romance rather than impropriety. But now . . .

And she had kissed this stranger! Or rather he had kissed her, but the distinction would scarcely matter.

She rose to her feet. "Who are you?"

He stood. "I should be crushed that you do not remember although we have never been formally introduced." He swept a curt bow. "Viscount Beaumont, my lady, at your service."

The name struck a familiar chord. "Have we met then?"

"Not really." Beaumont shrugged. "I am a friend of Lord Helmsley."

"Of course." How could she forget? Viscount Beaumont, Randall, or rather Thomas called him Rand. She'd seen him only briefly once, in a darkened library, but his name was all too familiar. Beaumont had taken part in an absurd, and highly successful, plan to dupe her sister Marianne into accepting marriage with Thomas less than a fortnight ago. She couldn't suppress a twinge of gratitude for his role in uniting the couple. "And an excellent friend too from all I've heard."

"One owes a certain amount of loyalty to one's friends." He paused as if considering his words. "As well as to one's country."

At once the mood between them changed, sobered. She studied him for a long moment. He was tall and devastatingly handsome, and before someone had thrown a knife at her she would have noticed little more than that. Now she noted the determined set of his jaw, the powerful lines of his lean body like a jungle cat clad in the latest stare of fashion. And the hard gleam in his eye. She shivered with the realization that regardless of his charming manner, his easy grin, and the skill of his embrace, this was a dangerous man.

She met his gaze directly with a courage she didn't entirely feel. "What is going on, my lord? Who were they?"

"It would be best if you knew as little as possible," he said in an irritatingly firm manner.

"Then all is well since I know nothing at all," she snapped. "I did no more than over-hear a few comments and the next thing I knew, knives were whizzing by my head."

"One knife," he said absently and fixed her with an intense stare. "What exactly did you hear?"

"Nothing that made any sense or seemed of any real significance." She shrugged and re-peated what she'd overheard. "Is it important?"

"No." He shook his head thoughtfully. "It wasn't what you heard that makes you a threat but what you saw."

"How can I be a threat? I told you I didn't see anything."

"Would you recognize them if you saw them again?"

"Once again, my lord." She emphasized each word. *"I didn't see them."* The man might well be handsome and dashing but his comprehension of the English language was questionable.

"They don't know that," he said as if he was talking more to himself than to her, his manner more considering than concerned.

She stared in disbelief. "Surely they'll know that if we pretend this whole thing never happened. Once they realize you have no idea who they are —"

"Who one of them is," he corrected.

"Whatever." She waved an impatient hand. "Once they realize I didn't identify them to you, they'll know they have nothing to fear from me and I'll have nothing to fear from them. There will be no problem. You did say it would be impossible to find anyone wishing to blend into the crowd?"

"I did."

"Well, then we must simply leave it at that." She stepped closer to him. "You must promise not to tell anyone about this. I never came in here. I never saw them." She glanced at the knife on the floor and grimaced. "I never saw *that*. You never saw me. We were never alone here together. You never —"

"Kissed you?"

"Kept me quiet." She crossed her arms over her chest. "It scarcely counted as a kiss."

"Perhaps not the first," he murmured, "but the second —"

"Promise!"

"Very well," he said slowly, "you have my word not to reveal what has happened here unless . . ."

"Unless?" She stared in suspicion.

"Unless it becomes necessary." The look in his eyes brooked no argument.

"That's something at any rate." She stepped to the door, then turned back. "Thank you" — she waved a wide gesture at the room — "for everything."

"For saving your life?" He swept an exaggerated bow. "It was entirely my pleasure."

"It wasn't a mistake, was it?"

He raised a brow. "That's yet to be determined."

"Not saving me." She rolled her eyes at the ceiling. "This whole incident. It wasn't a case of mistaken identity or anything remotely like that, was it?"

"No."

She sighed. "I didn't think so." She started to leave, then once again turned back. "Is

Prince Alexei in danger?"

Beaumont considered her question for a moment, and she wondered if he was deciding how much to tell her or if to say anything at all.

"Never mind," she said. "Your silence says a great deal." She swiveled back toward the door but his voice stopped her in her tracks.

"I doubt that he's in any mortal danger. Politically, however . . ." She could hear the shrug in his voice.

Encouraged and more than a little curious, she turned to face him. "Politically?"

His expression was noncommittal.

"I have a great number of other questions."

"I am not surprised."

"You're not going to answer them, are you?"

"No."

"But it does have to do with the prince, doesn't it?"

He didn't respond.

"You are . . ." She struggled to find the right words although it was probably too late to worry about such details now. "You are not a . . . a villain, are you? What I mean to say is that you are to be trusted. You are on the side of —"

"Good instead of evil?"

"Well, yes."

"Overly dramatic but you could put it that way I suppose." He chuckled. "I am currently charged with protecting the interests of my king and my country. As a representative of the crown, yes, you can trust me."

She blew a relieved sigh. "I had thought as much but —"

"You needed to hear me say it."

"Yes, I did." She smiled in gratitude. "I must get back. Again you have my thanks." She pulled open the door and cautiously glanced down the corridor. The hallway was empty. She stepped out of the room and closed the door behind her. If she could make it back to the ballroom unnoticed, she could pretend this entire incident had never happened.

But what of Alexei? Strange, he seemed of rather less importance at the moment. His proposal would have to wait. Not that another day really mattered. He could declare his intentions as easily tomorrow as tonight.

She made her way back to the ballroom, turning her attention once again to the prospect of becoming a princess and away from intrigues and unexpected dangers. She was confident the incident was at an end, and it was easy to wipe away all thoughts of wicked men and their wicked knives from her mind.

What proved a bit more difficult was ignoring the lingering memory of a strong, male body pressed against hers and the passionate kiss of a dangerous man.

Rand stared at the closed door for a long moment. A scant hour ago he would have wagered a small fortune that this mess could not get any more complicated. He would have lost.

The beautiful Lady Jocelyn was now smack in the midst of it all.

He walked over and picked up the knife from the floor. It was unremarkable in appearance, of a style made predominantly in the Baltic regions. Quite common and therefore worthless in determining ownership. But lethal in the right hands. And it had quite nearly skewered the lovely lady's neck.

He uttered a short curse at the thought of what would have happened if he'd arrived so much as a split second later. Of course, he'd had no idea she was in the room. The man he was watching had escaped his observation and apparently met with his accomplice in the darkened shadows out of doors. Rand and his men were checking each room with access to the terrace or gardens in hopes of uncovering the very meeting Lady Jocelyn had stumbled upon. It was only a heightened sense of danger that had served him well during the war years that led him to the right door.

Why she had been in the music room anyway?

She'd started to say something . . . Of

course. He snorted with disdain. She was here to meet Alexei. Rand had missed most of the season thus far, only returning to London a few weeks ago, but he couldn't fail to miss hearing of the woman who had apparently attracted the attention of the crown prince of Avalonia. The incomparable Lady Jocelyn Shelton.

He had to admit she was indeed incomparable and wondered why he'd barely noticed her at their brief earlier meeting. With golden hair and eyes only a shade darker, the rich color of honey, she stood a bit taller than most women, which only served to increased comparisons to the perfection of a Greek statue. Her family connections were excellent and her dowry was obviously substantial.

For a man seeking a wife, she was the prime pick of the lot this year. And who would have suspected the surprising amount of courage, perhaps even intelligence, hidden in that enticing package? Another woman would have been hysterical at such a narrow escape.

No, he amended the thought. Strike intelligence. If she was there to meet Prince Alexei she wasn't nearly as smart as she might appear. The prince was notorious for his amorous liaisons, and while rumor was rife that he was looking for a bride, Rand suspected even Lady Jocelyn's sterling qualifications would not be up to snuff for a royal match.

If the prince wished to meet with the lady privately, Rand would wager his intentions were not particularly honorable.

For his part, Rand wanted nothing to do with the prince. Yet here he was, charged with the task of protecting the heir to the Avalonian throne from the intrigues that surrounded him.

It was only Rand's family connections that placed him in this awkward position in the first place. And given those connections he could scarcely refuse a request from the Foreign Office to return to service, unofficially of course, to look into the prince's charge of a conspiracy to discredit him centered right here in London.

Prince Alexei had specifically asked the government for Rand even though the two men had never actually met until his arrival in England. No doubt the prince had assumed the distant blood connection between them would assure Rand's loyalty. Blasted man.

Rand had no desire to further his acquaintance with the prince or his country. Whatever hereditary Avalonian title he might hold was nothing more than a mildly amusing bit of history. He was the sixth Viscount Beaumont. The son of his father and an Englishman to his very soul. His loyalty was to his sovereign and the land of his birth. So if the country he had long sworn to defend did

of their sight tonight. Once she was safely back at Effington House, he would make Thomas aware of the situation and they would determine further steps.

And if in the process, he was forced to kiss her again, well — he grinned — such was the price of duty. Still, he sighed and firmly pushed away the memory of her delectable body pressed against his, he could not allow such thoughts to color his judgment. It was duty, plain and simple, that compelled him to protect her.

And he couldn't help but consider, in the cool analytical portion of his mind unfettered by inconvenient thoughts of guilt and honor and desire, that it was rather unfortunate there was no way to encourage Strizich to go after the fair Jocelyn and right into Rand's hands. Strizich would undoubtedly reveal all he knew once captured. It was a pity there wasn't some way to use her as bait.

Still, it was entirely possible that one way or another, she already was.

Chapter 3

"Are you quite all right?" Marianne's concerned voice pulled Jocelyn from her thoughts. The older girl leaned across the closed carriage and placed her hand on her sister's arm. "You are unusually quiet."

"Am I?" Jocelyn said absently and wondered why it was taking so long to travel the brief distance home to Effington House.

"You are indeed and for that we should all be exceedingly grateful," Becky said. "You'd been anything but quiet until we entered the carriage."

Jocelyn stared unseeing out the window into the night. She couldn't deny Becky's charge. Jocelyn had indeed been overly spirited and unusually animated since what she thought of as *the incident*.

She hadn't wanted to think of it at all and indeed at first had tried to ignore the whole thing. She'd returned to the reception as if nothing of any consequence had happened. In truth, she really didn't believe she was in any danger. Still, she'd found herself chatting

50

nervously and laughing too brightly and jumping at any unexpected movement. She'd made certain she was surrounded by suitors or friends or family every moment. And when an elderly gentleman had dropped a plate she'd uttered a short scream at the sound, then laughed to cover her terror.

And terror was exactly what it was. It clogged her throat and thudded in her chest and tensed the muscles of her shoulders.

"She's probably behaving so oddly because the prince has yet to declare himself," Becky said smugly.

Alexei. She'd scarcely given him more than a momentary thought since the incident. How very odd when he was all she could think about before someone had tried to kill her, yet afterward he'd barely entered her mind.

"I still don't trust him," Thomas murmured.

"Of course you don't, Thomas," Marianne said. "And we don't expect you to. It's part of your charm."

Jocelyn barely heard the conversation around her. Even if the prince did not dwell in her thoughts, in those rare moments when she was not preoccupied with hiding her fear, that annoying viscount did. Or more precisely, the kiss of that annoying viscount. And the way he'd held her . . . and how safe she'd felt in his arms.

"She'll be insufferable once she becomes a princess." Becky sighed.

"I shall quite enjoy being insufferable," Jocelyn murmured in an absent manner.

"More insufferable," Becky said pointedly.

At last the carriage pulled to a halt. For once Jocelyn was grateful for Thomas's typical refusal to wait for a servant to open the door. She was as impatient as he to escape from the confined space. He pushed open the door, jumped down, and turned to assist Marianne, then Becky. Jocelyn pulled her cloak more tightly around her, drew a deep breath, and allowed Thomas to help her out. The group gathered in the pool of illumination cast by the gaslights on the street, then headed toward the impressive front entry of Effington House.

The door swung open in welcome and Jocelyn breathed a sigh of relief. Even though the Shelton sisters had only lived there for a few months, right now it was home. And home had never looked so safe. She reached the first step, and chaos erupted around her.

Without warning a sharp retort sounded, echoing in the dark night. One of the bricks framing the door a scant few feet in front of her exploded, scattering shards of red clay over the walk. Shouts sounded from somewhere behind her.

"Bloody hell, that was a shot!" Thomas

seized Marianne and shoved her into the house. "Quickly! Now!"

For less than a moment, fear froze Jocelyn where she stood. Then panic gripped her and she grabbed Becky and pulled her toward the door.

Another shot rang out. Another spray of fragments burst from the brick façade.

"Get in the house!" a voice yelled from the shadows. She recognized it at once. Giddy relief flooded her with the immediate, and probably absurd, belief that if Beaumont was here all would be well.

She and Becky stumbled over the threshold. Thomas slammed the door behind them. "Mansfield," he barked at the servant standing stunned in the foyer. "Get my pistol!"

In the back of her mind, Jocelyn noted how very absurd Helmsey's order sounded here in the grand, marble-floored foyer.

Before the butler could move, pounding sounded at the door. Thomas hesitated.

"Let him in," Jocelyn said quickly and started forward. "He could be —"

Thomas glared. "Who could be —"

"Thomas!" Beaumont's urgent voice called from behind the door. "Let me in."

"It's Beaumont." Jocelyn reached for the door.

"Rand?" Thomas jerked the door open. "What in the name of all —"

Beaumont brushed passed him and Thomas snapped the door shut in his wake. Beaumont's gaze flicked over each of them as if assessing damage, then settled on Jocelyn. "Is anyone hurt?"

"No one seems to be." Marianne caught her breath and glanced around the gathering, then nodded. "I think we're fine."

"But confused as hell." Thomas glared at his friend. "What is going on, Rand? Why was someone shooting at us? And more to the point: who was shooting at us?"

"I have my men trying to find him now." Beaumont addressed Thomas but his gaze stayed on Jocelyn.

"Your men?" Thomas said slowly. "I see."

"Well, I don't," Becky said.

"Neither do I," Marianne added. "Perhaps you should explain it to us all."

Thomas nodded at Beaumont. "That's up to him."

Beaumont stared at Jocelyn as if there were no one present but the two of them. As if once again he would take her in his arms. "Are you sure you're all right?"

She stared back. He had already saved her once tonight. If not for him . . . Abruptly anger, intense and unreasonable, wiped away her fear. If not for him, none of this would have happened. "No thanks to you."

His eyes widened. "My dear lady, I can scarcely be blamed for —"

"You can be blamed for all of it!" she snapped. "Every horrible thing that has happened to me tonight can be blamed on you!"

"What horrible things?" Marianne's voice rose.

"Horrible things? Really?" Becky said eagerly. "How very exciting."

"It wasn't the least bit exciting," Jocelyn said sharply. "It was quite terrifying and it was all his fault."

"My fault?" Disbelief washed across Beaumont's handsome face. "How is it my fault?"

Jocelyn planted her hands on her hips. "If you had been doing whatever it is you're suppose to be doing that vile man would never have had the chance to try to kill me."

"Kill you?" Shock colored Marianne's voice.

"Bloody hell," Thomas said under his breath.

"That is horrible," Becky murmured.

"If you had stayed where you were supposed to be you wouldn't have been in danger in the first place." Beaumont stepped toward her in a decidedly menacing manner. "But instead you were behaving like a common trollop."

"A trollop? How dare you!" She drew back her hand to slap him but he caught her wrist.

"Now, now." Anger snapped in his dark eyes. "I wouldn't allow you to hit me before and I shall not allow it now."

"Why did you want to hit him?" Becky stepped forward but Marianne pulled her back. "Is he the one who tried to kill you then?"

"No." Jocelyn wrenched free of his grip, her voice dripping with disdain. "He kissed me."

Thomas snorted.

Becky snickered.

"Oh dear," Marianne murmured.

"I saved your life." Beaumont's tone was hard.

"*That* would save *my* life." Becky nudged Marianne. "He's really quite —"

"Quiet," Marianne's voice was firm.

"Hah!" Jocelyn scoffed. "I wouldn't have needed saving if you had —"

Beaumont cut in. "Or rather if you hadn't left the reception for a private rendezvous with the prince —"

"You did *what?*" Aunt Louella's voice rang from the stairway.

All eyes turned toward the stairs. Aunt Louella stood leaning on the rail, a diminutive figure who somehow towered above them all and who now quivered with indignation.

Jocelyn groaned to herself and stepped forward. "It's not quite as bad as it seems —"

"No?" Aunt Louella hobbled down the steps and Thomas moved to help her. "Then how bad is it?"

"He wanted to meet me privately because he was going to ask me to marry him," Jocelyn said staunchly.

Beaumont scoffed. "I scarcely think that was the proposal he had in mind."

Jocelyn shot him a scathing glare and wished she had something far more lethal to fling at him.

"I never did trust him," Thomas muttered.

Aunt Louella's gaze slipped from Jocelyn to Beaumont and back. "I fail to attend one gala and the next thing I know you are off arranging clandestine meetings, with a prince no less, and —"

"And don't forget someone trying to kill her," Becky said brightly.

Jocelyn winced. Silence fell over the assembly. Aunt Louella's eyes narrowed. "I want to hear everything. Mansfield, take their wraps. All of you into the parlor. Now."

A few minutes later they had arranged themselves in the parlor. Aunt Louella and Marianne shared a sofa. Becky sat on another, Jocelyn chose a chair, and both men stood by the mantel. The room was heavy with tension and thick with the scent of the dozen or so bouquets sent by the prince in recent days.

Jocleyn's mind raced for an acceptable excuse for her behavior. Of course, if she'd actually met Alexei there would be no need to explain anything. She'd be betrothed to a

. prince and well on her way to becoming a princess. Aunt Louella could scarcely complain about that.

"Now then." Aunt Louella settled back and pinned Jocelyn with an unflinching gaze. "Start from the beginning."

"Very well." Jocelyn drew a deep breath and related everything from the moment the prince had requested their meeting to the knife imbedded in the door frame by her head.

"I gather this is where you come in." Aunt Louella gestured for Beaumont to begin. "If you please."

Beaumont picked up the story but left out a great deal, including the part where he'd kissed her. Jocelyn was at once grateful and annoyed.

"Then those were shots I heard in the street?" Aunt Louella asked.

Beaumont nodded. "We'd thought, since we were unable to apprehend them, they would realize Lady Jocelyn was no threat and would not try to harm her again. Obviously . . ." He paused and cast Jocelyn an apologetic look. She pointedly turned away. "We were wrong."

Aunt Louella studied him for a long moment. "You're lying, my lord."

"Aunt Louella," Marianne started but her aunt waved her still.

"That's not at all what you thought is it?"

Aunt Louella shook her head. "If you truly believed there was no danger to Jocelyn, why did you come here tonight?"

"Indeed." Jocelyn frowned and stared at Beaumont. Everything had happened so fast she hadn't considered that point. "Why were you here?"

Beaumont looked like a boy caught with a stolen cookie. "Well, you see . . . That is . . ."

"I know." Becky jumped to her feet. "He was here because if the villians came back to get Jocelyn he'd be able to catch them." Excitement rang in Becky's voice. "Don't you see? It was a trap and Jocelyn was the . . ." Realization dawned on Becky's face. "Oh my," she murmured and dropped back on the sofa.

"Bad move, old man," Thomas said under his breath.

"The bait?" Jocelyn's eyes widened and her voice rose. She got to her feet. "You used me —"

"Not really," Beaumont said quickly.

"As bait?" She stared in stunned disbelief and stepped closer. "Like cheese for a mouse? Or a rat dangled before a cat?"

"Not deliberately." He held up a hand. "However, I knew there was a possibility —"

"Why didn't you tell me?" Her voice had an odd, high sound suspiciously close to a scream but she didn't care.

"Why would I?" He stepped to her and gripped her shoulders. She tried to pull away but he held her tight. "Look at me," he ordered. She stared up into his eyes. Dark and endless and, God help her, to be trusted. "What would you have done if I told you?"

"I don't know. I could have —"

"You could have done nothing." His tone was firm. "Absolutely nothing. You simply would have been scared."

"More frightened than I was already? That's hardly possible." She jerked free and turned away, wrapping her arms around herself. "I have been terrified since it happened."

"Oh dear, Jocelyn." Marianne stood and crossed the room to Jocelyn and enfolded her sister in her arms. "You should have told me."

"And you should have told me," Thomas said to Beaumont.

Beaumont blew a long breath. "I was going to tell you in the morning. Though we were at the ready, I honestly did not expect anything to happen tonight."

"It scarcely matters." Marianne stroked Jocelyn's hair much as she had when they were very small. And now, as then, Jocelyn's fears eased. "It's all over now."

No one said a word.

"Thomas?" Marianne's question hung in the air.

Jocelyn pulled free from her sister and swiveled toward the men. "It is over, isn't it?"

Beaumont and Thomas exchanged glances.

"Is it over, Rand?" Thomas asked in a sober voice that chilled her blood.

"I don't know," Beaumont said simply. "I wish I did."

"Then what do you propose we do?" Aunt Louella's tone was matter-of-fact, as if they were discussing a matter of no more importance than the daily menu.

"First of all, we shall have to make sure she's protected." Thomas drummed his fingers on the mantel. "There is an army of servants on staff here and I shall alert them to deny entrance to strangers. I can also hire additional —"

"It's not enough," Beaumont said slowly. His gaze met Jocelyn's. "She will be in danger as long as she remains in London."

"Then she shall leave London immediately," Thomas said firmly. "We shall take her to the country. We'd planned to leave for Effington Hall in a few days anyway. We shall simply go at once."

"No." Beaumont's tone was hard and unequivocal. "As long as she is with you, you are all in danger. Any one of you could have been shot tonight."

"That does make it all somewhat less exciting, doesn't it," Becky said with a sigh. "It would be rather annoying to be shot by accident."

Marianne cast her an irritated look.

"Well, it would," Becky muttered.

Marianne ignored the younger girl. "Besides, Effington Hall would be the first place anyone would look for her."

"I could go home then." Jocelyn looked from face to face, hoping to find a glimmer of agreement anywhere. "To Shelbrooke Manor. There's no one there but the servants and with Richard still away no one would ever think I would —"

"Shelbrooke Manor is as obvious as Effington Hall," Thomas pointed out. "We need to find a place unconnected to her. To any of us."

"Then there is nothing else to be done." Aunt Louella folded her hands in her lap and directed her words to Beaumont. "You shall take charge of her."

"What?" Jocelyn whirled toward her aunt. "You can't be serious. What on earth do you mean by that?"

"I mean, my dear child, that this man is clearly the only one qualified to truly protect you and keep you out of the hands of these madmen."

"Him?" Jocelyn waved disparagingly at Beaumont. "How can you say that? He's done a terrible job of it so far."

"That may well be. Still" — Aunt Louella

turned toward Beaumont — "from what's been said here, and a very great deal that hasn't, I gather you are in the employ of the government. Our government, that is."

Beaumont nodded. "At the moment."

"And I am also aware that he is an old friend of yours." She glanced at Thomas. "Is that correct, my lord?"

"I have known him for years," Thomas said.

"And is he a good and honorable man?"

"He is, my lady, as well as a true and loyal friend. I would trust him with my life." Thomas grinned wryly. "I have trusted him with much more."

"Very well then." Aunt Louella nodded in satisfaction. "It is settled."

"Nothing is settled as far as I'm concerned," Jocelyn said.

Her aunt ignored her and directed her attention only to Beaumont. "Do you know of a place where she will be safe?"

Beaumont thought for a moment, then nodded slowly. "I believe I do."

"I don't care," Jocelyn said stubbornly. "I'm not going anywhere. And I'm not going anywhere with him."

She stepped to her aunt and knelt on the carpet before her. Jocelyn had always been her aunt's favorite. The only one of the Shelton sisters who truly understood the value of a season in London and fine clothes and a good match.

Jocelyn took the older woman's hands and gazed into her eyes hoping against hope that if she'd ever had any power to persuade her aunt she had it tonight.

"Aunt Louella, if I were to go with him, no matter how legitimate the reasons, my reputation would be ruined. And any chance for a good marriage, let alone a match with a prince, would be destroyed. My very life would be over."

"But you would still have a life, my dear Jocelyn. And that is the overwhelming consideration in all of this."

Jocelyn's voice took on an edge of panic. "But you've never allowed me, or any of us, to do anything that that could be considered the tiniest bit improper. Surely you can see the potential for scandal here. Regardless of the circumstances, I can't believe you would ever permit me to go away with a man, any man, let alone a virtual stranger."

"You're right, child. I would never permit that." Aunt Louella cupped Jocelyn's chin in her hand and gazed into her eyes. "You shall have to marry him first."

Chapter 4

The pronouncement hung over the room like a sentence of condemnation. Shock was apparent on every face. No one said a word.

Jocelyn couldn't believe her ears. How could her aunt suggest such a thing? But Aunt Louella had that look in her eyes that declared her decision was not open for discussion.

"Never!" Jocelyn got to her feet. "I can't! I won't!"

She looked at Beaumont. His jaw was clenched and his lips pressed into a firm line as if he was trying not to protest.

"If it is a question of marrying him or losing my life at the hands of a lunatic" — Jocelyn raised her chin defiantly — "I'd rather die."

"It appears there's a very good chance you will if you refuse," Aunt Louella said.

"Then shoot me right now and be done with it because I won't do it. I absolutely will not marry him." Jocelyn shook her head vehemently. "Besides, I'm supposed to marry the prince. I know he's about to ask me and once he does . . ."

"But he hasn't asked you and I cannot allow your life to rest on the possibility that he will." Aunt Louella gestured at the floral arrangements filling the room. "These are lovely tokens but they do not mean Prince Alexei's intentions are entirely honorable. I quite agree with Lord Beaumont's assessment on that and Lord Helmsley's as well. Any man, regardless of whether he is a prince or not, who seeks a private meeting with a young lady is not to be trusted."

"But obviously he did not wish to propose publicly." For the first time, Jocelyn wondered if indeed she had been mistaken as to Alexei's intentions. He hadn't actually said the word *marriage*. Could she have been wrong? Her cheeks flamed at the realization that perhaps his desire was not for marriage at all.

"This should be done as soon as possible," Thomas said. "A special license can be arranged for in the morning."

"No!" Jocelyn's gaze darted from one face to another. Marianne's expression was sympathetic, Thomas's was resigned, and Becky looked as if this was an exciting adventure and not the end of her sister's life. Or at least the life she had planned.

Beaumont didn't say a word.

Jocelyn stared at him. "You can't possibly want this."

Beaumont considered her for a moment, then chose his words with care. "My wishes scarcely matter at this point. In many ways, as you have pointed out, I am indeed to blame for this situation. Therefore" — his gaze bored into hers — "it is my responsibility to correct it."

"Oh, that's all any woman could ask for, isn't it?" Jocelyn snapped. "To be married off to correct a mistake?"

"It doesn't seem quite fair," Marianne murmured.

Becky scoffed. "But much fairer than one of us being killed by accident."

Jocelyn swiveled toward her aunt. "Even if your suspicions about the prince are correct, and I don't believe they are, I could still make a better match than" — Jocelyn waved at Beaumont — "than him!"

"I too would prefer to be shot rather than wed, my lady, but that does not seem a viable option." Beaumont's voice was grim.

"Jocelyn!" Aunt Louella said sharply. "Stop this at once."

"No, I won't stop it." Jocelyn knew how petty she sounded but she couldn't help herself. All her hopes and dreams were crashing in around her, and she refused to let them die without a fight. "I'd planned to marry a prince. Or at the very least a marquess. And look at him. He's not shabby but I daresay he doesn't have a great deal of money. I have certainly never so much as heard of him and he's only a mere viscount!"

"I think he looks quite delicious," Becky said with a grin. "I'd marry him."

"Thank you, my lady." Beaumont smiled and directed a bow toward the younger girl.

"Becky, do keep still. And Jocelyn." Marianne sighed. "You're being terribly rude."

"I'm not being rude, I'm being honest. You are all quite willing to marry me off to someone I barely know, and I need to make each and every one of you realize this is a horrible, horrible mistake." She whirled toward Beaumont. "Do forgive me, my lord. I don't wish to be impolite and I am grateful for your intervention earlier tonight, but aside from the arrogance of your manner and admittedly your friendship with Lord Helmsley and a few other odds and ends that have surfaced this evening, I know nothing whatsoever about you. So, in truth, this is not entirely personal."

"And for that I am most grateful." Beaumont folded his arms across his chest and leaned against the mantel. "I can only wonder, now that you have denigrated my character and my title and my fortune, what's next? Would you care to cast aspersions on my ancestry? Or would you rather wait until we are man and wife and you know of my many other flaws to continue your tirade?"

Jocelyn grit her teeth and glared at him. "You are most annoying, my lord."

"And you are spoiled and at the moment at least, rather insufferable." His gaze traveled over her in an assessing manner. "While you are not unpleasant to look at —"

"Not unpleasant?" Jocelyn gasped. "I'll have you know men have compared my hair to spun gold and my eyes to moonlight."

"Men who, no doubt, were interested in meeting you in the privacy of an empty music room." The pleasant tone of his voice belied the loathsome nature of his words.

Sheer outrage choked her response and she could do nothing more than sputter.

"In addition, your character is apparently quite shallow, your intelligence is suspect, your behavior is not unlike that of a child, and I have serious questions about your morals. In short, my dear lady, were I to select a bride of my own choosing you would not be my first choice." He smiled sweetly, and once again Jocelyn wanted to hit him.

"Oh, this is starting out well," Marianne said under her breath.

"We should make the arrangements at once," Thomas said.

"No, wait. Please." Jocelyn pressed her fingers to her temples and tried to think. Surely there was some way to avoid this disaster. "What if . . . what if I go with him but . . . but we bring Aunt Louella as a chaperone.

And servants." She addressed her plea to Marianne, possibly her best hope among this group for salvation. "Lots and lots of servants."

"Impossible," Beaumont said. "We will have to travel quickly and by horseback."

Aunt Louella shook her head. "I can't possibly ride a horse in this state."

"And the fewer people who know about this the better," Beaumont added.

Jocelyn glared at him. "You are enjoying this, aren't you?"

"Perhaps a bit. It always helps to find amusement in dire circumstances." He shrugged. "I am reconciled. Nothing more. And unfortunately, I cannot see another way to save both your life and your reputation."

"Dearest Jocelyn," Marianne said softly. "There doesn't appear to be any choice."

The inevitability of it pressed in on her. Jocelyn's heart sank. "There has to be something."

"Consider for a moment, child," Aunt Louella's voice was gentle. "How you would feel if something were to happen to Marianne or Becky because of you. You would never forgive yourself."

She was right, of course. They were all right. Even that blasted Beaumont. It could all be blamed on her. If she'd never gone to meet Alexei none of this would have happened. And her life would not be ruined.

"Very well then." Jocelyn squared her shoulders. "I'll marry him but" — she turned toward Beaumont — "the moment this is resolved I want an annulment."

"An annulment is exceeding difficult to get," Aunt Louella said.

"Wouldn't you have to be insane for that?" Thomas asked Beaumont.

"What makes you think I'm not?" Beaumont muttered. "I'm marrying her."

Jocelyn ignored him. "Or a divorce then."

"Even harder." A smile quirked the corner of Beaumont's mouth. "The best you can hope for, my dear, is to be a young widow."

"I shall work on that." Jocelyn fairly spit the words.

"It appears we are all in agreement then." Aunt Louella nodded firmly. "Come, Becky, help me up the stairs. Marianne, go with Jocelyn and start packing her things." Becky assisted Aunt Louella to her feet. The older woman paused. "Jocelyn, my dear, I know this is not what you've planned for your life but I am confident all will work out well. He is a good man. You could do far worse."

"I could do far better," Jocelyn muttered.

"As could I." Beaumont swept a sarcastic bow.

Aunt Louella's gaze lingered first on her niece, then Beaumont. "You may very well suit each other better than you think now. You have already shared a kiss."

71

"How did —" Jocelyn started.

"As one gets older, one realizes eavesdropping is not the sin it has been portrayed. Now then, as I was saying, the two of you also share a passionate distaste for one another. Many newly wed couples do not even have that much in common." She leaned on Becky and started toward the door, then stopped and glanced back at Beaumont. "You did say this all came about because the men involved believe Jocelyn will identify them, thus ruining their plans?"

"Yes," Beaumont said cautiously.

Aunt Louella chuckled. "Delicious irony there, don't you think?" She turned and let Becky help her from the room. "I do so love irony . . ."

Jocelyn stared after them. "I am glad one of us is finding this amusing."

"Two of us." Beaumont's voice sounded behind her.

A dozen scathing comments rose to her lips but she refused to give him the satisfaction of a response. "Come along, Marianne, apparently I have to pack for my" — she gritted her teeth — "wedding."

"One bag, no more," Beaumont called. "We will have to travel quickly and we will be on horseback."

"One bag? I can't possibly —" She started to turn, then caught herself. No, there would be plenty of time later to trade barbs with the arrogant viscount. "Very well." She continued toward the door.

Behind her she could hear Marianne's lowered voice and Thomas's reply. It scarcely mattered what they were saying. Jocelyn's fate was sealed. She would never be a princess. Never be more than a mere viscountess. She held her head high and marched out of the room.

If it wasn't for the threat her presence posed to her family she'd stay right here and take her chances. Run the risk of another shot in the night or a knife flung at her head or poison in her luncheon meal or any number of other ways to meet her demise. At the moment, danger of any kind was far preferable to marriage to Randall, Viscount Beaumont.

At the moment, she'd rather be dead.

"She's not as bad as she seems." Thomas took a sip of his brandy and studied his friend. The men had retired to the library, allegedly to discuss arrangements, but right now Rand wanted little more than to indulge in Thomas's excellent liquor for the rest of the night.

"Oh?" Rand raised a brow. "In what way?"

"Well." Thomas thought for a moment. "She is pretty."

"She's exquisite." Rand could well see why men had compared her hair to gold and her eyes to moonlight. Although they were mistaken. Her eyes were definitely the color of honey. Warm, tempting honey. "And she knows it."

"That she does." Thomas chuckled. "Are you going to tell her you have money?"

"What? And spoil her martyrdom? Let her believe what she wishes for now. Besides, my finances are nothing compared to yours and I doubt the lovely Jocelyn would be happy with anything less. The Beaumonts have made and lost any number of fortunes through the generations while your family" — he raised his glass in a salute — "has always managed to keep its money."

Thomas lifted his glass in response. "We Effingtons are clever when it comes to funds. Still, your fortune is quite respectable. Even impressive."

"We have succeeded in holding on to it through the last three generations. That's something at any rate. I daresay, though, it's not impressive enough for the fair Lady Jocelyn." Rand chuckled in spite of himself. "She really is somewhat mercenary."

"That she is." Thomas grinned.

"Not precisely the quality I would wish for in a wife." Rand heaved a heavy sigh.

"What one wishes for and what one gets are often decidedly different." Thomas drew a long sip, then continued. "And often decidedly better."

"Ah, words of wisdom late in the night," Rand said wryly. "Pity your philosophy will not hold true in this case."

"Perhaps," Thomas murmured.

For a long time, neither spoke, sharing the kind of companionable silence known only to men secure in the knowledge of lasting and loyal friendship.

It was somehow fitting to be in this room on this night with this friend. Seated in these very chairs, through the years of their acquaintance, he and Thomas had shared any number of brandies and traded any number of confidences and discussed any number of women. It was here a few months ago that Thomas had first complained of having the Shelton sisters in his charge for the season. And then later, this was where they had hatched a somewhat drunken, but nonetheless successful, scheme to convince Lady Marianne to accept Thomas's proposal of marriage.

"Are you familiar with her background?" Thomas said casually.

"Familiar enough, I suppose." Rand sipped his drink and thought for a moment. "I know her brother, Richard, is the Earl of Shelbrooke and married to your sister, Gillian. I know they are currently somewhere in America awaiting the birth of their first child."

"And what of her father?"

"He was something of a gambler if I recall."

Thomas snorted with disdain. "An unsuccessful gambler and in truth a bit of a wastrel. His wife died when the sisters were very young. Afterward the old earl squandered the family fortune and left his daughters, four of them altogether, practically penniless. They grew up in the country, at Shelbrooke Manor, a grand old house once that had fallen into appalling disrepair. Richard used to try to fix things there himself."

Thomas leaned forward. "They weren't complete paupers, you understand. From what Marianne has said, I gather it was a kind of genteel poverty. Richard was rather wild in his youth and not around at all until after his father died. Then he did what he could to recoup the family's finances but" — Thomas shrugged — "it was not until last year when he married Gillian and they inherited a tidy fortune that the lives of his sisters finally improved."

"I didn't know."

"The perfectly attired, elegant, and admittedly spoiled Lady Jocelyn you see today has not had an easy time of it." Thomas settled back in his chair. "If she revels in her family's newfound fortune, and indeed views wealth and an impressive title as the path to happiness, I daresay it's understandable."

"I suppose it is." Rand downed the liquor in his glass and held it out for a refill. It was difficult to reconcile this Lady Jocelyn with the childhood Thomas had described. And difficult as well to equate it to his own. As a boy, he'd never questioned where the money for good food or fine clothing or excellent horses had come from. He'd never had to. "Still, it is an explanation, not an excuse."

Thomas started to respond, then held his tongue and instead picked up the decanter on a table beside him and obligingly filled Rand's glass. Good. Rand preferred not to hear anything else tonight that might put his future wife in a better light. It was his responsibility to keep her safe, and if that meant marriage, so be it. There would be time enough to make peace with the idea, and the lady, later. Tonight he wanted nothing more than to wallow in the self-pity of having to marry a woman not of his own choosing.

Odd, he'd liked her a great deal more on their first meeting tonight than he did now. And admittedly quite enjoyed kissing her and, more, her reluctant, but present nonetheless, response. Of course, earlier this evening he was saving her life. Now she claimed he was ruining it.

"Are you taking her to the Abbey then?"

"No, but I will admit that's the first place I thought of, and frankly I wouldn't mind a good long stay." Rand's London townhouse was more than comfortable but it was the Abbey, nestled in the hills of Bedfordshire, that he considered home. It had been months since he'd been back. "Especially since my mother is not in residence at the moment."

"I gather that would make the Abbey more attractive."

Rand blew a short breath. "Infinitely. Every time I see her of late she is compelled to mention her desire to see me wed and the need for a Beaumont heir. She's driving me mad."

"Will she be pleased then about this turn of events?"

"She would be pleased if I were to bring home a bride with two heads and warts. Given Jocelyn's family connections I'm certain my mother will be ecstatic." Rand chuckled. "However, I am also exceedingly grateful that I can avoid introductions for a while. I believe my mother is in Italy at the moment. Given her passion for gossip, and our need for secrecy, I'm grateful for her absence.

"I'm hopeful that as of now, my involvement in all this is still unknown. Should that change, while Beaumont Abbey is not as obvious as Effington Hall or Shelbrooke Manor as a sanctuary for Jocelyn, if someone was trying to locate me, the Abbey is the first place anyone would look."

Thomas pulled his brows together. "If you're not going to the Abbey, then where . . ."

"Do you recall my mother's stepbrother? My Uncle Nigel?"

"Lord Worthington, isn't it? I vaguely remember you speaking of him. Is he still alive? He must be . . . what?"

"Past seventy now, and yes, he's still around." Rand chuckled then sobered. "He's been quite ill of late and I was afraid we'd lose him. That's where I've been for most of the season. But he's a stubborn old goat and he pulled through. Thank God. He'll probably bury us all.

"At any rate, I thought Worthington Castle would be the best place to wait until this matter is resolved. I'm afraid my uncle has let it run down a bit but it's not intolerable."

"Jocelyn's always wanted to live in a castle," Thomas murmured.

"I doubt if this was what she had in mind. Still, it's probably the last place anyone would expect the incomparable Lady Jocelyn to be."

"The incomparable Lady Beaumont, you mean."

"Damn it all, Thomas, I've never considered myself a romantic sort. I've always thought I was rather practical. The kind of man who sees what needs to be done and does it." Rand pulled himself to his feet and paced the room.

"The kind of man who feels it's his duty to participate when his country is at war," Thomas said quietly.

"I suppose, although admittedly at first I saw it all as a grand adventure and great fun." The muscles of his face tightened into the hard expression that came without thinking whenever talk turned to Rand's activities during the war.

In the beginning, intelligence work was little more than a game. Exciting and exhilarating, a gamble with high stakes. But all too soon he realized the stakes were not merely high but a matter of life and death, not just for him but for the faceless thousands of British troops who would be affected by the accuracy of the information he gathered and conveyed. And with the realization came fear. The kind of fear known only to those who held the fate of other men in their hands. Fear that sharpened his senses and honed his skills and made him more than he'd ever imagined he could be.

Perhaps that was the problem tonight. He simply hadn't been terrified enough to do a good job. He might well be now. He would not allow someone, anyone, to lose his life because he did not do his job. Not in the past. Not ever.

"You're not a romantic sort?" Thomas prompted.

"What? Oh, yes." Rand shook off the memories of the past. "I am not prone to flowery phrases or" — he cast Thomas a grin — "poetry. Yet, whenever I've considered marriage I've thought . . ."

He groped for the right words and continued his pacing. What did he think? His footsteps brought him from the light cast by the lamps to the deeper shadows of the library and back. It struck him as a fitting metaphor for his life. "I thought . . ."

"You thought?"

"I thought I'd at least *know* the woman. Probably even like her. Definitely desire her. And more, actually *want* to spend the rest of my days with her." His thoughts jelled even as he spoke the words. "I've never particularly considered love but I have always thought, or at least hoped, it was a possibility.

"My parents loved each other. And since my father's death my mother has been in love a dozen times or more."

Thomas choked back a laugh.

Rand couldn't resist a grin. "At least she has claimed to be in love. But never enough to give up the title of Viscountess Beaumont, so perhaps not." He shook his head. "Even though my father is gone, I believe Mother married for life. Hers as well as his."

He glanced at Thomas. "As I suspect I will. Because I further suspect there will be no annulment, no divorce."

"Either would be extremely difficult." Thomas studied him carefully. "Are you sure there is no other choice here but marriage?"

"No. I wish I was." He ran his fingers through his hair. "I don't even know for certain if there is any continuing threat. All I do know is that should anything happen to Lady Jocelyn, it would be my fault. And I cannot allow that. So" — he uttered a strained laugh — "I am about to be wed."

"It could be worse," Thomas said helpfully. "She could be ugly."

"Come now, Thomas." Rand sank back down into his chair. "An ugly girl would be grateful for a husband regardless of the circumstances. I'd much prefer a bride's gratitude to her hatred."

"I doubt that she hates you."

Rand cast Thomas a dubious glance.

"Perhaps, at the moment . . ." Thomas smiled weakly.

"Nonetheless." Rand heaved a resigned sigh. "She is to be my wife." He shook off the melancholy the words brought. There were far more serious things to consider at the moment than his future wife's feelings. "Now then, about tomorrow . . ."

Briefly they went over the arrangements for the next day. It was simple enough. Rand would get a special license and Thomas would quietly secure a minister to marry them right here in the house. It was unorthodox but Thomas was confident Effington money would smooth the way.

The rest of the family would make a great show of leaving for the country at dusk. While Thomas, Marianne, Becky, and Aunt Louella headed by carriage in one direction, Rand and Jocelyn would travel by horseback in the other. It was an odd hour to start a journey but Rand felt it was imperative to leave London under cover of darkness.

"Enough of this." Rand sat his glass on the table and got to his feet. "I have arrangements to make."

In spite of the late hour, he would go at once to speak with his superior, the man who'd gotten him into this mess. Now that Rand had ascertained there was indeed at least a political threat to the prince, it was imperative that the investigation continue, albeit with someone else at its head. He would also request permission to leave the man's name with Thomas simply as a precaution. He hoped his friend would never need the information, but it was best to be prepared for any eventuality. It shouldn't be a problem. As the son of the Duke of Roxborough, the Marquess of Helmsley was above reproach.

Thomas stood and studied him in an offhand manner. "Regarding whatever it is you're doing?"

Rand bit back a smile. As intensely curious

as Thomas no doubt was, he could count on his friend not to ask untoward questions. In the years after Napoleon's defeat, while Thomas had now and again casually asked about Rand's wartime activities, he'd never pressed for answers. Rand's secrets remained secret.

"Precisely." Rand grinned. "Although I have a few personal arrangements to make as well if I am to leave the city tomorrow." He started toward the door. "With luck, this will be resolved soon and we can return from the country. At any rate, Prince Alexei will return to Avalonia within the next few weeks, and I'm confident that will put an end to any danger for" — he tried not to choke on the word — "my wife."

Thomas walked him to the door and clapped a hand on his shoulder. "It's not so dreadful, old man. I'm about to be shackled myself."

Rand restrained the urge to point out the differences between Thomas and Marianne's impending nuptials and his own. The difference between eager and resigned. Between love and, well, not even tolerance at the moment.

"*Shackled* does seem the appropriate word."

"One way or another" — Thomas's tone was abruptly somber — "I'm certain all will work out."

"I wish I shared your confidence, Thomas.

I'm only certain I can keep her alive. Beyond that . . ." Rand blew a long breath. "The idea of living with a woman who detests me . . ." He shook his head. "I don't know what's going to happen."

"It seems to me the two of you will be spending a great deal of time together. Alone. Perhaps," Thomas said slowly, "that time could be put to good use."

"What do you mean?"

"I simply mean I've seen you charm more stubborn women than Jocelyn."

Rand stared at his friend. "You're suggesting I seduce her?"

"If anyone, especially Marianne, were to accuse me of that I'd deny it to my dying breath but" — he grinned — "that's exactly what I'm suggesting."

"Seducing Jocelyn," Rand murmured. "What an intriguing idea."

Thomas raised a brow.

Rand laughed. "Very well, more than intriguing. You yourself pointed out she's not ugly. It has a certain amount of appeal." At once he remembered the feel of her delightful body against his. "A great deal of appeal."

"I'm surprised you didn't think of it yourself."

"As am I. I'm afraid the overwhelming specter of wedded bondage quite obscured the more pleasant aspects of wedded bliss.

However, now that you have brought it up . . ." Rand grinned. "Thank you, old man."

Thomas shrugged modestly. "One does what one can for one's friends."

Rand laughed. Seducing Jocelyn would not be at all easy. She would not fall quickly into his bed. But by God, it was a challenge he was well up to.

He already had the lady's hand. Now he just needed to win her heart.

"I hate him." Jocelyn lay crosswise on her bed and stared up at the ceiling. "I hate him with every breath in my body."

"Nonsense." Marianne's tone was brisk. "You don't hate him at all. What you hate are the circumstances."

"Pardon me if I don't see a great deal of difference between the circumstances and the man." Jocelyn heaved a heartfelt sigh. "My life is over."

"Your life is not over." Marianne settled on the foot of the bed. "It will simply be somewhat different than you'd imagined."

"Somewhat different? Hah." Jocelyn rolled over onto her side and rested her head on her hand. "That's easy for you to say. You're about to marry a future duke. An Effington. And the man you love. I was *supposed* to marry a prince."

"Jocelyn." Marianne studied her sister for a

moment. "Did you love him then? Prince Alexei, I mean."

Jocelyn plucked at the coverlet, then sighed. "No. But I'm confident I would have someday."

"You may well grow to love Beaumont someday as well."

"First I have to like him," Jocelyn muttered.

"I like him. Quite a bit actually." Marianne's voice was thoughtful. "Beyond that, I think he's trustworthy and honorable. He's been an admirable friend to Thomas. And he has a charming sense of humor and an excellent imagination."

Jocelyn knew the tale of her sister's involvement with Beaumont. Marianne had written a series of stories for a Sunday paper based loosely on her relationship with Thomas. When Thomas had found out, he'd convinced Beaumont to play the role of a suitor Marianne had fabricated as a way to teach Marianne a lesson.

"And don't forget he's quite dashing and extremely good-looking." Becky sauntered into the room and dropped a small bag on the bed. "And his shoulders are extraordinary."

And he does have the most amazing dark eyes. Annoyed, she pushed the thought away and eyed the valise suspiciously. "What is that?"

"Aunt Louella told me to bring it to you,"

Becky said. "It's for your things."

Jocelyn sat up. "But that's entirely too small. I can barely fit a decent ball gown in that."

"Dearest," Marianne said gently, "I doubt if you'll be attending many balls in the immediate future."

"Of course not. I'm being exiled. To someplace quite dreadful no doubt." Jocelyn groaned and flung herself back on the bed. Marianne was right, of course. There would be no balls. No galas, no soirees, no routs. No fun of any kind. "Then just throw a few old dresses in there. It scarcely matters, I suppose. I don't even know where he's taking me but I daresay it won't be the tiniest bit enjoyable. Probably some horrible little cottage in some nasty little village."

"He could take me to a horrible little cottage," Becky said with a grin.

"You're welcome to him." Jocelyn propped herself up on her elbows and considered her younger sister. "It's a pity we don't look more alike. Oh, we share a similar height but your hair is distinctly red. Of course, a wig would —"

"Jocelyn," Marianne snapped. "Don't even think about it."

"It was just an idea." Jocelyn grimaced. "I'm desperate. If I don't think of something I'll be the Vicountess Beaumont by this time tomorrow."

"There are worse fates," Becky said pointedly. "Death for one."

"At the moment, death does not seem especially worse."

"Isn't there anything about him that you like?" Marianne rose from the bed and moved to the wardrobe. She pulled open the doors and studied its contents.

Becky crossed her arms and leaned against a bedpost. "I like him."

"You don't have to marry him," Jocelyn said.

"He once told me he was a spy," Marianne mused. "Of course, I didn't believe him at the time. Now, I wonder . . ."

"A spy." Becky's eyes sparkled at the thought. "How very exciting."

Jocelyn wasn't sure if the idea of Beaumont as a spy made him more palatable or completely unacceptable.

"You must like him a little," Becky said. "You did kiss him, after all."

"Not exactly," Jocelyn said quickly. "He kissed me." And admittedly, it was a lovely kiss, the memory of which even now made her insides warm and her stomach flutter. A kiss that made her wonder, in spite of herself, what else this man could make her feel. Abruptly she sat upright. "I hadn't considered that at all."

"Kissing him?" Becky smirked. "I have."

"No. At least not just kissing him."

Jocelyn's eyes widened and her gaze met Marianne's. "What shall I do if he . . . that is, he'll be my husband. Legally, and what if he . . . well" — she swallowed hard — "demands his . . . rights?"

"I doubt Beaumont is the kind of man who would force you to do anything against your will," Marianne said firmly, pulling a gown from the wardrobe.

"Except marry him," Jocelyn said.

"Jocelyn." Marianne folded the dress and handed it to Becky, who tossed it into the bag. "I think you should keep in mind that Beaumont doesn't especially want to marry you any more than you want to marry him. He's only doing out of a sense of responsibility and honor. He's doing it to save your life."

"What life I'll have left won't be worth saving."

Marianne heaved an exasperated sigh. "I do wish you'd stop being so selfish about this."

"Well, I wish I'd stop being so selfish about this too," Jocelyn snapped. "I know how I sound and I hate myself for it. But I can't seem to help it. It's how I feel."

"I daresay most women would jump at the chance to marry a man like Beaumont. And he's very mysterious, which just makes him all the more attractive," Becky said. "You may not know Beaumont at all but I think he's already figured out your nature. You sound like a spoiled, shallow, insufferable child."

"Becky!" Jocelyn stared in stunned disbelief. "How can you say such a thing?"

"I am sorry. That was mean of me. I know you're overset and therefore allowances should be made." Becky moved around the bed, sat beside Jocelyn, and gazed into her eyes. "And I know, even if he doesn't, that you're not really spoiled, shallow, and insufferable, at least not all the time."

"Thank you," Jocelyn said dryly.

"And I also know this is dreadful for you. But he's really not all that bad. Why, I'd wager eventually you'll have a wonderful life together."

"No, we won't. I don't see how we could." Jocelyn got to her feet and turned to Marianne. "You have to promise me, when this is over and you're the Marchioness of Helmsley with all the money and power of the Effington family behind you, you'll do everything you can to help me procure an annulment or a divorce."

Marianne shook her head. "I don't know if that's even possible."

"Marianne." Jocelyn took her hands and met her gaze firmly. She drew a deep breath. "I'm doing this as much for you and Becky, more really, as I am for myself."

"What a selfless heroine she is." Becky

sighed dramatically. "Willing to sacrifice herself for her sisters' safety."

Jocelyn ignored her. "*I'm* willing to take the risk of staying right here but I can't put *you* in danger."

"Is she willing to sacrifice her virtue as well?" Becky said in a stage whisper.

"Quiet," Jocelyn snapped but kept her gaze on Marianne. "All I'm asking in return is that you help me escape from this marriage when the time comes."

"But perhaps our fair heroine forgets there would not be a threat in the first place if she hadn't —"

"Becky!" Jocelyn whirled toward the younger girl. "If you say one more word I shall —"

"Stop it at once, both of you," Marianne ordered. "Becky, you are not helping."

"Will you promise me then?" Jocelyn held her breath.

Marianne nodded slowly. "I promise to do what I can to ensure your happiness. Whatever that entails."

Jocelyn heaved a sigh of relief. Marianne's vow wasn't, in truth, very much, but it was at least something to hold on to, a tiny raft to keep Jocelyn's spirits afloat. If she could cling to the belief that marriage to Beaumont was not permanent, she could take whatever came. At least for now. "Thank you."

"You do realize annulment or divorce will

not really put things right. It will not erase your marriage as if it never existed." Sympathy shown on Marianne's face. "Even if we manage to keep all of this secret, there is no way to privately obtain the dissolution of a marriage. Word will get out. There will be a certain amount of scandal." She shook her head. "You will not be able to pick up your life as if nothing has happened."

"I know." Even as she said the words Jocelyn realized, deep down inside herself, she did indeed know her life would change forever. And nothing would ever be the same.

"Now, you must make me a promise," Marianne said firmly. "Promise that you will keep in mind the fact that Beaumont too is making a sacrifice. That his life too will be changed irrevocably. And give me your word that you will at least try to accept this marriage for however long it may last." She pulled her closer and kissed Jocelyn's forehead. "We have been through far greater difficulties in our lives and survived. You will come through this unscathed."

"Will I?" Jocelyn murmured.

"I for one have no doubt of it." Becky grinned. "It takes a certain strength of character to be spoiled, shallow, and insufferable. A weaker nature couldn't handle it at all."

For a moment no one said a word. Then all three sisters burst into laughter.

"Thank you, Becky." Jocelyn laughed. "No

one quite puts me in my place the way you do."

"Now then," Marianne said with a smile. "Do I have your word? That you will at least try to be an acceptable wife." Jocelyn opened her mouth to protest but Marianne cut her off. "Within reason, of course."

"Very well. I promise. I will do my best to be rather less insufferable and to be an acceptable wife and a better person as well, I suppose." Jocelyn sighed. "And I will try to remember he is in very much the same boat I am. But not tonight." She smiled weakly. "Tonight I want to feel sorry for myself. And I want my sisters to be terribly sympathetic and I want you" — she looked at Becky — "to see if you can find any sweets in the kitchen that we can all share."

"Now that's the best idea I've heard tonight." Becky started for the door, then stopped and turned back. "You know, Beaumont might have had the solution all along."

"Oh?" Jocelyn raised a brow.

"Well, while there is a certain stigma to annulment or divorce there's none to being a widow." Becky's voice carried a feigned note of innocence. "And didn't Beaumont say the best you could hope for was to be a young widow?"

"Becky!" Marianne groaned. "Don't give her any ideas."

"I've had that one already, thank you."

Jocelyn wrinkled her nose. "It didn't seem particularly practical."

"Oh well." Becky shrugged. "At least he's handsome."

With eyes that seemed to see into her very soul.

"And amusing," Marianne said.

And arms that promised comfort and security.

"And wonderfully mysterious." Becky nodded.

And a kiss that warmed her toes.

"It would be rather a shame to waste all that," Jocelyn murmured. "I suppose I'm not spoiled enough to want Beaumont dead just so I can be his widow.

"Pity, I can't see myself being his wife either."

Chapter 5

"We're here." Beaumont's voice jerked Jocelyn awake.

"Here where?" Jocelyn pulled herself upright and shook her head in an effort to wake up.

How long had she been on that blasted horse anyway? She'd never particularly envied men the freedom to ride astride, she'd never ridden much herself, but it would be infinitely easier for an endless ride like this than her sidesaddle. Every muscle and joint in her body ached.

It was dark, obviously late in the night. The second night of their journey. At least she thought it was the second night. She'd long since lost any real sense of time.

The last twenty-four-plus hours were a blur of high emotion and deep exhaustion. Immediately after their brief but nonetheless awkward wedding ceremony, her sisters, her aunt, and Thomas had started off for Effington Hall in a coach Jocelyn would have gladly killed for, accompanied by a raft of servants.

Jocelyn and Beaumont had slipped away on horseback, alone, in an opposite direction.

They'd ridden through the night, stopping at daybreak only to exchange horses. Beaumont would allow them to pause now and then to share the surprisingly tasty bread, cheese, and wine he'd brought with him and take care of personal needs. From what she could tell, they traveled on little-used roads. Beaumont was unfailingly polite and really rather considerate. Still, his sense of urgency communicated itself to her, and she refused to complain. Or at least not too often.

She dozed off and on, amazed anyone could rest on a horse at all but finding a bit of refuge in sleep. Fortunately her mount followed his without any particular effort on her part. Good. The last thing she wanted to admit to him was that she'd never been a more than adequate rider. It was difficult to ride with confidence when one couldn't see where one was going.

Their positions made it impossible to talk. She was grateful for that too. Jocelyn had decided to stop feeling sorry for herself and to accept her fate but had no idea how to go about getting to know this man. *Her husband.*

Somehow the flirtatious banter she'd perfected during the season did not seem particularly appropriate to her current circumstances. Fluttering her fan and gazing in a wide-eyed, adoring manner while commenting on something of no substance whatsoever didn't equate to fleeing for her life, newly married to a virtual stranger. Besides, she'd spent most of the journey being far too weary to do more than struggle to stay on the blasted creature beneath her.

Jocelyn slid off the saddle and into Beaumont's arms. "I can walk, thank you." She pushed out of his embrace and took a step. Her knees collapsed beneath her.

"Apparently you can't." Amusement sounded in his voice. He hoisted her into his arms and started toward the door.

"Annoying man," she murmured and snuggled against him. He was infinitely more comfortable than the horse. "I am so tired." She rested her head against his chest.

He shifted her weight and hammered with his fist on a great wooden door. At once she was fully awake. "Where are we?"

"Worthington Castle." He pounded again.

"A castle? Really?" Her mood lightened. How bad could exile be if she were to spend it in a real castle?

"Really." He glanced down at her. The light of the moon shadowed the planes of his face and she could see his grin. She had the strangest desire to feel the warmth of his skin. What would he think if she rested her palm against his cheek? "However, it might not be exactly —"

Without warning the door creaked open a

wide crack. A suspicious face peered out at them. "Stop making that bloody racket! It's the middle of the — my lord!"

"Good evening, Nick."

At once the door swung fully open. A short, plump gentleman, somewhere between forty and ancient, clad in a dressing gown that had seen better days and a brightly colored nightcap, beamed at them. "My lord, we had no idea . . . That is, we were not expecting . . ." He turned and bellowed into the depths of the building, "Flora!" then stepped aside and urged them in. "What are you waiting for? Come in, come in."

Beaumont stepped over the threshold into the dim light. Sconces mounted on stone walls cast flickering light over a huge entry area. Arched stonework soared upward into a blurry darkness. Their voices echoed hollowly in the distance.

"It's good to see you again so soon, my lord." Nick peered out the door, then looked at Beaumont. "No carriage?"

"No. Just the two horses."

In spite of the familiarity of his address, the servant was obviously too aware of his position to say anything further. But curiosity colored his face.

"Beaumont," Jocelyn said under her breath.

He set her on her feet but kept his arm around her. Before she could protest the intimate gesture, she swayed slightly. His arm

99

tightened and she was thankful for the support. And his thoughtfulness in providing it.

"This is Nick — Nicholas Harper. He is the house steward and his wife, Flora, is the head housekeeper, but in truth" — Beaumont lowered his head in a confidential manner — "they rule the castle."

Nick chuckled. "Go on with ye, lad."

"Nick, I'd like you to meet" — he paused slightly and she wondered if it was difficult for him to say the words — "Lady Beaumont."

"Lady Beaumont?" Nick's bushy brows drew together under the nightcap, then his eyes widened with realization. "Lady Beaumont!"

"My wife."

"It's lovely to meet you," Jocelyn said cautiously.

"Married." Nick grinned and shook his head. "I never thought I'd live to see —"

"Nicholas Harper, what on earth is going on out here?" A female version of Nick hurried into sight. She was precisely his height and build, and in the faint light Jocelyn couldn't be entirely sure, but it looked like her dressing gown matched his. "Who would be —" She pulled up short at the sight of Beaumont.

"Good evening, Flora." Beaumont turned toward the housekeeper and lifted her hand to his lips. "You are as beautiful as ever."

"Watch yourself or you'll be turning my head with your fancy words, Your Lordship." Flora giggled and Jocelyn could have sworn a blush accompanied it.

"And this, Flora," Nick said significantly, "is Lady Beaumont."

"Lady . . ." Flora's mouth dropped open and she stared unabashedly.

"Good evening," Jocelyn said.

"As I live and breathe. *Lady* Beaumont." Flora shook her finger at Beaumont. "Shame on you, my lord, you never said a word."

"There wasn't a word to say when I left. It all happened" — he glanced at Jocelyn, and laughter sparked in his eyes — "rather quickly."

"Love is like that. Sneaks up on you when you least expect it." Nick nudged Flora. "Don't it, my sweet?"

"Stop that kind of talk right now." Flora's tone was reproving but there was affection in her glance.

"I haven't heard from you so I assume my uncle is still doing well?" Beaumont looked from Flora to Nick.

"Better even than when you left." Flora nodded.

"Excellent," Beaumont said. "I assume he's asleep?"

"Oh my, yes, has been for . . ."

The conversation swirled around her about this heretofore unmentioned uncle and their travels and a dozen other things but Jocelyn's tired mind couldn't grasp the words. She had any number of questions but was too weary for any attempt at making sense. The warmth of the room seeped into her bones and she wanted nothing more than to lie down and sleep. She tried not to yawn and failed.

"Oh dear, you must both be exhausted. Imagine coming all the way from London on horseback. Whatever possessed you?" Flora clucked. "It will take far too long to wake a maid; I'll make up your room myself right now." She started off, her voice trailing behind her. "No carriage. Tsk, tsk. Isn't that the silliest thing you've ever heard . . ."

Beaumont directed Nick to get their luggage, such as it was.

"Two rooms," Jocelyn murmured and sagged against her husband.

He chuckled and picked her up once again, and once again she didn't protest. Regardless of whatever she might not like about this man, she did rather like being in his arms.

He carried her up the stairs and she had a vague impression of vast space. In some part of her mind not fogged with fatigue she wondered exactly where he was taking her, and more to the point, what he would do when they got there. She knew it was an important question but couldn't seem to remember why.

He laid her gently on a bed that might well have been the softest thing she'd ever felt.

Perhaps it was only soft in comparison to the horse, but its warmth enfolded her. She struggled to remember what it was that was so important — something she had to say to Beaumont. Something she needed to make clear.

Whatever it was it paled in comparison to the enticing lure of clean linen and the seductive comfort of a soft mattress. And in the last moment before blissful sleep claimed her she wondered where Beaumont, where her *husband,* was going to sleep.

"Jocelyn?" Rand said softly, staring down at the exhausted figure on the bed.

She murmured something unintelligible and was obviously deeply asleep. Rand was nearly as weary as she. He had pushed them hard, driven by the urgent need for speed and the possibility of pursuit.

He'd seen nothing to indicate that and had caught only occasional glimpses of the handful of men he'd arranged to follow them at a discreet distance. They would patrol the castle grounds, as unobtrusively as possible, until Rand received word from London that any possible threat was at an end. Even so, Rand did not completely let down his guard until their arrival at the castle. His constant vigilance took as much a toll on him as the grueling ride itself.

Before leaving town he had turned over the

information he'd gathered to his superior and was essentially no longer involved in the investigation. If, at some point, Jocelyn admitted she could indeed identify the man he'd sought, he would deal with it. He suspected her inability to do so had more to do with fear than anything else. Still, it was of no consequence at the moment. He was out of it now and his only job was to keep Jocelyn safe.

And here he could do just that. Worthington Castle was as much home to him as the Abbey and every bit a sanctuary. Now he could relax in the bed that had always been his whenever he'd visited Worthington.

However, said bed was already occupied.

They hadn't discussed it but he was fairly certain she would not wish to share. Not that it mattered right now. Even the attractive picture presented by the lovely Lady Jocelyn could not overcome the weariness that engulfed him. And he was not about to sleep on the floor or a less than appealing chair.

He pulled off his coat and tossed it aside, then considered her. There was no determining how long she'd sleep. At least through the night and possibly well into the next day. He was certainly tired enough for that. Well, he couldn't allow her to sleep fully clothed. She'd toss and turn and no doubt disturb his rest to boot. She still wore her cloak as well as her clothes. There was only one thing to do. She wouldn't like it one bit but he hoped she was too deeply asleep to notice.

He drew a deep breath and pulled off one shoe, then the next. Rand sat on the bed beside her and propped her up against him. Somehow he managed to remove her cloak and her pelisse. She murmured occasionally but did not awaken. Pity. It would have been so much easier if she had.

He could have called Flora to help, of course, but it would have seemed an odd request for a newly wed husband. He didn't want either Flora or Nick to question his relationship with his new wife. They were as dear to him as family and he didn't want them to know his marriage was not what it appeared. Whether Jocelyn liked it or not, they were indeed man and wife. It was imperative they behave accordingly, for his pride as much as for her safety. He'd married a woman out of necessity rather than choice and he preferred to keep that fact private.

Still, when he'd thought of his wedding night, or more accurately the second night of his marriage, he really rather hoped the lady in question would be conscious.

Rand struggled with the tapes and ties of her gown. Blast it all. He'd undressed any number of women in his life, but never without their willing assistance, and with Jocelyn he was battling a dead weight. Finally he removed her dress, leaving her in her chemise and stockings. That would do.

He got to his feet and studied her. Damnation, but she was lovely. Especially now with her mouth shut and her features relaxed in sleep. Her form was tall and slender, her hips nicely curved, her breasts firm and full. Her long lashes rested dark against her cheek and her blond hair was tousled on the pillow about her head like a cloud of gold. If he had to marry a bride not of his choosing, well, he certainly could have done worse.

She'd been remarkably decent on the ride here as well. A few minor complaints, but all in all she'd seemed determined to make the best of it. Had she too realized they could well spend the rest of their lives together? She'd been polite and even pleasant during their rare breaks on the road. Admittedly he was surprised by her demeanor and during their long silent hours together wondered if he was mistaken about her after all. It was a hard ride for him and no doubt even more difficult for her. He had to admire her resolve and even her courage.

With a start he realized he was not at all averse to this marriage. And realized as well Thomas's suggestion of seduction would be most pleasant. His stomach tightened at the thought. Most pleasant indeed.

Still, this was not the time. He wanted her fully awake and, more, wanted her to want him. Just as he wanted her.

He wanted her? Rand laughed softly and shook his head. When had that happened? Perhaps it was when he'd accepted the fact that she could very well be his wife for the rest of his days. Or maybe it was the way she'd instinctively snuggled against him when he'd carried her in his arms. Or possibly he had wanted her from the moment he'd pressed his lips to hers to stifle her scream.

He rubbed a weary hand across his eyes. It really didn't matter, he supposed. The difficulty would lie in making her want him. It might well take a while, but then they had a great deal of time together ahead of them.

He grabbed the coverlet folded at the foot of the bed and tossed it over her. She sighed and burrowed beneath it. *An exceedingly pleasant task.* He pushed aside the thought, disrobed, and circled to the other side of the bed. Rand blew out the candle, pulled back the sheets, and slid between them. There were layers of linens and blankets between the two of them. Jocelyn could scarcely complain about sharing the bed, although Rand was confident she would do so anyway.

He didn't really care. His body was tired, his mind was muddled, and he wanted nothing more than to fall into the welcome arms of oblivion.

He closed his eyes and waited for sleep. Instead he found himself listening to the gentle breathing of the woman beside him. Alert to the rustling of covers when she shifted position. Cognizant of how easy it would be to reach out and pull her into his arms and forever into his life.

And wondered if she dreamed of princes and palaces.

And wondered as well what it would take to make her dream of him.

Lord, she'd had the oddest dreams.

Jocelyn shifted and burrowed more deeply beneath the covers. She'd dreamed she'd been riding on a horse forever and was cold and tired and . . . married.

Her eyes snapped open and she stared into the sleeping face of Randall, Lord Beaumont.

She opened her mouth to scream, then clamped her lips shut tight. No. Screaming would only wake him up and she preferred him asleep right now. At least until she gathered her wits about her. Besides, the last time she had screamed, or tried to scream, he had quieted her with a kiss and she didn't want that to happen again. At least she didn't think she wanted that to happen again. No, she definitely didn't want that here and now. Perhaps later . . . Oh dear, it was all so confusing.

And it was all too horribly real. It wasn't a dream even if it could be likened to a nightmare. She groaned to herself. She was Lady

Beaumont. Viscountess Beaumont. And the man lying beside her was — she swallowed hard — her husband.

He hadn't kissed her again, had he? Or done anything else? A barrier of sheets and blankets separated Beaumont's sleeping form from hers. That was a good sign. Cautiously she lifted up her coverlet and winced. She didn't remember taking off her clothes but apparently somebody had. She pushed aside the thought of who that somebody might be. At least she still wore her chemise and stockings. Beaumont's shoulders were bare and he no doubt wore nothing else but the blankets. He struck her as the kind of man who would sleep unclothed.

She couldn't help but notice that Becky was right. His shoulders were extraordinary. Was the rest of him as nicely put together? He was certainly one of the handsomest men she'd ever met. Had circumstances been different she might well have been interested in him. Of course it scarcely mattered now. Now she was his wife.

She propped her hand under her head and studied him. If it hadn't have been for Alexei, who did in fact embody her childhood fantasy, she might have been extremely interested in Beaumont. Even if he was only a mere viscount. And apparently not a terribly wealthy viscount at that. Still, the man had an air about him, mysterious and attractive, and was really quite appealing. At least when he was asleep. And he had brought her to a castle. She'd always wanted to live in a castle.

Beaumont's eyes flickered open and she stared straight into their dark, endless depths. Her stomach fluttered and she realized how close she was to him. How easy it would be to lean forward. To brush her lips —

"Good morning."

She said the first thing that popped into her head. "Is this your castle?"

"My, you are mercenary." A wry smile lifted his lips.

She shrugged but had the good grace to blush. "I'm not mercenary, just curious."

"Well, in that case." He propped himself up on his elbow. "It will be someday but at the moment, no. The castle is owned by my uncle."

"And he is?"

"Uncle Nigel. Lord Worthington." His smile grew. "The Earl of Worthington."

"Oh." She thought for a moment. An earl wasn't bad at all. And an earl's wife was a countess. "Then you will someday be —"

"Viscount Beaumont, nothing more." He laughed at the disappointment she tried, and failed, to hide. "I am sorry, my dear, but my uncle is my grandmother's stepson and in truth no blood relation to me at all. Our ties are no more than those of affection and his title will die with him, though, God willing, not for a very long time. However, Worthington Castle is not entailed and therefore will come to me one day."

"I see." That was something at any rate. "You can't fault me for asking."

"I can, but I won't." He studied her with an air of amusement. "Do you have any other questions?"

"Why are you in my bed?" she blurted.

"Actually you are in my bed."

"I was here first." She pulled her brows together. She couldn't really remember how she'd gotten here at all but she was fairly certain she was first. "Wasn't I?"

"This is not a territory to be claimed by the first to plant a flag. Regardless of who was in this bed first, this is where I have always slept, and quite well I might add, and I have no intention of sleeping elsewhere." He met her gaze firmly. "Not now, not ever."

She gathered the blanket more closely around her. "What exactly do you mean by that?"

"I mean, my dear lady wife, this is my bed and this is where I shall sleep."

"Then I shall sleep elsewhere as I have no intention of sharing your bed." She raised her chin defiantly. "Not now, not ever. Surely there is another bedchamber I can occupy?"

"A dozen or so but you're not going anywhere." One naked shoulder lifted in a casual shrug. "You are my wife and you shall share my rooms."

"How barbaric of you." She sat up and glared down at him. "Civilized couples do not share bedchambers."

"Beaumonts have never been especially civilized." He flashed her a wicked grin. "We quite prefer it that way."

"Then I shall sleep on the floor," she said loftily.

"As you wish, but I warn you, the floors are made of stone and even at this time of year are extremely cold and damned uncomfortable."

She heaved an exasperated sigh. "You are determined to make this difficult, aren't you?"

"Not at all." The smile remained on his face but his eyes were serious. "I am determined to make this work."

"You are? Why?"

It was his turn to sigh. "Because, my dear Jocelyn, I checked into the possibilities of annulment or divorce the morning of our wedding, and either takes years to accomplish. Therefore, we are essentially stuck with each other for a very long time."

It was interesting, though unsurprising, to note he had taken the time to uncover the details of dissolving their marriage. Marianne had also managed to come up with the same information before the wedding. Jocelyn knew full well this marriage was likely to be permanent or, at least, last untold years. Even not consummating their union would not guarantee its dissolution unless, of course, he was unable to do so. Jocelyn didn't doubt for a moment that Beaumont was very, very able. Still, consummation did not seem like a wise move if she had any hope of escaping this marriage someday. And Marianne had promised to do whatever she could at some indeterminate time in the future.

"But surely, Beaumont —"

"My given name is Randall although I have never been particularly fond of it. Therefore my close friends call me Rand. As should my wife," he said pointedly. "Now then, if there is nothing else." He sat up and swung his legs, his bare legs, over the side of the bed.

"Wait!"

He stopped and raised a brow. The covers had fallen to his waist, revealing a chest that was every bit as impressive as his shoulders. A smattering of dark hair dusted hard planes of muscle and drifted low to disappear beneath the blanket. She'd never seen a man's chest before but had no doubt this was a magnificent specimen. Perhaps there was something to be said for consummation after all.

"Yes?" he prompted.

Her gaze jerked to his. "I . . . um . . . well, I mean . . ."

"Yes?" His gaze slipped from hers to travel

downward and at once she realized her blanket too had fallen. She yanked it up to her chin. His gaze met hers and a lazy smile curled his lips. The memory of his mouth on hers washed through her, and once again she wanted to lean forward and —

"Did you have another question?" Amusement and something else lit his eyes. Something more. Something very, very dangerous.

She drew a deep breath. "I want to know if you . . . if I . . . if we . . . if last night . . ."

"Absolutely not." He shook his head in a slow, solemn manner. "Not last night."

She blew a long sigh of relief and ignored a vague sense of disappointment. "Oh, well, I just . . . wondered. The last few days are all rather jumbled in my head and my memory is somewhat fuzzy and I —"

"Of course, we did arrive the night before last." She widened her eyes and he laughed. "And I, you, we did nothing but sleep."

He reached out and took her hand and pulled it to his lips. "And I can assure you when I, you, *we* do something other than sleep in this bed . . ." He brushed his lips across the back of her hand. Heat flashed through her. His gaze simmered and her breath caught. "You will remember it."

For an endless moment she could do nothing more than stare at him. Stare into his seductive, midnight eyes. And she knew if he wanted her right now, she would be his. Willingly. The realization snapped her back to her senses and she withdrew her hand.

"I daresay we will both remember it," she said with an air of confidence she didn't entirely feel.

"Excellent." He laughed again. "You may well be more intelligent than I had thought."

"Oh, thank you, my lord. Rand." She fluttered her eyes at him in an exaggerated manner. "I am so flattered by your reassessment of my character. And what else was there? Ah yes. Am I still as shallow as you originally thought? Still as spoiled, and are my morals still in question?"

"Shallow and spoiled? Let me think." He crossed his arms over his naked chest and she tried to ignore how his various muscles flexed with the movement. He leaned back against the pillows, considered her question, and grinned. "Probably."

She burst into laughter and was rewarded by his surprised expression. "You are an honest man, Rand. I will give you that." She tilted her head and cast him a well-practiced and most flirtatious smile. "And what of my morals?"

"I'm not entirely certain at the moment. And more, not at all sure if I want to be wrong" — a slow smile spread across his face — "or if I very much want to be right."

She laughed again. Marriage to Lord Beaumont — to Rand — might be rather more enjoyable than she had imagined.

"It's past time we were both up and about." He cast her a warning look. "I am going to get out of bed now."

"As you wish."

"And I have nothing on," he said.

"I didn't think you did." She smiled sweetly.

He stared in disbelief. "Are you just going to watch me then?"

"Unless you need assistance, but I'm sure you can dress yourself." She twisted, plumped up the pillow behind her, then settled back. There was something quite delightful about turning the tables on him. "This is, as you have so kindly pointed out, my room as well as yours. And, as I have no intention of rising at the moment, I think I shall indeed simply sit here and think about my marriage and all it entails."

"Aren't you even going to turn your head?" Indignation rang in his voice.

It was all she could do to keep from grinning like a lunatic. Teasing Rand was the most fun she'd had in days. And who would have imagined the man would be so modest? Well, it was his turn to be uncomfortable and annoyed.

"I could, I suppose, but I too am curious about my morals. Other than that insignificant incident of meeting with the prince —"

"The insignificant incident that got us into all this."

"Yes, that's the one. Aside from that, I've never really confronted the question of my morals. So it seems to me this is something of a test."

"I have no clothes on." He ground out the words.

"That's why it's a test." She cast him her brightest smile. "Will I look or will I close my eyes?"

"This doesn't bother me in the least, you know."

"Well, it isn't a test of your morals, now, is it? I've never been in a situation like this before, whereas I have no doubt endless numbers of women have seen you without clothing."

"Not endless." He huffed. "But a considerable number."

"And were there any, oh what's the word I'm thinking of . . ." She paused thoughtfully. "I know. Complaints?"

"None whatsoever." He glared as if questioning her nerve to so much as suggest such a thing.

"Then I'm confident I shall have none either." She waved him off. "Do go on. Don't mind me."

"I won't." He was obviously reluctant to stand up. "My clothes are in the dressing room behind that door." He nodded toward the near wall. "Your bag is there by the wardrobe. I was up briefly yesterday and stopped the maids from unpacking. I didn't want them to disturb you."

"Your thoughtfulness is most appreciated."

"Yes, well, I am definitely getting up now." He didn't move an inch.

"Rand, may I ask you one more question?"

"Of course." Relief crossed his face at the reprieve.

She widened her eyes in feigned innocence. "Who, precisely, removed my clothes?"

He stared at her for a long moment. Slowly, he smiled with genuine admiration. "Well played, Jocelyn." He looked like a man who had just discovered the world was not at all as he thought it was. "Very well played."

He chuckled, and before she could respond he was on his feet, striding across the room. Her face warmed at the sight of his nicely sculpted backside. The rest of him quite fulfilled the promise of his shoulders.

He needn't have worried about what she might or might not see. Within a few steps he was nothing more than a large flesh-colored blur. Did he know about her sight problem? She couldn't remember if it had been mentioned or not but surely Thomas had told him. Still, it was of little consequence.

He did keep his back to her and while she never would have admitted it to him, she was grateful. She wasn't entirely sure she was ready to see a *completely* naked man. She wasn't particularly ready to see a naked rear end either, but causing him this bit of discomfort was certainly worth it.

From the moment of their first meeting he had, after all, had the upper hand, and she was quite tired of it. And tired as well of feeling as if absolutely everything in her life was totally out of her control. This was a minor victory but a victory nonetheless.

He disappeared into the dressing room. Jocelyn slipped out of bed and winced. Every muscle in her body was stiff and sore. Gingerly she made her way toward the large brown smudge on the far wall that she hoped was the wardrobe. She found her bag at once, opened it, and pulled out a dress. This would do. She had no idea how quickly Rand would reappear and preferred to be fully clothed when he did. Then she could find a washbasin although it was more than likely in the dressing room. She threw the garment on over her head. It was a simple day dress and she could fasten it without assistance.

She picked up the valise, brought it to the bed, and sat down to see what else her sisters had managed to fit into the far too tiny satchel. She pawed through the bag and found her hairbrush, several other items, and a small, oblong package, wrapped in tissue and tied with a blue ribbon. A note was tucked under the bow. She pulled the paper free and unfolded it.

Dearest Jocelyn,

Some day you might well wish to see beyond the tips of your fingers and then you will need these.

> *Yours with affection,*
> *Marianne*

Whatever did she mean? Jocelyn untied the ribbon and pulled off the paper. A pair of spectacles lay in her hand.

Jocelyn drew her brows together in annoyance. Marianne knew full well Jocelyn would never so much as consider wearing glasses. Part of that shallow nature of hers, no doubt. She turned the spectacles over in her hand. Marianne had probably ordered these made specifically for Jocelyn. Well, she could try them on, she supposed.

She slipped the wires over her ears and glanced up.

The room jumped out at her and she started. Then stared.

It was as if a gauzy fabric was lifted from the world. The walls, a gray stone with subtle patterns of subdued color, were sharp and distinct. The ceiling soared upward overhead, held aloft by carved stone arches. With every

120

discovery, her excitement grew. There was indeed a wardrobe against one wall, a clothespress against another, and a brightly colored tapestry on a third — beside the door to the dressing room, she noted with satisfaction. Two well-worn chairs sat in front of a massive fireplace. A multipaned, leaded glass window framed streams of morning light, a built-in cushioned seat nestled beneath it. She flew to the window and pushed it open.

Green hills rolled away toward eternity. Here and there trees stretched upward toward the heavens. Clouds like fluffs of down drifted overhead. And good Lord, was that a lake in the distance? It was amazing. She could see forever. Maybe even farther.

She leaned her elbows on the stone sill, rested her chin in her hands, and gazed out in fascination. Why hadn't anyone told her about this? She ignored the voice in the back of her head that said Marianne and nearly everyone else in her family had. Over and over again.

"Jocelyn?" Rand called from the dressing room.

She snatched the spectacles off her nose, hid them in the folds of her skirt, and whirled away from the window. It was a rather shallow and terribly vain reaction, but she had only just started trying to improve her character and it was absurd to expect miracles. "Yes?"

"I'm coming out in a minute and I warn you, I will be fully clothed."

"Don't tease me, Rand," she said absently, fingering the glasses in her hand. How incredible that something so insignificant could change her world so completely. "My spoiled nature simply can't handle it."

His laugh echoed through the room.

She smiled with satisfaction. She had bested him earlier and the lovely feeling of success lingered even now. Better still, he wasn't at all upset by her victory but rather impressed. She didn't believe she'd ever impressed a man before, at least not in this particular manner.

The realization pulled her up short. The admiration in his eyes had nothing to do with how she looked and everything to do with who she was. Her wit and her mind as opposed to her face and her figure.

It was the nicest compliment she'd ever had.

Chapter 6

It was a very large castle.

At least that was Jocelyn's impression. Rand led her through the broad corridors and down the wide spiral stone stairs of the ancient building. In the manner of an excellent tour guide, he pointed out the various chambers and their uses. They passed a chapel and any number of smaller rooms. She couldn't possibly remember it all nor could she see much of what he commented on unless it was close at hand. She promised herself to explore later without him and with her spectacles. She also vowed to work harder on her problem with vanity, part of her promise to be a better person.

"And this is the gallery." Rand stepped into a grand corridor that overlooked the lower floor. "That's the great hall below us. It was originally used for feasts and sundry public events. Now it serves the purpose of a parlor, albeit a very large parlor. There's also an enormous dining hall. I'll show you that later."

"It's a very big castle, isn't it?" she said under her breath.

He raised a brow.

"I'm curious, Rand." She huffed. "Not mercenary."

"I didn't say a word." He grinned, then continued, "It is indeed rather large, although I understand it was not unusually big for the standards of its time, around four hundred years ago. You must remember castles like Worthington housed not just a lord and his family but servants and soldiers, knights and priests and any number of others. It was very much a self-contained community."

He strolled along the wall lined with the gilded, elaborately framed portraits of an endless number of Worthington ancestors. Jocelyn trailed behind, intrigued by the paintings almost as much as by the man. Rand was casually dressed in breeches and a crisp, loose linen shirt scandalously open at the throat. It was entirely improper yet completely fitting. It suited him and suited their exile. He looked very much like the confident master of the castle. Or master of anything he wanted.

"There used to be a dozen or so outbuildings for tradesmen and the like, all hemmed in by a towered wall. The buildings were torn down in the last few centuries and the wall itself is little more than a memory in some spots and a ruin in others."

He cast her a significant look. "Castles are exceedingly expensive to keep up."

"No doubt," she murmured, ignoring the pointed nature of his comment.

"Two of the towers, and much of the wall between, have survived. They're on the north side of the castle. One tower is nearly in ruins but the other is in excellent shape. In recent years, or at least before my grandmother died, it was used as guest quarters although it's closed up at the moment. I was allowed to stay there on my own as a boy. It was quite an adventurous undertaking. I can show it to you if you like." His manner was offhand as if he didn't particularly care if she wished to see his boyhood sanctuary or not.

"That would be lovely. But I must admit I am rather confused by all of this. You've obviously spent a great deal of time here yet apparently this is not your ancestral home. But your grandmother lived here." She shook her head. "Just who in your family is whom and what is what?"

"It's really not all that complicated." He shrugged and stepped a few paces down the gallery and nodded at a portrait. Jocelyn followed and stood by his side. "This was my grandmother."

The painting depicted a woman not much older than Jocelyn. With dark hair and darker eyes, Rand's eyes, and a faint wistful smile.

"She's lovely," Jocelyn said.

"She died, oh, nearly twenty years ago now." Rand studied the painting. "She was really quite remarkable. One of the few truly courageous people I have ever met."

"Really? How so?"

"She was not British by birth. After her first husband was killed, she was forced to flee her homeland with her infant daughter, my mother, and little more than the clothes on her back and this." Rand gestured at a small painting hung beside his grandmother's portrait.

Less than a quarter the size of the painting of his grandmother, the work depicted a handsome man with an air of supreme confidence. The painting was the smallest she'd seen in the gallery thus far, scarcely more than a miniature, not more than nine inches square, but was nonetheless mounted in an overly ornate, baroque frame similar to all the others. "This was my grandfather."

"He looks very young." And quite wealthy. "Where were they from?"

"A small kingdom somewhere near Prussia." He shrugged in dismissal then continued. "He was only a few years older than his wife when he was killed. At any rate, Grandmother made her way to England and the old earl, Nigel's father, took her in. He was in his fifties at the time and she was no more than three-and-twenty. He married her to keep her safe."

"Is it a family tradition then?" she teased. "Marrying women to keep them safe?"

"She was a good and dutiful wife to him for all the remaining years of his life," he said staunchly.

"I see." And obviously he expected good and dutiful wives to be a tradition as well.

"My mother grew up here. After she married my father, the fifth Viscount Beaumont, Nigel returned to the castle and has lived here ever since."

Something about his story struck her as odd. As if there was some detail of significance he had failed to mention. It probably wasn't important, still, its omission was intriguing. Was there something he didn't want her to know?

"I gather your mother is not here now?"

He laughed. "My mother is off conquering the capitals of Europe. My father died shortly after I returned home, four years ago, and my mother has seen fit to travel the world since then." He shook his head in tolerant amusement. "I can't fault her for it. She too was —"

"Yes, yes, a good and dutiful wife. You've mentioned that already." And if he mentioned it once more Jocelyn would be compelled to try to smack him again.

"I thought it bore repeating." He laughed. "Now then, if you've had quite enough tales of my ancestry, it's time you meet my uncle.

127

He was quite a rake in his younger days and still has an overly flirtatious manner. He's a bit eccentric now with a tendency to say whatever comes into his mind but I expect you'll like him. Shall we go?"

"Not yet. You've talked about history, but beyond a few comments about your childhood and the acknowledgment of countless women who have seen you naked, you've mentioned very little of your own past. If I am to be a good and dutiful wife I should know all there is to know about you." She folded her arms and leaned against the wall under the forbidding stare of a grim matron dressed in Elizabethan garb. "Marianne says you were a spy."

Rand glanced at her with an amused smile. "You are curious, aren't you?"

"Would you prefer mercenary?" she asked. "Now tell me."

"I scarcely know what to say." His voice was thoughtful. "*Spy* is a rather nebulous term, don't you think?"

"I think it's quite specific."

"No, not at all." He shook his head. "I think a term like *officer* or better yet, *general,* now that's specific."

"Rand."

"I suppose *prime minister* or *king* is also quite specific. As are *tailor, baker, gardener* —"

"Rand!" She glared with irritation. "You are such an annoying man." Obviously he was not about to answer her question. "No wonder you make me want to slap you. Or scream with frustration."

"I wouldn't advise trying to hit me. Again. That's not been overly successful for you thus far. As for screaming . . ." He rested his hand on the wall beside her head and leaned closer. She couldn't help but note that he was just the right height, taller than she but by no more than six inches. "I shouldn't be at all averse to your trying."

"Why?" she asked even though she knew the answer. Her gaze slipped from his eyes to his lips and back, and her heart thudded in her chest.

"Why?" He placed two fingers under her chin and bent forward. "So that I can shut you up of course."

His lips met hers softly at first, no more than a whisper. Without thinking, she rested her palms on his chest. She could feel the heat of his body and the beat of his heart through the fine fabric and noted an answering echo in her veins. His lips pressed harder against hers and she opened her mouth slightly in response. His arms wrapped around her and he pulled her closer, and an urgent sense of need swept through her.

She slid her hands higher, over his hard shoulders and to the back of his neck. His tongue met hers in a shocking intimacy, and warmth spread from his touch through her body to curl her toes. Her fingers tangled in his hair. His hands splayed across her back. She pressed harder against him, reveling in the feel of his body close to hers, her breasts against his chest, her hips against his. She wanted to . . . what? Devour him? Yes, that was it. And wanted him to devour her. And wanted . . . more.

He drew his head back and gasped, staring into her eyes with a look that could only be desire. A desire she realized she shared.

"This is probably not the place," he said slowly.

"No, of course not." She struggled to catch her breath. "Still . . ." She drew his lips back to hers. "I am certain I feel a scream coming on."

Again his lips crushed hers and all thoughts of place and time vanished. Her hands explored the warm flesh of his neck and ran across the tensed muscles of his back. He pulled his mouth from hers to trail kisses along the line of her jaw to her neck just below her ear. His hands slipped to the small of her back and lower still to caress her derriere.

She moaned with pleasure and jerked her head back to give him greater access.

And promptly smacked her skull hard against the stone wall.

"Jocelyn!" Rand pulled away and stared at

her with concern. "Are you all right?"

"Yes. Of course." His face swam before her and she shook her head to clear her vision. "I'm fine." She tentatively felt the back of her head and winced. "Except for this."

"Let me see." He gently turned her around and ran his fingers carefully over her head. "There's no blood."

"That's something," she murmured. It certainly did hurt enough to be bleeding.

"But there will be one hell of a lump in a minute." He turned her to face him. He frowned and stared into her eyes. "Look at me."

"Gladly." She raised her lips to his.

"No, I just want to look into your eyes. To make certain you're all right." He held her face between his hands and his gaze searched hers. He might well be looking for signs of injury, but she was far more interested in studying those mysterious eyes of his. They were brown. No, darker. Nearly black. She'd thought they were dangerous before. Now she knew.

She wasn't sure exactly what he'd seen but abruptly he released her and stepped back. As if he'd seen something he didn't expect. Or something he didn't want. Surely this man of experience had no reason to fear anything he saw in her eyes? "I think you're fine."

"I'm sure I am." Were they talking about

her head now or something else?

"It might throb a bit for a while."

"Oh, I'm certain it will." At least *she* was no longer talking about her head.

"We should probably do something to relieve the ache."

"Oh, we should," she said a shade too eagerly. "We most definitely should do . . . something."

"Come along then." He grabbed her hand and started off, practically dragging her along behind him. "Flora will know what to do."

"Flora?" She hurried to keep pace with him. "I don't want Flora. I want . . ." At once she realized they had indeed been talking at cross-purposes. Well, it was probably for the best. In spite of the amazing passion of their kiss and the startling but wonderful sensations she found in his arms, she doubted she was ready for anything more. At least not yet. And in truth her head did hurt quite a bit.

What would have happened if she hadn't hit her head? Would he have carried her back to their room? Or would he have taken her right here on the stone floor of the gallery? Or would she have taken him? She choked back a laugh at the thought and winced.

"Rand?" One would have thought the man was running for his very life.

"Yes?" he said over his shoulder.

"First, would you slow down?"

"Sorry." He came to an abrupt halt and she nearly skidded into him.

"Thank you," she muttered. "And secondly, the next time you wish to stop me from screaming, do you think it can be done without flattening me against a wall?"

Jocelyn's laughter echoed in the breakfast room. Uncle Nigel grinned with unfettered delight. And Rand kept a close eye on his wife.

He watched Jocelyn as surreptitiously as possible. He didn't want her to think he was at all worried, and she did appear to have recovered. But she had cracked her head rather hard. He'd seen blows to the head before and knew they were tricky devils. Still, her eyes had been clear and her pupils looked normal and he doubted she had any injury of consequence. Even so, he preferred not to take chances. It was his charge to keep her safe from whatever harm might befall her.

"Didn't think I'd ever see the boy wed. He's two-and-thirty now, you know," Nigel said with a nod.

"As old as that?" Jocelyn cast Rand a look of feigned astonishment. "Why, I'm surprised he can still feed himself."

She was obviously recovered.

"I'd say he's got some life left in him." Nigel chuckled. "Takes after his uncle. Feared he'd take after me too much though."

He leaned toward her as if about to impart a great secret. "I never married myself."

"Of course not, my lord, how could you possibly have wed?"

Nigel's eyes narrowed suspiciously. "What do you mean by that, girl?"

"Why, only that, from what I've heard, of course . . ." She glanced from side to side and lowered her voice in a confidential manner. "Your marriage would have broken the hearts of half the women in England."

Nigel stared at her for a moment, then cackled with laughter. "Very good, my girl. Very good indeed." He wagged his finger at his nephew. "She's a prize, boy. Good head on her shoulders and a sharp wit. Brains in a woman is just as good as beauty. Better even."

Jocelyn beamed at the compliment.

"Not hard to look at either. Not at all." He settled back and assessed her with a wicked gleam in his eye. Rand was too young to know firsthand of his uncle's rakish days, yet right now he could clearly see the rogue the elderly gentleman had once been.

"Pretty hair. Good skin and she's tall enough." He glanced at his nephew. "I always liked them tall. Long legs, you know. Shapely. Are her legs —"

"Excellent, Uncle," Rand said quickly. "She has extraordinary legs."

Jocelyn lifted a brow and Rand shrugged

apologetically in response. He had no desire to let his uncle, or anyone else in the household, know he was not overly acquainted with Jocelyn's legs. Although he had seen them when he'd taken off her clothes and could honestly say they were, in truth, extraordinary.

"Yes, indeed. Always did love long legs," Nigel mused, obviously no longer considering Jocelyn's legs in particular but long legs in general. Or long legs he had known. "Legs that could wrap themselves around a man's —"

"Uncle!" Rand snapped.

Jocelyn stared in stunned fascination.

"Come now, boy. You can't tell me she hasn't wrapped her legs —"

"That's quite enough," Rand said quickly.

An odd, strangled sound came from Jocelyn. Tears welled in her eyes and she sniffed hard.

"Pardon me," she choked out the words. Was she upset by Nigel's bawdy commentary? "I have something in my" — she pressed her lips tight together but her eyes simmered with laughter — "throat." No, she was definitely amused. Rand's estimation of her notched upward. Again.

"Uncle, you really shouldn't —"

"Now, now, Rand." Nigel scoffed. "She's a grown woman and married to boot. Married to you, no less." He nodded at Jocelyn. "I'd wager there were any number of broken hearts when you snared him."

Rand groaned.

"I'm sure women are even now throwing themselves off bridges in despair," Jocelyn said with mock solemnity.

"You're bloody well right about that." Nigel nodded smugly. "I said he takes after me. Damned proud of that. Of him." He lowered his voice. "The man's a prince, you know."

"Uncle." A warning note sounded in Rand's voice. He'd really rather not bring up the subject of princes. They hadn't spoken of Alexei once since their arrival. Rand knew at some point they would, although this was not the right moment.

"He speaks highly of you as well," she said with a smile.

Nigel ignored her. "I'd wager you never thought you'd be married to a prince."

"A prince of a man," Rand said quickly.

"Well, there was a moment or two, maybe a decade . . ." Jocelyn murmured.

"I believe that's enough talk of princes," Rand said firmly.

"That would make you Princess Jocelyn." Nigel's forehead furrowed with thought. He shook his head. "Sounds silly. Doesn't suit you. Lady Beaumont suits you much better."

"Perhaps," she said lightly and met Rand's gaze.

In that moment, the oddest sensation swept

through him. The same feeling he'd had this morning when he'd looked into her eyes to check her injury. It was at once uncomfortable and rather, well, remarkable. He'd known seducing the fair lady would not be a chore but wondered if he could grow to care for her as well. Or if perhaps he already did.

A look of surprise flashed across her face. Did she feel the same?

She pulled her gaze from his and turned back to his uncle. "Lord Worthington, I must confess I don't know a great deal about my husband's past. However, I imagine you have any number of embarrassing stories to tell."

"I daresay I can come up with one or two." The elderly man chuckled and launched into a recitation of Rand's misdeeds stretching over the past thirty years.

Jocelyn murmured appreciative comments and laughed more often than not. Rand paid only cursory attention to his uncle's tales. He was far more interested in observing the woman he'd married. Scrutiny that had nothing to do with the lump on her head.

She was rather more than he'd expected. He wasn't entirely sure what he had expected from Jocelyn but it wasn't this. Blast it all, the woman was, well, nice. She treated Nigel as if he were a suitor and worthy of her attention, rather than an old man. She flirted easily with the elderly gentleman and it was apparent Nigel was becoming quite charmed by her.

As, admittedly, was his nephew.

Since their marriage he had wondered more and more if he had misjudged her. Based his conclusions on little more than her reputation in society, which, in truth, never hinged on significantly more than a lady's charms and her behavior in public.

She'd been remarkably uncomplaining on their grueling journey. She hadn't been overly distraught at finding herself in his bed this morning. Indeed she'd been extremely clever and quite witty. And her kindness to his uncle indicated a generous nature. None of which meshed with the shallow, spoiled picture he'd had of her.

Perhaps he was wrong. Perhaps fate had led him to the one woman he could well spend the rest of his days with.

"Now." Jocelyn's curious tone, pulled him from his reverie. "Tell me about his days as a spy."

Although at this particular moment he would have gladly traded curious for mercenary.

"I don't think —" Rand started.

Nigel cut in. "Nonsense, my boy. There should be no secrets between a man and his wife. I may not have known the state of matrimony firsthand but I know that much. Secrets will destroy a marriage faster than even infidelity." He paused and a shadow passed through his eyes, as if he reflected on something in his own past. His own secrets. Nigel's eyes cleared and he directed his words to Jocelyn. "About this spying business."

She leaned forward eagerly. "Yes?"

Rand held his breath.

Nigel shook his head. "I'm sorry to say, child, I don't know anything about that. Don't know for sure if it ain't nothing more than gossip."

Rand started at the old man's blatant lie. Lord Worthington might have become something of a recluse but he'd always had friends in high places. Rand knew full well his uncle had maintained his contacts in London and through them had kept a close eye on his nephew's activities during the war.

"Oh well." Jocelyn settled back in her chair with a disappointed sigh. "It scarcely matters, I suppose. I was simply" — she tossed Rand a teasing smile — "curious."

"Let the past stay in the past, I say." Nigel smacked the table with the palm of his hand and nodded sharply. "It's over and done with. It doesn't do anyone any good to look back. With the exception of myself, of course.

"And now." Nigel grabbed his cane and got to his feet. "I've got work to do."

"My uncle is writing his memoirs," Rand said.

Nigel wagged his brows at his nephew.

"Plenty of long legs in there." He chuckled. "I miss 'em, I can tell you that. Knew lots of long legs in my day."

Jocelyn's eyes widened. "It does sound . . . interesting."

Rand grinned. "I for one cannot wait to read it."

"Not until I'm dead, my boy. Or maybe to-morrow. Haven't decided yet. Stop in the library later and see how it's going." Nigel turned his attention to Jocelyn. "Good to have a pair of long legs in the castle again. Puts life back in the place."

"Do you need help, Uncle?" Rand rose to his feet.

"Not from you." Nigel waved at a maid positioned by the door. "Rose will help me." He lowered his voice. "I don't have many pleasures these days and leaning on a sweet young thing to help me get around is the best I can do." He glanced at the approaching plump, middle-aged woman. "Course she ain't sweet or young but my eyes ain't what they used to be either." Once again he chortled with laughter and Rand joined him.

Rose rolled her eyes toward the ceiling, stepped to the older man's side, and wrapped her arm around his waist. Nigel leaned on his cane and draped his free arm over the woman's shoulder. His gaze met Rand's and he winked.

"Come along now, my lord," Rose said and led him toward the door. "And I'll have none of your tricks today."

"Tricks? Don't know what you mean, girl."

The couple stepped through the stone archway, their voices drifting after them.

"They'll be none of that poking me with your cane."

"It's not my cane." Nigel's cackling laughter echoed behind him.

Rand met Jocelyn's startled gaze and they burst into laughter.

"He's really quite . . . um . . ." She grinned up at him. "Outspoken?"

"At the very least." Rand shook his head and sat back down at the table. "I think he likes you. Very much."

"All of me or just my legs?"

"All of you, especially since he has not seen your legs."

"You said they were extraordinary."

"They are." He paused. *As, I suspect, are you.* "I hope he didn't embarrass you."

"Not at all." She leaned forward, rested her elbow on the table, and propped her chin in her hand. "Did he embarrass you?"

"No." He smiled. "Not overly, that is."

"He's rather wise, isn't he?"

"Well, he's in his seventies," Rand said thoughtfully. "He's seen quite a bit and no doubt learned quite a lot."

She grinned. "About women."

"Among other things."

She absently traced the design on the tablecloth with her forefinger. "I liked what he said about leaving the past in the past."

"So did I." He studied her for a moment. "You were really very kind to him."

She looked up at him. "You sound surprised."

"It's just that he's an old man and he can be rather dotty at times —"

"I didn't find him dotty at all. I thought his mind was quite sharp."

"I only mean he says things he probably shouldn't and —"

"He says exactly what he thinks. I rather admire that." Her words were measured. "Obviously that's one area in which you do not take after your uncle."

"I beg your pardon." He stared at her indignantly. "I say precisely what I think."

"Do you really?" She got to her feet.

"Of course I do." He rose at once. "Don't be absurd."

"Add it to my list of failings." Her eyes narrowed and his stomach churned. He had obviously done something to anger her but for the life of him he had no idea what it was.

"You're surprised I was kind to your uncle because I have nothing to gain from it. Because I am too shallow to enjoy the company of a charming old man without some kind of compensation."

"No, that's not what I thought at all." Of course, there had been a moment when perhaps . . .

She must have read the thought on his face. Her eyes flashed. "I have a splitting headache, my lord, and I am retiring to my rooms. Alone."

"Our rooms," he said without thinking.

"Our rooms." She fairly spat the words at him. "However, I should be most grateful if you would absent yourself from *our rooms* for the remainder of the day. I realize that request is selfish on my part but I'm afraid I am too spoiled to care." She turned on her heel and started toward the door.

Rand wasn't entirely certain what had just happened but he knew it wasn't what he'd intended. Hadn't he tried to compliment her? "Jocelyn, wait, I didn't mean . . . My uncle is quite taken with you."

She halted and her shoulders heaved with an irritated sigh. "He's quite delightful and I like him very much."

"He thinks I made an excellent choice."

"And what do you think?" She whirled to face him. "Do you think you made an excellent choice?"

"Possibly."

"Possibly?"

He winced. He'd never been stupid enough to actually tell a woman what he really thought before. Why on earth did he choose now to reform? It was her accusation about not saying what he thought that no doubt did it. He held up his hands helplessly. "Probably. I meant probably."

"What you meant is that in spite of how nicely we've been getting along or how hard I've been trying or the fact that you scarcely know me at all — in spite of well, *everything* you're still convinced I'm shallow, spoiled, selfish, and stupid."

"I never actually said stupid." And wasn't that a point in his favor?

"It was implied," she snapped.

Apparently not.

"In the interest of saying what we think" — Jocelyn crossed her arms over her chest — "I don't believe Lord Worthington is quite as wise as I had originally thought."

"Why not?" he asked cautiously, knowing he would not like the answer.

"Because his assessment of you is unrealistic. He sees what he wants to see. He's convinced I've married a prince. Obviously he's never met a real prince." Her gaze traveled over him with disdain. "Since, in reality, what I wed was a toad. Good day, my lord." She turned on her heel and stalked out of the room.

"A toad?" he called indignantly. "I am hardly a toad."

He stared after her. He'd never lived with a woman before, and apparently there were things he was going to have to learn about the temperamental creatures. Like when to say what he really thought and when to keep his mouth shut.

Her charges weren't at all fair. He did realize he'd been wrong about her. Pity he hadn't managed to convey that. Well, he had the rest of their lives to straighten everything out between them. And he'd start today.

She was rather magnificent when she was angry. Like a golden avenging angel. All that passionate fury wrapped in a delectable package. How magnificent would she be when her passion was directed in a much more enjoyable manner?

He smiled slowly. He'd always rather relished making up with women. Usually it required the presentation of a little bauble, much champagne, and a sincere apology. Making up with Jocelyn might be more of a challenge. She was his wife, after all, and that no doubt changed a woman's perception of what was forgivable and what wasn't.

Still, he'd faced far greater challenges in his life.

He ignored the voice in the back of his head that pointed out this wasn't merely a challenge.

This was his wife.

Chapter 7

"Now then, my boy." Nigel sat behind his desk and studied his nephew over the rim of the spectacles he used for reading. "Don't you think it's time you told me everything?"

"I thought you wanted to discuss your memoirs?" Rand resisted the urge to squirm as he had as a boy when confronted by that same look in his uncle's eye and that same tone in his voice.

"I know all about my life. I want to know about yours."

"There really isn't anything to tell," Rand said cautiously.

Nigel snorted. "Don't bam me, boy. It's been less than a fortnight since you were last here and there was no talk of a wife when you left."

"Admittedly, the wedding was rather sudden."

Nigel narrowed his eyes. "Is she increasing?"

"No," Rand said quickly. "Of course not."

"Don't look at me like that. You can't

blame me for asking. It's the usual reason for a hasty wedding."

"Well, it's not the reason for this one."

"Then what is?"

"There's nothing out of the ordinary here, Uncle."

"No?" Nigel raised a white brow. "You arrive here in the middle of the night, on horseback, with a bride in tow. I'd scarcely call that ordinary."

"I couldn't wait for you to meet her," Rand said staunchly.

"You can do better than that." Nigel scoffed. "Few women of quality I know would agree to travel all the way from London on horseback."

"Jocelyn is an accomplished rider." The lie rolled smoothly off Rand's tongue. Jocelyn sat a horse with all the confidence of a mouse clinging to the back of a tiger.

"Hah. She's not the type." Nigel shook his head. "The best horsewomen I've known tend to look a bit like their steeds. Your lady doesn't bear even a faint resemblance to a horse. And in that, my boy" — Nigel grinned — "I congratulate you."

"Thank you." Rand grinned back. "I must admit she is indeed —"

"Why'd you bring her here?" Nigel's eyes were as sharp as his voice. "Why didn't you bring her to the Abbey?"

"I told you I wanted you to meet her."

"I don't know how you've managed to survive this long, Rand. I do hope you lie better to other people than you do to me."

"I'm not —"

"Stuff and nonsense, my boy. I've known when you were lying since you were old enough to get into mischief. And I suspect mischief is exactly what you're into now." Nigel leaned back and studied him. "No one in their right mind would bypass the Abbey with its excellent staff and comfortable surroundings for a crumbling castle with a bare minimum number of servants."

"It doesn't have to be quite as crumbling, you know," Rand said pointedly and not for the first time.

"When it's yours, you can bring it back up to snuff. I see no reason to waste the funds necessary to do so now. I like it this way. It suits me." Nigel narrowed his eyes. "But you've changed the subject. Why did you marry this girl? Why the haste? And why are you here?"

His uncle was right. Rand never could lie to him. At least not well. Rand considered the questions for a long, silent moment. This was Nigel's home, and simply by bringing Jocelyn here he had more or less involved his uncle in the situation. Besides, he could trust Nigel with his life. Or Jocelyn's.

"Very well, Uncle." Rand drew a deep breath and quickly outlined the story.

"Better than I thought." Nigel chuckled then sobered. "I gather you don't believe she's in any real danger here?"

"I don't know. Probably not, but" — Rand shook his head — "I have men stationed on the property as a precaution. I suspect those involved in this conspiracy have better things to do than chase Jocelyn across the country. I doubt they'll take the time or make the effort to find her. However, as I cannot be sure of that, I refuse to take any chances."

"I can see why my talk of princes annoyed you, eh? Didn't want her dwelling on thoughts of what she lost? Or considering what she might have gained?"

"Something like that," Rand murmured.

"Who knows you're here?"

"The man I was working for, of course, and Thomas. We both thought it best if we kept it from Jocelyn's sisters. The fewer who know the better.

"With luck, I'm out of it now. Unless, of course, Jocelyn is able at some point to give us a description. She says she didn't see the men involved but I suspect she's simply put it out of her mind. Fear and all that. Not that I blame her. But for the moment, I've nothing further to do with it all. Jocelyn is my only responsibility."

Nigel studied him silently, and once more Rand felt as if he were a child again. "So what are you going to do about her?"

"I'm not going to *do* anything about her." In truth, Rand had very specific ideas about what he hoped to do about Jocelyn, beginning with an apology that was totally out of proportion to his crime but an excellent idea nonetheless.

"Come now, she's a beautiful woman. And your wife. More than likely for the rest of your life."

"I did think I would try to get to know her better."

"Get to know her better." Nigel chuckled. "Never heard it put quite that way before."

"Thomas suggested I seduce her." Rand grinned. "It seemed like a good idea."

"Damned if I don't agree with him. Smart man. I know his grandmother. Fine-looking woman in her day . . ." Nigel's face took on a familiar far-off expression. For the moment, his uncle was looking at sights and memories only he could see. Nigel's memoirs would be fascinating reading and more than likely quite scandalous.

"Uncle?" Rand prompted.

"Quite a beauty if I recall." Nigel sighed. "Now then, where was I?"

"Seduction?"

"Ah yes. Excellent idea but, in this case, seduction alone is not enough."

Rand snorted in disbelief.

"Think what you want, but I know what I'm talking about." Nigel tapped his pen thoughtfully on the desk. "Seduction is all well and good but it's, at best, an intermediate step. Sharing your bed is one thing, sharing your life is entirely different."

"I don't understand," Rand said slowly.

"Sometimes you're thicker than a newel post. Pay attention, boy." Nigel leaned forward. "You're, no doubt, in this arrangement for as long as you live. But passion alone doesn't last. By itself, it's not enough."

"What are you saying?"

Nigel blew a frustrated breath. "I'm saying you can't merely seduce her; you have to court her with an eye toward more than her bed." Nigel aimed an accusing finger at him. "Blast it, Rand, you have to make her love you."

"I don't know if I can do that." Rand shook his head.

"Of course you can. Unless . . . she isn't in love with that prince, is she?"

"I don't think so." No, he was fairly certain, if love was involved between Jocelyn and Alexei it was her love of his title and his wealth and his love of her beauty.

"Good." Nigel nodded with satisfaction. "She does already like you, you know. I can see it in her eyes."

"Then you see more than I do."

"I see that you like her as well. It's a damned good start. Some couples don't have that. Have you kissed her yet?"

"Yes." Rand drew the word out slowly.

The old man's eyes twinkled. "And did she kiss you back?"

"Yes." Rand grinned. "And with a fair amount of enthusiasm as well."

"Then you're halfway there." Nigel settled back in his chair. "Women are odd creatures, Rand. For them, desire more often than not goes hand in hand with love. That's where they differ from us. Win her heart first, Rand. And be patient. It will be worth the wait. There's nothing more loyal, more delightful, and more passionate than a woman in love. And nothing better for a woman than the love of a good man." He considered his nephew for a moment. "How do you feel about her? Deep down. In your gut. Where it counts."

"I don't know," Rand said simply. "At first I thought she was no different from many other young women I see during the season. Not a thought in her head beyond snaring the most eligible husband available. I thought she was self-centered and spoiled and stubborn."

"And now?"

"Now I *know* she's stubborn." Rand grinned, then sobered. "Marrying me meant her life would not turn out as she'd planned. And she did it more to keep her sisters safe than out of any concern for her own life. That was scarcely the act of a spoiled nature.

152

In that I was wrong.

"She's taken everything else in stride with remarkably few complaints and relatively good humor. I do think I've misjudged her."

"That's all very well and good but how do you *feel* about her?"

"I like her. Quite a bit actually." Rand considered the question for a moment. What were his feelings for Jocelyn? He wanted her, he was certain of that. And wasn't there something more? Something in the pit of his stomach when he gazed into the amber depths of her eyes? "Beyond that, Uncle" — Rand shrugged — "I don't really know."

"Excellent. That's a good place to begin. By George, I'd be worried if you did know at this point." Nigel smiled with satisfaction. "I daresay the two of you will suit well together. She'll make you a fine wife eventually." Nigel raised a brow. "And will you do as well as a husband?"

Rand started. "I hope so."

"Hope ain't enough, boy. If you want loyalty, respect, and affection you have to return it in kind. In spite of whatever misadventures I may have had in my younger days, I never dallied with a married woman. Considered it a point of honor. If you want fidelity from her, you have to be prepared to offer it in return."

"I fully intend to be faithful for as long as this marriage lasts. Forever if need be." Rand meant every word. Nigel was right. It was a point of honor, and Rand had never been especially impressed by men who kept mistresses or had affairs outside the marriage bed. His father hadn't been such a man and neither was Rand. "In that, I have had excellent examples to follow. My father and . . ." Rand met the older man's gaze firmly. "You."

For a long moment neither man said a word, but then words were not necessary. It was an unspoken vow between them that this one subject would not be discussed aloud. Never discussed aloud. If someday Nigel chose to discuss the one true love of his life, Rand would be there to listen. Until then, the privacy of Nigel's past would remain unbroken.

"I envy you, boy. You're just at the beginning of a new life. I suspect with the fair Jocelyn, it will be a journey with any number of intriguing twists and unexpected turns and, no doubt, one hell of a trip. No, on further consideration" — he chuckled — "I wouldn't be you for anything in the world. I couldn't stand the turmoil."

"I'll try to survive," Rand said wryly.

"You'll have a damned fine time too. There's a lot to be said for turmoil." Nigel's eyes twinkled wickedly. "And nothing better than a woman with long legs."

"Good evening, my lord." Jocelyn nodded

stiffly, then stepped to the opposite end of the long table in the immense dining hall, ignoring the place set next to her husband. She seated herself and glanced around. "Isn't Lord Worthington joining us?"

"Since his illness he tires rather easily. He's already retired for the evening." Rand smiled and gestured to the chair beside him. "Wouldn't you prefer to sit here? Where we can talk?"

"No thank you, my lord," she said coolly. "I prefer to sit right here and I'd rather not talk."

"Very well." He gestured to a maid, Ivy if Jocelyn remembered correctly. She and Rose were Flora's sisters. Rose was a widow and Ivy was married to a man who served as stable master for the handful of Worthington horses as well as farmed a portion of the castle's land.

In addition to the maids, Jocelyn had also met the cook, Mrs. Dudley. And that, together with Flora and Nick, was the extent of the castle's minimal staff.

Ivy collected the dishes and silver, brought it to Jocelyn's place, and set it before her. The look on the older woman's face was clearly disapproving but she didn't say a word. The staff there might be meager but it was well trained. Ivy arranged the setting, fetched a glass of wine from the sideboard, then left for the kitchen.

"How was your day?" Rand called.

"Very nice, thank you."

She'd spent much of the day exploring the building, spectacles in hand, and avoiding Rand. She simply didn't know what to say to him. What to expect. And what would happen next between them. It hadn't been particularly difficult to avoid her husband. He'd occupied much of his day ensconced with his uncle in the library. Not that his lack of attention bothered her. Or perhaps it did, but only a little.

The castle was an adventure in itself. Even when, now and then, she'd take the wrong turn and lose her way, it was still quite exciting. After all, she'd never lived in a castle before. She found any number of rooms not in use, with massive pieces of furniture hidden under dusty covers. There was evidence of renovation and remodeling, but somewhere in the distant past. Much of the building was in need of repair.

She'd paused for a few minutes in the chapel and noted with unexpected pleasure the air of serenity in the obviously little-used room. She'd discovered a relatively new billiard table in a chamber near the library and wondered if Rand played. And if, during their exile here, he'd teach her to play. She rather liked the idea. Besides, one didn't need to see far to be able to master the game.

She'd also gotten over her anger at Rand, and surprisingly quickly. Grudgingly she'd admitted to herself she couldn't really blame the man for thinking the worst of her. First impressions were lasting and she hadn't been especially gracious during their initial encounters. Still, she was trying and it wasn't at all fair of him not to give her a chance.

"And your day, my lord?"

Even at this distance, she could see the muscles in his jaw clench at her repeated use of the formal address. Good. There was something quite lovely about irritating him.

"It would have been much improved by the presence of my wife."

Ivy returned to the hall with a large soup tureen. She ladled a healthy serving into Jocelyn's bowl, then headed toward Rand's end of the table.

"*I* was remarkably easy to find should anyone have attempted to do so. *I* was not hiding behind closed doors all day" — she paused for emphasis — "my lord."

"Blast it all, Jocelyn." Rand got to his feet. "This is absurd." He strode the length of the table and sank into the chair next to hers. Jocelyn stifled a smile at the indignant look on Ivy's face. "This is much better. Now we can talk."

Jocelyn sipped her soup and watched Ivy bring Rand's utensils and place them in front of him, then return for his glass, and once again for the tureen.

Jocelyn had realized earlier in the day she might have been somewhat oversensitive. And, on reflection, had decided Rand hadn't meant his words in an unkind manner. Still, she did want an apology. The thoughtless nature of his comments called for at least that. And if she'd learned nothing else about men in recent months, she'd learned that it was best to keep them off-balance and, if at all possible, confused. It gave women a certain amount of power and control in a world in which so much of their fate was not in their own hands.

"I told you, I do not wish to talk." Jocelyn stood, picked up her bowl and her wine, strode to the other end of the table, and seated herself.

"Well I do." Rand got to his feet and started after her.

"My lord." Ivy's voice rang with exasperation. She thrust his bowl and his glass at him. "Would you be so kind as to take these with you?"

"Of course," he muttered, accepted the offerings, and returned to his original chair. Ivy scurried after him, filled his bowl the moment he sat down, then nodded with satisfaction.

Jocelyn rose again.

Rand stood once more.

Ivy looked warily from one to the other.

"I am prepared to follow you to the ends of the earth if I have to," Rand declared.

"Lord help us all," Ivy muttered, setting the tureen on the table with a sharp thump and stalking from the room.

"With soup in hand if need be." Determination rang in his voice and Jocelyn had no doubt he would do just that.

For a moment, in the dining hall with its stone walls and echoing spaces, she saw him as he might have appeared in this very place centuries ago. Standing strong and tall, a knight of old, bold and resolute, courageous and unwavering. Handsome and noble and . . . hers. Something deep inside her warmed at the thought.

She planted her hands on her hips and tried not to smile. "And would you be so determined, my lord, if it wasn't soup but oh, say, a piece of bread or a slice of cheese?"

His brows pulled together. "Of course."

"Oh? What if it was a bit of quail or a fruit tart?"

He stared at her suspiciously, then the corners of his lips curved upward. His words were measured. "I would follow you through the streets of London itself waving a joint of beef in one hand and a jug of ale in the other if I had to."

"Very well then." She sat down primly. "We can talk."

"Good." He grinned with satisfaction and

159

settled back into his chair.

"Well?" she prompted.

"Well what?" He downed half his wine in one long swallow.

"What did you wish to say?"

"Well." He sat his glass on the table in a deliberate manner and drew a deep breath. "First of all, I am sorry if I offended you this morning. It was not my intention and I —"

"You're forgiven," she said blithely.

"I am?" Confusion crossed his face. "That's it? That's all I have to do?"

"Unless" — she fluttered her lashes in an exaggerated manner — "you brought me flowers."

"No."

"Flowers would have been customary for an apology or, between a husband and wife, expensive jewelry." She paused. "I gather you don't have some exquisite bauble either?"

"No," he shook his head but his lips twitched as if he resisted a smile.

"Never forget my mercenary nature, Rand. However, as you have neither jewels nor flowers" — she waved a hand in a dismissive manner — "it's of no real consequence." She smiled over the rim of her glass. "But next time, I shall expect, at the very least, flowers."

"I'll remember that." He took her hand and raised it to his lips. His gaze meshed with hers. "I promise the next time, my apology will be accompanied, at the very least, by flowers." His breath was warm on the back of her hand. His lips rested on her skin for less than an instant but heat spread from his touch.

"You do that so well," she murmured.

"I wish I could swear there would not be a next time." His eyes simmered with an entirely different kind of pledge. "Vow to you there will never be a need for my apologies but . . ."

She could lose herself in those eyes.

"That's, no doubt, too much to hope for," she said, her voice annoyingly breathless.

Drown in their dark depths without struggle, without regret.

"Ah, but sometimes hope is all we have."

Rand's words lingered in the air. Shimmering with promise. Fraught with unspoken meaning. Silence stretched between them.

"We should probably . . ." Jocelyn withdrew her hand and gestured at her bowl. The moment had at once become strained and awkward and Jocelyn gratefully turned her attention to the meal.

"Ivy will be quite indignant if we don't eat."

Jocelyn sipped at her soup. Rand did the same. For long moments the only sounds in the room were the discreet noises of a meal being dutifully consumed. There were a dozen things Jocelyn wanted to say but the words were difficult to find.

Finally Jocelyn set down her spoon and squared her shoulders. "I have been doing a great deal of thinking about our situation."

"I'm not sure I like the sound of that."

"No, it's nothing untoward. Or at least I don't think it is." Jocelyn pulled a breath for courage. "It seems to me that as we are married now, and will more than likely be married for a very long time, the first thing we need to do is to become better acquainted with one another."

"Excellent idea." Rand's voice was serious but laughter lurked in his eyes. "How do you propose we begin?"

"To start with I think you need to understand a few things about me. About my life." She paused to pull her thoughts together. "If indeed I am spoiled —"

"And shallow," he added, obviously holding back a grin.

She ignored him. "I haven't been spoiled for very long. That is, we, my sisters and I, didn't grow up at all pampered. My father —"

"Yes, I know," Rand said quietly.

"I should have realized you would." She sighed. "No doubt my father's reputation was well known."

"Not at all. Thomas told me of your background."

"Oh." That was something at any rate. She'd always hated the thought that when people looked at Jocelyn, her father's failings came to mind. "Then you know it has only been in the past year, since Richard married Thomas's sister and they inherited an impressive fortune, that we have had any money to speak of. And I must confess" — she leaned forward eagerly — "it's been wonderful."

"Has it?"

She brushed aside his amusement. "It has indeed. For the first time in our lives we had new clothes and a fine carriage and trips to London and a roof that didn't leak."

"All that," he murmured.

"I know you think this is quite humorous —"

"Not at all." He leaned back in his chair and studied her. "I want to hear more."

"You're teasing me now but I forgive you." She thought for a moment. "Do you have sisters?"

"No," he said cautiously. "Why?"

"If you had sisters you'd understand." She pushed aside her soup bowl, clasped her hands, and rested them on the table. "For the most part, women are dependent upon men for their survival. There's little we can do to earn our own way. That's simply the way life is and it's never particularly bothered me."

She pulled her brows together. "Of course, I do have a sister, Emma, who paints and sells her work, but she's in Paris and the

French are so much different than we are about things like art. Besides, she's married as well, so she has no real need to support herself. And there is Marianne, who writes and actually earns money from it. But Emma and Marianne are rather rare exceptions. The only real way — the only acceptable way — for a woman to do well in this world is to marry well. You can't fault me for wanting to make a good match."

"I see," he said slowly.

"Do you?"

"I do indeed. You had your heart set on a prince and got a viscount instead."

"I knew you'd understand." She cast him her brightest smile. "So you do realize it wasn't so much that I am, or rather was, shallow but simply disappointed. Which was only natural under the circumstances."

"The circumstances being that you ended up with a viscount instead of a prince." His manner was matter-of-fact.

"Exactly." She beamed at him.

"You know, Jocelyn," Rand said slowly, "I have been considered, on occasion, quite a good catch."

"Oh, I have no doubt of that," she said quickly. "Your title, while not overly impressive, is still quite respectable. You're really rather dashing and ever so attractive with a wonderfully mysterious air about you. All that spy nonsense no doubt. In addition, you laugh easily and I do like that."

"I shall probably need to keep a sense of humor about me," he said under his breath.

"Indeed you shall. We both shall. Otherwise our circumstances would be quite dire." She sat back and studied him carefully. "I do hope I haven't offended you."

"Not at all," he said wryly. "One quite enjoys hearing one's failings balanced against one's attributes."

"I was simply being honest. In truth, I was only doing what your uncle suggested. You remember. He said there shouldn't be secrets between husbands and wives. Besides, you of all people should understand my feelings about money."

"Should I?"

"Most certainly. Rand." She lowered her voice confidentially. "I have been through the castle and while it is, on one hand, quite impressive and extremely interesting, it's also staffed by a mere handful of servants, far too few for a building of this size, and it has obviously seen better days. I'd wager the roof leaks, doesn't it?"

"Only when it rains."

"I suspected as much." A thought occurred to her and she sat up straighter. "I say, this is your uncle's home, though, isn't it? Not yours?"

"Yes?" The word was cautious.

"Then surely you have another home somewhere? Where your mother lives when she's not traveling" — Jocelyn's eyes widened with realization — "which does take money and —"

Rand held up a hand to quiet her. "My mother has a small inheritance that funds her travels. And yes, I do have a residence elsewhere, rooms in London and a modest house in the country."

"How modest?" she said hopefully, envisioning a nice-sized but not ostentatious country house.

"Very modest."

"Oh well." The country house shrank to a small cottage. She shrugged. "That's that then."

Rand narrowed his eyes. "I'm surprised that you don't sound more disappointed."

"So am I." She laughed. "It's really no worse than I expected." She considered him thoughtfully. "And what of you, Rand? What did you expect?"

"What do you mean?"

"You married me to protect me. Out of a sense of honor and responsibility. Quite admirable, I admit," she added quickly. "But surely, when you considered marriage, when you thought about the type of woman you wanted as a wife, I was not the first person to come to mind."

"Perhaps not," he said carefully. "Admittedly, I had not planned on marriage at this particular time."

"What did you want in a wife?"

"Oh, I don't know. A good dowry, of course." He flashed her a grin. "But then you have that."

"You will have to speak to my brother when he returns," she murmured. Until now, she hadn't given her dowry a thought. It was substantial, although Jocelyn wasn't certain of exactly what it entailed. After all, she hadn't planned on marrying this season. She pushed aside a twinge of irritation that her dowry would be the first thing Rand mentioned. Still, she of all people could scarcely fault him for considering the financial aspects of marriage.

"But that was not a prime consideration." Rand got to his feet, strolled to the sideboard, and grabbed the open bottle of wine. "I suppose when I thought about the woman I would one day marry, most of all, I wanted someone with a fair amount of intelligence."

"How very odd of you." She stood, picked up her glass, and held it out to him. "Most men I've met aren't the tiniest bit interested in a woman's mind."

"I gather you speak from your vast experience." He refilled her goblet. "This was your first season, was it not?"

"It was a very long season and nearly at an end," she said loftily. "Besides, you needn't be overly intelligent to recognize what is right before your nose." She sipped her wine and studied her husband. "In spite of your claim that you value intelligence in a mate, tell me, Rand, the first time you meet a woman, are you thinking about her mind?"

"Admittedly I might not —"

"And when you ask her to dance" — she stepped closer — "or brush a kiss across the back of her hand in that well-practiced way you have, are you considering how witty and clever she might be?"

He stared down at her with a smile of amusement. "You consider the way I kiss a lady's hand to be well practiced?"

"Isn't it?"

"I prefer to think of it as a natural gift."

"Call it what you wish. It's scarcely relevant at the moment." She pointed her glass at him. "And you, my lord, are evading the subject."

"If I am it's because your questions are entirely unfair. You're talking in generalities. Every woman is different and therefore my reaction to every woman is different."

"All right then, let's be specific. When you met me was it my clever repartee that you noticed first or the low cut of my gown?"

He choked on his wine and she hid a smile of satisfaction.

"Well?"

"I should say it was your bold manner," he said smoothly, recovering nicely.

She raised a brow.

"Very well. The first thing I noticed about you" — he eyed her over the rim of his glass — "was your response to my quieting your scream."

"And would you have quieted me in the same manner if I had been as ugly as a troll?"

He hesitated.

"Aha." Triumph rang in her voice. "I thought so."

"On the contrary, it was necessary and I would have done much the very same thing had you been as ugly as a troll. Or even uglier." His eyes flashed wickedly. "I just wouldn't have enjoyed it as much."

"But you enjoyed it because I'm pretty."

"Yes, you are."

"Very pretty."

"Some would say exquisite."

"It's a natural gift." She grinned and he laughed. "Emma was the artistic one, Marianne the dreamer, Becky the hoyden, but I have always been the pretty one.

"It takes a bit of effort to be the pretty one, you know. You must be ever aware of dress and manner. And natural gift or not, one finds it necessary to practice the fluttering of a fan." She fluttered her fingers as if she held a fan. "The artful tilt of the head." She tilted her head and gazed up at him. "The flirtatious yet not too inviting smile." She cast him her best enticing smile,

169

the very one guaranteed to make men forget their own names.

"It seems to me it takes rather a lot of effort to be the pretty one," he said mildly.

"Indeed it does."

"And you have perfected it to a fine art." He raised his glass in a toast.

She returned the salute. "Indeed I have. And all to one purpose."

"Making a good match."

"Exactly."

"Pity to have gone through all that trouble to end up with a mere viscount."

"It is ironic, isn't it. Aunt Louella would appreciate it. She does so love irony. However" — Jocelyn trailed her fingers along the edge of the table — "it may well be for the best."

"As your new husband, I find that rather encouraging."

"It's not always easy to be the pretty one. The one expected to make an excellent match because, frankly, nothing else is expected of you."

"You were well on your way to doing just that until circumstances intervened."

"Yes, I was. But . . ." Just how much could she confide in this man? Her husband? She'd never told another soul, not even Becky. And she did want him to think better of her. "Lately, I had begun to wonder if there shouldn't be more to life than fine gowns and eager suitors and grand parties." She shot him a pointed glance. "Mind you, I quite enjoy fine gowns and eager suitors and grand parties."

"No doubt."

"It was what I had always wanted, always dreamed of. Yet it had all begun to feel rather insignificant and somewhat pointless." She sipped at her wine and widened her eyes in feigned innocence. "I was beginning to fear I wasn't nearly as shallow as I — and everyone else — believed."

He laughed. "It must have been something of a shock."

"You're teasing me again, but yes it was extremely surprising. I had waited all my life for a season in London with the express purpose of being acclaimed a diamond of the first water. Of being the toast of the season and, eventually, making a brilliant match. And the first part, at any rate, did indeed happen.

"It simply wasn't as satisfying as I'd expected." She studied him curiously. "Odd, don't you think?"

"Not at all." Rand shrugged. "The problem might well be that you *do* think, even if no one credits you for it. I know I had not particularly expected it."

"I do hope you're not disappointed."

"Not at all. It seems I may be the one who has inadvertently made a brilliant match.

Beauty and brains. I could scarce want for more."

Nor could I. The thought flashed in her head. Perhaps, just as she'd said, it was indeed all for the best. Rand was an honorable man. Regardless of his less than lofty title or the minimal size of his fortune and every other thing she'd always thought necessary for a secure future, perhaps this was a man a woman could depend on. A man she could depend on.

"Pardon me, Your Lordship, my lady." Ivy stood in the doorway, arms crossed over her chest, a murderous look in her eye. "If you don't mind my saying, Cook won't be pleased to know she's ready to send in the rest of the meal and you two ain't hardly touched what's already here."

"We can't have that," Rand said in a serious manner that belied the twinkle in his eye. He stepped to Jocelyn's chair and held it out for her.

"It would be unforgivable." Jocelyn returned to her chair and allowed him to seat her, ignoring the accidental brush of his fingers on her shoulder and the delightful shiver that raced through her at his touch.

They turned their attention first to the remainder of their soup and next to the succulent roast of beef Ivy presented. They ate dutifully and drank rather a lot and laughed more than Jocelyn would have thought possible.

And they talked. About all manner of things. He was impressively well read. And while she had never been particularly interested in books, she was surprised to find the schooling offered through the years from her aunt and her older sisters had well prepared her for intelligent discussion. It was something of a delightful shock to discover she could hold her own with him.

Jocelyn had never talked to a man like this before. Without pretension or artifice. Without concern as to whether she said too much or too little. With more attention paid to the substance of her comments rather than the delivery.

The candles in the elaborate, old-fashioned candelabra on the table burned low. Jocelyn reluctantly noted the lateness of the hour. It was obviously past time to retire. Whatever that entailed. Jocelyn wasn't at all sure she wanted to know.

She drew a deep breath and stood. "Well, it has been a long day and . . ."

"Indeed." Rand got to his feet quickly. "And tiring as well."

"Then I shall be going." She inched toward the archway leading to the stairs. "To my rooms. To *our* rooms."

"Quite right." His brow furrowed. "Our rooms."

"Are you" — she swallowed hard — "coming?"

"You know" — his expression brightened — "I do believe I should like a brisk ride before bed. Would you care to join me?"

She stared at him. "It's dark."

"Oh, I'm certain there's plenty of moonlight or starlight. I've always enjoyed riding at night."

"Do you? It sounds rather . . ." At once she realized exactly what he was trying to do and relief swept through her. Was he as nervous about what came next between them as she? She nodded eagerly. "It sounds delightful."

"Then that's what I shall do then."

"Wonderful. And I shall" — she moved toward the exit — "go to . . . that is to say . . . retire." She turned and tried not to race for the stairs. Tried to keep her steps measured and relaxed. As if her pulse were not racing and her heart was not beating wildly in her chest. As if she were not at once terrified he would change his mind and be no more than a step behind her.

And just as terrified that he would not.

Jocelyn pulled her wrapper more tightly around her and paced her bedchamber, *their* bedchamber. What exactly would happen when Rand joined her for the night? She had no doubt he would indeed join her. What she didn't know was precisely what he would expect when he did.

She glanced at the bed. It was immense, impressive, a remnant of another time. Dark wooden posts spiraled upward from each corner. Heavy brocade hangings draped from top rails. A more fanciful imagination would have likened it to the den of some giant, lurking threat. A creature of some sort. A dragon or other monstrous beast. Ready to devour. To consume. Pulsing with erotic menace.

She blinked hard to clear the image. The bed once again was nothing more than a bed. And no more daunting than any other piece of furniture one would use for . . .

She pushed the thought from her mind and with it the accompanying vivid images of entwined bodies and low murmurings of intimate secrets and . . .

She wrapped her arms around herself and paced faster. There was no need to be nervous about this. Hah. There was every reason to be nervous about this. She'd never been a bride before. Never had a wedding night. Never shared a marriage bed. Never experienced anything more than a kiss.

The bed drew her gaze like an irresistible force. Did it have to be so big? So overwhelming. Why, it quite dominated the room. A huge, looming portent of doom. The site of her demise. The place of her inevitable downfall.

And surely it was the flickering candlelight

and her poor vision that made the covers un-
dulate like that?

Perhaps she could avoid Rand altogether.
Put off this — she cringed at the very
thought of the word — *consummation.* Her
husband was not a beast. He would never
force her, take her, against her will. In truth,
he was, well, rather surprisingly wonderful.
With his dark, mysterious eyes that made her
insides melt. And the square set of those
broad, muscled shoulders that proclaimed
confidence and power with every step he
took. And the way he laughed and the way
he listened.

And the way he looked at her. As if she
wasn't merely the woman he had to marry
but the woman he wanted.

The woman he wanted.

A delightful warmth washed through her at
the idea. He was her husband and he did
have certain rights and . . .

And why not?

The thought stopped her in her tracks.
Certainly she was a bit apprehensive, but
then wasn't every bride? And when she considered it, in a completely honest way,
weren't her feelings right now as much excitement as dread? As much anticipation as
unease? Perhaps . . . more?

She looked at the bed once more. Odd. It
no longer seemed threatening but, well, inviting. Even tempting. Possibly . . . seductive.

And when Rand returned . . . what?

She stepped to the wardrobe and found her spectacles where she'd discreetly hidden them. She slipped them on, then moved to the window, sank onto the seat and stared out into the dark night. The glasses were of little help but at least at the window she would hear the approach of his horse. Her gaze drifted upward and her breath caught.

The sky was alight with a hundred, no, a thousand stars. Bright, tiny points of pure magic. She'd never seen stars before and had never imagined the sheer glory of the heavens.

She leaned against the window frame and stared up into the night sky. It was the most amazing thing she'd ever seen. Unexpected and enchanting and perfect.

And she couldn't help but wonder what else of enchantment the night might hold.

Rand stood on a rise some distance from the castle and leaned against the ancient oak that had served as refuge and fortress and everything else a boy needed during the visits of his childhood. The tree was as much a constant through the years as the castle. Unchanging and solid and forever. A comforting anchor in an adventurous life.

A life that once again had taken an unexpected turn.

He gazed at the figure silhouetted in the

window in the west wing of the building. His window. No, *their* window. It was a startling thought, at once odd and yet somehow right. He'd never before considered the day he'd share his rooms or his life. Never thought significantly about marriage. It had been . . . what? Three days since their wedding? They'd passed in such a blur he'd scarcely had time to consider the full meaning of his actions.

Oh, certainly between the discussions he'd had with Thomas and Nigel and even Jocelyn herself, he was well aware this marriage was forever. But had the truth really sunk into him before now?

Lady Beaumont. His wife. That too was both strange and fitting.

How did one go about getting one's own wife to fall in love with him? Surely tonight had been a good start.

He'd never been in love before so far as he knew. Certainly he would have noticed such a thing. Oh, he'd enjoyed the company of any number of women through the years, but love? No. He had hoped, somewhere in the back of his mind, to find what his parents had shared. He'd rather expected when the right woman came along he would be struck at once by love, like a bolt from the heavens. It was a ridiculous idea, of course, and had never happened, and now he was married.

He had no idea how to make a woman fall

in love with him. In point of fact, he'd always avoided women who might possibly do just that.

Desire more often than not goes hand in hand with love.

Perhaps that was the answer. Perhaps he had to make her want him before she could love him. In that respect this was very little different from any seduction. He'd never had any difficulty with seduction before, but when he thought about it, he'd never been involved with a woman when the attraction between them, and the desire, was not mutual. When the games, the rituals, of mating were not born of experience on both sides. With no expectation of a future and no commitment beyond the here and now.

This was entirely different. Both the circumstances and the woman. In spite of Jocelyn's flirtatious manner and air of confidence, she was very much an innocent. He'd never attempted to seduce a virgin before. Never tried to awaken desires never before experienced. Never particularly wished to.

His uncle was right. He would have to be patient.

Rand sank down on the cold ground and settled his back against the oak. He knew the meaning of patience. Knew the importance of waiting for the right moment to move or strike or put forces into play. Knew as well the failures that came with acting too quickly, with impulse rather than thought.

The shadow in the window hadn't moved. What thoughts were on Jocelyn's mind tonight? Did she share his growing desire? Did she wonder what it would be like when he joined her in their bed for more than slumber? Did she long for the heat of his body against hers? Ache for the touch of his hand on her naked flesh, the taste of his skin on her lips, the caress of his fingers where she'd never known a man's touch before? Did she yearn for the moment when the passion of their kiss exploded into something more? Something uncontrollable. Something magnificent.

He shifted uncomfortably and blew a long breath. That was enough of that.

Win her heart first, Rand. And be patient.

Patience? Was his character strong enough for that? With every minute spent in Jocelyn's presence, and every minute away from her, he wanted her more. Wanted to run his hands along the curve of her hip, kiss the full swell of her breast, feel the long stretch of her legs entwined with his . . .

Rand groaned aloud. He would never be able to keep his hands off her if he continued to think along these lines. He had to focus on something else. He'd checked with his men again tonight, and as he'd expected, they had nothing untoward to report. And nothing further to occupy his mind for the minutes, even hours he was determined to wait here. He wanted her to be asleep when he returned. Otherwise . . . well, he could not guarantee he could resist the temptation of the delectable Lady Beaumont.

Would she resist if he came to her right now and took her in his arms and made her truly his? Perhaps not, given her response to their kisses. But would she then regret it?

No, it was too soon. His plan to make her want him as much as he wanted her was sound. Or if not sound, it was at least a plan. And the only one he had. Besides, didn't women always want what they couldn't have? He ignored the thought that Jocelyn was turning out to be unlike any woman he'd ever met and unlike any expectations he'd had of her.

Patience? Never had the word seemed so daunting. But if that's what it would take, then so be it. His future and hers were at stake. It wouldn't be easy. But then achieving anything of worth was never easy.

He'd wait until she was asleep, then join her in bed. The same way he had on their first night. If it took night after night of sharing the same bed to make her want him, so be it. She'd be insane with desire. It was a good way to start a marriage and well worth the trouble.

If he didn't go mad first.

Was she thinking of him? Wanting him? Longing for him?

He watched until the figure in the window vanished, and at last the light went out. And still he sat and watched and tried not to dwell on the lovely creature lying in his bed but considered instead the odd turn his life had taken.

And wondered as well if the marriage, the wife, he'd had no choice in might well have been the best decision of his life.

Chapter 8

Damnation. Jocelyn sat upright in the huge bed and glared at the empty spot beside her. She certainly hadn't meant to fall asleep but it had gotten so late and she was so tired. She'd tried to wait for Rand to return to their room. To their bed. And obviously he had at some point, judging by the crumpled covers on the other side of the bed.

Then why hadn't he awakened her?

She punched a pillow, jammed it behind her back, crossed her arms over her chest, and tried to think. Surely after yesterday's kiss and the truly wonderful time they'd had last night he'd want to share her bed for more than just a restful night's sleep. Although, judging by the state of the covers, his sleep was anything but serene. Good. She hoped he'd tossed and turned all night and hadn't had so much as a single second of peaceful slumber.

His restlessness certainly hadn't bothered her. She heaved a frustrated sigh. She wished it had. She wished she'd awakened to find his long, hard figure stretched out beside her. To hear the sound of his breathing in the dark. To feel the warmth of his body next to hers in the night.

Jocelyn groaned, grabbed his pillow, and buried her face in it. How could this have happened? She wanted him. Wanted everything that was supposed to happen between a man and a woman. Between a husband and a wife. His faint spicy scent of man and heat still lingered on his pillow and surrounded her. It was intoxicating. He was intoxicating. And the way he made her feel when his lips pressed hers or his hand touched hers or she looked into his eyes, everything about him was quite, quite intoxicating. And not nearly enough.

Was this then love? She jerked her head up and stared unseeing into the distance. Or was it simply desire? Hah. There was nothing simple about it and nothing familiar either.

She'd never been in love. Not once. Never particularly considered it one way or another. Certainly her brother and two of her sisters had found love but love had no bearing on her own plan for her life.

As for desire, she'd never given that any consideration either. It was not the type of thing a well-bred young lady *would* consider. If she and her sisters were nothing else, they were indeed well-bred, and Aunt Louella had seen to it they were properly raised. But properly raised or not, Jocelyn recognized desire when she saw it. She'd seen it often enough in the eyes of men when they looked at her.

She definitely wanted Rand, *desired* Rand, in every terrifying and exciting sense of the word.

But he didn't want her!

Of course. That's why he didn't wake her up. He was probably relieved she was asleep. No doubt he made every effort not to make a single sound. The inconsiderate beast. His pride insisted on sharing their bed, *his bed,* but there was nothing more to his presence there than that.

Anger, disappointment, and an annoying touch of pain mixed together in a confusing wash of emotion. She threw his pillow across the room with all the strength she could muster and resisted the urge to scream. How could he not want her? Men always wanted her. She was the pretty one!

She threw back the covers, slid out of bed, and stalked back and forth across the floor.

How could this have happened? Oh, certainly Rand had said he prized intelligence in a wife above anything else. She snorted in disdain. Jocelyn still didn't believe such nonsense. Rand was a man, after all. Besides, hadn't she proved to him she was not the empty-headed twit he'd expected?

No, she was smart enough and definitely

pretty enough. But apparently, for whatever reason, she wasn't enough. She just didn't appeal to him.

Perhaps the problem was with him and not her? Good Lord, a prince had wanted her. Why didn't her blasted husband?

Still — her step slowed — Rand was not completely immune to her charms. It was apparent in the way he'd kissed her. Why, who knew what would have happened in the gallery if she hadn't hit her head. No. She knew full well what would have happened, and he probably did too. He'd definitely wanted her then.

And she'd make him want her again.

Her chin lifted with determination.

How difficult could it be? He was a mere man and she had been practicing the art of flirtation her entire life. Flirtation carried to a higher level was seduction, wasn't it?

If it was pride and his desire to keep up appearances that kept him in her bed, then it was her pride and desire that would ensure he did something more there than sleep.

By God, as her husband the man had certain rights, and as his wife she had a duty to make certain he got them.

The only question now was where to begin. She would obviously continue to demonstrate her intelligence but that was entirely too subtle and could take forever. Besides, she had no idea how to entice him with her mind. No, she had to rely on tried-and-true methods with Rand.

She stepped to the wardrobe, pulled open the doors, and stared at the few dresses she'd brought with her. They were all terribly practical and horribly modest. Not at all the kind of thing to make a man take notice. Still, she selected one and studied it thoughtfully. Perhaps there was some benefit after all to a childhood in which sewing and mending were required activities. If she removed the fichu and the lace, and lowered the bodice a bit . . .

She scowled at the frock. She had hoped never to have to pick up a needle again and, in truth, had never been especially good at it. Perhaps Flora could help her. She stepped to the door and flung it open.

Flora stood there, balancing a tray in one hand and about to knock with the other. Her eyes widened with surprise.

"Good day, my lady." In spite of her burden, Flora managed to drop a quick curtsy. "His Lordship thought you might want a bite to eat."

"Lord Worthington?" Jocelyn asked. "How considerate of him."

"No, no, not that lordship. Dear, dear it's always confusing with the two of them here. No, it wasn't Lord Worthington although he has been known to be considerate on occasion." Flora swept past her and into the

187

room. Jocelyn followed on her heels. "It was your husband. He and his uncle ate quite some time ago. Morning is nearly over."

"It is, isn't it." Jocelyn hadn't realized it but she had slept quite late. Not surprising, given how late she had stayed up waiting for Rand. "I hope I haven't caused you any trouble?"

"Not at all, my lady." Flora set the tray down on a table near the huge stone hearth. "I expect it will take rather a while before you're fully recovered from your travels." The older woman shook her head in disapproval. "I can't imagine what Lord Beaumont was thinking, dragging you halfway across the country on a horse." She clucked her tongue. "Men don't have half a brain in their heads sometimes."

"Yet they do value it in others," Jocelyn said under her breath.

"Now then." Flora pulled up a nearby chair. "You sit right down and eat something. You need to keep your strength up."

Jocelyn sat down and stared at the plate Flora, or more likely Cook, had prepared. It was heaped with cold meats and coddled eggs, accompanied by several healthy slices of toast in a holder, a pot of jam, and a cup of tea. It was substantially more than Jocelyn normally ate in an entire day.

"I do appreciate it but" — Jocelyn looked up at the housekeeper — "I can't imagine ever needing this much strength."

"Now, now, my dear. I daresay the trip isn't the only thing taking its toll."

Jocelyn picked up a piece of toast and nibbled on the corner.

"You're newly married and I know what that's like. I'd wager His Lordship kept you up half the night."

Jocelyn choked and Flora flew around the chair to pound her thoroughly on the back. Did everyone in this place say exactly what they thought?

"I'm fine." Jocelyn grabbed the cup of tea and took a quick swallow of the tepid brew. "Really. Quite all right."

"Dear, dear, I am sorry." Flora sighed, pulled up another chair, and hesitated.

"No, please." Jocelyn waved at the chair. "Do join me."

"If you're sure." Flora plopped into the chair with another sigh. "We're overly casual here, I fear, and no doubt not what you're used to. Not up to the standards of London. It was different when the countess was alive."

"Lord Beaumont's grandmother?"

Flora nodded. "Oh, she was a lovely woman, she was. With the kindest heart you'd ever want to meet. Knew her place too. Made sure His Lordship kept up the castle, and the staff, the way his father had. And her not any older than him."

Jocelyn shook her head. "I'm afraid I'm a bit confused."

"It is confusing, I suppose, if you're hearing it all for the first time." Flora chuckled and settled back in her chair in the manner of a master storyteller about to impart a tale. "The countess, well, she wasn't the countess then, of course, was younger than Lord Worthington when she married his father. Even so, she wasn't a bit flighty as you might think. No indeed, she was a good and dutiful wife to him."

"So I've been told," Jocelyn murmured.

"They were married more than a dozen years until his death. It was a good marriage, or so I've heard. I didn't enter service here until much later." Flora thought for a moment. "I started right about the time your husband's mother left to marry her viscount. It would be, what? Somewhere near five-and-thirty years I would think. So long ago . . ." Flora shook her head at the realization. "At any rate, that's when the present Lord Worthington, then the young Lord Worthington, that is, returned home for good."

"I've heard he was quite a rake in his day." Jocelyn grinned.

"Oh my Lord, yes. And so handsome he was too. And charming with that glib tongue of his. You couldn't blame any woman for falling in love with him." Flora leaned forward confidentially. "I had a bit of a fondness for him myself when I was a girl."

Jocelyn laughed. "I can well imagine. Odd that he never married."

Flora opened her mouth to say something but then appeared to think better of it.

"Flora?" Jocelyn studied her curiously.

The older woman's brow furrowed with indecision. "Every family has its secrets, my lady. It ain't my place to reveal them."

"This family is my family now." Even as she said the words she realized they were true. And realized as well she quite liked the idea. "I would never do anything to cause Lord Worthington the slightest harm or a single moment of embarrassment." She smiled. "I am already exceedingly fond of him. He has lost none of his charm with the years, you know."

Flora chuckled. "No, indeed." She paused, then drew a deep breath. "It scarce matters now, I suppose. The countess passed on, oh, twenty years ago."

"The countess?" Jocelyn stared for a moment, then what Flora hadn't yet said became abruptly clear. She sank back in her chair. "Rand's grandmother? That's why his uncle never married?"

"He loved her," Flora said simply.

"His father's wife," Jocelyn said softly.

"Mind you, some of what I know is before my time. But my mum was in service here before me, and she said they fell in love the moment they set eyes on each other but it

191

was too late. She was already married to his father. That's why he stayed in London so much. He scarcely ever came home in those years." Flora sighed. "It pained him too much to be around her."

"Did his father know how they felt?"

"I don't know. Mum told me nothing was ever said and neither the countess nor His Lordship ever showed their feelings. And she was a good wife. Never so much as a hint otherwise." Flora shook her head. "But you never really know what secrets there are between a husband and wife."

"I suppose not," Jocelyn murmured.

"Even after his father died, His Lordship didn't come back to stay until Lord Beaumont's mother married and moved away. Course they couldn't do nothing about their feelings then neither."

"The scandal, of course." Jocelyn nodded.

"Scandal, my foot." Flora snorted. " 'Twas the law that kept them apart. Even though she weren't a blood relation to him, in the eyes of the law she was his stepmother and always would be." Flora shook her head mournfully. "It was a tragedy for them both, it was."

"How very sad." This was obviously what Rand had failed to tell her in the gallery. She could see why he wouldn't mention it even if she was not about to condemn his uncle and his grandmother for loving each other. Still,

Rand scarcely knew her well enough to know that. Yet. "But they were able to live together here."

"Oh my, yes. They were great friends and companions for the rest of their days. They never did anything that would say otherwise, so much as any of us could see." Flora wiped an errant tear from her eye. "But you could tell from the way they looked at each other their feelings were as strong as ever. From the moment they met until the day she died." Flora sniffed. "I ain't never seen a love like that and I doubt I'll ever see it again."

Flora fell silent, and for a long moment neither woman spoke. Jocelyn didn't think she'd ever heard a story quite so sad before. She couldn't imagine a love so strong it would last a lifetime in secret. Her heart ached for Nigel. And perhaps for herself.

Was his nephew capable of such a love? Was she? Abruptly she realized she wanted more from Rand than his merely desiring her. She wanted his love. And wanted to love him in return.

"Now, my lady." Flora's brisk tone pulled Jocelyn from her thoughts. Flora nodded at the dress still in Jocelyn's lap. "Did you have something you need mended?"

"Not exactly." Jocelyn shook out the dress. "I brought very few clothes with me and I was hoping maybe we could make this a bit more, well, interesting." Quickly she explained what she had in mind.

"I see." Flora raised a curious brow. "Don't know that it's necessary, you being newly married and all. Still, it's better to keep his interest right from the beginning than lose it and start over."

Jocelyn laughed. "My feelings exactly."

Flora plucked the garment from her hands and examined it. "Shouldn't be hard. The removal of the lace alone should do the trick. Won't take more than a few minutes I should think." She looked up at her. "I do believe we have some old gowns of your husband's grandmother around here somewhere. She was not as tall as you; still there might be something you'd like. They're not the fashion now — Lord, they'd be more than forty years old — but beautiful all the same. Silks and satins and the like. If you'd be interested . . ."

"Oh I would." Jocelyn nodded eagerly. She could well imagine how she'd look in the gowns of another era. With wide skirts and sensuous fabrics and low-cut bodices. She'd be a vision. Any man's fantasy. And surely irresistible to one man in particular.

They chatted for a few more minutes about inconsequential matters and Flora took her leave, promising to alter the dress at once and return within the hour, then look for the older gowns.

Jocelyn ate absently, the story of Nigel's

tragic love lingering in her mind. She wanted to be loved like that. Wanted it fiercely. How strange when she'd been fully prepared not more than a week ago to marry without giving love a second thought. Everything, her life, her future, her desires had changed since then.

She had changed.

Resolve filled her and she smiled wickedly. Or perhaps she hadn't changed much at all.

And perhaps, at least if the love of the man you wanted was your husband, the best place to work your way into his heart was in his bed.

"It seems to be me that while you know everything about me, I know very little about you." Jocelyn gazed up at Rand from beneath a fetching straw bonnet, one she'd brought with her from London precisely because she knew it framed her face perfectly.

Jocelyn sat on a blanket beneath an old oak on a grassy rise a short distance from the castle. Rand reclined beside her. She'd asked him to show her around the grounds in the belief that if she was going to get this man to care for her, she had to spend as much time with him as possible. He had agreed without hesitation, even going so far as to ask Cook for a picnic basket.

It had been an excellent meal and an excellent afternoon. They'd spoken of all kinds of meaningless matters and she'd learned he liked Shakespeare, had a fondness for large dogs, and detested asparagus. He also had the most intriguing flecks of green in his dark eyes when the sun hit them in just the right way.

Now, however, it was time for more serious matters.

Rand laughed. "What exactly do you wish to know?"

"Well, let me think." She kept her voice nonchalant, as though their conversation were of no importance. It was, of course. She wanted to know everything there was to know about this man who was her husband. She reached into the basket, pawed through the remaining fruit tarts and other leftover morsels, pulled out an apple and a paring knife. "Tell me about being a spy."

"No," he said with a grin.

"Why not?"

"First of all, no true spy would ever admit to being a spy. It would quite defeat the purpose."

"But you were —"

He raised a brow. "How do you know that?"

"Why, I . . ." She huffed in annoyance. "I suppose I don't really, do I?" She brightened. "However, I do know you were working for the government as recently as last week."

"One can perform all sorts of services for

one's country without being a spy," he said mildly.

She studied him for a moment. "You are an annoying man, aren't you?"

"And you are an intensely curious creature." He plucked the apple from her hands, took the knife, and began to peel the fruit.

"At least you no longer consider me mercenary," she murmured, watching the deft way he handled the knife.

"I'm not entirely certain curious is much better." He pressed the back of the blade with his thumb and slowly turned the apple, the peel dangling from the fruit in one long curl.

"Why?"

His fingers were long and strong, his motions sure and competent and altogether mesmerizing. "A curious woman can get herself into all kinds of trouble."

"Can she?"

The peel fell to the blanket, a scarlet spiral against the pale coverlet.

"Isn't there some superstition children have about the peel of an apple forming the initial of a future spouse?" Rand poked at the peel with the knife. "It doesn't particularly look like an initial other than perhaps a curved P."

"Prudence perhaps? Or Patience?"

"Or Patricia?" He laughed. "Surely there are more but I can't think of any others."

"Philomena." She nodded and grinned. "Or Prunella."

He grimaced in exaggerated horror. "God save me from a woman named Prunella."

"I daresay you're already saved as you're already married," she said with a laugh.

"Absolutely. And as that is the case . . ." He rearranged the peel into a reasonable approximation of a J. "That's much better."

Her gaze met his. "Is it?"

He nodded slowly. "Yes, I believe it is."

She leaned forward until her lips were close to his. He wanted to kiss her. She could see it in his eyes. But he didn't want it enough. Not yet.

She took the apple from his left hand, the knife from the right, and straightened. He drew a shuddering breath and she smiled to herself. This was indeed a very good start.

"Tell me, Rand" — she cut a slice from the apple — "about your family. Your mother perhaps."

"My mother?" He frowned in surprise and the tension between them vanished.

Jocelyn groaned to herself. *His mother?* What a stupid thing to ask him about. The last thing a man needed to be reminded of at a moment like this was his mother. And it had been going so nicely too.

"Yes," Jocelyn said with a resigned sigh. As long as she had brought up the subject she might as well continue. "My mother died when I was very young and I scarce remember her at all. I rather look forward to meeting yours."

"She'll like you, I think." He studied her for a moment. "I suspect she always feared I'd marry some milk-and-water miss."

"And she wouldn't like that?" Jocelyn took a bite of the apple slice and noted the way Rand's gaze focused on her mouth. She chewed slowly and deliberately.

"Not at all. She's rather an independent sort herself." Jocelyn took another bite and Rand swallowed hard. "Led my father on quite a merry chase, I believe."

She cut a second slice, started to take a bite, then held it out to him. He accepted it, his fingers brushing hers, and electricity again sizzled between them. He popped the piece into his mouth, a drop of apple juice lingering on his lips.

Without thinking she reached out to brush it away. He grabbed her hand and licked the juice from her finger.

Rand turned her hand over and kissed her palm, and a shiver ran through her. His gaze met hers and she saw her own desire reflected in his eyes.

He pulled her down to him slowly as if they moved in a dream. Their lips met and time itself seemed to pause, then all restraint between them vanished. He jerked her into his embrace and her arms wrapped around him with a need she'd never known. His lips were hard and demanding and she demanded in return. Her mouth opened and his tongue met hers and delight swept through her. He tasted of apples and heat and desire. She wanted him and all that wanting him meant.

His hands were on her back, then lower, caressing her derriere, and they rolled together off the blanket and onto the grass. She lay on top of him, feeling every inch of his long, hard length beneath her. She wrenched her lips from his to kiss his face, his neck, and the pulse beat at the base of his throat. His scent, his touch filled her, surrounded her, conquered her.

His hands slipped along her sides and down the length of her legs until her skirt slipped up and he touched her bare skin. She gasped and shifted to lie face-to-face with him in the grass. His leg wedged between hers and she could feel the evidence of his arousal pressing into her. Fear flickered, then was swept away by the more powerful urgency of need. His hand cupped her buttocks beneath her dress, pulling her more tightly against him. His head dipped to the swell of her breast revealed by the low bodice and she strained against the fabric wanting only his touch, his kiss.

His hand slipped between her legs to the moisture she could feel there and to a place she'd never been touched before. Indescribable sensation shot through her and she sucked in a hard breath. "Oh dear Lord, Rand."

He stilled.

"Rand?" She pulled her head back and stared at him.

"No." His expression hardened. He yanked her dress down into place, then got to his feet. "This is neither the time nor the place."

"Is it ever?" She sat up and struggled to clear her fogged senses. "Why on earth not?"

"It's not the way to begin a marriage." He ran his hand through his hair in obvious frustration.

"Isn't this the way most people begin a marriage?" She grabbed his offered hand and he pulled her to her feet. She glared at him. "After all, you are my husband and you have certain rights."

He stared at her and a smile tugged at the corner of his mouth. "I know."

"Well then?" She fisted her hands on her hips and glared. "Shouldn't you insist on them?"

He moved closer and straightened her bodice. "This is entirely too low."

"I know." *Thank you, Flora.* Not that it did any good. His whole attitude was quite annoying. She slapped his hand away. "Don't change the subject."

"I'm not. When you and I are ready to be married in the truest sense of the word, I want all to be right between us." He cupped her chin in his hand and brushed his lips against hers.

"This seemed rather right to me," she muttered.

"I want more from you than a moment of passion on the side of a hill where anyone could see."

"I thought it was more than a moment of passion on the side . . ." She drew back and stared at him. "What do you mean anyone could see?"

He hesitated.

"Rand," she said slowly. "It seems to me Worthington Castle is rather remote, precisely why we're here in the first place. We are some distance from the nearest village and, at the moment, some distance from the castle. Who exactly are you worried will see us?"

He blew a long breath. "I have a few men patrolling —"

"You have a few men? Here?" She looked about in disbelief. "I thought you said once we were out of London, that there wasn't any danger?"

"I did."

"But you don't believe it?"

"I do," he said without hesitation. "I just don't want to take any chances."

She crossed her arms over her chest. "Is there anything else you haven't told me?"

"Not a thing." He shook his head, his lips pressed into a firm line.

She studied him for a long moment and didn't believe him for a second. There was probably no end of other things he hadn't mentioned. He hadn't told her about his uncle and his grandmother either, although she really couldn't fault him for that. He was loyal and protective of those he cared about. And once, he'd probably been a damned fine spy. Because, whether he wished to confirm it or not, the man obviously *had* been a spy and was probably well used to lying when the occasion called for it. No doubt he felt justified in not being entirely truthful where her safety was concerned.

"I don't believe you." She gathered up the blanket and the basket and thrust them at him. "But I shall not press you at the moment." She started off down the hill.

"What do you mean?" he called after her.

"You said it yourself, Rand, there are all kinds of trouble a curious woman can get into."

"Jocelyn." There was a warning in his voice and she disregarded it. After all, while whatever secrets he had about his past life as a spy or his most recent work for the government were intriguing it wasn't what interested her most. Abruptly she realized she could trust him. Regardless of what secrets he kept she could trust him with her life and trust him without question. And someday, perhaps, trust him with her heart as well.

What truly held her curiosity right now was what it would take to get him into her bed.

What did the man consider the right place and the right time? And whether it would be as wonderful as she thought.

And exactly what he meant by wanting more from her than passion.

Chapter 9

This wasn't working out at all the way he had planned.

Jocelyn sat next to Uncle Nigel at the dinner table chatting brightly, laughing a great deal and using each and every flirtatious skill she possessed to turn the old gentleman's head. Not that Nigel was putting up the least bit of resistance. No, in point of fact he was giving at least as good as he got, and looking a good twenty years younger for the effort.

Had it been another place, and another man, Rand might have been annoyed at the attention being paid his wife and the attention she was paying someone else. Particularly given her appearance tonight.

She looked like something from a dream. His dreams to be exact.

She usually wore her blond hair piled on top of her head. Tonight it fell loose in soft careless curls to caress her shoulders. Her eyes caught the candlelight and gleamed with enjoyment. Her skin glowed almost as if she was lit from within by excitement or secrets. And she'd donned the most amazing silk and satin confection. A dress even he could see was a good thirty years out of fashion. Still, it suited her.

Its full skirt rustled provocatively every time she so much as breathed, although how she could take even a single breath was beyond him. The bodice was tight-fitting, defining her waist, laced with ribbons up the front. The ivory-colored satin was barely a shade different from the peach and cream hue of her skin. And if he'd thought the neckline of the dress she'd worn today was low, it was positively modest compared with what she had on now.

It was scandalous. It was outrageous.

And absolutely delectable.

Jocelyn directed a question to him and Rand responded without thinking.

Nigel raised a brow. "Do you really think so, my boy?"

"Indeed," Rand murmured with absolutely no idea what he'd just agreed with.

Nigel and Jocelyn exchanged glances and yet another laugh. It was rather annoying to be excluded from the conversation. Although it didn't really matter at the moment. He hadn't been able to concentrate on much of anything since their aborted picnic this afternoon.

He wasn't sure why he had called a halt to

what would surely have led to a delightful afternoon of lovemaking under blue skies.
Damn it all, one would have thought he was
the skittish virgin and she the experienced
rake. Regardless of what he had said, it
wasn't the possibility of discovery that had
stopped him. His men were stationed along
the perimeter of the castle grounds a good
distance away and completely out of sight.
The chances of being spotted by them, or
anyone, were practically nonexistent.

"And I'm certain you agree?" Jocelyn
turned toward him, her honey-colored eyes
brimming with laughter.

"Of course." Rand nodded absently.

"I knew it." Jocelyn turned back to Nigel,
and once again the conversation continued
without him.

He'd realized it on the hill today. He didn't
just want it to be right for her. He wanted it
to be right for them. Because it was important for the rest of their lives to start out
right with the woman he . . . what? Loved?

Nonsense. She was the woman he'd married. The woman he'd had to marry, and love
played no role in it whatsoever.

Jocelyn leaned toward Nigel, and once
again Rand noted the appallingly low cut of
her gown. He was bloody well glad she
wasn't wearing something like that around
someone like Alexei.

Where had that thought come from? It felt

suspiciously like jealousy. Regardless of her words, did she indeed care more for Alexei than she'd let on? Had she wanted the prince for more than his title and his wealth? Although it scarcely mattered, she was Rand's now.

"I was hoping he'd teach me," Jocelyn said with a sidelong glance at Rand.

And Rand wanted her.

"He's quite accomplished at it." Nigel nodded. "I'd say it was something of a natural gift."

Wanted her in his bed.

"But you've never —" Nigel started.

Wanted to feel the heat of her skin next to his.

"No." She sighed. "I haven't really had the opportunity although I am exceedingly curious. It sounds quite enjoyable."

Wanted her writhing with pleasure beneath him.

"I toyed with the idea when we were at Effington House earlier in the season." Jocelyn shook her head. "There were any number of gentlemen who would have been more than willing to instruct me."

Wanted her to call out his name in the throes of passion.

"He's acquired a bit of a reputation for it, at least among his friends."

In the grip of love.

"Be aware, though, I have on occasion

heard him whoop with triumph accompanied by a rousing *well played*." Nigel chuckled.

Abruptly the words registered in Rand's mind and shock coursed through him.

"Uncle!" Certainly allowances had to be made for Nigel's age but this was too much. "I daresay I have never — nor would I. And to say such things in the presence of a lady, especially my wife, is . . ." Rand's gaze shifted from his uncle's look of astonishment to Jocelyn's confused expression. At once his cravat felt exceedingly tight around his neck. "What were we discussing?" he asked carefully.

"Billiards, Rand." Jocelyn stared at him as if he was quite insane, and perhaps in truth he was.

"She wants you to teach her how to play." Nigel's voice held an innocent note but his lips twitched as if he held back a grin, and his eyes glittered with silent laughter.

"I noticed the billiards room and I would very much like to learn the game." Jocelyn studied him cautiously. "It's not an unfitting pursuit for a woman. I know the dowager Duchess of Roxborough plays, as did Marie Antoinette."

"Lovely women. Both of them. I may have played with the duchess once myself. Or perhaps it was the queen. Or maybe both." He leaned toward his nephew in a confidential manner. "I am still speaking of billiards here,

209

Rand. Wouldn't want you to mistake my words." Nigel grinned wickedly. "Again."

"I do appreciate that," Rand said under his breath.

"After dinner then?" Jocelyn continued to consider him curiously.

"After dinner?" Rand stared at her across the table. Gad, she was lovely. She quite took his breath away. He wanted —

"Billiards, Rand," Nigel said pointedly. "She's talking about billiards."

"Yes, of course, billiards." Rand nodded firmly, belying the odd flustered feeling that gripped him. "After dinner. Excellent."

He made it a point to concentrate on the conversation throughout the remaining courses, actually managing to add a coherent comment or two in the process and eliciting an occasional appreciative laugh. Still, he couldn't ignore the tumult of emotions swirling in the back of his mind.

What had the woman done to him? He was a clear-thinking, intelligent man. Passion, lust, had always had a place in his life, but never before had it been the only thing he could think of. And never before had it centered on a single woman to the exclusion of any other rational thought.

Blasted woman. It was her fault. If she didn't look so bloody enticing and wasn't so obviously willing and . . .

And she did want him, didn't she? Wanted

him as much as he wanted her?

And if she wanted him, wasn't it entirely possible that perhaps she loved him as well?

"Now then," Rand said, obviously warming to his duties as tutor. "The object of the game —"

"I know the object of the game, Rand." Jocelyn rolled her gaze toward the ceiling. "You have one red ball and two white balls. You hit them with this stick —"

"It's called a cue."

"Whatever." She shrugged. "I've watched people play. It's very much like croquet only on a table without the wickets."

"Something like that." He nodded at the table. "Go ahead."

"Very well." She leaned across the table, positioning her cue as best she remembered and attempted to smack the nearest white ball. Her cue glanced off the side and the ball dribbled off at an angle. She glanced up at Rand. "That wasn't very good, was it?"

"No indeed." He chuckled. "But you're not holding the cue properly. Here, watch how I do it." He eyed the balls on the table, lined up his cue, and stroked it smoothly. It rolled straight into the red ball, propelling it into the nearest pocket.

She raised a brow. "Your uncle was right. You do know how to play."

"I quite enjoy billiards." He strode around

the table, studying the remaining two balls. She liked the confident way he moved. Like a man with a purpose. A man who knew what he wanted and how to go about getting it. Her stomach fluttered at the thought. "I played a great deal when I was last here."

He took another shot, striking the remaining ball and sending it into another pocket. He pulled the balls from the pockets and tossed them back onto the table. "I was here for rather a long stay when Nigel was ill. Of course, I helped manage the estate for him, but there was little else to do and he slept a great deal."

Rand circled the table, taking a shot now and then, nearly always successful. He was a pleasure to watch, graceful in a masculine sort of way.

"Nigel mentioned to me once how much he liked the game so I had the table sent up from London in the hopes that once he recovered he would enjoy taking it up again. When he felt better we played together, and Flora tells me he has indeed been playing in my absence." Rand took another shot, then straightened. "Care to try again?"

"It doesn't look terribly difficult." She studied the table, selected a position, and tried once more. This time her ball smacked the red ball with a solid thunk. She smiled with satisfaction. "Much better, I think."

"We'll make a billiard player of you yet."

Rand grinned. "Now then, allow me to show you . . ."

They played for a long while with Rand explaining as they went along. Jocelyn realized the game took far more skill than she'd expected. Still, it was enjoyable, even if a bit frustrating.

There was a chandelier directly above the table that lit the playing surface but little else in the room. The atmosphere was distinctly cozy, even intimate. Perhaps her concentration would be better if she wasn't so acutely aware of Rand's presence. Awareness that grew with every passing minute.

She caught herself brushing past him a bit closer than necessary and wondered if he noticed. She found herself studying the curve of his neck when he leaned over the table and the way his dark hair curled over his starched collar. She noted the fine fabric of his jacket stretched taut over his broad shoulders and how the muscles of his back rippled beneath the cloth. And remembered exactly how that back had looked without any clothes at all. And wondered why it seemed so hot in here now.

"Your turn." His gaze caught hers and he smiled. A distinctly rakish sort of smile as if he knew full well what she was thinking.

"Is it?" She turned away to hide the annoying blush she knew colored her face. Blasted man. What was he doing to her anyway? This afternoon she wanted nothing more than to give herself to him right there in the grass, and tonight little more than a knowing smile on his part had her quite disconcerted.

She drew a deep breath and leaned over the table. Still, this afternoon passion had simply erupted with no hesitation and no conscious thought. Now desire seemed to hover in the very air like an omniscient presence. Pulsing and growing with every word they spoke and every word they didn't. Threatening and terrifying and exciting.

"You're really not holding that right, you know," Rand said softly.

"No?" Her voice was barely more than a whisper. She swallowed hard and straightened. She met his dark gaze directly. "Perhaps you would be so kind as to show me the proper way to . . . to . . ."

"My pleasure." He leaned his cue against the table and stepped to her side. She turned back to the table and he moved behind her. So close she could feel the heat of his body through his clothes and hers.

"Hold it like this." His breath teased her neck and a shiver ran through her. He wrapped her right hand around the cue, his fingers lingering on hers. "Now lean forward and place it on the table." She did so and he shifted slightly to her side. He positioned her other hand on the table to help support the cue. His arms were around her, his presence engulfed her, and she could barely hear his words over the beat of her heart.

"Now then." His voice was low against her ear. "Just pull back slowly" — he fit his actions to match his words — "then push forward, in a nice easy stroke."

The cue hit the ball but Jocelyn scarcely noticed. She didn't move so much as a single muscle. "That wasn't very good, was it?"

He kissed the side of her neck, and her knees threatened to buckle. His voice was low. "It was very good."

She held her breath. His lips trailed down the curve of her neck and his warm hand slid up her arm to push the neckline of her gown over her shoulder. He kissed her shoulder and she shuddered with delight.

He straightened and drew her up with him. She closed her eyes, lost in the sensation of his hands on her bare skin. He pushed her hair aside and kissed the back of her neck, then nudged her dress off her other shoulder. His fingers lingered on her skin, lightly caressing, and she reveled in the intimacy.

He wrapped his arms around her, pulling her against him. His hands skimmed over the satin of her bodice and higher to cup her breasts. His thumbs circled her nipples through the fabric and she felt them harden with his touch. Her head dropped back against him and he nuzzled her neck. She could barely breathe and didn't care.

She turned in his arms and her lips met his with an eagerness that surged through her, captured her, controlled her, sweeping away all judgment and reason. She shoved at the shoulders of his jacket until he shrugged it off and it fell to the floor. She kissed his lips, his jaw, his chin. His lips moved over her face, her throat, her shoulders. She tugged at his cravat and yanked it free. He fumbled with the ribbons on her bodice, the complicated ties and bindings.

"Bloody hell," he muttered against her skin. "Damned dress, I can't —"

"Just rip it, Rand." She gasped. "Now."

He didn't pause to protest but gripped the delicate fabric in his hands and tore it down the middle. The confining tightness of the bodice vanished, replaced by a glorious freedom and spiraling anticipation. He moved to kiss her breasts and she braced her hands on the edge of the table behind her. His lips moved over her, tasting and teasing until she wondered if she'd swoon from the sheer delight of it. He pulled a nipple into his mouth and suckled until she moaned with pleasure.

He wrapped his arm around the small of her back and pulled her upright. She gazed into his eyes, black with passion, a mirror of her own consuming desire. She gathered his collar with both hands and, with a strength she didn't know she had, ripped his shirt down the front, her gaze never leaving his.

Surprise shot across his face, followed by wicked amusement. His voice was low. "I rather liked that shirt."

"I like it better now." Her sultry tone matched his. She placed her palms on his chest and ran her hands slowly upward to his shoulders, then leaned forward and flicked her tongue across the dark ovals of his nipples. He sucked in a hard breath, and she reveled in the new and intoxicating sense of power brought on by his reaction. He pulled her tight to him, his mouth capturing hers, conquering hers. Or was she the conqueror and he the conquered?

Her naked breasts crushed against his bare chest, hot and hard and powerful. She marveled at the exquisite feeling of flesh to flesh, heat to heat. She pressed closer, needing more. His grip tightened, demanding more. She slid her hands down his back to the curve of his buttocks and let her fingers roam over the tight fabric of his trousers. His hands dropped to her skirt and he gathered it up impatiently until it was bunched up between them. At once she regretted the stupidity that had led her to wear the old-fashioned gown with its yards of fabric.

Rand paid it no mind. His hands skimmed over her hips and around to the flat of her stomach and lower until his palm cupped her and his fingers slipped between her legs. She shuddered at his touch, slick and sensual and overwhelming. His fingers stroked back and forth and her world narrowed to that one point of pleasure. Time and place vanished and all she knew, all she wanted to know, was the indescribable tension tightening inside her and the throbbing ache that pulsed through her veins.

Without warning he stopped, and before she could protest, grabbed her waist and hoisted her up and backward onto the table. He started to climb up after her.

Abruptly she realized that in another moment it would be too late. To prevent what she wanted. What they both wanted. To turn back. She pressed her hand to the center of his chest. "Rand?"

"What?" His glazed gaze met hers.

"Is this the time and the place?"

"No?" It was more a gasp than a word.

"Do you care?"

He drew a shuddering breath. "No."

"Neither do I." She grabbed the remains of his shirt and pulled him toward her.

He tumbled or perhaps leapt or maybe just fell, it scarcely mattered and she didn't care. Somehow they were both on top of the table struggling to find overheated flesh amid a tangle of torn satin and linen and silk. He pushed her skirts up and she tugged at his trousers, with fear and anticipation. Hand and mouth, lips and fingers were everywhere in a frenzy of touch and taste and desire. She realized he'd managed to remove his trousers, and his long legs were naked next to hers. She reached down for him, at once excited and afraid. Her fingers wrapped around his arousal, larger and harder than she'd expected and surprisingly smooth beneath her fingertips. Steel cloaked in velvet.

He groaned with her touch, then shifted to hover over her, his knees on either side of hers, his forearms braced on the table.

"Jocelyn." His gaze searched hers. "Are you —"

"Yes." She tried not to wince. "I know what . . . that is, I've been told . . . prepared . . ." She grabbed what was left of his shirt and pulled him down to whisper against his lips. "I understand any discomfort is well worth it."

"Oh indeed," he murmured, and she tried hard to believe him. He reached between them, and she felt his hand guide himself into her with a slow, measured pace. "Well worth it."

She tensed in spite of her resolve to relax, and clung to the belief that, ultimately, according to Marianne, this would be wonderful. It certainly had been up to this moment. Now, however, it was distinctly . . . odd. Not uncomfortable, simply . . . unusual. If this was as bad as it got, it wasn't unpleasant at all. Rand paused, apparently this was it and she was a bit disappointed. All that had happened before he had actually, well, *entered,* was much, much more exciting.

"Hold on to me," he whispered in her ear.

"Hold on —" Before she could finish the sentence he pulled back, then thrust hard and deep into her.

Searing pain shot through her and she opened her mouth to scream. He clamped his lips over hers and held her tight. Her body throbbed around his, ached with invasion, with trespass. She wanted to stop. Now. It wasn't at all pleasant. Not the tiniest bit wonderful.

But Rand wouldn't let her go, wouldn't let her move. His mouth remained on hers, his embrace unyielding. After a few moments, the pain abated, and she relaxed slightly. He moved within her slowly, tenderly. She braced herself and waited and grudgingly admitted it wasn't perhaps as bad as she'd thought. She moved tentatively in response to him. Not bad at all. In truth, with each of his easy thrusts it grew nicer. And nicer yet when she lifted her hips to meet his.

His rhythm increased and she matched his tempo, that elusive sense of bittersweet tension she'd felt before once again coiling deep within her. They moved together faster and he thrust deeper into her and she pushed harder against him. Her breath came in short gasps. Her blood pounded in her veins. Her heart thudded hard in her chest and she felt or sensed or heard his beat in unison. In a tiny fraction of her mind not absorbed with sheer sensation and unbelievable pleasure she noted that it was indeed well worth it.

And when she thought she simply couldn't survive another moment, and knew without doubt she would surely die if she didn't reach whatever elusive height she was striving toward, yearning for, she exploded around him. Her back arched and her body shuddered and great waves of ecstasy crashed through her until she gasped for breath. And he thrust once again, hard and deep, and joined her with a deep shudder of his own and a groan that was at once pain and joy.

He shifted and rolled onto his side, taking her with him. For a long time they clung to each other, struggling to catch their breath, waiting for the beat of their hearts to slow and the world to stop spinning.

At last he released her and propped his head on his hand. His shirt hung off his shoulders in tatters and he gazed at her with a dazed expression and a bemused smile. "This wasn't exactly how I'd envisioned our first time together."

"No?" She smiled slowly, caught in the most wonderful, lazy, satisfied feeling. She wanted nothing more at the moment than to lie right here. Or perhaps she did. "What did you have in mind?"

"I had imagined, oh, I don't know." He grinned. "A bed perhaps? I had hoped to make this, well —"

"Memorable?" She reached out and caught the hanging shreds of his shirt in her hand. "I know I shall never forget it."

"It was quite remarkable."

"Yes, it was. Quite remarkable." She pulled him closer. "Well played, my lord." Her lips met his. "Well played indeed."

A Treatise on Princes and Princesses and Other Related Matters
by Lady Jocelyn Shelton, age 10

Part Two: On Princesses

A princess should never have sweets more than once a day, no matter how much she likes them, or she will get fat which is not at all attractive. And she should never have a mustache.

A princess should not be vain even if she is very, very pretty.

A princess should be kind and good hearted and hardly ever want someone's head cut off unless they are truly, truly bad. Even then she should probably send them off to live on an island somewhere in the middle of an ocean where they can be bad all they want and no one will be bothered.

A princess should have grand jewels that sparkle all the time but should never be smug about it to ordinary girls who are not princesses even if they have been mean to her.

A princess should have lots of ladies in waiting and other servants but should always

223

be nice to them and give them her old clothes.

And she should be willing to give up everything for her prince.

Chapter 10

"My lord, husband." Jocelyn nuzzled the ear of her sleeping husband. It had been three glorious days and equally glorious nights since their game of billiards, and it wasn't enough. She wanted to be with him every moment of every day. And in his arms every night.

She eased herself up on her elbow. She did rather like watching him sleep, but then she rather liked watching him do anything. Liked the sleek way he moved or the wholehearted way he laughed or the way he looked at peace with the world when he slept. And the way he made her happy.

She'd never been so happy, never dreamed she could feel like this, and had wondered, in the past few days, what she had done in her life to merit it. Certainly she'd never been quite as shallow and spoiled as Rand had thought her to be at first, but she'd definitely never been good enough to deserve such bliss. Of course she hadn't achieved the title and fortune she'd always wanted, but oddly enough it no longer mattered.

Surely *this* was love. She couldn't be certain, of course, but what else could it be? Oh, the wonders of lovemaking were enough to change a woman's outlook on the world, but even the excitement to be found in their bed or the billiard table or the stables or that lovely, secluded spot by the lake did not fully account for the tumultuous emotion that held her in its grip. A feeling that was at once sweet and tense, gentle and fierce. She wanted to laugh aloud at the sheer joy of it.

No, this was undoubtedly love and undoubtedly he felt the same. How could it possibly be otherwise? And couldn't she see how he felt right there in his dark, wonderful eyes?

"Rand." She nipped at his earlobe. His eyes remained closed but his lips quirked upward. "You're awake. I knew it."

She threw her leg over his and shifted to settle on top of him, grateful that neither of them had felt the need to retrieve scattered nightclothes last night.

"And you're insatiable." His eyes opened and gazed into hers.

"I know." She feathered kisses along the line of his jaw. "It's a natural gift."

"Thank God."

She loved lying on him like this, as if she were completely in charge and he at her mercy. As if she could do whatever she wanted with him. It gave her a wonderful sense of power. It was false, of course; he could extricate himself whenever he wished. Still, it was a delightful game.

"What shall we do today?" She straddled him and sat up.

"Well . . ." He frowned as if he were actually considering her question but his fingertips drifted idly along her legs. "I can think of one thing."

"After that." She leaned forward, her hair falling around them like a curtain, and brushed her lips provocatively across his in a manner she knew he could not resist, then stretched out on top of him, her legs entwined with his. His manhood nestled between her legs.

"Rand," she said idly, very aware of his growing arousal. She folded her arms on his chest and stared into his eyes. She nodded at the wicked-looking scar that ran from his collarbone diagonally to end just below the pit of his arm. "How did you get this scar?"

He shrugged as best he could, given his position. "It was a mishap. Nothing more."

She raised a brow. "A mishap?"

"A mishap, a mistake. It's of no real consequence."

"Did you get it when you were a spy?" she teased.

He heaved a long-suffering sigh. "It's at times like this that *mercenary* has a certain amount of appeal." He grabbed her wrists and quickly rolled over to place her beneath him. He anchored her wrists with one hand above her head and pinned her legs with his. "And past time to teach you a lesson about the price of curiosity and the sanctity of a man's rest."

"I scarcely think your sleep is sacred." She looked up at him with feigned innocence. "And the last time you attempted to teach me anything it was billiards and look what that led to."

"I know," he growled with a wicked look in his eye, and anticipation shivered through her. He threw aside any covers that remained on the bed and ran his free hand slowly up the length of her. "Now it's time to learn what happens to women who awaken men prematurely."

"Is it?" She practically purred the words. With her hands over her head and her body fully exposed, she felt at once delightfully helpless and completely aroused.

He ran his hand over her, his touch no more than a teasing whisper, trailing his fingers over the flat of her stomach and tracing a lazy pattern up and over her breasts. He kneaded one nipple lightly until she moaned and arched upward.

"No, no, none of that." He lowered his head and took her breast in his mouth and suckled slowly, then turned his attention to the next, until she thought — no, she knew — she would faint from the sheer pleasure of his touch.

"You do that" — she panted for breath — "rather well."

He raised his head and his dark eyes smoldered. "You yourself said the manner in which I kissed your hand was well practiced." His hand slid down her stomach and slipped between her legs. "Do you want to know what else I am well practiced at?"

"No." She gasped. "Yes."

She was already wet with wanting and his fingers slipped over her, toying and teasing in an ever increasing rhythm. She wanted to thrash and buck beneath his touch but he held her firmly, her immobility heightening her excitement. Until finally that bubble of tension inside her she likened to fine crystal burst.

He rolled over and pulled her on top of him, guiding her hips and sliding into her as if they were made for each other. She wondered if there would ever come a time when she didn't delight in the remarkable feel of him hot and hard within her. And marveled that one man and one woman could fit together so perfectly. So naturally. Halves of the same whole.

They moved together in unison, their senses attuned to each other. Their bodies in harmony. He thrust faster and harder and she matched his movements with her own. The bed creaked beneath them. The room itself throbbed around them. The world stilled and held its breath.

He groaned beneath her, and she could feel him surge within her. And her fists clenched and she gasped with the mindless joy of release and waves of erotic pleasure.

She collapsed on top of him, satisfied and happy, with no desire ever to move again.

At last he chuckled, and she grinned with the movement of his body beneath hers, lifting her head to gaze into his eyes.

"Well," he said firmly but his eyes twinkled. "That should teach you."

Errant tendrils of blond hair glowed golden in the midday sun. Standing in the meadow north of the castle, Jocelyn looked like a forest sprite or an unfettered goddess of nature.

"Archery?" Jocelyn studied the bow in his hand with obvious distaste, and the illusion of a spirit of the earth vanished. "You're not serious about this, are you?"

Rand laughed. "Of course I am. We have been spending far too much time indoors of late."

"Oh?" She raised a brow. "I believe the stables are out of doors as is that charming area by the lake."

"Nonetheless." He tried and failed to hold

back a satisfied smile. "There is no finer time of year in this particular corner of the world than late spring, and I for one should like to enjoy it. A brisk ride with my wife by my side would be acceptable, but I could not fail to notice the skill with which you sit a horse. However" — he shrugged — "if you would prefer to ride —"

She reached for the bow. "Charming sport, archery. Always meant to take it up."

"Excellent." He shaded his eyes with one hand and pointed with the other. "I've set up a target on that stump. Do you see it?"

"You mean that stump?" She waved at the target.

He laughed. "I mean the only stump out there."

"I know what you meant," she said loftily. "Now what exactly do I do?"

"First you need to hold the bow properly." He pulled an arrow from the quiver on the ground, stepped behind her, and put his arms around her to position the bow.

"I see." She twisted her head and grinned at him. "A great deal like the instruction for billiards, isn't it?"

"No." He kissed her firmly. "Now pay attention." She grimaced and turned her head back. "Notch the arrow —"

"Do what?"

"Place the groove here in the feathered end of the arrow, along the gut of the bow." He showed her as he explained and she grudgingly followed his directions. He positioned her properly, guided her in pulling back the arrow, and helped her shoot. The arrow missed the target, but not by much.

"Not bad for your first attempt." He stepped back and handed her another arrow. "Your turn."

"I can scarce contain my excitement," she muttered and accepted the arrow.

She stood as he had shown her and proceeded to take an inordinate amount of time notching the arrow. But then they had all the time in the world and he was a patient man.

Patient? He chuckled to himself at the thought. Apparently not when it came to Jocelyn. His scheme to resist her charms until she wanted him hadn't lasted very long. Or rather hadn't taken very long. And the days since then had been, well, glorious.

At last Jocelyn sighted the arrow, took careful aim, and let it fly. It missed the target by a good thirty feet.

"How was that?" she asked.

"Excellent if you were aiming for France." He pulled his brows together and shook his head. "Remember what I told you about aiming. Look along the length of the arrow and line it up with the target."

She looked as if she were about to protest, then gritted her teeth and grabbed another arrow from him. He bit back a grin. She was too stubborn to admit defeat. He quite liked that about her.

Once again she took her time. Just as he was beginning to question his own capacity for patience, she shot the arrow. He would not have thought it possible, but this attempt went even farther afield than the first.

"There." She nodded with satisfaction. "How was that?"

"Interesting. Most people tend to do better with practice though," he said mildly and handed her another arrow.

She took it with reluctance, gazed at it ruefully, then looked up at him. "Rand, do you really think intelligence is more important in a wife than beauty?"

"I do," he said without hesitation and grinned. "However, I count myself fortunate to have a wife with both."

"But, given a choice, you would rather have a woman with a mind than one that is merely pretty?"

"Of course."

"And honesty between a husband and wife is truly important?"

"Always." *For the most part.*

She nodded thoughtfully. "Do you recall what your uncle said about secrets?"

"As you have reminded me more than once, how could I possibly forget?" He studied her curiously. Something was obviously bothering her.

"Then you agree that secrets should not be kept from one another?"

He hesitated.

"Unless it has to do with the sanctity of the British crown, government, or the country's honor." She huffed with annoyance. "I fully understand why you insist that exceptions be made when it comes to national interests, and furthermore I accept it, annoying as it may be."

"In that case" — he grinned — "I do indeed agree."

"Good." Her expression was worried and a twinge of fear stabbed him. Good God, how serious was this? He moved toward her. "Jocelyn?"

"Wait." She stepped away and fumbled with the wide ribbon sash of her dress, then turned her back to him for a moment. A cold hand squeezed his heart. At last she turned and faced him.

A pair of spectacles was perched upon her pert nose.

He stared in stunned disbelief. "Spectacles?"

"I knew it. I knew you didn't mean a word you said." She snatched the glasses from her face. "I never believed you for a moment. All that nonsense about intelligence over beauty."

"All this was about eyeglasses?" Relief rushed through him. "All your talk about secrets and honesty?"

"Yes." She met his gaze directly. "And you

may make as much fun of me as you want over the matter. I don't care."

The absurdity of it all struck him and he burst into laughter.

"It's not that funny." She crossed her arms over her chest and glared. "I know you think I'm quite vain and perhaps I am but I explained it to you once. I was always —"

"Yes, I know. You were the pretty one." He struggled to hold back another laugh.

"It sounds so ridiculous when you say it," she muttered. "But it's who I am. It makes me as much *me* as your being a mere viscount or a spy —"

"I am not —"

"— makes you who you are."

"Nonsense. It's not the least bit important. Not to me anyway." It was ridiculous but she was extremely overset. He forced a semblance of composure and held out his hand. "Let me see those."

Reluctantly she passed him the spectacles. He held them up to his eyes. The far distance jumped out at him. "Good Lord, these are strong." He looked at her. "Is your vision this bad?"

"I can see you," she snapped.

He stepped away. "Can you still see me?"

She sighed. "Yes."

He took a few more steps. "Now?"

"Yes."

He moved again to stand about ten feet

from her. "What about now?"

"You're starting to get a bit fuzzy around the edges."

He started off. "Stop me when —"

"Stop." She wrinkled her nose. "That's it. You're nothing more than an indistinct blob now."

He was barely fifteen feet away. "No wonder you couldn't hit the target, you couldn't see the blasted thing." He returned to her side and handed her the spectacles. She hesitated, then took them and slipped them on. He cupped her chin in his hand and gazed into her eyes through the glass. "They're not all that unbecoming, you know. You're just as pretty as ever."

She looked a bit appeased but pulled away from him nonetheless. "Oh, certainly you have to say that now. But if I'd been wearing these when we first met, you'd scarcely have given me a second glance."

"That's absurd." He studied her with a critical gaze. "They don't detract at all. If anything they give you an air of intelligence that quite complements your appearance."

"Do you really think so?" A hopeful note sounded in her voice.

He tried not to grin. As silly as he thought her attitude was, he could well understand how a woman who'd never been valued for more than her looks would fear anything that might affect them. Even an intelligent woman.

"I really do." He smiled down at her.

"Thank you," she said with a reluctant smile of her own.

"And should I have met you wearing those spectacles I would have been even more intrigued than . . ." The truth slammed into him and pulled him up short. His eyes widened with realization and he stared. "You didn't see those men at all, did you?"

"What men?" She glanced around. "Is there someone here?"

"No, not here." Impatience sharpened his tone. "In the music room at the prince's reception. The ones who tried to kill you. You didn't see them."

"No, how could I?" Her brows pulled together in irritation. "I told you at the time I didn't see them."

"I thought you were just saying that. I thought you were just scared."

"Of course I was scared. Some vicious fiend had thrown a knife at my head. Only a complete fool wouldn't be scared."

"But you didn't see them."

"We've established that. You can stop repeating it."

"I'm repeating it because I'm trying to understand." He turned on his heel and paced. Pieces of a puzzle he hadn't realized existed fell into place. She wasn't scared of the truth. Hadn't wiped her mind of the faces of the brigands because of fear. She really hadn't seen them. But they didn't know that. Nor, apparently, did anyone else. "How long have you worn those spectacles?"

"I haven't," she said cautiously. "I found them in my bag when we arrived at the castle. Marianne had had them made for me. She's been badgering me for years to get me to try them. Apparently she assumed, now that I was married, I needn't worry about my appearance."

"Does anyone outside your family know about your vision?"

"You!" she snapped.

"But if you hadn't been so vain —"

"And shallow and selfish too, no doubt." She ground out the words.

"— and had consented to wear spectacles years ago, the world would have known. And known as well you couldn't possibly recognize anyone from across a room."

"What are you saying?"

"I'm saying, my dear wife, if your need for eyeglasses was public knowledge, then your life would never have been in danger because no one would have feared your identification of them."

"And you would not have had to marry me." Her voice was level.

"That goes without saying." He started to pace again. In a part of his mind not grappling with the implications of this new information he noted Jocelyn's unusually quiet manner but disregarded it for the moment. He thought back to that infamous night. "Now I understand what your aunt meant about the irony of the situation."

"Aunt Louella always did appreciate irony." Her tone was cool.

He laughed wryly. "What a colossal joke. On both of us. Forced to wed because of —"

"My vanity?" The hard note in her voice caught his attention. Her face was composed but her eyes gleamed. "I believe we've established that as well as the state of my sight."

He stared at her. "Surely you can see the absurdity of all this."

"In point of fact, I can't. I don't find anything here the least bit humorous."

"Come now, Jocelyn." Rand drew his brows together. "Your life is threatened. You, we, are forced into a marriage neither of us wants simply because you refused to wear spectacles." He shook his head. "Add to that the now vanished hope that you would recall the faces of the men —"

"You thought I might still be able to identify those men?" Jocelyn's eyes widened.

He shrugged. "There was always a possibility —"

"Did you bring me here hoping they would follow?"

"Of course not. I brought you here to keep you safe."

"Really? You used me as bait once before.

How do I know you didn't do it again? How do I know all that nonsense about your responsibility and protecting me wasn't just a convenient lie?" Anger flared in her eyes. "After all, dishonesty is more than acceptable when issues of government affairs are at stake." She whirled around and started back toward the castle.

"Wait just one moment." He grabbed her arm and jerked her beck to face him. "I never lied to you about my reasons for bringing you here. Your life was in danger and it was your own fault. More so than I originally thought. You're the one who hasn't been entirely truthful."

"Me?" She gasped with disbelief. "When have I lied to you?"

"You didn't tell me you couldn't see!"

"You didn't ask!"

"It was a lie of omission and equally as bad. You should have told me."

"How could I possibly know you didn't know? That Thomas or someone else in the family hadn't told you? Besides, I never actually hid it from you." Her chin lifted in defiance. "I told you nothing but the truth. I didn't see them. I couldn't identify them."

"But if you had told me *why* you didn't see them —"

"Would it have made a difference?"

"Blast it all, yes. Of course it would have."

"How?"

"I would have found a way." His voice rang with determination. "Somehow I would have made certain that word of your problem reached the right ears. The threat would have vanished. Your life would have gone on just as you'd wanted. As would mine. We never would have had to marry. All of this could have been avoided."

"All of it?"

"Yes!" Hurt flashed in her eyes, and at once he realized what he'd said and his heart dropped. "No! I didn't mean that the way it sounded."

"Didn't you?" She tried to pull out of his grasp but he refused to release her.

"No! Not in the least! Damn it all, Jocelyn!" His gaze searched hers; his voice was intense. "You're my wife!"

"Am I?" The question hung in the air between them. The moment stretched taut with accusation and denial. "Or am I just the woman you married?"

He stared at her, stunned. He didn't know how to answer. What to say. What she wanted, needed to hear.

She wrenched free, turned on her heel, and stalked toward the castle. Her back was stiff with fury, the lines of her body rigid with anger.

"Jocelyn, wait!" He started after her. What had he done to her? He hadn't meant anything the way it had sounded, and on reflec-

241

tion it didn't sound good. Without warning she stopped and whirled toward him.

"May I go home now?" Her voice was cool and remote and didn't fool him for a second. He'd seen her angry before but he'd never seen her like this.

"Of course." Was she going to forgive him? "I'll escort you back to the castle."

"No, I want to go home. Back to London." She brushed a strand of hair away from her face, and for a moment her composed façade cracked, and his heart twisted at the pain he saw. And the knowledge that it was entirely his fault. "Or Shelbrooke Manor."

He shook his head. "I can't allow that."

"Why not?" Her eyes narrowed. "Because I'm your wife?"

"Not entirely, but that enters into it."

She snorted with disdain.

"The circumstances that brought all this about remain the same," he said carefully. "There is still a threat. Nothing has changed."

"Nothing has changed?" Her voice rose. "How can you say that? Everything has changed. I thought . . ." She wrapped her arms around herself and gazed off into the distance. Even with the spectacles he knew she was staring at nothing that could be seen. "I thought or maybe I just hoped . . ." She shook her head and met his gaze. "Perhaps I am not the least bit intelligent after all."

"I can't let you leave," he said softly and knew he'd never said anything so true in his life.

"Then I shall stay. Where I am safe and protected." She laughed, a short, bitter sound. "Where nothing can hurt me." She turned and started back toward the castle.

He watched her stride off, awash in a sea of helplessness. What had he done? And what could he do now? He hadn't meant for it to turn out like this. Of course he was annoyed at discovering what a farce his life had become, but he hadn't meant to blame her for that. He'd lost his head. Wasn't thinking. Said things he shouldn't have.

And he'd hurt her more than any knife or gun ever could.

He pulled his gaze away from her and spotted the bow and quiver. He'd collect them now and come back for the spent arrows later. It was far more important to stay by Jocelyn's side. To try to convince her that he hadn't meant to hurt her. That he was indeed glad he'd married her. That it might well be, that she might well be, the best thing that had ever happened to him.

He started after her. She needed to know that he cared for her. Deeply. More than he'd ever cared for any woman. Maybe it wasn't mere affection. Possibly he even —

"Rand," Jocelyn called over her shoulder, an odd note in her voice. He picked up his pace and in two long strides was by her side. She stood gazing at a point past the castle. "Being able to see may not be as beneficial as I'd assumed. For example . . ." She nodded and he followed her gaze.

In the far distance three riders headed toward the castle from the south. From the direction of London.

"I have no idea if they are friend or foe," she murmured.

"Nor do I." Rand shaded his eyes against the sun low in the afternoon sky. "From here I can't tell if they are my men or not but I doubt anyone meaning any harm would approach in quite so direct a manner. Regardless, we shall be prepared. Come on." He grabbed her hand and started toward the castle. "And by the way, *I* am your friend." His clipped tone brooked no argument.

"Then I have little to fear from my foes," she snapped.

He ignored her. Time enough later to settle what was between them. They hurried toward the castle. He doubted Jocelyn had ever before moved so fast, and he had to admire how she gamely kept up with him. Fear did that to a person. Or anger. They skirted around a tower, scrambled over part of the crumbled wall, dashed through the overgrown rose garden, sprinted the final distance, and practically fell into the building.

"Nick!" Rand barked the order the moment he stepped foot inside. The servant appeared almost at once. "Fetch my pistol." Nick vanished.

Rand turned to Jocelyn. "Stay here." He started toward the stairs. "Don't worry."

"I'm not." She folded her arms over her chest. "There is probably nothing to worry about, exactly as your first instincts indicated. Oh, there is a slim possibility I shall be killed, in which case my troubles shall be over, or you shall be killed" — she smiled in an overly sweet manner — "and my troubles will still be over."

"Excellent, Jocelyn. People who are angry have little room left for fear."

"Then I shall more than likely never be scared again."

"You can't stay angry at me forever."

"Would you care to wager on it, my lord." The look in her eyes indicated he'd lose. At the moment, anyway. Still . . .

"Yes." He turned and headed for the stairs. "We'll settle this later."

She called after him. "If there is a later!"

"There will damned well be a later," he muttered to himself, taking the steps two at a time. There would be a tomorrow and a day after and an entire lifetime with her whether she liked it or not. And blast it all, she would like it eventually. He would make sure of it.

He reached the upper floor, sprinted down

the hall and into a room with a window facing south. He grabbed the spyglass he'd placed there for just such a purpose, put it up to his eye, and brought the approaching figures into focus.

At once he recognized the two outside riders as his men. As for the man who rode between them . . .

He clenched his jaw and slowly lowered the glass.

"Bloody hell."

Chapter 11

"The least you can do is tell me what's happening," Jocelyn snapped.

Rand brushed past her, his manner terse and preoccupied, and headed toward the door. He muttered something she couldn't hear. It was annoying not to know what was going on but then when *wasn't* the man annoying? His arrogance simply added to her anger. Anger she held close right now as a barrier against anything deeper. Anything painful.

"Stay here," he ordered.

"I think not." She marched after him.

He stopped and turned so quickly she nearly ran into him. He clenched his teeth and glared down at her. "Stay here."

There was a hard warning in his eyes and she bit back the sarcastic retort that was on the tip of her tongue.

He turned away, threw open the door, and strode outside. At once she stepped after him and slipped behind the open door, hidden from sight but able to hear. Or at least able to hear if Rand and the others weren't speaking in such abominably low tones. At her husband's direction, no doubt.

"My lady," Flora whispered behind her. "I doubt His Lordship would want —"

"Nonsense, Flora. I'm sure he simply wants us to be quiet." Jocelyn moved closer to the wall on the off chance she could see something of the scene outside through the crack between the door and the jamb. The effort was futile. Blasted castle was simply too well built.

She recognized Rand's voice drawing closer and immediately moved away from the door, back to the spot where he'd left her.

He stepped over the threshold, his expression grim, and shot her an odd, assessing look. He nodded at Flora. "If you would prepare a room, it appears we have a guest."

"A guest?" Jocelyn tried to see around him. "Who on earth . . ." Her eyes widened and she whipped her spectacles from her face.

"My lady, I have counted the minutes since our last meeting." Prince Alexei Frederick Berthold Ruprecht Pruzinsky strode into the room as if he had no doubt as to his reception. He stopped in front of her, bowed, then took her hand and drew it to his lips. His voice was low. "I have missed you, my dear Jocelyn."

"Lady Beaumont," Rand said in a hard voice. Jocelyn ignored him and cast Alexei her brightest smile. "Your Highness. How delightful to see you again."

"You are as lovely as ever." Alexei's eyes bored into hers.

"It's Lady Beaumont now," Rand repeated firmly.

"So I've heard." Alexei stared down at her with a knowing smile. "What a pity."

"Not at all." Rand stepped to her side and glanced pointedly at Alexei's hand still holding Jocelyn's. The prince released her, but his gaze lingered on her. "We suit well together." The blatant lie jerked Jocelyn's attention away from Alexei. Rand smiled at her in an overly affectionate manner. She wanted to smack him.

She stepped pointedly away and favored Alexei with her complete attention. "You're right, Your Highness, it's been entirely too long." She looked around him. "But surely you've not come all this way alone?"

"I left the rest of my party some distance back. At a dreary little village a good two hours or so away." He stripped off his gloves. "I thought, as Beaumont had taken such pains to conceal your whereabouts, it seemed wise." He glanced at Rand and smiled. "Did I do well, cousin?"

Cousin?

"I find it hard to believe they allowed you to travel alone," Rand said before Jocelyn could get in a word.

"No one *allows* me to do anything." Alexei's voice carried a note of amusement. "I do precisely as I wish. It is a privilege of power."

"How did you find us?" Rand said.

"It was not at all difficult." Alexei shrugged. "I am a prince of a sovereign nation on good terms with your own and a guest in your country. When the man I have specifically requested to look into a matter involving my security simply vanishes, and a dolt of a peasant is put in his place, surely you don't think I would let the incident pass without inquiry?" Alexei slapped his gloves on his palm. "I simply asked where you were and why. Yet another advantage to power."

The prince turned his attention to Jocelyn. "I do hope you have not been harmed in any way."

"No, not at all." She flashed a quick glance at Rand to see if he had noted the subtle sarcasm in her comment. He had.

"I should never forgive myself if any harm came to you because of me." Alexei's tone was both sincere and intimate. Perhaps too intimate. Yet gratifying just the same.

"How kind of you to say so."

"Forgive me for interrupting" — again Rand stepped closer to her — "but other than your concern, appreciated, of course —"

"Most appreciated," Jocelyn added.

"— why, exactly, are you here, Your Highness?"

"Because you are the only man I trust. The only man in England, perhaps in all of Europe as well, who I know does not wish to see my father deposed and my brother, sister, and I thrown out into the streets or worse. Come now, cousin, I couldn't possibly allow my fate to rest in the hands of that imbecile who replaced you."

There it was again. *Cousin.*

Jocelyn pulled her brows together. "Forgive me for asking, Your Highness, but you've called Lord Beaumont *cousin* twice now, and I find it extremely curious."

"Do you? Why? What do you call your cousins?"

"I scarcely think —" Rand began.

"Actually, I have no cousins, but if I did" — she shook her head — "I suppose I would call them *cousin.*"

"Precisely why I call Beaumont *cousin.*" He studied Rand and raised a brow. "Have you been keeping secrets from your lovely wife, *cousin?*"

"Not at all." Rand shrugged as if his answer didn't matter, but it did. "I simply didn't feel it necessary to mention a remote familial relationship."

Jocelyn turned to her husband and studied him carefully. He had that look about him. Granted, they had not been together long, but she'd been with him long enough to recognize the firm line his lips took on when he was not being entirely truthful. She narrowed her eyes. "Exactly how remote is it?"

"Really rather insignificant." Rand's manner was offhand. "I can scarce remember the details myself."

"You wound me deeply, cousin." Alexei sighed. "Disavowing the nature of our relationship so cavalierly. I realize family relations are complex but I scarce think it overly difficult to recall *our* connection." He turned to Jocelyn. "His grandmother was my father's older sister. The only daughter of King Frederick the Third."

The import of Alexei's declaration struck her and she could barely get out the words. "Then he is . . ."

"A cousin," Rand said sharply. "Nothing more."

"Nothing more? Come now, Beaumont." Alexei snorted. "Through your mother you are a direct descendant. By the ancient rules of heredity in my country that disregard gender and consider only bloodline, you are fifth in line to the throne after myself, my brother and sister, and another cousin. I'd call it neither especially distant nor nothing." He cast Jocelyn a wry smile. "My dear, your husband is a legitimate heir to the crown of Avalonia. In truth a prince of the realm."

"I have never had any interest in nor pursued any claim to the throne," Rand said quickly.

Alexei waved away his declaration. "Nonetheless, you remain a member of the royal family."

Jocelyn stared in disbelief. "A prince?"

Alexei eyed her with amusement. "Indeed he is. And you, my dear Jocelyn —"

"Lady Beaumont," Rand said through clenched teeth.

"Hardly." Alexei scoffed. "As your wife her title is far more significant than a mere viscountess. By virtue of her marriage to you she may legitimately be called" — he paused dramatically — "Princess Jocelyn."

For a long moment, shock held Jocelyn's tongue. A myriad of thoughts and emotions whirled in her head. Rand? A prince? Through no fault of her own she'd married a genuine prince? Perhaps it was simply the element of surprise, but it wasn't nearly as wonderful as she'd thought it would be. She stared at her husband. "Were you planning on mentioning this?"

"There was nothing to say," Rand said slowly.

"Nothing to say?" She struggled to keep her voice calm against a rising tide of anger. "Given the circumstances of our marriage, don't you think I deserved to know?"

"It's a hereditary footnote." Rand's voice was firm. "Nothing more significant that that."

"I consider it extremely significant," Alexei said mildly.

Jocelyn ignored him, her attention fully on her husband. "Why didn't you tell me?"

Rand crossed his arms over his chest. "It's not important."

"I've always thought it rather important," Alexei murmured.

"And . . ." A look of unease flitted through Rand's eyes. "You didn't ask."

"And therefore you didn't tell me?" Her voice rose at hearing her own words thrown back at her. "Doesn't that make it a lie of omission? And isn't that just as inexcusable as any other kind of lie?"

"I never lied to you." Rand shook his head.

"Hah!" She poked her finger against his chest. Hard. "You went on and on about my having married a mere viscount instead of a prince knowing full well you were a prince."

Rand grabbed her hand and stared into her eyes. "I didn't lie to you."

"Oh? Even if you discount your lie of omission, and you were the one who so vehemently declared that to be reprehensible" — she glared up at him — "what about the virtue of honesty between a husband and wife? The importance of there being no secrets between a husband and wife? Didn't you say that to me?"

"Well, yes," he said grudgingly, "something like that."

"Exactly like that." She pulled her hand away. "And within the hour as well."

Alexei cleared his throat. "Dear me, have I come at a bad time?"

"Yes," Rand snapped.

"No," Jocelyn said in unison with her husband. She drew a deep breath and turned to Alexei. "Do forgive me, Your Highness, it has been a rather long and extremely enlightening day. My husband has been teaching me the finer points of archery." *As well as deceit.*

"Archery?" Alexei cast her a skeptical smile. "I had not thought you to be interested in such out-of-doors pursuits."

"It is amazing what one can find interesting on occasion." She forced a light note to her voice. "Besides, you never know when you will be forced to use such a skill. I daresay with a bit of practice I may well be able to actually hit a target I aim for. Preferably moving."

Alexei laughed. "I do hope there is no danger in your mistaking one target for another?"

Jocelyn slanted a quick look of disdain at her husband but kept a pleasant smile directed at Alexei. "Not at all, Your Highness. I suspect when I am ready to shoot something my aim will be accurate. Now then, I find I am a bit overtired and therefore will retire to my rooms until dinner." She extended her hand and Alexei took it at once. "You will join us?"

"Nothing could keep me away." He brushed his lips across her hand, his gaze meeting hers. "Until then, Jocelyn."

She smiled and withdrew her hand, then nodded curtly at Rand. His jaw was clenched and he looked like anything but a hospitable host. Of course he wasn't, in truth, the host here, was he? For the first time since Rand had discovered her poor eyesight, genuine amusement touched her. Nigel would no doubt enjoy this new turn of events.

She swept out of the room at a brisk pace and didn't falter until she shut the door of her rooms, their rooms, behind her. She leaned back against the door, and the control she'd kept firmly in check dissolved.

A marriage neither of us wants.

Her eyes fogged with tears. Certainly neither had wanted this marriage at the beginning but everything had changed since then. At least for her. Apparently not for him.

A marriage neither of us wants.

She swiped angrily at her eyes and stalked across the room. He didn't care for her. Not one bit. In spite of how close they'd grown in recent days. Or how close she'd thought they'd grown. She'd talked to him of things she'd never told anyone save perhaps her sisters and never imagined she'd tell a man. Any man. She'd shared all her secrets with him. Oh, certainly they weren't as significant as royal blood but they were important to her.

Yet in spite of everything that had passed between them he harbored some absurd belief that she could prove useful to whatever he was involved in. It was yet another lie and scarcely one of omission, although he would probably term it such.

A marriage neither of us wants.

How could he say it? And worse, how could he mean it? She wanted it. Wanted him and wanted him forever. Wanted to be Lady Beaumont and nothing more than that.

And now he was a prince.

She bit back a bitter laugh at the sheer absurdity of it all. She'd wanted a prince and instead married a viscount who was, in truth, a prince. Now that she'd been foolish enough to fall in love with her husband, what he was — prince or pauper or spy — didn't matter at all.

The realization stopped her in mid-stride. She was indeed in love with him. Pain swept away any lingering doubts. A wrenching, searing ache that overwhelmed her. She wanted to cry. She wanted to scream. Only love could possibly hurt this much. Only knowing, even now, that he regretted their marriage could cause this much anguish. Wound this deeply.

And she'd believed he'd loved her back.

She sank down onto the bed and covered her face with her hands. How had this happened to her of all people? Jocelyn Shelton had never looked for love. Never particularly wanted love. Love played no role in the selection of a husband. No, all she'd wanted was position and wealth. There was no question of love when she'd planned to marry Alexei.

Aunt Louella would appreciate the irony.

Jocelyn had a prince after all.

Perhaps . . . An odd thought struck her. She raised her head and stared unseeing across the room.

Rand had to care about her, at least a little. And not just because of any information he'd hoped to learn from her or any trap he might have set. She did tend to believe him about that if nothing else. Regardless of his intentions on the night they'd met, he was not the kind of man who would put a woman's life, his wife's, in danger deliberately.

No, she'd seen something wonderful in his eyes and not just in the throes of passion either. No matter what he'd lied about, or simply failed to mention, she couldn't believe he didn't have some affection for her. Maybe even love. His actions alone indicated that. Perhaps he hadn't considered love any more than she had until now. Perhaps all she had to do was make him realize it.

Jocelyn stood and crossed to the window. She pulled out her spectacles, put them on, then settled in the window seat. This had become her favorite spot to consider her life. It was as if gazing out at a world sharp and distinct and serene brought her own thoughts clearly into focus.

Perhaps the way to make her husband realize his feelings was with the unwitting help of the man she'd planned to marry in the first place.

The setting sun cast a soft pink glow on the countryside.

She loved him and she was going to make him realize he loved her as well. If she was wrong, if he didn't love her, well — she squared her shoulders — it wouldn't make the least bit of difference. He could scarcely break her heart any more than he already had.

Randall, Viscount Beaumont, prince, spy, or whatever else the blasted man might be, was still simply a man. And no match for a Shelton woman determined to get what she wanted.

She caught sight of the stump that had served as her archery target. For this particular sport, she had no doubt of her aim or the precise location of her target.

After all, in spite of everything, she had managed to marry a prince.

"I imagine the two of you have any number of things to discuss so I shall take my leave." Nigel got to his feet and started toward the library door. Rand and Prince Alexei rose at once.

"I didn't mean to disturb you, Uncle," Rand said. "I merely wanted to introduce you to His Highness. We can certainly —"

"Nonsense. This is the most private room in the place. Besides, I was finished for the day." He waved at a serving cart near his desk. "Rand, you know where the brandy is. I expect the two of you may well need it."

"I am most grateful for your hospitality, Lord Worthington," Prince Alexei said respectfully, and Rand's estimation of the man grudgingly rose. "I know it must be somewhat unsettling for guests to intrude on your solitude without warning."

"Think nothing of it." Nigel chuckled. "Haven't had so much fun in a long time." He moved slowly toward the door, then stopped and pinned Rand with a considering look. "Flora tells me there was quite a commotion when His Highness arrived. Sorry I missed it. Apparently your wife did not take the revelation of your heritage well?"

The prince coughed, then smiled blandly.

"You could say that," Rand muttered.

"I told her you were a prince." Nigel shook his head. "And I warned you about secrets."

"Yes, well, that's neither here nor there at the moment," Rand said quickly.

"Keep your head about you, boy," Nigel said sharply. "You'll be no good to anybody if you don't. As for you" — he studied Alexei for a moment — "you behave yourself."

Rand groaned to himself. Only Uncle Nigel would dare to talk that way to royalty. Regardless of Rand's personal opinion of Alexei, he was still a prince, and the position alone deserved a modicum of respect.

Alexei's eyes widened in feigned innocence. "My dear sir, I am nothing if not well behaved." He flashed Nigel a wicked grin. "Or at least very good."

Nigel laughed and Alexei joined him. The kind of laugh shared by men who recognize a kindred spirit. And why not? Nigel had been just as much of a rake in his day as Alexei was now. Still, the immediate bond between the two men rankled.

A few more pleasantries were exchanged and Nigel took his leave. Rand immediately stepped to the cart and poured two glasses of brandy. He passed one to the prince, then took a healthy swallow from his own glass. There was nothing quite as good as good brandy to put life in its proper perspective.

Prince Alexei casually wandered around the edges of the vast room and inspected the books on the shelves. "Quite an impressive collection."

The Worthington library was one of the few rooms in the castle with wood paneling as opposed to the stone walls found elsewhere. Shelves of books reached from the floor upward to a height unreachable by any means other than a ladder. As a boy, Rand had often wondered precisely what volumes were housed so close to heaven and so far out of reach of man. Again today, as he had as a child, he vowed to himself someday to climb to the top shelves to discover what treasures might be hidden there.

"Nigel is exceedingly fond of books as was his father and, I gather, any number of earlier earls." Rand studied the prince's perusal of the volumes and wondered when the man would bring up the true reason for his unexpected appearance. Rand was impatient with idle conversation, yet reluctant to move toward anything more significant. Let the prince make the first move.

Prince Alexei swirled the brandy in his glass and glanced at Rand. "You don't like me very much, do you, cousin?"

"I scarcely think that's of any importance, Your Highness." Rand shrugged.

"Probably not." Alexei moved to one of two comfortable, upholstered chairs positioned before Nigel's desk and sank into it. "Still, I find it rather curious."

"Do you? Why?"

"In spite of our family ties, we hadn't met

until my arrival here in England and we've had nothing more than a single, brief conversation since." The prince narrowed his eyes. "You don't know me well enough to like or dislike me, yet your opinion is obvious."

The accuracy of the statement was unsettling. The prince was right, of course. Rand had little on which to base his immediate dislike of the man, yet there it was. Still, he'd always prided himself on being fair-minded. "I do apologize, Your Highness, I —"

"Please, call me Alexei," the prince said with an impatient sigh. "Regardless of your acknowledgment of our connection we are indeed cousins and I do relish those moments when I can be a mere relation rather than the heir to the throne. However, I shall make you a bargain."

"Oh?"

"If you call me Alexei, I will try not call you *cousin*." He grinned. "You obviously hold no fondness for that particular title."

Rand bit back a smile. "My family, my friends, call me Rand."

"Excellent. And do sit down." Alexei waved at the other chair. "It's bad enough to have you glowering at me without you towering over me as well."

Rand raised a brow. "I was not aware I was glowering."

"You have glowered since the moment we met. It's quite annoying."

"My apologies." Rand settled into the second chair.

"Accepted." Alexei took a thoughtful sip. "I must say, I am surprised to find you here rather than at Beaumont Abbey. As your grandmother is no longer living, I would not have expected you to come to Worthington."

"Nor would anyone else, which was precisely the idea." Rand raised a shoulder in an offhand shrug. "Outside of a handful of acquaintances, few people are aware of the close nature of my relationship with Lord Worthington."

"I certainly had no idea. And my information is usually so accurate," Alexei murmured.

"Your information?"

"Surely you of all people understand the necessity of knowing all there is to know about a situation before venturing into it."

"And what situation would that be?" Rand said carefully. "My information is also usually quite accurate, and I understood the purpose of your visit to England is nothing more significant than attendance at a symbolic ceremony."

"Ceremonies are convenient, are they not? State functions, events, celebrations . . . weddings."

Rand's own wedding flashed through his mind and with it thoughts of his lovely wife, who was no doubt at this very moment planning her widowhood. "*Convenient* is not the word I would choose."

"Perhaps not." Alexei chuckled. "However, this particular occasion provided me with a reason to come to England and the opportunity to at last make your acquaintance. It is always best to know those who might wish to usurp your position."

"I have no interest —"

"Yes, yes, I know." Alexei sighed. "I do hope my information on that matter was accurate as well?"

"Understand this, Alexei, I am an Englishman. This is my country, my home, and here is where my loyalties lie. I have no desire to claim any title or position that might be mine through a quirk of heredity. You needn't worry yourself about any intentions on my part."

"Still" — Alexei considered him thoughtfully — "circumstances can change. As can attitudes."

"Not mine," Rand said firmly. He sat back and studied his cousin. "Is that why you requested my assistance? To determine for yourself my interest in the crown?"

"You do get to the point, cousin — excuse me, Rand — and I will be candid as well." Alexei blew a long breath. "I was not aware of any specific plot when I first asked your government to assign you to investigate, although admittedly plots and conspiracies in

Avalonia blossom on a regular basis. Usually, whenever it looks as though the crown might pass to the next in line. Conspiracies and reason are as much a tradition as the ceremonies of state."

"I had heard that your father was ill. My condolences."

"He had improved somewhat when I left." Alexei fell silent for a moment, then drew a deep breath. "I don't know how much you know about the country of your ancestors, so permit me to expound for a moment."

He leaned forward. "We are a tiny kingdom, maintaining a tenuous presence between the greater powers of Prussia, Russia, and Austria. We cling to our independence through a precarious mix of alliances, treaties, and goodwill. It is a balance that we have maintained for the last few centuries, but I cannot predict what the future may bring. Yet the threat to the stability of my country does not, at the moment, come from without but from within.

"We are not an unhappy people for the most part. In general the standard of the lives of the population is probably better than here in England. Controversy and insurrection in Avalonia do not come from the people." He chuckled in a humorless manner. "No, it is the royal family that is its own worst enemy."

"Once again, Alexei, you have nothing to fear from me on that account."

"And that, my dear cousin, is both a blessing and a pity. Avalonia could make good use of a man of your caliber. Not on the throne of course." Alexei lifted his glass in a wry salute.

Rand returned the toast, then drew a long swallow of the liquor. If nothing else, it seemed the prince had the best interests of his country at heart. Perhaps he had misjudged Alexei. He seemed to be doing that a lot lately.

"However, should you ever wish to return to Avalonia and acknowledge your position as a prince, it would be of great benefit to your country."

"*Your* country, not mine."

"In spite of our obvious distrust of one another, I suspect we would do rather better as allies than enemies. You could be of great assistance."

Alexei paused as if deciding how much to say. "At the present time I suspect any immediate threat comes from the Princess Valentina. She too is a cousin, next in line for the throne after my brother and sister and a step before you in succession. Her father was King Frederick's youngest son, your grandmother's brother. She is overly ambitious, quite lovely, and far too clever for a woman. There is nothing more dangerous than a beautiful woman with intelligence and ambition."

"No doubt," Rand murmured.

"Whatever you have stumbled upon, I suspect her fair hand is involved. Although, without proof . . ." Alexei shrugged. "Did I mention she was clever?"

Rand nodded. "Regardless, you don't seem worried."

"I'm not." Alexei laughed. "I am well used to countering Valentina's efforts. I sincerely doubt my life is in danger, merely my crown."

"If there was not a particular plot you were aware of, although there obviously is one now" — Rand chose his words with care — "why did you request my help? After all, I have been away from this sort of work for a few years now. I've done little more than tend to my estate and my uncle's affairs. And your own sources tell you I have no interest in the crown."

"It was an indulgence, nothing more. As there is some kind of conspiracy afoot after all, it seems my indulgence was a blessing." Alexei sipped his brandy in a far too casual manner. "You represent a third branch of the direct line of descent in the royal family. Given that, do you doubt why I wanted to meet you for myself?"

Rand studied him for a long, thoughtful moment. "Actually, Alexei, I do."

Alexei laughed. "You are as clever as I'd

heard. Very well then, Rand, I have not been entirely honest."

Rand raised a brow. "Imagine my surprise."

"With my father's health in question it is entirely possible I will ascend to the throne within the year." A shadow passed across Alexei's face. "Valentina and her supporters have taken the opportunity to sow seeds of unrest. For the most part, my father has ruled wisely but he is not infallible and has made enemies. As have I."

His gaze met Rand's. "I need a means to pull my country together before it is too late. To engage the hearts and minds of the people and rally their support behind my father and myself before there is no choice left but bloodshed. I am looking for a symbol. Of the monarchy and the country, of tradition and history, of prophecy and legend. And of the future."

"Correct me if I'm wrong, but it seems to me vague, legendary symbols are exceedingly hard to find."

"You are right on one count — this is exceedingly hard to find but it is not in the least bit vague." Alexei's gaze searched Rand's. "I am looking for the heavens."

Rand smiled. "And the moon and the stars, no doubt."

"Exactly." Alexei sipped his brandy. "The legendary Heavens of Avalonia. The moon, the sun, and the stars."

Rand pulled his brows together and stared. "I gather you're not referring to a celestial configuration?"

"Not at all. The Heavens of Avalonia are a set of rare and precious jewels representing the sun, the moon, and the stars, or points of the compass. They were set in a wide gold cuff and traditionally worn by the queen or the eldest princess. The moon is a large opal, the sun a ruby matching in size, and the four smaller stars are diamonds."

Rand let out a low whistle. "They must be worth a fortune."

"You could say a king's ransom. In fact, I think they once might have been a king's ransom." Alexei studied him intently. "You've never heard of them?"

"No." Rand shook his head. "I gather they're missing."

"They have been lost for half a century. They vanished during the last major political upheaval, fifty-two years ago to be precise. The Heavens disappeared at approximately the same time —"

"— that my grandmother fled the country." At once Rand understood. "You think I have them."

"Do you?" Alexei's eyes gleamed with intensity.

"No."

"Your grandmother never mentioned them, then?"

270

"My grandmother died when I was thirteen. She never would have confided such a secret in a mere boy." But would she have confided in Nigel? Rand preferred to keep that thought to himself but he would speak to his uncle. "My mother has never spoken of them either. I've never heard of the Heavens until today."

"Perhaps," Alexei said slowly.

Rand stared. "You don't believe me."

"I don't know you well enough to believe you or not." Alexei's tone was mild.

"Well said." Rand grinned. "Cousin." He got to his feet, took Alexei's empty glass, and moved to refill the glasses. "So tell me, if these jewels have been missing for fifty years, why is it only now that someone has come looking for them." He pulled the stopper from the decanter and poured the brandy.

"They are only displayed for state occasions and no one realized they were gone. Apparently truth is indeed a casualty of war.

"I learned of this completely by accident and, in recent weeks, have managed to piece together the story. As far as I've been able to determine, the jewels were discovered missing in the dark days after the insurrection. The king's control of the country was still tentative, as was obviously his control of his daughter."

"I understood the queen sent her away or at least encouraged her to flee." Rand

271

stepped to Alexei and handed him a glass. "Besides, you can scarcely fault her for disappearing. Her husband had been killed, her country was in chaos. She feared for her own life and the life of her daughter."

"I can fault her for taking her country's heritage with her."

"You don't know she did," Rand pointed out. "There are any number of cases throughout history in which a country's treasures have vanished during war or unrest. All you know is that the Heavens vanished at the same time she did. You yourself admit it was an extremely chaotic time."

"True enough, I suppose." Alexei paused then continued his story. "At any rate, it was thought revealing their disappearance would only cause further turmoil. The king had a replica of the cuff created, complete with false gems, as a temporary measure. When he died, somehow the truth died with him. It's only recently that this has come to light.

"I do hope I do not have to tell you the discreet nature of this information. Only a handful of people, including my brother and sister, are aware of this. Now, as then, it is imperative this is not revealed."

"Why?"

"There is a legend about the jewels. Avalonia will stand as long as the Heavens."

"Rather vague, isn't it?"

Alexei chuckled. "It's a legend. However,

superstition is a powerful thing. If it's known the Heavens are missing, particularly at this uncertain moment, it will be used against my father and me and taken as a sign that we should not rule."

"And if you had the jewels, there would be no question as to who is the rightful king."

"Precisely. The Heavens are a powerful symbol, exactly what my country needs at the moment." Alexei paused. "Would you give them to me if you had them?"

"Yes," Rand said without hesitation, then grinned. "But of course, you don't know me well enough to believe me."

Alexei laughed, then sobered. "I long ago learned not to underestimate Valentina, but I doubt she knows about the Heavens. Therefore, whatever the underhanded scheme is that you have happened upon probably has nothing to do with the jewels."

"Probably not." Rand was reluctant to voice the thought uppermost in his mind.

"Come now, Rand. We are being honest, are we not?" Alexei's gaze trapped his cousin's. "I assume you are far more experienced in matters of this sort than I. What are you thinking?"

Rand drew a deep breath. "The men Jocelyn interrupted were willing to kill to keep her from identifying them. One I am familiar with. He's nothing more than a hireling but dangerous nonetheless. I suspect the other may well be an official in your government. Probably of high rank. Perhaps even someone well known to you. Someone you have no reason to distrust." He paused to choose his words. "I would guess that, at best, their purpose here is to discredit you. At worst —"

"Assassination?" Alexei's tone was matter-of-fact. Obviously the threat of murder was nothing new to him. Still, it was always difficult to accept that someone wanted you dead for whatever reason.

Rand nodded. "Possibly."

"Probably." Alexei sipped his brandy thoughtfully. "I want you to know I am not a fool. I spoke directly, and privately, to your superior. And I took every precaution in coming here. No one knows precisely where I am. When I left my entourage, I headed alone in one direction, then doubled back. I am confident I was not followed." He chuckled ruefully. "It was really quite an enjoyable game."

"With exceedingly high stakes," Rand said mildly.

"I am well aware of the stakes." Alexei paused. "I am not a coward but I would prefer not to risk the life of anyone else. Are we safe here?"

"As safe as anywhere, probably safer, I suppose." Rand nodded slowly. "I have good and loyal men posted. Not enough to hold back an army but enough to ensure we are not caught unawares."

"If you agree, I should like to remain for the next few days until it's time to return to London. If I do not appear at the ceremony it will be used against me. Disreputable scoundrel, unfit to rule, that sort of thing."

"I understand."

"You know, cousin." Alexei considered him with a pensive half smile. "I find I rather envy you at the moment."

"Do you? Why?"

"You are master of your own life. Your freedom is relatively unfettered." He laughed softly. "And no one wishes you dead."

Jocelyn's face flashed in Rand's mind. She was angry enough to wish him dead although she'd probably be happy just making his life miserable.

"In addition . . ." A wicked spark shone in Alexei's eye. At once a feeling of unease washed through Rand. "You have a remarkably lovely wife."

Chapter 12

Laughter rang in the dining hall and the evening meal had the festive air of a party.

A party to which Rand did not feel particularly invited.

No one had snubbed him. He simply didn't find Alexei as entertaining as Nigel did. He saw no reason to fawn over him as did Ivy, Rose, and Flora. And he could not for the life of him understand why Jocelyn was obviously enraptured by his charms.

And he didn't like for a moment the way Alexei was just as captivated by Jocelyn.

The meal itself was long since over, and it was well past the time when ladies should retire, leaving gentlemen to their after-dinner refreshment and discussions. However, since the only lady present was Jocelyn, and she showed no interest in leaving, the group still lingered around the table. A gathering made tolerable to Rand only by Nigel's excellent cognac. However reclusive the elderly man may have become he still stocked an outstanding cellar.

"Do tell us, Alexei, about the . . ."

Rand kept an overly pleasant smile plastered on his face until he thought his very skin would crack. He forced a mellow and lighthearted tone to his voice. He chuckled in the appropriate places. And he had yet another glass of cognac.

In spite of the liquor, Rand noticed the subtly intimate manner in which Alexei directed a question to Jocelyn. The wicked light in his eyes when he smiled at her. And the way he looked at her as if she were a rare delicacy and he an eager connoisseur.

And not once did Rand reach across the table and grab Alexei by his royal cravat. He prided himself on his restraint.

He did, however, note the way Jocelyn leaned toward Alexei when asking a question, barely a fraction of an inch, of course, but lean nonetheless. The way she tilted her head to look at the prince in an overly beguiling manner. The way her gaze meshed with his cousin's as if they were the only two in the room. Rand totally disregarded the fact that she behaved much the same toward Nigel.

And not once did Rand jump to his feet, grab her hand, and haul her out of the room, no doubt kicking and screaming every step of the way. That too was a mark of his self-control.

"You should visit Avalonia someday, cousin,"

Alexei said. "I daresay you would like it."

"Would I?" Rand said as pleasantly as possible, vowing to himself never to step so much as a single foot upon the soil of Avalonia.

"I have always wanted to travel. I would quite like to see the capitals of Europe." An annoyingly enthusiastic note sounded in Jocelyn's voice, and Rand expanded his private promise to include all foreign lands.

"Your grandmother always spoke highly of the country of her birth," Nigel said. "I suspect she missed it a great deal."

"I should think it's quite difficult to live out your life so far away from home," Alexei said. "I've scarce been gone a full month, yet already I feel the need to return. Still, there are obligations I must attend to here."

"Official duties?" Jocelyn asked.

"My life consists of very little save official duties." Alexei chuckled. "But yes, this is in fact the purpose of my visit to England. The Society for the Preservation of Anglo-Avalonian Brotherhood is celebrating a century of peace between our two countries."

Rand knew about the ceremony and the gala to follow but had never given it a second thought. Now it struck him as rather absurd. "Correct me if I'm wrong, Alexei, but I do not recall there ever having been anything *but* good relations between England and Avalonia."

"Hence the celebration," Alexei said blithely.

Rand studied Alexei carefully. Was it possible that this event was staged simply to give Alexei a legitimate opportunity to come to England and search for the Heavens?

"It is always wise to cement the friendship that binds our two countries." Alexei smiled in an all too polished manner.

Not just possible but indeed quite probable.

"Besides, we have a great deal in common," Alexei added. "You have a parliament to advise your king and assist in governing. We have a council of ministers that serves essentially the same purpose." Alexei thought for a moment. "Although I do think the overall attitudes of our respective peoples are dramatically different."

"How is that, my boy?" Nigel asked.

"It seems to me the British, at least the nobility, are rather staid, even stuffy, when it comes to the enjoyment of life. Your society has any number of silly rules and antiquated regulations."

"Every society has rules of some sort," Rand said mildly.

"Of course, as do we. It is, as I said, a simple matter of how people look at life. For example, take our views on marriage."

"Marriage?" Jocelyn laughed. "I cannot imagine that people everywhere don't see marriage in essentially the same way."

"Not at all, my dear. While divorce is as difficult and complex in Avalonia as it is here, we accept, far better than you, I believe, how, well" — Alexei shrugged — "mistakes can occur."

"Mistakes?" Jocelyn pulled her brows together curiously. "What do you mean?"

"As I understand it, annulment of a marriage in this country is quite complicated and can take a rather long time. Years perhaps. In my country, although admittedly it is not an everyday occurrence, it can be accomplished with discretion and little more than a petition to the king and a royal decree."

"Really?" Jocelyn murmured. "How interesting."

Rand scoffed. "Come now, there must be more to it than that."

"Most certainly." Alexei nodded. "The dissolution of a union is not to be taken lightly. The king gives a great deal of weight to the circumstances of the match. Were both parties willing participants? Was there excessive familial pressure? Was the marriage performed for matters of, say . . . safety or protection?"

"Surely every case is different?" Jocelyn said, clearly fascinated by the topic. Far too fascinated.

"Indeed it is. And individual circumstances are thoroughly considered. However, anyone finding themselves in an unwanted marriage because of a situation pertaining to the security of the royal family would be most favorably looked upon."

"I have no interest in an annulment," Rand said under his breath.

Jocelyn ignored him, an intent look on her face. "But you're talking about Avalonia. Certainly such an annulment would not be accepted in England?"

"Countries do extend other nations the courtesy of acknowledging their laws. It is true that two British subjects could not simply travel to Avalonia and request an annulment; I dare not think of the chaos that would ensue should that be permitted. However, the circumstances would be quite different if one of the parties in question was of Avalonian descent." He paused. "And of royal blood."

Jocelyn tossed Rand a pointed glance, then turned back to Alexei. "How very interesting."

"In theory perhaps. However, I personally have no interest in an annulment," Rand repeated firmly.

"Even so," Jocelyn said to Alexei, "you're saying it is possible."

"Quite possible. I only mention it at all because I am well aware of the factors that led to your, how to tactfully say it, hasty nuptials." Alexei's gaze shifted from Jocelyn to

Rand. "I feel somewhat responsible for the situation you find yourselves in."

"You needn't." Rand said sharply. "Jocelyn and I suit well together."

"Still, it's always good to know options exist." Jocelyn's gaze met Rand's. Her honey-colored eyes glowed in the candlelight, and he hadn't the least idea exactly what she was thinking. Unease washed through him. "Don't you agree?"

"No," he said sharply.

She raised a brow.

"In my day, a marriage was a marriage forever," Nigel said. "Two people shackled together were bound for the rest of their days." He sipped his drink. "Longer even."

Rand drew a deep breath. He was being ungracious but he didn't feel particularly kind toward anyone who gave Jocelyn so much as a slim hope of dissolving their marriage. "I do appreciate the information, Alexei, but Jocelyn and I are quite content with our union regardless of the manner in which it began."

Jocelyn emitted something that might have been a snort or a cough and covered her mouth with her hand. Rand cast her a scathing glare and she smiled sweetly in return.

She turned toward Alexei. "Nigel is right, Your Highness, regardless of the manner in which it came about, marriage is quite permanent in this country. For the most part. Even so" — she extended her hand to Alexei — "I am so grateful for the considerate nature of your suggestion."

Alexei raised her hand to his lips and gazed deeply into her eyes. "It is the least I can do for you."

Rand clenched his jaw and once again congratulated himself on not giving in to his immediate urge to bash Alexei's smiling face.

"Now then." Jocelyn slowly pulled her hand free. "Do tell us more about your family. I have seen the portraits of Rand's grandparents but I know nothing else about the heritage the two of you share."

Alexei launched into an entertaining recitation of the long and noble history of the royal family of Avalonia.

Rand paid cursory attention and participated with an occasional nod or vague murmur. His attention was fixed firmly on his wife. Jocelyn was wearing another of those damnable old-fashioned gowns that compressed her waist to a size a man's hands could easily fit around and barely constrained her delectable bosom. She flirted and flattered and teased in the manner in which she'd admitted she had practiced all her life. Lessons obviously well learned. She was nothing short of glorious and looked and sounded and behaved, well, like the princess of some magical realm. Or a man's deepest desires. He could scarcely fault Alexei for the gleam in his eye.

It was to be expected, he supposed. She was a captivating woman, and no doubt many men would look, or had looked, at Jocelyn in much the same way. And no doubt it would annoy him just as much in the future. Still, other men were not Alexei. Not the man she had once set her cap for.

But, damn it all, Jocelyn was his wife. And he had no intention of giving her up.

Her laughter rang in the room, accompanying his realization that the emotion gripping his gut was nothing less than jealousy. It was an entirely new sensation and he didn't like it one bit. Still, it was probably inevitable when one cared for one's wife.

And he did care for her. More than he would have thought possible. Perhaps, just perhaps, it was love.

The thought struck him that this was a very good way to begin their lives together.

Alexei said something and Jocelyn responded with a flirtatious smile and a seductive flutter of her lashes. Rand's jaw clenched.

Of course, before he could explore his own feelings, he had to pacify hers. Had to clear up that mess he'd caused this afternoon and make sure she understood he hadn't the slightest regret about marrying her.

And make sure she understood as well he would never let her go.

★ ★ ★

"Before you say anything, I believe I owe you yet another apology." Rand's voice sounded behind her.

Jocelyn sat in the window seat gazing out at the starry night through her spectacles. It was really quite amazing. She couldn't help but regret the vanity that had kept her from appreciating such a remarkable sight until now.

"Jocelyn?"

She heard him close the door firmly and turned toward him. "One apology, Rand? I would have thought you owed me a dozen."

"Only a dozen?" He stepped toward her with a tentative smile, one hand behind his back. "That's much better than I anticipated."

She'd already decided to forgive him for nearly everything. Certainly there was the possibility she was simply fooling herself but she doubted it. After all, in spite of anything he might have said aloud, his behavior at dinner spoke volumes. The nasty looks he'd cast Alexei, the grim set of his lips, his obvious jealousy, and his adamant refusal to so much as consider the annulment Alexei offered all strengthened her belief that he did indeed care for her.

She simply had to make him realize it.

"And this time . . ." He drew his arm from behind his back to reveal a large bouquet of

285

white roses from the garden. He held them out to her. "I have come prepared."

She studied him for a minute. "Did you mean what you said?"

"I realize that jewelry would be appropriate as well but at the moment all I could —"

"No." She huffed. "Not about being prepared. About what you said this afternoon."

His brows drew together. Obviously the man had no idea exactly to which of his assumptions, half truths, or misstatements she referred.

"No." He drew out the word carefully. It was as much a question as an answer. He appeared so perplexed she was hard pressed not to laugh aloud.

"You don't know what I'm talking about, do you?"

"Of course I do." But clearly he didn't.

"I can certainly understand it. There were so many ill-thought things you said this afternoon." She got up from the seat and walked toward him. "When you said this was a marriage neither of us wants. Did you mean it?"

"Well . . ." His brow furrowed and he looked as if he were debating the merits of any number of answers.

Perhaps she should take pity on him. "You said a marriage neither of us *wants*. Not *wanted*. Did you mean to say that? Did you mean that at this particular time, right now,

286

today, this very moment, you do not *want* this marriage?"

His expression cleared and he shook his head firmly. "No. Absolutely not. What I do mean is that I do *want* this marriage. I misspoke today. I should have said *wanted*. I didn't mean to say *wants*. It was a slip of the tongue. I was quite disconcerted and —"

She grabbed his jacket with both hands and pulled his lips toward hers. "Then do shut up and kiss me."

He dropped the roses and wrapped his arms around her. His lips crushed hers and an impossible sense of joy flooded through her. Surely no man could kiss like this without affection. Surely he cared for her. He might well be annoying but he was an annoyance she would treasure for the rest of her days.

At last he pulled back and stared down at her. His gaze searched hers. "You are no longer angry then? I am forgiven?"

"For the moment." She grinned. "But I cannot promise how long that will last. You have the most irritating tendency to say exactly the wrong thing. However, I have already begun to realize, for the most part, they are unwitting mistakes. Fortunately for you, I am intelligent enough to understand that."

He laughed. "I am indeed a lucky man."

"That you are," she said primly. "Especially

since you have no idea how to behave with a woman."

"I have a very good idea how to behave with a woman." His gaze slid to the bed, then back to her. "And I would be more than happy to demonstrate."

She laughed and pushed out of his arms. "That's not what I meant and you know it."

"Pity," he said with a wicked grin and knelt down to retrieve the roses.

"Now then." She studied him for a moment. "Why didn't you tell me you are a prince?"

He paused, then continued picking up the flowers. His tone was guarded. "For the very same reason you didn't tell me you couldn't see. You didn't —"

"Yes, yes, I know I didn't ask." She waved away his comment impatiently. "Even you must admit the two things are not at all equal in importance. My, well, secret I suppose is relatively insignificant —"

He glanced up at her and raised a brow.

"Come now, you know it is. Besides, I did tell you I hadn't seen those men and you simply took it the wrong way."

"Nigel told you I was a prince" — a slight smile quirked his lips — "you simply took it the wrong way."

"They are not the same thing and you know it."

"Nonetheless." He stood and handed her

the roses. Their delightful fragrance sur-rounded her and she wondered how any man could fail to realize how difficult it was for a woman to remain angry when presented with such beauty of sight and scent. She glanced around the room, then headed toward a pitcher.

"I don't consider myself a prince, you know," he said, his tone sober.

Jocelyn placed the flowers one at a time in the pitcher and waited.

"I didn't tell you because it's not important to me. I hardly ever think of it." He paused and she turned toward him. "It plays no role in my life. I don't consider it significant."

"Alexei apparently does."

His expression darkened. "Alexei's world is not mine. He was raised to become the next ruler of Avalonia. I was brought up to be the Viscount Beaumont. I am quite content with my lot in life." He shrugged in a rather help-less manner that tugged at her heartstrings. "I can't expect you to understand."

"Explain it to me then."

He studied her as if deciding if she really wanted to know what he thought. "I am an Englishman." His words were deliberate and measured. "This is my country and King George is my king. My king and my country have my full allegiance and my complete loy-alty. I have been willing in the past to lay down my life for England and should do so again without question if called upon.

"Earlier today you said being pretty was very much a part of who you were, although I daresay I find those spectacles perched on your nose more and more seductive." He shot her a wicked grin, then sobered. "The sixth Viscount Beaumont is who I am. It is ingrained in my very nature. In my soul, as it were. And England is my home.

"Avalonia holds no interest for me, nor does any hereditary title from that land. It does not engender feelings of loyalty or desire. It is a spot on the map. Nothing more. I daresay I shall never even visit the country, nor do I particularly want to."

"I know this will sound mercenary and I am trying very hard to reform my nature but, Rand" — she heaved a sigh — "you could be, in point of fact you are, a prince. Think of it. A real prince. And think of everything that goes along with it. Wealth and position and . . . everything."

"And you could be a princess, exactly as you wanted." A wry smile quirked his lips but his eyes were solemn. "Knowing that can never be, do you think perhaps, not now of course but someday, you could be happy being a mere viscountess? Lady Beaumont and not Princess Jocelyn?"

Her heart fluttered in her chest. "Lady Beaumont?" She walked toward him slowly. "Instead of Princess Jocelyn? That is quite a choice. Hmmm. Let me think." She stepped in front of him and placed her hands on his chest, then slid them up to his shoulders. "If I remain Lady Beaumont do I get to keep Lord Beaumont as well?"

"If you will have him." He slipped his arms around her and drew her close. "I have no desire to end this marriage, Jocelyn."

"No annulment then?" She gazed up at him.

"No." His tone was adamant, and surely that was love she saw in his eyes.

"Very well. Besides, your uncle was right." She grinned. "Princess Jocelyn doesn't suit me nearly as well as Lady Beaumont does."

Rand laughed and pressed his lips to hers in a kiss long and tender and absolutely delightful. And she kissed him back with the certain knowledge that she would quite enjoy being nothing more than Lady Beaumont and with the growing desire only Lord Beaumont could trigger. His lips moved from her mouth to kiss her throat, and she gasped with enjoyment and more than a little anticipation. He nibbled up the side of her neck to her ear, and she wondered just how hard the floor beneath them would be or if they could make it all the way to the bed.

"Stay away from Alexei." His voice was low against her ear.

At once all desire vanished. She pulled her head away and looked at him. "What did you say?"

He cast her a firm look. "You heard me."

"I must have heard wrong." She pushed out of his arms and took an unsteady step away.

"I doubt that. However, I am more than happy to repeat it. Stay away from Alexei. I don't like the way he looked at you, and furthermore" — he crossed his arms over his chest — "I'm not overly fond of the way you looked at him."

"Don't you trust me?" She narrowed her gaze.

"I don't trust *him*," he said staunchly. "He has a considerable reputation. One he did his best to earn."

"You think I am too . . . too" — she clenched her teeth — "stupid to recognize that?"

"Not at all. But you are young and as such could be extremely susceptible to someone like Alexei."

"Do you believe I would be unfaithful to you?" Her voice rose.

He hesitated no more than a heartbeat but it was enough. "Not deliberately, of course. However, he is a man of considerable charm, and in spite of your successful season you are still very inexperienced —"

"You have certainly provided me with a great deal of experience!"

"I meant in the ways of disreputable rakes like Alexei." He spoke as if he were talking to a small child or some feebleminded creature who needed to have things explained as simply as possible. It was most condescending and altogether infuriating. "You could easily find yourself in a situation where you could be, well, swept away —"

"Swept away!" She couldn't believe her ears. "You think I would allow myself to be swept away?"

"I swept you away."

"Hah! If I recall the sweeping was entirely mutual!"

"Exactly. Besides, you were willing to meet with him privately once," Rand said pointedly.

"It certainly wasn't for purposes of being swept away!"

"Not on your side, perhaps, but I have no doubt what Alexei intended during that ill-fated rendezvous of yours."

She gasped with indignation. "He intended to ask me to be his bride! *His* princess!"

Rand snorted. "Come now. As an intelligent woman surely you cannot still believe that?"

Whether she did now or not wasn't the least bit relevant. She certainly had at the time. "You don't trust me!"

"Of course I do," he said quickly but not quite quickly enough. "It's Alexei I don't trust. And therefore, as your husband, I am telling you I don't want you near him."

Shock stole her breath. "Is that an order?"

"Call it what you will. I would not have put it that way but if you insist . . ." A challenging light shone in his eyes as if he were daring her to protest. "I am indeed ordering you to desist this ongoing flirtation with Alexei."

"There is no flirtation and" — she struggled to keep her voice cool and level — "I don't take well to orders."

"Nonetheless you will obey this one."

She stared in disbelief. Was the man completely insane? Had jealously driven him stark raving mad? Or was he nothing at all like the man she thought he was? "I will do precisely as I wish."

"Not when it comes to Alexei." Determination rang in his voice.

"When it comes to anything at all. It may well be time we completely understood each other, my lord. I will entertain requests. I will give due consideration to petitions or entreaties. I will even acquiesce to a rare demand, but I will not be ordered about like a servant. I am willing to fulfill my obligation as your wife and your viscountess but I will not be treated in any way less than those positions deserve. Not even by you."

"I am your husband." He looked so indignant she would have laughed if she hadn't been so angry.

"I don't especially care. Now," she ground out the words, "get out."

"Now *that* sounded like an order."

"How very astute."

Rand stalked to the door. "I am only leaving because I have nothing more to say at the moment." He jerked open the door. "As far as I'm concerned the subject is closed. I have made my position perfectly clear."

"Your position?" She sputtered with rage. "Your position!" Jocelyn whirled around, stalked to the pitcher of roses, and grabbed it.

"Don't throw that at me," he warned.

"Is that an order?"

"Yes!"

"I don't take orders!" She flung the pitcher with all her strength.

He ducked behind the open door a split second before the pottery shattered against the wall barely a few feet from his head in a satisfying spray of water and white petals. There was something to be said for being able to see well enough to aim.

He glanced at the scattered roses and raised a brow. "Well, that's the last time I accompany an apology with flowers."

"Hah! There aren't enough flowers in the world! Now get out!"

"Another order, my dear? You should know I'm not fond of them either. I'm leaving now only because that's exactly what I had planned to do." He smirked, backed out, and slammed the door.

She stared at the closed door wishing she had something, anything, to fling once again and struggled to slow her breathing to a more sedate rate.

That certainly hadn't gone at all well. Not in the least what she'd had in mind. Why, at this very moment he was supposed to be sharing her bed doing all those lovely things to her she had grown quite fond of in recent days. And she should be doing equally lovely things to him in return.

She crossed her arms over her chest and paced. She did tend to think better on her feet. What, precisely had gone wrong? Nothing she could pinpoint on her part. It was his fault, all of it.

Of course, she had set out to make him jealous. And had, perhaps, paid a bit too much attention to Alexei in the process. Still, she'd made it a point to favor Nigel equally, although that had slipped Rand's notice. There was the distinct possibility she'd gone a bit too far.

It was that question of trust that was disturbing. Of the two of them, Jocelyn would have thought she was the one who would be unwilling to trust. Her father hadn't been the least bit reliable, and even her brother could not be depended on for much of her life, although ultimately he had made up for it. But hadn't she trusted Rand right from the beginning?

For Rand, trust might well require a leap of faith. And love.

It was, no doubt, his secretive government background that made him so hesitant to trust her as completely as she trusted him. She'd not given him any reason to distrust her, at least not since their marriage. Oh, certainly she had once planned a private meeting with Alexei, but that seemed like a lifetime ago even if, in truth, it was little more than a week. She'd done nothing to betray Rand, nor did she intend to, even if, with Alexei's presence, the opportunity might arrive. No, she was as content with her lot as Rand's wife as he was with his position in life.

Perhaps she simply needed to make that clear to him, although, at the moment, he well deserved to stew in his own turbulent juices. A night apart would probably do him good.

He was undeniably jealous and that was exactly what she'd wanted. She'd simply never expected that jealousy on the part of a man went hand in hand with stupidity.

Her husband had quite a bit to learn about women in general and especially about his wife. He had to learn when to speak and when to keep his mouth shut. He had to learn to trust her. And he had to understand she never had, and never would take well to orders.

Well, he certainly told her!

Rand stalked through the wide corridor.

If he wished to issue orders, he would bloody well issue orders. His position was perfectly understandable.

He stomped down the spiral stone stairs. That's the way it would be. There would be no debate, no discussion. He was the husband. She was the wife.

And apparently he was sleeping by himself.

His step slowed with the awful realization that he was something of a fool. He groaned aloud. How could he have thought, even for a moment, that she would respond well to his issuance of orders. In point of fact he hadn't thought. He'd simply opened his mouth and the most outrageous things flowed out.

Certainly he was well within his rights to insist that Jocelyn stay away from Alexei, but it wasn't necessary to sound like an unyielding general commanding disobedient troops. He should have known she wouldn't take it at all well. Who would?

He strode into the shadowed library and headed straight for the brandy decanter, aided by the light from the still-burning fire in the hearth.

What was it about the blasted woman that made him firmly put his foot in his mouth every time he was with her? She'd lull him into some sort of vulnerable state where all was going well and just when he'd relax enough not to watch every word, he'd say something absurd again. So far he'd called her shallow, accused her of lying, indicated he regretted their marriage, and now had approached her in a manner guaranteed to overset her. What was wrong with him?

He tossed back two full glasses of brandy in quick succession, then poured another.

"Argue about Prince Alexei, did you?" Nigel's amused voice came from a chair near the fireplace.

"It's that obvious?"

Nigel snorted.

Rand started toward the chair opposite his uncle's, pausing only long enough the grab the decanter. "She's turned me into a complete and total idiot, Nigel."

Nigel chuckled. "That does tend to happen."

Rand collapsed into the chair. "What? Insanity? Is it a by-product, then, of marriage?"

"Not necessarily of marriage but" — Nigel paused — "perhaps of love."

"Love? Hah," Rand scoffed. "If this is love, I want no part of it. It's driving me mad. She's driving me mad." He leaned forward and rested his forearms on his legs. "Tell me this, Uncle, am I a reasonable man? An intelligent person? Do I rely on logic and rational thinking to make decisions?"

"I have always thought so."

"As have I, but apparently I've changed." He sank back and drained his glass. "Whatever reason and good sense I might have previously possessed has vanished. Gone. Like that." He tried to snap his fingers but oddly enough couldn't quite manage. Instead he refilled his glass and sighed heavily. "It's a pity."

"What is?"

"I've been felled by a mere woman. She might as well have cut off my hair like, oh, who was that fellow?"

"Samson?"

"That's him. He trusted a woman and look what happened to him."

"Jocelyn has given you no reason to distrust her."

"I have no reason to trust her either." And wasn't that a point in his favor? It did seem rational at the moment. "People have to earn trust. When you trust blindly, well, terrible things can happen. Battles can be lost. People can die."

"This is not war, Rand," Nigel said gently.

"It feels like war," Rand muttered. "Different battlefield, that's all."

"I'm confident you can trust your wife."

"Hah. She didn't want to marry me, you know." He lowered his voice in a confidential manner. "She wanted to marry *him*. She wanted to be a princess." He smiled smugly.

"I could make her a princess if I wanted. I don't, but I could."

"Tell me something, my boy, does Jocelyn trust you?"

"Of course," he said indignantly, then raised his glass and grinned. "I saved her life."

"And then you were forced to take any decision she might have made as to the *rest* of her life away from her," Nigel said gently. "Not your fault, of course, but there it is. Still, she has not held that against you, has she?"

"No."

"She has tried to make the best of it, has she not?"

"Yes."

"Even to the point of being your wife in every sense of the word?"

"Yes."

"And have you tried as well to be the husband she deserves?"

"Well . . ." Rand resisted the urge to squirm. Had he indeed made an effort to make their marriage work? Or had he simply let events unfold as they would?

Neither of them had had any choice initially. Marriage was the only option if he was to take her away and keep her safe. He hadn't really considered until now what she'd been forced to give up.

Oh, not Alexei. Rand was confident

Alexei's intentions toward Jocelyn had never been especially honorable. But Jocelyn could have made a far better match than the sixth Viscount Beaumont.

Yet it didn't appear she regretted it. No, she seemed to be making the best of their marriage. In those rare moments when he wasn't drawing her annoyance, she seemed to be enjoying their newfound life together. She laughed a great deal and he rather liked the sound of it. In his rooms and in his bed. And she'd certainly scarcely hesitated to join him there.

"I don't want to end this marriage, Nigel." Even as he said the words, Rand realized they'd never been truer.

"Why?"

"Because I . . ." *Why?* That was the real question, wasn't it? It wasn't simply a matter of honor, although at this point he had, for all intents and purposes, ruined her. Nor was it any concern of scandal. Like it or not, scandal would definitely accompany any dissolution of their marriage. It had nothing to do with pride or responsibility.

"You what?" Nigel pressed.

Rand stared into his glass as if the answer were there, floating in the amber-colored liquid. The color of her eyes.

"I don't want to give her up," he said quietly. "Ever."

"Because?"

"Because . . ." He drew a deep breath and

met his uncle's gaze. "I don't think I could live without her. I don't want to live without her. Not a day, not a minute." He shook his head. "She's not at all what I first thought I wanted in a wife, yet with every day she is more and more exactly what I want. Or maybe what I need. I can see my life stretching out before me with her by my side and I like what I see." He shrugged. "It's all quite perplexing."

"It's love, my boy."

"Do you really think so?"

"Let's consider the facts here." Nigel paused. "Do you find her confusing? Is it as if you are totally off-balance when it comes to her?"

"Yes."

"You find yourself doing irrational things, making unreasonable demands? Behaving very much like a fool?"

Rand blew a long breath. "Without a doubt."

"And do you want to challenge any man who so much as casts her a smile?" Nigel grinned. "Up to and including beloved uncles?"

"Not beloved uncles." Rand laughed, then sobered. "But anyone else. Charming princes in particular."

"Given all that, plus your admission that you want to spend the rest of your days with her" — Nigel chuckled — "it certainly sounds like love to me."

Rand had considered the possibility, of course. But never having experienced the maddening emotion, it was not at all surprising he hadn't recognized it. Of course he was in love. Or insane, which might well be the same thing.

Rand shook his head. "It's not at all pleasant, is it?"

"It has its moments."

"I can scarcely wait," Rand murmured. He swirled his brandy and considered the intriguing way it coated the side of the glass. "What would you suggest I do about it?"

"Given the way you stormed in here, I suggest you do nothing more tonight. I would suspect she is little more pleased with you than you are with yourself at the moment. After that . . ." Nigel shrugged.

"After that is the question," Rand said wryly.

"I see it's time for the benefit of my vast years of experience. Very well then." Nigel studied him for a long moment. "Give her the credit she deserves, Rand. See her for who she is, not who you thought she was. She's not perfect, no woman is, but in truth she is a far cry from the spoiled, pampered debutante you originally believed her to be. She is both intelligent and courageous, and has shown a great deal of fortitude in making the best of her situation. Her life is radically different than her dreams yet, to my knowledge, she has not held that against you."

Nigel shook his head. "You must have been born under a lucky star, boy. I don't know how it happened, but in the odd unexplained ways of this world, you may well have stumbled upon the one woman who could make you truly happy." The older man leaned toward him. "There are those who believe for every man there is just one woman. For every soul, one mate. Fated, one for the other. Destined to be together. I suspect Jocelyn may well be yours."

Rand narrowed his eyes. "Why do you think that?"

Nigel grinned. "Because in the days since you've been here, there is a lightness in your step, a look in your eye, and an air of contentment, even happiness about you."

"That's absurd." Rand laughed. "I haven't felt the tiniest bit happy or content." *Or had he?*

"The confusion of love often tends to obscure the joy. At least in the beginning. It gets better, my boy." Nigel chuckled and sank back in his chair. "Before my cache of sage wisdom is completely exhausted, let me tell you something else. I would wager my last penny your wife is in love with you as well."

Rand brightened. "Do you think so?"

"I realize she's not nearly as idiotic about it as you, but yes. I've seen the way she looks at you. For an old man, it's rather enchanting to see that look in a woman's eye again." Nigel fell silent, and Rand knew his uncle was looking back through the years. To the look in the eye of another woman in love. At last he spoke, his voice quiet. "Let her know how you feel. Don't lose her because she thinks you don't care about her."

"Then I should tell her?"

"Have you heard a word I've said?" Nigel huffed in annoyance. "It's no good dispensing advice if no one listens."

"Sorry," Rand murmured.

"Now, pay attention. No self-respecting woman can love for long without being loved in return. You wouldn't want the kind of woman who could. Whiny, clinging creatures. However it happened, you have found yourself a good woman. You'd be a fool not to make certain she knows exactly how you feel.

"You have the opportunity for the sort of happiness that is rare in this life." Nigel aimed a firm finger at him. "Don't muck it up."

Chapter 13

Jocelyn stepped into the parlor and pulled up short. The room was empty save for the prince, who appeared to be examining the area around the fireplace. "Alexei?"

His head snapped toward her and she could have sworn he scowled at her interruption. But at once a pleasant smile appeared on his face, and she thought it must have been nothing more than a trick of the late afternoon light.

He straightened and turned to face her. "Jocelyn, my dear, how lovely you look today."

"Thank you." She cautiously returned his smile.

His forehead furrowed in a frown. "What is that on your nose?"

"Spectacles." She'd quite forgotten she had them on and resisted the impulse to snatch them off. "I was looking for Rand. Have you seen him?"

Alexei shrugged dismissively. "I spoke to him earlier. He said he was going to check on his men."

"I see." She pulled her brows together. She hadn't spoken to Rand all day. It was most disquieting. She had assumed or expected or perhaps simply hoped he would have sought her out first thing this morning for yet another apology. One she was willing, once again, to accept on the condition that he understood she would not be ordered about.

It was odd the way she rather enjoyed fighting with him. It was more than a little exhilarating, although not nearly as enjoyable as making up. She was certainly ready to make up, with everything that entailed. She'd waited for him most of the day and now was determined to track him down. He was such an annoying man and in spite of it, or perhaps because of it, he had thoroughly captured her heart.

"I do hope he'll return home soon," she murmured.

"I'm certain the ride will do him good. He seemed somewhat under the weather when I saw him and a bit preoccupied as well." Alexei studied her. "Is something amiss?"

"Not at all," she said blithely. "Why do you ask?"

"No particular reason except my cousin appeared even more grim today than usual." Alexei chuckled. "But then he does tend to wear an unrelentingly forbidding expression when he is in my presence. Tell me, Jocelyn, does your husband ever smile?"

She bristled at the question but maintained her own smile. "Oh, he does more than that. In fact, he finds a great deal of humor in life and can be most amusing himself. He grins, he chuckles, he even laughs."

Alexei raised a brow. "Laughter? From Viscount Beaumont? I can scarcely picture such a thing."

"Whether you can or not, it's true nonetheless."

"Perhaps." Alexei smiled ruefully and Jocelyn could see a vague resemblance to Rand she'd failed to notice before. The two men were of a similar height and build although her husband's hair and eyes were darker. The prince's features were finely boned whereas Rand's were more strongly defined. Alexei was a handsome man but Rand was, well, *right*. At least for her. Odd how it had turned out that way.

"I must confess, my dear, I have been concerned about you," Alexei said in an offhand manner. He clasped his hands behind his back and wandered along the perimeter of the room.

"Nonsense." She laughed in spite of a touch of unease at his words. "There's nothing to be concerned about."

"Come now, Jocelyn. I know the circumstances that led to this farce of a marriage of yours. I cannot believe you're happy about it all."

"I'm quite happy. Thank you for asking."

"You could have had so much more." He paused and studied a tapestry hanging on the wall. "Do you ever think about that, Jocelyn? What you might have had?"

"No." The answer came without hesitation and at once she realized the truth of it. From the moment she'd married Rand she'd been far too busy discovering what she'd gained to dwell on what she'd lost. Yet another indication that she wasn't shallow after all. She smiled at the revelation. "Not in the least."

"I don't believe you."

"Believe as you wish. It's quite true."

"Please, my dear, I am not some dim-witted peasant." He continued his casual perusal of the room. The odd thought struck her that his meandering appeared almost methodical, as if he were searching for something. Ridiculous idea, of course. Obviously all Rand's talk of Alexei's untrustworthy nature had colored her view of him. "When last we spoke, I told you that you were a woman well aware of your own worth."

She laughed. "That does seem rather a long time ago now."

"Still, has anything changed?"

"Everything has changed," she said firmly.

"Let me see your hands." He stepped toward her.

"My hands?" Instinctively she held them behind her back. "Why?"

"Just show them to me."

Reluctantly she presented her hands. He took them in his, glanced at them, then met her gaze. "He has not given you a ring to mark your marriage?"

"There's scarcely been time." She tried to pull her hands away but his grasp was firm. She hadn't even noted the lack of a ring before now, and she and Rand had not discussed it. "Besides, we've been here since we wed and there's been no opportunity —"

"But surely he's presented you with some bauble to commemorate the bonds of wedlock? A necklace or a bracelet? Something of his mother's or perhaps his grandmother's?"

"No, nothing." She tugged at his hands. The blasted man had a grip of iron.

"But every family has some trinkets." He frowned thoughtfully, then brightened. "What about jewels? Diamonds or rubies —"

"No." She jerked her hands free and glared with annoyance. Alexei held on to a subject with the same determination he'd held her hands. "I daresay there is little possibility of anything of the sort. He hasn't a great deal of money, you know."

"Hasn't he?" Alexei mused, a curious expression on his face. "I had thought . . ."

"What?"

"It's of no significance." He shrugged.

"Well, as Rand is not here, I should probably . . ." She turned to leave.

Alexei caught her hand, swung her around, and pulled her into his arms. "I would have given you jewels. You should be showered in jewels."

She stared up at him indignantly and wondered how, prince or not, she had ever wished to marry this particular man. "It's rather too late for that. Now do let me go."

"Is it too late?" His gaze slipped to her lips. "I wonder."

"This is absurd, Alexei, now if you don't —"

His lips crushed hers. Panic and anger surged through her and she struggled against him. He was decidedly stronger than she'd expected.

"Unhand my wife."

Jocelyn's heart plunged and her breath caught. She pushed hard against Alexei, who at the same instant released his grip, and she stumbled out of his grasp.

Rand stood in the doorway, tall and handsome and exceedingly, well, grim. His gaze flicked over her as if looking for evidence of what obviously appeared to be a mutual indiscretion.

She squared her shoulders and resisted the impulse to explain. From the hard, nearly expressionless, rather dangerous look on Rand's face, she knew it would have been futile. She really had done nothing wrong, although he probably wouldn't see it that way.

"I'm glad you finally decided to make an appearance." She planted her hands on her hips. "Where have you been?"

His gaze locked on Alexei but he directed his words to her. "Out."

"Well?" She heaved a resolute sigh. "Aren't you going to say something?"

"Keep your hands off my wife," Rand said to Alexei, his voice hard.

"Not to him." She huffed. "To me."

"No."

"Why on earth not?" She crossed her arms over her chest. "You must admit this looks bad."

"Very bad," Alexei murmured.

"I know how it looks," Rand said. "I further know exactly what I saw when I walked in here."

"Aren't you going to demand an explanation?" she asked.

"Not from you." His gaze met hers. "I am not a fool, Jocelyn, even if, where it concerns you, I may appear so on occasion. However, my eyesight has always been accurate and I recognize when an embrace is mutual and when it is not."

She widened her eyes and stared. "What are you saying?"

"I'm saying, my dear wife" — he blew a short breath and rolled his gaze toward the ceiling — "that as difficult as it may be to keep my wits about me when it comes to you —"

"Yes?" She couldn't hide the eagerness in her voice.

"I have spent much of the day on horseback, accompanied by my own thoughts and, well" — his manner was reluctant — "damn it all, Jocelyn, I trust you."

She stared in disbelief, then beamed at him. "As well you should."

"As well I should." He grinned sheepishly.

"This is all very touching and I am so grateful to have been witness to it but you do need to understand, cousin." Alexei moved closer to Jocelyn. "Regardless of her marital state, I still have certain feelings for Jocelyn."

She stepped quickly away. "Whatever feelings you may have are certainly not returned."

They ignored her.

"Your feelings are no longer significant." Rand's gaze locked with Alexei's.

"Not in the least." Jocelyn nodded. They paid her no heed. It was as if Alexei and Rand were alone.

"I am not accustomed to having my wishes disregarded." Alexei narrowed his eyes.

"Perhaps it's time you became accustomed to it." Rand's tone was unyielding.

"I can provide Jocelyn with everything she's ever dreamed of," Alexei said.

She shook her head. "I no longer —"

"She is my wife and I will provide for her."

Rand's hands curled into fists at his side.

"Really? As a mere viscount? You could give her a great deal more." Alexei's words carried a deeper meaning and at once Jocelyn realized they were no longer talking about her.

"I do not wish for more."

"Do you not feel any sense of obligation." Alexei's eyes flashed. "Of duty?"

"I do indeed." Rand's tone was firm. "To *my* king and *my* country. And *my* wife."

The two men glared at each other. Tension shimmered in the air. Any minute they would be at each other's throats or worse, issue a challenge both would feel obligated to meet.

"Stop it this instant." Jocelyn stepped between them. "I'm not entirely sure what this discussion is about but you're both behaving like children."

Alexei shrugged. "As you wish."

She turned to her husband. "Rand, did you —"

"Beg pardon, Your Lordship." Nick stepped into the room, an uneasy expression on his face. He moved to Rand's side and murmured something in a low tone. Rand nodded.

"I shall be back in a moment." Rand cast her a quick smile, then turned and followed Nick out of the room.

"Now then, my dear, where were we when we were interrupted?" Alexei stepped toward her.

She glared at him. "Are you mad?"

He reached for her and she slapped his hand away.

"Stop that nonsense at once. You're going to make him think there really is something between us."

"Well, isn't there?"

"No." She heaved an annoyed sigh. "And in truth, there wasn't a great deal to begin with. Surely this is not the first time a woman has said no to you?"

Alexei frowned and shook his head. "I certainly can't recall another instance."

"Then do feel free to revel in this new and unusual experience!"

"Come now, I can't believe you mean a word of what you're saying." He stepped closer and at once she moved away. "Besides, I am doing no more than picking up where we left off."

"I have no desire to pick up where you — not we, but *you* — left off." She pulled a steadying breath. "I am flattered, truly I am, but I am now wed. And frankly happy with my fate. I realize there was a point when you wished to marry me —"

"What?" Alexei's brows pulled together.

"When you wished to marry me," she said slowly.

He laughed. "Whatever would make you think such a thing?"

"You said I was the one you wanted." Her

words were measured.

"And so you were. In point of fact you still are."

She studied him for a long moment, at last accepting the truth Rand had known all along. The truth even she'd begun to suspect. "When we were to meet in the music room, didn't you wish to propose?"

"How absurd." He scoffed. "I did have a proposal in mind, but certainly not one of marriage. Surely you are not as naïve as to have expected anything else."

"Apparently I was," she snapped.

"Now that you realize my intentions, I do hope you are not overly upset?"

"Overly upset?" She clenched her teeth. "While it is always upsetting to discover you are not nearly as intelligent as you thought, I am not overly so. I am, however, furious."

"With me?" His eyes widened in surprise. "Why? Naïve or not, you couldn't possibly have believed that a prince, the heir to a throne, could marry a —"

"A what?"

"A woman not of royal descent. Princes do not marry based on mere emotional whims." He shook his head. "No indeed, when I marry it must be to a princess of royal blood with connections to a country that would prove beneficial to my own. A royal marriage is a political alliance, not a love match. I can only hope that when the time comes, I will find a bride who is not only suitable but to my liking as well."

She struggled to keep her voice level. "Then your proposal?"

"It would have been the usual sort of thing." His manner was offhand, as if discussing nothing more significant than an outing in the park. "I would have provided for your every whim. An excellent home, fine clothes, jewels. We would have been together for however long we both wished. It would have been quite enjoyable for us both." He shrugged. "You needn't be angry about it. I would have been quite generous."

"I am angry. At myself more than at you." She whirled away from him and paced the room. "I can't believe I was such a fool."

Alexei raised a brow. "Your flattery will quite turn my head."

She cast him a scathing glare. "Don't you dare be insulted. I am the one who has been insulted. To think that you, that I . . ." She clenched her fists and drew a deep breath. "I suppose I should be grateful to you."

"Well, I *was* going to make you an excellent offer."

"Not about that." She snorted with disdain. "I wouldn't have accepted. But if I hadn't agreed to meet you, I never would have been in that music room. My life never would have been in danger. And I never would have married the man I love."

"The man you love? Good Lord." He groaned. "You're in love with him? That certainly does muddy the waters. How on earth did that happen?"

"How?" She stared in disbelief. "Well, let me think. He is honorable and amusing, courageous and kind, not to mention quite attractive. He rescued me from certain death. He sees there is more to me than a pretty face. Aside from a few ill-chosen comments on occasion, he has done everything possible to ease the rather shocking state of abrupt matrimony. In short, he treats me like, well, a princess."

"No jewels though," Alexei murmured.

"And when he kisses me" — she smirked — "he warms my toes."

"I could warm your toes." He grinned wickedly.

"You will never have the chance. You have played me for a fool, Alexei, and I have learned my lesson."

"I . . ." He drew a deep breath, then straightened his shoulders. "Please accept my apology. I truly had no idea you misunderstood my intentions." He studied her carefully. "So, you love him and he claims to trust you. It seems all has turned out well."

She raised her chin. "Quite well."

Rand stepped into the room, his gaze pinned hers. "Jocelyn."

There was something odd in his tone and a

tremor of fear shivered through her. "What is it? What's the matter?"

"It seems we have another guest."

"Another . . ." A tall figure stepped into the room and her breath stilled.

"Richard?" The word caught in her throat.

"At your service, little sister." Richard Shelton, the Earl of Shelbrooke, stood grinning in the doorway.

"Richard!" Her eyes fogged with tears and at once she was in his arms, laughing and crying at the same time.

"Are you well, Jocelyn?" he murmured against her ear.

"Yes. Now." She drew her head back and smiled up at him. "Oh, Richard, I have missed you so." She peered around him. "Is Gillian with you? And the baby?" She gasped. "Are they here? Are they all right?"

"They are safely ensconced at Effington Hall with the rest of the family. My wife and" — he chuckled — "my daughter."

"A daughter! How delightful!" She hugged him once again. "I can't wait to meet her."

"She is every bit as beautiful as her mother." He grinned with pride. "Although after dealing with you and your sisters through the years, I must admit I was hoping for the less grueling demands of a son. However, I have quite fallen in love with her."

She stepped out of his arms and studied him. It had been nearly a year since they'd last seen each other and she could scarcely believe he was there. "You look wonderful."

"As do you." He raised a brow. "Spectacles?"

She raised a shoulder in a self-conscious shrug. "I've discovered the unexpected pleasure of being able to see."

"Apparently much has changed in my absence," he said dryly.

"You can't imagine. I have a great deal to tell you. So much has happened and I —" She pulled her brows together thoughtfully. "When did you get back and what are you doing here?"

"We arrived at Effington Hall a few days ago, unexpectedly I might add. I suspect the letter detailing the specifics of our return home will come in the next week or so, if we're lucky." He shook his head in disgust. "At any rate we arrived just in time to attend a wedding. Lady Helmsley sends her regards."

"Lady . . . Marianne!" She beamed at him. "Oh how lovely. Is she happy?"

"Indeed she is, although I must confess to being a bit disgruntled myself." Richard pulled off his gloves one at a time, his words as measured as his actions. "When we discovered Gillian was with child and we could not return to England in time for the season I had promised you and your sisters, I left you all in the care of my dearest friend. I assumed you would have successful seasons, enjoy the pleasures of London — theater, museums, and the like. However, upon my return I find" — he met her gaze directly and she resisted the immediate urge to wince — "one sister has engaged in penning scandalous stories —"

"They weren't that scandalous," she said quickly.

"— based, apparently, on her amorous adventures —"

"Loosely based. Very loosely. In point of fact" — she forced a lighthearted laugh — "there was scarcely any truth to them at all and I'd hardly call them amorous."

"And another sister" — he narrowed his gaze — "compelled to wed a virtual stranger —"

"Have you met my husband," she said brightly, waving in Rand's general direction.

"— and forced to flee London for her very life."

"It does sound bad when you put it that way," Alexei murmured.

Jocelyn shot him a quelling glance. She had quite forgotten Alexei was there but the last thing she needed at the moment was his comments. She slanted a quick look at Rand and caught the quiet assurance in his gaze. At once she knew he would allow her to handle her brother but would be there if she needed him.

"It's not as bad as it sounds, Richard." She cast him a reassuring smile.

"I daresay it can scarcely be as bad as it sounds." His gaze was steady. "However, now that I have returned I'm certain all can be resolved to everyone's satisfaction."

"What do you mean 'resolved'?" She didn't like the look on his face. The inflexible, older brother, I-know-best expression. Unease trickled through her. "Exactly why are you here, Richard?"

"I should think it's obvious, Jocelyn." His gaze bored into hers. "I am here to take you home."

Chapter 14

"Take me home?" She stared at her brother for a long moment, resisting the immediate impulse to laugh. He would not take it at all well but he was so amusing when he had that tone in his voice.

"Exactly," he said in a lofty manner.

"I think not." She shook her head and grinned. "For the moment, Richard, this is my home. And home for now and always will be at my husband's side."

"She does not take well to orders, you know," Rand said mildly. "Did you really think you could walk in here and dictate to this particular woman?"

"Not for a moment." Richard sighed. "I've never been able to tell her, or any of my sisters for that matter, what to do. However, I did think it was worth a try." He looked at Jocelyn. "I had no idea what to expect, you know. What I was told by Thomas and the others did not paint a very attractive picture."

"It didn't start out that way," Jocelyn admitted. "But I think it's turned out rather nicely."

"Has it?" Richard studied her carefully. "Are you happy?"

"Quite." She traded smiles with her husband and wondered how long it would be before they were alone together again.

"You're going to let her stay with him then?" Alexei asked.

"If that's what she wants." Richard smiled down at her. "Thomas speaks quite highly of Lord Beaumont. And any man who can get her to wear spectacles is obviously a better man than her brother."

"If she was my sister I'd drag her out of here kicking and screaming if necessary," Alexei said idly.

Richard looked at him with a frown of annoyance. "Who are you?"

Something that might have been a laugh or a snort or more likely a bit of both sounded from Rand. "Lord Shelbrooke, may I present His Royal Highness, Prince Alexei of Avalonia."

"Prince . . ." Richard's mouth dropped open and he stared unabashedly. "Bloody hell."

"My sentiments exactly," Alexei said with a smirk.

"Ignore him, Richard," Jocelyn said firmly. "He doesn't like it, but it serves him right."

"I could have you shot for that in my

country," Alexei murmured.

"A prince." Richard chuckled and pulled his gaze from Alexei back to his sister. "As I was about to say, I'm pleased, of course, but somewhat surprised. I would not have expected you of all people to be content with, well" — he waved vaguely at the room — "this. Your ambitions for a match have always been considerably grander."

"I know. It's really quite remarkable. I'm not sure I can explain." She hooked her arm through her brother's elbow and led him to the nearest sofa. They sat down and she pulled her thoughts together. "As you well know, I had always hoped — well, planned really — to marry someone with a far more impressive title than a mere viscount."

"I know I shall never tire of the way *mere* always seems to come before viscount," Rand said wryly.

She ignored him. "Beyond that, you know how much I truly dislike being poor. I had always thought to marry someone with a great fortune, at least as great as yours, and, well, I didn't."

Richard narrowed his eyes. "He doesn't have money?"

"Oh he's not impoverished," she said quickly. "At least everything I've noticed indicates he has some money." She glanced at Rand. "You're not, are you? Impoverished, I mean."

Rand hesitated. "About that, Jocelyn, I should tell you —"

"No." She held out her hand to stop him. "I don't want to hear the exact state of your finances at the moment. It's simply not significant." She turned back to Richard. "I will still get my dowry, won't I? And it is substantial, isn't it?"

Richard frowned. "Yes, of course, but —"

"Then we shall be fine," she said firmly. "We shall always have a place to live. He has a lovely cottage somewhere —"

"A cottage?" Alexei snickered.

"Jocelyn," Rand stepped toward her, "I really must —"

"Not now." She quieted him with an impatient wave. "Someday this castle will be his as well. Oh, I know it's in a sorry state, and in truth crumbling down around us, but it has a great deal of charm and I've become quite fond of it."

"Have you?" Richard stared at her as if she were a complete stranger and he'd never seen her before now.

"Indeed I have. And, Richard." She leaned toward her brother in a confidential manner. It was important to make him understand. "I don't care about any of it. It doesn't matter to me. Not his title, not his money or lack thereof. None of it." She shook her head in amazement. "I still can't quite believe it myself."

"Nor can I," Richard murmured. "This is not the same sister I left behind." He glanced at Rand. "What have you done to her?"

Rand grinned and shrugged in a rather satisfied manner that didn't bother her for a moment.

"Well, his kiss does warm her toes," Alexei said helpfully.

A hot blush swept up Jocelyn's face.

"That's more than I needed to know," Richard said under his breath.

Rand cleared his throat. "While I do appreciate the assistance, I would prefer —"

"Come now, cousin," Alexei said. "We are all family, aren't we?"

"Family?" Confusion colored Richard's face. "Cousin?"

"That's the ironic part. Or one of them anyway," Jocelyn said. "As it happens, Rand is Alexei's cousin and by blood a prince of Avalonia. Even though he has no interest in ever claiming the title, which on one hand is something of a pity but on the other simply doesn't signify as it doesn't matter to me in the least.

"So you see" — she cast her brother her brightest smile — "I have ended up with a prince and a castle after all."

"A prince and a castle," Richard said slowly, obviously trying to take it all in. The poor man was completely befuddled. Not that she blamed him. It was all rather convoluted. He smiled weakly. "Next you will tell me there's a dragon around the place somewhere."

"I much prefer to think of myself as a wizard." Nigel stepped through the doorway. Richard immediately got to his feet.

Rand stepped forward. "Lord Shelbrooke —"

"Richard," Jocelyn said. "And Rand and Nigel. Do call each other by your given names. As Alexei pointed out, we are all family here."

"Very well, Richard, this is my uncle, Lord Worthington, Nigel." Rand grinned. "A most remarkable man, and I have always thought of him as something of a wizard."

"Only with words, my boy, but I relish the comparison." Nigel leaned on his cane and studied Richard, as if assessing his character along with his appearance. "About time you showed up."

Richard started. "I was unaware of any of this until my return —"

"Come to rescue her, did you?" Nigel's eyes narrowed. "She doesn't need it, you know."

"As I have just now discovered." Richard smiled and bowed. "To my great pleasure."

Nigel chuckled. "Glad to hear it."

"Blast it all, I nearly forgot." Richard's brow furrowed. He drew something from the pocket of his waistcoat and approached

Nigel. "I was asked to give this to you."

"What is it?" Rand frowned and moved closer.

"It's mine is what it is," Nigel said pointedly. "Don't get many letters." He unfolded the paper and squinted at it. "Can't read a word of it anyway. Flora!" He bellowed over his shoulder.

Flora poked her head in, no doubt already listening at the doorway. Jocelyn bit back a grin. She'd wager Ivy, Rose, and Nick were out there as well.

"Fetch my spectacles."

Flora nodded and vanished. Nigel hobbled to the nearest chair and settled into it.

"At least tell me who it's from," Rand said firmly

"Don't know yet," Nigel snapped. "Haven't read it."

"Richard?" Rand turned to her brother, and Jocelyn noted the change in her husband's attitude from a moment ago. His stance, his voice, the way he moved was sharp, hard, no-nonsense, with a tense sense of purpose about him. Abruptly the very air around them grew heavy and taut.

Richard obviously noted it too. His gaze met Rand's; his tone was sober. "It was given to me by the man you worked for."

Rand studied him and waited, with that silent, expressionless look that always brought to mind his private past and the secrets she would never be privy to. Apprehension gripped her.

Richard drew a deep breath. "Thomas refused to tell me exactly where you were. We nearly came to blows about it but he was adamant." Richard chuckled wryly. "He was quite impressive."

"He is a loyal friend," Rand said quietly.

"Yes, he is. To us both. It was a difficult position for him, and I regret having put him in it. Nonetheless, I was as determined as he." Richard shrugged. "He finally directed me to your superior, who agreed I was no threat and revealed your location."

Flora returned with the spectacles. Nigel placed them on his nose and scanned the note.

The room waited.

"Well, well, this is a bit of a pickle," Nigel murmured, his gaze still on the letter. At last he looked up. "The ceremony the prince is to appear at has been moved ahead to three days from now —"

Alexei frowned. "On whose authority?"

"It doesn't say." Nigel studied the paper. "You are all to return immediately and as discreetly as possible."

"Very well." Rand's tone was resolute. "We shall be off at once."

"Hold on, boy, there's more. It also says there are efforts afoot to make certain he does not arrive in time." Nigel's gaze met

Rand's. "The roads are being watched."

"We'll simply take a roundabout route," Rand said. "We'll be accompanied by my men. I have no doubt we can get through."

"But probably not without incident." Nigel shook his head. "You're talking about a group of what? Five or six men traveling together? That's bound to attract attention. According to this, any confrontation on the roads with whatever brigands are involved would be as detrimental as Alexei not putting in an appearance at all."

"Still —" Rand started.

"This is politics, boy, don't forget that," Nigel said sharply. "It's not as clear-cut as war but every bit as dangerous. You can't just ride out of here like a band of knights of old. No indeed. Won't work at all." He tapped the note thoughtfully. "You need a plan. Possibly even a disguise."

"Ridiculous." Alexei snorted. "I am certainly not going to go skulking about the countryside —"

"If you want to save your crown and, no doubt, your hide as well, you'll set aside that royal pride of yours and pay attention." Authority rang in Nigel's voice, and abruptly Jocelyn realized his nephew might not be the only one in the family with an adventurous past. "We have to come up with an idea, a good one, and we have precious little time in which to do it."

Silence fell over the room and Jocelyn took the opportunity to study the faces of the men around her. She couldn't help noticing they were rather a handsome lot. Not that their appearances had limited them in any particular way. No, their minds were considered much more important than their looks. It really wasn't at all fair how men were judged on intelligence and ability whereas women, more often than not, were judged only on beauty. Women were scarcely ever given the credit for even the simplest things and were bound by all sorts of ridiculous conventions about deportment and behavior regarding every aspect of their lives from how they danced at a ball to how they sat a horse to how they traveled . . .

"Women," Jocelyn said aloud. "That's it." She jumped to her feet. "That's the answer."

"Jocelyn." Rand shook his head. "I know you are trying to help —"

"Be quiet and listen to me for a moment." She paced a few steps, trying to organize her thoughts. It was a wonderful idea, if a bit wicked. And she had no doubt they wouldn't like it at all. Still . . .

She stopped and turned to face the gathering. "If indeed a band of men would be noticed at once, a carriage of women would be all but invisible."

"Women?" Alexei laughed. "I scarcely think —"

"I am doing the thinking at the moment and this is a wonderful idea." Excitement sounded in her voice and she turned to her husband. "You and Alexei will dress as women. Nick can drive the carriage. If it took a full day and night for us to travel here by horseback, how long will it take to return to London?"

Rand nodded thoughtfully. "Three days and nights, maybe less, if we stop for nothing more than to change horses."

"You'd make it just in time by carriage," Nigel said.

"Well?" She stared at each of them in turn, her gaze finally settling on Rand. "What do you think?"

He considered her for a moment. "I think I would never fit in your clothes."

"Of course not, don't be absurd." She laughed. "But I suspect between Flora, Rose, and Ivy we can certainly come up with something suitable."

"That we can, my lady," Flora's voice sounded from the hall.

"Grand idea, my dear. I'm damned proud of you." Nigel chuckled. "Brains and long legs too. You're a lucky man, Rand."

"I have already realized that, Uncle." Rand's dark gaze meshed with hers and she wanted nothing more than to throw herself into his arms. "It's an excellent plan, Jocelyn. No one would suspect two female travelers of being anything other than what they appeared."

"Oh, not two women." She shook her head. "Three."

"Three?" Rand's brow furrowed.

"Absolutely." She crossed her arms over her chest and grinned. "I'm going with you."

"Absolutely not," Rand said without a second thought. "I will not permit it. I won't allow it."

Jocelyn raised a brow.

"This is not an order, Jocelyn. It is a . . . a demand. You did say you would agree to an occasional demand. I consider that a promise and I'm calling it in. I demand you remain here."

"I would if I could, dear husband, but I can't." Jocelyn shook her head, her gaze brimming with amusement. "You need me."

"This is not a game, Jocelyn. And not the least bit funny," Rand said sharply. "Furthermore, I am perfectly capable of taking care of myself."

"I'm certain that you are. You are a wonderfully competent gentleman and probably have all sorts of curious skills I can't even guess at, but" — she shrugged — "you have no idea how to behave like a lady."

"She's got you there, boy. And I believe I said *all* of you had to return." Nigel studied the letter. "It says right here your presence

and your wife's are required at the ceremony."

"I do not want —"

"Regardless, those are your orders. I
daresay it's due to her involvement in this
mess although there's no explanation given."
Nigel eyed him firmly. "Besides, haven't you
sworn to protect Jocelyn? You can't very well
do that if you leave her here."

"She'll be safe here," Rand said staunchly.

"Will she?" Nigel asked. "Think about it. If
the roads are being watched it's likely your
whereabouts are known. Can you leave her
behind knowing that?"

Rand's gaze slid from Nigel to Jocelyn.
Neither his uncle nor his wife was the least
bit inclined to comply with his wishes. Not
that he really had much choice in the matter.

"When you put it that way, I suppose I
would rather have her where I can keep an
eye on her. I am not happy about it though."
He blew a short, resigned breath. "Very well,
you may come. On one condition." He fixed
her with a firm gaze. "And this is not debat-
able, Jocelyn. You will do precisely as I say
without argument. And that includes following any *orders* I might issue. Do you understand?"

"Of course." Jocelyn's eyes widened innocently. "I will follow your requests —"

"She can scarcely say the word," Alexei
said in an aside to Richard.

336

"— without question." She smiled in an overly sweet manner, and Rand knew she didn't mean a word of it.

"Well, if she's going, I'm going." Richard stepped forward.

"Richard." Jocelyn laid her hand on his arm. "I think it would be best if you stayed here. At least for a few days. With Rand gone . . ." She looked at her husband.

Rand understood at once and agreed. "I would rest a lot easier if you would stay, Richard. I daresay once we're gone there shouldn't be any problems but I hate to leave my uncle here alone should any difficulty arise."

Richard thought for a moment, then nodded slowly. "You're quite right, of course. Certainly I'll be happy to remain for a bit."

"Appreciate the thought but I don't need a watchdog," Nigel said gruffly. "Will need your help, though. With the diversion."

"What diversion?" Rand said. He didn't like the sound of that one bit.

"You don't think you can drive off just as you please? Sometimes I wonder about you, boy." Nigel shook his head in disgust. "You're going to need some sort of diversion. Something to attract attention in one direction while you go in the other. Done all the time in my day."

"When Arthur was king, no doubt," Alexei murmured.

Nigel quieted him with a pointed look. "As I was saying, you need a diversion. Something big. I was thinking we could" — his gaze met Rand's — "burn down the castle —"

"No!" Rand said at once.

"Not the castle!" Jocelyn gasped.

"Uncle," Rand moved closer to his uncle. "I do appreciate the offer, but —"

"Nigel." Jocelyn stepped to the older man's chair and knelt down on the floor beside him. "Don't even think it. We would never allow you to make such a sacrifice."

"This is your home. The home of your father and his father before him." Rand's gaze searched his uncle's. "I know what it means to you."

"You would lose a legacy as well," Nigel said mildly.

"That scarcely matters." Rand shook his head.

"It's not important," Jocelyn said at the same time.

Nigel's gaze slipped from Rand's to Jocelyn's and back. "I expected no less. From either of you. However" — he chuckled — "I was not about to burn down Worthington Castle. I was going to suggest setting a fire in the ruins of the northeast tower. It would scarcely be a loss. There is more than enough wood in the structure of the thing for an impressive blaze. It's far enough from the castle proper for safety. In addition, unless these old joints of mine have failed me altogether, we'll have a decent rainfall in the next few hours."

"It could well work," Richard said thoughtfully. "If your man will show me to the area, I'll take a look."

"Nick." Rand barely got the word out before Nick was in the room. Quickly he explained the proposal. Nick asked a few pertinent questions, then he and Richard left.

"We have perhaps two hours before sunset. I propose we leave as soon after that as possible," Rand said, his mind churning with the myriad details that needed to be attended to before then.

"Then we'd best get going," Jocelyn said brightly and stood.

"This is not a picnic, my dear. It is not an outing in the park." He didn't wish to scare her but he did want her to understand the serious nature of what they were about to embark on. Whoever wanted to keep Alexei from returning to London would not hesitate to stop him by whatever means necessary.

"I realize that. I do understand the risks and the possibility of danger. However." She stepped close and gazed up at him. "I shall be with you and therefore I am not the tiniest bit worried." She smiled and her eyes shimmered with a far different meaning than her words. "I trust you."

He wanted to take her in his arms and tell

her how much she'd come to mean to him. Kiss her until her toes did indeed grow warm and her senses muddled. Tell her once again he trusted her. With his life if need be, and more important with his heart. Without thinking he reached for her.

"Do keep yourself under control, cousin," Alexei said mildly.

"He's right, my boy," Nigel chided. "Plenty of time for that sort of thing later. Right now you've got to get yourself ready. I daresay it's going to take a while if you're to be presentable and believable as women. The only thing either of you has going for you is long legs.

"Although in this case," Nigel snorted, "it's not going to be nearly enough."

Chapter 15

Nigel was right.

Rand and Alexei stood before the two cheval mirrors Jocelyn had had the maids set up in her room. She'd thought it would be easier to turn two dashing lords into two passable women here, where she had everything necessary near at hand, rather than another room, but perhaps the chapel would have been a better location. A bit of prayer wouldn't hurt.

Jocelyn, Ivy, Flora, and Rose studied their handiwork. The two men studied their reflections. Jocelyn wondered if she should make some comment, but she wasn't certain if she should be honest or tactful.

"Well, I'll say one thing for them," Flora said at last. "They're not pretty."

"No indeed." Ivy shook her head.

Rose nodded. "I'd call 'em ugly."

"*Ugly* is such a harsh word," Jocelyn murmured. "Appropriate perhaps, but harsh."

Flora considered the two men. "They are fine-looking gentlemen but not even handsome as ladies."

341

"I'm not certain if we should be offended or pleased." Alexei adjusted one of the leghorn hats Flora had found stored with Rand's grandmother's clothes. The hats were wide and would hide their faces better than anything else, even if they weren't quite as fashionable as they might once have been.

"Definitely pleased." Rand's voice was wry. "I believe for a man to be called an *ugly woman* is something to be preferred."

"We're not especially stylish either, are we?" Alexei said with a frown of annoyance.

"Humph." Flora huffed but held her tongue. She had graciously sacrificed her best dresses and was obviously not pleased at hearing they were not the latest stare of fashion. Especially as she and the maids had quickly fashioned wide ruffles for the hems to disguise the fact that these women were overly tall, had unusually large feet, and were wearing men's boots as well as breeches beneath their skirts. Jocelyn vowed to make certain Flora's gowns were replaced by something thoroughly up-to-date and even a touch frivolous.

"I doubt we'll have to fear for our virtue," Rand muttered.

"Perhaps not but you'll do, both of you." Jocelyn struggled to keep the amusement from her voice. She was grateful they'd gotten the two men to come this far and didn't want to do anything that might make them change their minds now. Neither man was especially thrilled at the thought of their female impersonation, although both agreed they had no other plan. "Besides, we'll be in the carriage nearly the entire time. With luck no one will get more than a glimpse of either of you."

"I feel like an idiot." Rand directed a raised brow at his wife. "An ugly idiot."

"At least yours fits. Mine binds." Alexei stretched his arms out in front of him and craned his neck in an attempt to look over his shoulder. "See. Across the back. It's too tight."

"I think it's your bosoms." Rand surveyed him critically. "The dress wouldn't be as tight if they weren't so large. I think your bosoms are too big."

Alexei looked down at his overstuffed chest. "Can bosoms ever be too big?"

"Not real bosoms perhaps, but I think in your case . . ." Rand considered him thoughtfully. "No question about it: they're definitely too big."

"Are you sure?" Alexei studied his reflection. "I thought they were just right for a man of my height."

"Possibly. Or it could be that they're simply" — Rand tilted his head — "off-center."

Alexei adjusted his bust with both hands.

Ivy tittered, Rose snickered, Flora choked

back a giggle, Jocelyn's eyes watered with the effort of holding back laughter.

"I think that's better," he said to Rand, "don't you?"

"Much." Rand nodded somberly.

"I think you're both, just, well" — Jocelyn sniffed hard and tried not to choke on the words — "lovely."

"Oh, you do, do you?" Rand yanked her into his arms and dipped her backward. She stared up in surprise. A teasing light sparked in his eyes. "Lovely, eh?"

"My yes, my lord, you are quite fetching." She wrapped her arms around his neck. "A diamond of the first water, the brightest star in the heavens, an incomparable among incomparables."

"You just want me because I'm pretty," he growled.

"Oh no, my lord." She widened her eyes in an innocent manner. "I am much more interested in your —"

He cut her off with a kiss, firm and fast and full of promise. Just when her toes started to warm, he drew back and grinned. "Never been kissed by a man in a gown before, have you?"

"I've never suspected it would ever be a possibility."

"Nor have I." He laughed and pulled her upright. "Now then, if you are ready —"

"I need just a minute more to finish

packing my bag." She turned to Flora and the other women. "Cook was going to pack a hamper. Would you make certain that's been done and it is put in the carriage?"

The three bobbed curtsies and took their leave. Peals of laughter sounded in the hall. Apparently the older women could not restrain themselves anther minute.

"Go on." She gave Rand a little push. "I shall follow momentarily."

"Do be quick about it." Alexei sighed. "The sooner we are off, the sooner we will be in London and the sooner we can remove these ridiculous clothes. Although" — his gaze traveled over Rand in an assessing manner — "I do believe I am the prettier of the two of us."

"Then you shall, no doubt, be asked to waltz first," Rand snapped and headed toward the door.

"I didn't say he was unattractive, although one doesn't always need to state the obvious, just that I am prettier." Alexei grinned at Jocelyn. "I hope I have not offended him."

"I'm certain he'll recover."

Alexei strode after Rand, and she made a mental note to explain to them both how ladies, even tall ladies with overstuffed bosoms and large feet encased in men's boots, walked properly.

A cackle of laughter sounded from the hall, followed by muttering male voices. A moment later Nigel appeared in the doorway.

"You've done a decent job, girl. As long as they keep their heads down, you travel by night and try like hell not to let anyone get a good look at 'em, you should be fine." Nigel chuckled and moved into the room. "I'd like to say I've seen less comely women in my time but I can't seem to think of any."

"As the wife of one of them I daresay I'm grateful for that." She grinned and stepped to her bag waiting on the bed. Nearly everything she'd brought originally was back in the satchel. Of course, she hadn't acquired anything new since they'd been here and she did think it appropriate to leave behind the few gowns of Rand's grandmother's she'd worn.

"I see you have plenty of room left in that bag of yours. Good." He turned toward the doorway. "Rose!"

Rose hurried in, a flat paper-wrapped package in her hand. She stepped to Nigel's side and handed it to him.

"Better things to do than this at the moment, you know," she said to him, then turned at once and left, muttering all the while. "Whole house in an uproar. Fires being set. Men dressing like women . . ."

Nigel shook his head. "Don't let her fool you. This evening is the most exciting thing that's ever happened to her."

Jocelyn laughed. "I can certainly understand that. It's probably the most exciting thing to happen to me in, oh well, at least since the last time someone shot at me and I married a man I'd barely met. Odd to realize so very much has happened in such a short time."

"Some of the best experiences of life happen when you're not looking. The twists and turns that come when you aren't prepared and you don't expect 'em. Love is like that, you know. Comes even when you might not be ready for it and hits you hard." He studied her sharply. "But I don't need to tell you that, do I?"

"No, you don't," she said with a quiet smile. "I understand exactly what you mean."

"Thought so." He nodded with satisfaction.

"My lord." She hesitated, then gathered her courage. She might not have another chance. "I was wondering . . . I saw the scar. Was he badly hurt?"

A shadow passed across Nigel's eyes. "His wound was serious, of course, but he recovered quickly. It was his, well, heart, I suppose, for lack of a better word, that suffered most."

Nigel paused, choosing his words carefully. "He was not a suspicious sort as a boy. He was easygoing and trusting. Refused to believe the worst about anyone. He was different when he came home. It might have been a combination of maturity and war or specifically connected to his injury. In truth he never told me exactly what happened. I suspect it involved betrayal of some sort."

"By a woman?"

"It's possible but I don't think so." He shook his head. "But then I have never asked."

"I see," she murmured.

"However, what I have seen of him recently, and most notably since you've come into his life, indicates his heart too has healed. And for that you have my thanks. Now then." He held out the package. "Take this with you. Rand should have it. It doesn't belong here. It never did."

She accepted the parcel and turned it over in her hand. It was square in shape, perhaps a foot across and a bit heavier than she'd expected. "What is it?"

"It's the portrait of Rand's grandfather. The one his grandmother brought with her from Avalonia." Nigel stared at the packet for a long moment and Jocelyn wondered if he was thinking of the unexpected twists and turns of life. If he was wondering what might have happened if he, and not his father, had been the one to meet and marry the desperate young princess. If he was thinking about love. "She wanted her grandson to have it. Even if he wants nothing else of his heritage, he should have this."

"Wouldn't it be wiser to keep it here until the next time we visit? When things aren't quite as, well, hectic?"

"Come now, girl. We're about to burn down a castle." Nigel's bushy brows drew together. "That brother of yours has taken no end of precautions, damned impressed with him by the way, and storm clouds are rolling in, but you never know for certain with fire. Can't be too careful. I promised his grandmother he'd get the portrait and I think the time is now."

"You do know, Nigel . . ." She tucked the portrait into her bag. "Should anything happen to the castle you are more than welcome to make your home with us at the cottage."

"At the . . . cottage?" Nigel said carefully.

"Absolutely." She closed the bag, fastened it, and smiled at him. "We would insist on it."

"You're very kind." Nigel studied her. "I'm quite pleased with how the quirks of life have caught the two of you so nicely and brought you together. My nephew is a lucky man."

"I feel rather lucky myself. It addition to all his other sterling qualities, it's quite pleasant to discover" — she smiled innocently — "that I shall never have to worry about his borrowing my clothes."

They drove a short distance from the castle and waited until the glow from the tower fire lit the evening sky.

"That's it then," Nick called down to them. A moment later the carriage lurched forward.

Jocelyn settled into the seat opposite Alexei, beside Rand, his leg pressed next to hers. His muscles were tensed and she knew he was alert to any possible problem. For those on the road and those they left behind. Rand's hand found hers in the dark and at once a sense of calm enveloped her. What harm could possibly come to her with this man at her side? In her life? Jocelyn vowed to herself to do whatever was necessary to make certain no harm came to him as well. For this journey and for rest of their lives.

They drove in silence for a good hour until thunder cracked overhead and lightning illuminated the sky. The heavens opened and rain poured down. Soothing relief filled the carriage, in stark contrast to the storm outside. Rand squeezed her hand and Jocelyn realized she'd scarcely breathed at all until now.

The downpour lasted for much of the next hour and ended as quickly as it had begun. The now muddy roads slowed their progress but Nick was experienced at the reins and they continued steadily onward, each turn of the wheel bringing them closer to London. Jocelyn dozed on and off, lulled by the rocking of the vehicle and the comforting warmth of the man at her side.

Rand spelled Nick at the reins so the other

man could rest, throwing on a coat over his gown and tucking the skirts in as best he could. Shortly before dawn, the men again exchanged places.

The hours passed at an inexorably slow pace. They stopped only for necessities and to change horses. The carriage was stuffy, overly warm, and even opening the windows did not help. Tempers frayed. Any comment from Alexei or Rand was met by the other man with a response that was sarcastic at best, snide at worst. They reminded her of petulant children and there were moments when she wanted nothing more than to smack them both.

Finally, a little after dusk, the carriage rumbled into the yard of an inn and shuddered to a halt. A moment later Nick pulled open the door.

"I'll see to the horses as fast as I can but it will take a bit," Nick said. "The place isn't overly busy but I'd suggest Your Lordships . . . er . . . Your Ladyships stay put."

"Very well." Rand sighed.

The trio sat in silence for no more than ten minutes.

"We'll stay beside the carriage," Rand said firmly, "but I think we all could use a breath of fresh air."

"Without a doubt." Jocelyn sighed with relief. She'd never been particularly bothered by enclosed spaces but right now, she desperately needed to escape the close confines of the carriage.

Rand moved to the door and allowed Nick to help him out. By the faint glow of the carriage light Jocelyn could see that the older man was having a difficult time keeping a grin from his face.

"One laugh from you and you'll regret it," Rand muttered. "I'm only accepting your help at all because it's damned difficult to move in these bloody clothes."

"Wouldn't think of laughing, my lord. This is serious business it is," Nick said as if laughter was the furthest thing from his mind and quickly turned to help Jocelyn out of the vehicle, hiding his face in the process.

Bright light shown from the windows of the inn and raucous laughter sounded from inside. At once Jocleyn was grateful there was no need to go into the facility.

Alexei climbed down and cast a disgusted look at their surroundings. "Another charming taste of the English at their best. I daresay, once I leave this country I shall never return."

"Englishmen everywhere are raising a toast at the thought." Sarcasm dripped from Rand's words.

"I don't see —"

"That's because you're —"

"Stop it at once, both of you," Jocelyn snapped. "Honestly, you two are like squabbling sisters. And I have had more than enough." She turned on her heel and stalked off, knowing full well it was impossible to leave them altogether yet needing at least the respite of a few yards distance.

"Jocelyn," Rand's voice sounded quietly behind her. "I am sorry. I know this is difficult for you."

"For me?" She whirled to face him. "It's difficult for all of us. Nick can barely keep his eyes open. You're no doubt as hot and sticky and cranky as I. And as for Alexei . . ." She glanced around Rand to see Alexei with crossed arms leaning in a bored manner against the carriage in a most unladylike position. "Regardless of what you or I might think of him, he has gone along with all this with a remarkably good nature."

"Good? Hah." Rand snorted.

"As good as yours," she said firmly. "I think he's behaving admirably."

"And I am not?" Rand said indignantly.

"Of course you are." She struggled to keep her voice cool and not lash out at him. "And you should be. After all, he has only a crown to look forward to. You" — she favored him with a suggestive smile — "have me."

He studied her for a moment. "Very well then. I'll behave. For now." He grinned slowly and leaned closer. "But I'll make no promises as to my behavior when we get home. When we are —"

"Do go away." A high falsetto voice rang in the evening air. "Leave me alone or you shall be sorry."

Jocelyn and Rand turned as one and started back.

"My, yer a big 'un you are." A stocky, grubby man a good foot shorter than Alexei stood leering up at him in a decidedly drunken manner. "I like 'em big. Like a woman with meat on 'er. Shows a 'ealthy appetite."

"Well, you wouldn't like me." Alexei's tone was imperious but had absolutely no effect on his admirer.

"Come now, luv, give 'ol 'Enry a little kiss." He reached for Alexei's arm.

"Now, now," Rand said in an overly high-pitched voice. He grabbed the besotted Henry by the scruff of his neck and pulled him away. "The lady said she's not interested so be on your way, good sir."

Henry's eyes grew huge and he looked from Rand to Alexei and back. "Bloody 'ell, there's two of 'em." He grinned a wide, toothless grin. "We could 'ave a good time, we could, the three of us."

"Not with you." Alexei sniffed. "And if you make one more improper suggestion my . . . my sister and I shall be forced to give you a proper setdown."

"Like a woman with spirit." Henry stepped closer to Rand and gazed up at him. "And

354

always been fond o' sisters, I 'ave. You —" Henry squinted and studied Rand's face in the shadow of the hat. His brow furrowed and his voice dropped. "Don't mean no insult, miss, but I think you be needing a bit of a shave."

"Heavens." Rand held his hand up to cover his face and choked back a sob. "I have never been so mortified. Jocelyn dear, do help me into the carriage." Jocelyn stepped to his side and assisted him into the vehicle.

"You beast," Alexei said and cuffed Henry on the back of the head. "How could you have been so cruel?"

"Yow!" Henry cringed with the blow. "Didn't mean nothing by it."

Nick stepped into view.

"Humph. You men are all alike." Alexei lifted his chin and climbed into the carriage. "You only want one thing from a girl."

Henry cast Jocelyn a brief glance, then dismissed her. Not enough meat, no doubt. He looked plaintively at the carriage door and called after the *sisters*. "I like a woman with a bit o' 'air on 'er."

"Get on with you now." Nick firmly grasped the lovestruck Henry's arm and steered him away, then returned to help Jocelyn into the carriage. He didn't say a word but it was apparent he was struggling not to laugh. Nick closed the door, and the moment the carriage started moving, laughter rang from his perch.

It was all Jocelyn could do not to join him. She sat in the darkened carriage and waited for someone to say something, firmly resolved it would not be she.

"Apparently," Alexei said at last, in the same high pitched tone he used with Henry, "Lord Worthington isn't the only one who likes long legs."

Shocked silence hung over the trio for a moment, then all three burst into laughter.

"Did you see his face when he said you needed to shave?" Jocelyn choked out the words between gales of laughter.

"His face?" Alexei laughed. "Did you see the drunken sot's eyes when he realized there were two of us? Sisters?"

" 'E likes 'em 'airy, 'e does." Rand's falsetto imitation of Henry triggered another round of laughter.

"Well, I do have to say one thing for our erstwhile swain." Alexei sniffed. "He has exceptionally good taste."

"Hardly." Rand laughed. "He preferred us to Jocelyn. I'd call his taste anything but good."

"That's simply because he likes them big. Meat on their bones and all that," Alexei said dismissively. "However, of the two of us, he liked me best." A grin sounded in his voice. "I told you I was the prettier."

Chapter 16

"We're here." Rand's tired voice awakened Jocelyn from a restless doze. She peered out the carriage window. It was late afternoon and they'd made much better time than they'd anticipated.

"Where, precisely, is here?" Alexei voiced the question uppermost in Jocelyn's mind.

"London," Rand said. "My townhouse. I suggest you change here, then go on to your hotel."

Alexei nodded. "Sound idea, cousin. I certainly can't present myself to my entourage dressed like this. As it is, there will be no end of recriminations because of my absence. I daresay they've all been wondering when I was going to return and where I've been."

"Some perhaps more than others." Rand's words were measured and his gaze met Alexei's, neither obviously willing to give voice to uneasy speculation.

The carriage door opened. Rand allowed Nick to help him down, Jocelyn and Alexei following close behind. They stepped quickly to the front door. Jocelyn caught a brief glimpse of the surrounding street but she recognized it at once as not merely respectable but quite a fashionable area. Far nicer than she'd expected.

The door opened and a stern-faced butler gazed out at them. "May I help . . ." The servant's voice faltered and his eyes narrowed suspiciously. "My lord?"

"Yes, Chesney, it's me." Rand stepped past him and ushered Jocelyn and Alexei into a fair-sized entry hall. "It's a rather long and bizarre story and I will be happy to give you all the absurd details at a later time. For now, please see to a change of clothing for His Highness and arrange for his transport to . . ." He glanced at Alexei.

"The Pulteney." Alexei pulled off his hat and thrust it at Chesney. "And do see to those clothes at once. I am most anxious to be on my way."

"No doubt," Chesney murmured, apparently too well trained to be overly shocked by the arrival of His Lordship and someone he referred to as *His Highness* in women's clothing. Jocelyn wondered if the butler had seen much stranger sights on Rand's doorstep.

"And have the maids draw a bath for Lady Beaumont —"

"Lady Beaumont?" Chesney's eyes grew even wider, all training forgotten. Regardless of what other odd occurrences might have

358

happened in Rand's home, apparently there had never been a Lady Beaumont before.

"I suppose I failed to mention that when I left." Rand passed a weary hand over his forehead, then realized he still wore his grandmother's hat and pulled it off impatiently. The butler reached to take it even though the man was obviously still in something of a daze. Jocelyn would have laughed if she hadn't been so tired.

"Chesney, I would like to present my wife." Rand cast her an affectionate smile. "Viscountess Beaumont."

"My lady." Chesney bowed. "Welcome . . . er . . . home."

"Good afternoon." Jocelyn favored him with her brightest smile. This was not the way she'd ever planned on meeting the staff of a new husband, but then nothing about marriage had even remotely resembled her preconceived notions.

Rand laughed. "I don't blame you for being a bit confused. I do promise to explain everything later."

"As you wish, my lord." Chesney's momentary lapse in decorum vanished and he was once again the consummate butler who'd opened the door. "We were not certain when to expect your return, my lord. You were not specific about your plans and I fear the household is perhaps not up to snuff at the moment."

Rand raised a brow. "I see. The mouse playing while the cat's away, eh, Chesney?"

Chesney bristled. "Not at all, my lord, it's simply that we are not entirely prepared for you and Lady Beaumont. However, we will do our best."

Rand chuckled. "That's all I ask."

Chesney looked past Rand and nodded almost imperceptibly. At once two maids and an equal number of footmen appeared in the hall. Chesney took them aside and issued orders like an officer commanding efficient troops. Within moments the maids were headed up the gracious stairway and one of the footmen had vanished into the deeper recesses of the house.

"Your Highness." Chesney gave Alexei something that was half nod, half bow. "If you would be so good as to accompany me."

"Excellent." Alexei sighed. "I cannot wait to get these wretched clothes off." He glanced at Jocelyn, his tone resigned. "Although I shall be eternally grateful for the kindness of the woman who loaned them to me. Furthermore, I shall make certain she is amply reimbursed for the garments as well as her trouble."

Jocelyn smiled with satisfaction. "It's no less than I expected from you, Your Highness."

"Yes, well, expectations are not always met. More's the pity." He stared at her thoughtfully, then turned and followed Chesney up the stairs.

Rand spoke to the remaining footman in a low voice and Jocelyn studied him carefully. In spite of how well she believed she knew him by now, there was obviously still a great deal he had neglected to tell her. Starting with this townhouse. This was not the home of a man of modest means.

The footman left the hall and Rand turned to her with a smile. "I have a few errands that cannot wait. Among them arranging for men to watch the house. I shall return in plenty of time to dress for tonight. Once this blasted Avalonian business is wrapped up, we should have no further involvement. Unless these plans too have changed, Alexei was to return to —"

"This is your house then?" she blurted.

"Well, I do tend to think of it more as my mother's. Of course she's rarely in London." He hesitated. "But yes, I suppose it is, in terms of legal ownership, mine."

"It's quite nice." She narrowed her eyes. "Even somewhat grand."

"Oh, I would scarce call it grand."

"I think it's past time you told me —"

Before she could finish he stepped to her and swept her into his arms. "I think it's past time I told you how thoroughly wonderful I think you are. We might not have made it here without you."

"I'm confident you would have arrived safely." She wrapped her arms around his neck and smiled up at him. Time enough later to discuss his finances. Right now she was more than willing to allow him to distract her. "Oh, certainly the two of you might have killed one another on the way."

"Fortunately you were there to make certain we behaved like proper" — he grinned — "ladies."

She laughed, then pulled him closer and brushed her lips across his. "Isn't the time for proper behavior past?"

"Um-hmmm." His lips trailed to the side of her neck and he nuzzled the point just below her ear. Delicious anticipation washed through her. "Alexei is to leave London tomorrow for Avalonia. Which means he and the conspiracies whirling about him will be none of our concern and out of our lives forever."

She could scarcely concentrate on his words and didn't particularly care. Her eyes drifted closed and she reveled in the sensation produced by his whispers against her skin.

"And we can begin our lives together."

"Indeed we can, dearest husband," she said softly.

"Dearest wife." His lips met hers in a gentle kiss. For an endless moment his mouth plundered hers, sweet with words he hadn't yet said but were there between them nonetheless. Lovely warmth spread from her toes upward.

He drew his head away from hers and smiled ruefully. "I have to go."

"I know," she said with a sigh.

"I won't be gone long." His dark eyes simmered with desire.

She smiled. "I know."

He didn't move. "I don't want to go at all."

"I know that too."

He was as obviously reluctant to release her as she was to let him. Still, she pulled away. "Go now, before I change my mind and insist you stay."

"I could help you change your mind." A wicked smile quirked his lips. "About my staying and any number of other things."

"No doubt you could." She laughed. "And I shall quite look forward to your attempts."

He turned to leave, then without warning turned back, pulled her swiftly into his arms, kissed her hard, and released her. He nodded and grinned. "Until I return, then."

"Until you return," she said in an altogether too breathless voice. And knew she would count each and every minute until then.

Jocelyn had never been in, nor had she ever seen, a bathing tub this big.

She sank down until the water came up to her chin and stretched her legs their full length and still there was room left. Steam rose in tiny little wisps and the heat flowed into her very bones. It was nothing short of heavenly. She could close her eyes and stay there forever.

The maids had explained that the huge, metal tub had been constructed to His Lordship's specifications and permanently installed in a room off Rand's bedchamber. They'd pointed with pride to the drain connected to a pipe that disappeared through a tight-fitting hole in the floor. They'd told her that while filling the tub was a bit of hard work, tidying up afterward was almost a delight. And both girls mentioned how pleased they were to work in such an up-to-date house.

Their comments gave Jocelyn a great deal to think about. As did the number of servants she'd seen thus far, the size of the house itself, the quality of the furnishings, and everything else. It was obvious Rand was somewhat better off than she'd assumed.

How much better off was the question. Was the cottage in the country truly a cottage or did he have another castle lurking about? Certainly his uncle's home was badly in need of repairs and had obviously not had much invested in its upkeep. Still, did that mean anything at all when it came to Rand's own property? Or rather properties. His townhouse was certainly impressive.

She sank a bit lower and blew a long breath, idly watching the water ripple away from her. Rand's financial status was an interesting puzzle even if it really didn't matter. She'd meant everything she'd said to her brother. She didn't care a whit about how much money Rand did or did not have even if she'd prefer that he not be completely impoverished. She'd already experienced a certain amount of impoverishment and that was quite enough, thank you. Still, it was nice to know Rand had some money, although admittedly with this particular man even impoverishment would be bearable. He meant far more to her than any possible fortune.

"I see you appreciate my tub." Rand stood leaning in the doorway leading to his, *their*, bedchamber, arms folded over his chest.

"It must have been dreadfully expensive," she said mildly.

He paused for a moment, then shrugged. "Dreadfully. Do you think I was overcharged?"

"Absolutely not." She sighed with delight. The hot water had done its work well. She was both relaxed and refreshed. "It's wonderful. I daresay I shall spend as much time as possible right here in the future."

"Oh you will, will you?" He straightened and stepped toward her. She resisted the urge to cover various parts of her body with the tiny cloth she'd used to wash with.

"Indeed I shall." She rested her head on the back of the tub and watched him through half-open eyes. "It's not merely pleasant, it's rather decadent."

"I've always been fond of decadence." He stepped closer. His gaze slid over the surface of the water, and her nipples hardened with the look in his eye. "I've always been rather impatient with meager tubs as well. This one is suitable for soothing overtaxed muscles or easing overworked minds."

"It has definitely worked its magic on me," she murmured.

He slipped out of his jacket and tossed it aside. "I will admit, however, that this isn't quite as self-indulgent as it appears. It was originally designed for a more practical purpose. After my return home, the pain in my shoulder was at times unbearable. I found soaking in hot water helped soothe the ache."

"What are you doing?" she asked idly, knowing full well what he was doing.

"Disrobing." He loosened his cravat and pulled it free. "I tend to do that before I get in the water."

"Oh? Do you feel the need to soothe an ache then?"

He raised a brow but she knew exactly what she had said and exactly how it had sounded. He unbuttoned his waistcoat. "Indeed I do."

"Aren't you afraid your valet will come in?"

"Actually, I don't have a valet. Chesney serves in that capacity when necessary although I have never had a great deal of trouble dressing myself. Or undressing myself." He removed the waistcoat and it joined the rest of his clothing. "And I have taken the precaution of locking the doors."

"You are prepared."

"I have also sent a footman to Effington House to fetch an appropriate gown for you for tonight's festivities."

"How efficient of you." She hadn't considered the question of what she would wear to the gala. The only dresses she had with her were still in her bag and wouldn't do at all for an event like this evening's. His thoughtful gesture warmed her heart almost as much as his touch.

"I do try." He drew his shirt off over his head, then pulled up a chair and perched on the edge to remove his boots.

"Just to make certain I understand your intentions, I gather you are planning on joining me?"

"Indeed I am." A wicked smile curved his lips. "Do you mind?" He stood and pulled off his breeches.

She ignored the question and studied him provocatively. "Have you ever had more than one person in this tub at a time?"

"Let me think." He furrowed his brow thoughtfully and stepped to the side of the tub. He was obviously more than ready to join her and just as obviously bathing was not what he had in mind. "Was she . . . ? No. Or the one with the . . ." He grinned down at her and shook his head. "No. Never."

"Are you certain?" Would she ever tire of staring at him naked? He was certainly well worth looking at. His scar was pink and puckered and she hoped there would come a time when he would tell her just how he got it. If not — desire shivered through her — well, she could live with not knowing all his secrets.

"I'm certain I would remember. I am certainly planning on remembering this."

She pulled her knees up to her chest to allow him room. He stepped over the side of the tub and lowered himself into the water. They sat facing each other, his smile a reflection of her own, then without words he reached for her and drew her to him until her knees straddled his legs and his hard erection nudged against her. Her arms slipped around his neck and her lips found his. His kiss was long and languorous as if they had all the time in the world, and indeed they did. Her tongue met his in a slow erotic dance heightened by the feel of water lapping against them. His hands slid down her back, and he cupped her buttocks and pulled her closer. She angled her hips slightly and he slipped into her. She sighed with the delightful sense of fullness. For long moments they did nothing but savor the feeling of connection.

Slowly he moved within her and she responded with a restraint to match his own. She closed her eyes and pulled her head back, arching her neck to allow him to kiss the line of her jaw and her throat. Her breasts pressed against his wet chest and she reveled in the feel of the smattering of hair rough against her sensitive flesh. The water encompassed them, enveloped them, embraced them.

Need coiled within her and he knew and responded. His thrusts grew deeper and she moved with him. Water smacked against the sides of the metal tub, in odd accord with their ever-increasing rhythm. They moved together faster and harder, and ecstasy filled her, surrounded her as liquid, as all-consuming as the water around them. She clutched at his shoulders, and his grip tightened on her derriere. The sound of water splashing over the rim accompanied their labored breathing and the thudding of her heart in her ears. And when she thought she would die with the sheer joy of it, glorious release exploded within her and she gasped with delight. And he thrust once more and his own release shuddered through them both.

She sagged onto his chest and listened to the rapid beat of his heart echoing her own and the calmer slap of the water against the tub. They lay together for long sated moments, wrapped in each other's arms. Peace flowed over her and through her as fluid as the water and she knew without any doubt that no matter what forces of fate had driven her into his arms, this was exactly where she was meant to be.

At last he chuckled beneath her. She raised her head and smiled into his eyes. His dark, endless eyes.

"And what, my lord husband, do you find so amusing?"

"My dear wife, that was not amusement. That was the sound of a man well satisfied with his lot in life." He brushed his lips across hers. "And his wife."

She grinned with a happiness that threatened to overwhelm her. "I daresay the maids will not be nearly as satisfied with theirs when they see this mess we've left for them to mop up. Half the water in the tub is now on the floor."

"They'll have to get used to it." His smile was lazy and more than a bit smug and didn't bother her in the least. "I'm not certain I shall ever bathe alone again."

A wicked light gleamed in his eye. "I find company is an excellent way to soothe any and all aches."

Chapter 17

Jocelyn glanced around the large ballroom at the home of Lord Westerfield, the gracious host for the Avalonian ceremony. She wasn't wearing her spectacles, yet she could sense the curious stares directed toward Rand and her.

Jocelyn hadn't for a moment considered the possibility of scandal the appearance of Lord and *Lady* Beaumont might trigger. So much had occurred in her life so quickly, the question of public reaction when she and Rand returned to London society hadn't even crossed her mind. Yet it should have. The last time she was at an occasion like this she was also the object of speculation. But then it had centered on the attention paid to her by a prince.

Even though the season was nearly at an end, she should have realized her absence would be noted and remarked upon. Of course the rest of her family had left town at the same time and they'd all assumed the ton would believe she had accompanied them.

Now, however, she was back. And married to someone entirely different than expected.

She and Rand had arrived just in time for the official ceremony with Alexei and the Prince Regent, which was little more than a few enthusiastic, and mercifully short, speeches, and exchange of gifts between England's heir to the throne and Avalonia's crown prince. This was accompanied by a round of toasts to continued goodwill between the two countries. After that the music and dancing had begun and the ball was under way in earnest. It was only then she realized she and Rand were as much a target of attention as were the royal figures in attendance.

"Rand," she said in a low voice. "Am I mistaken, or are we the subject of a great deal of curiosity?"

"Indeed we are." He chuckled. "Does it bother you?"

"No," she said slowly. "I simply did not expect it."

"I suggest we take advantage of it."

"Oh? And how would we do that?"

"By showing each and every one of the gossips here that ours was not a marriage forced by any set of circumstances but rather a love match."

A love match?

"And we shall begin right now. Take off your gloves and give me your hand."

"My hand?" She laughed but removed her gloves. "Why?"

"It strikes me that I have been remarkably remiss as a husband thus far." He took her left hand with his right and pulled something from his waistcoat with his free hand. "But I intend to rectify that right now."

She held her breath.

He slipped a ring on her finger, a large, oval sapphire encircled by diamonds. Jocelyn stared in disbelief. She'd never seen anything as lovely, or as blue, in her life. And never had she been given anything that meant so much. "Oh my."

"This was my errand today. I wanted something to match your eyes but I had to settle for this. The jeweler said sapphires were once believed to have protected the wearer from harm. It seemed somewhat appropriate given how we began." He paused. "If you don't like it, I can certainly return —"

"Never!" She sniffed back an unexpected tear. "It's beautiful."

"Good," he said with a sigh of relief and lifted her hand to his lips. "But it pales in comparison to its wearer."

"I shall never take it off."

"Not even when you play billiards? Or bathe?" he teased.

"Especially not when I bathe," she said staunchly, pulling her hand from his and holding the ring up to the light. "Never." She glanced from the deep blue gem to the darker hue of her husband's eyes. "You are not even a bit poor, are you?"

"Is that my curious wife asking or her more mercenary nature?"

"Curious," she said primly.

"I'm probably somewhat more financially sound than you thought," he admitted. "And I am willing to confess the details of my finances whenever you wish. At the moment, however" — he bowed dramatically — "my dear lady wife, we have never danced before, and I should like nothing better than this dance. A waltz, I believe." He held out his hand.

She put her hand in his, still somewhat dazed by both the ring and his declaration. *A love match.* Dazed and overwhelmed and amazingly happy. She smiled at him with all the love in her heart, not caring who noticed or what they thought.

They danced one waltz, then another and another still, disregarding any sense of what might or might not be proper. Delighting in the enjoyment of being in each other's arms, moving to the strains of the music. At last Rand led her off the dance floor, his hand holding hers even when they stopped. Quite improper. Quite wonderful.

"My dear Lady Beaumont."

Jocelyn and Rand turned. The Duchess of Roxborough, Richard's mother-in-law as well as Marianne's new mother-in-law, beamed at them. Jocelyn had met her a few times since her brother's marriage but was always surprised at the overtly warm reception.

"Your Grace." Jocelyn bobbed a curtsy.

"Now, now, none of that." The older woman took her hands and kissed her firmly on both cheeks. "We are family, my dear, what with your brother married to my daughter, my darling granddaughter your niece, and one of your sisters wed to my son. Why, I almost think of you as something of a daughter, and I did always hope for more than one. I am delighted to see you looking so . . ." The duchess stepped back and studied her for a moment. "Happy. Yes, that's the word. I am most pleased. And pleased by your choice of husband as well."

The duchess turned to Rand and extended her hand. He took it and bowed low. "Your Grace."

"I know your mother quite well, my lord. Lovely woman. I have not seen her for a while, what with her flitting about the continent and my extended trip to America, yet I have always considered her a friend."

Rand straightened. "Thank you, ma'am."

"I know as well you are a good friend of Thomas's." The duchess's gaze met Jocelyn's. "He and Marianne have planned a wedding trip to Italy but will return to London first. Within the next few days, I imagine, and look forward to seeing you. The rest of the family is still in the country but the duke and I . . ." She cast a glance around the room with a huff of annoyance. "He is here somewhere. He's always been somewhat difficult to keep track of at an event like this, not his favorite sort of thing at all, you know, although that's neither here nor there. At any rate, we decided it would be best to make an appearance here tonight."

She leaned toward them in a confidential manner. "We thought if we publicly acknowledged your union and made it clear to all concerned how delightful we think it is, and how fitting a match and how much we approve, well, there simply wouldn't be any nasty gossip to deal with. And any question as to the haste of your marriage would be put to rest." She smiled smugly. "I have already made it a point to mention with relentless frequency how yours is very likely the match of the season."

"Pardon my impertinence, Your Grace." Rand chose his words with care. "Am I to surmise that your explanation as to your purpose here is why I was ordered to bring Jocelyn to this event?"

"Of course." The duchess straightened and nodded at Jocelyn. "He's clever as well as handsome. I do congratulate you, my girl. You've made an excellent choice."

"Thank you, Your Grace," Jocelyn frowned

in confusion. "But how did you know we would —"

"Oh, I didn't." The duchess shook her head firmly. "But my husband did. He always seems to know everything about everything. How he does I will never know although he has any number of official and unofficial sources of information. Some rather mysterious. Now and then I quite give up trying to figure it all out but then my curiosity rises once again. I do believe my continuing quest to uncover all his secrets keeps our life together interesting."

She paused thoughtfully. "His mother, the dowager duchess, always seems to know everything about everything as well. I've never been able to determine how. The woman rarely leaves the country these days. The Effingtons are an odd lot but I am quite fond of them all." The duchess laughed affectionately, and Jocelyn and Rand joined her.

The lady was right of course. If the Duchess of Roxborough gave her public approval to a marriage, regardless of the haste or circumstances surrounding the match, no one would so much as utter a single word of condemnation. Jocelyn vowed right then and there to name their first girl Katherine after the duchess.

They chatted for a few more minutes. From what she could see, Jocelyn distinctly noted the earlier stares of scandalized curiosity had changed to something equally curious but far more approving, even envious. The duchess had done her work well.

"Your Grace." Alexei appeared before them and bowed. "How lovely you look this evening."

"Your Highness," the duchess said with a slight curtsy. "How kind of you to say, especially as we have never met."

"I am always most appreciative of beauty when it favors me with its presence," Alexei said smoothly. The duchess's brow quirked upward in a slightly skeptical manner. "Lord Beaumont, Lady Beaumont." He turned to Jocelyn and Rand. "I am pleased, as well, that you were both able to attend."

"Wouldn't miss it," Rand said dryly.

"No doubt." Alexei chuckled; his gaze met Jocelyn's but he addressed his words to Rand. "Would you do me the great honor of allowing me to dance with your wife?"

Rand hesitated.

"I believe I have promised this and every other dance to my husband," Jocelyn said quickly. The last thing she wanted to do was dance with Alexei. Particularly as it could well undo all the good the duchess had done.

"My dear, you really can't refuse him." The duchess was firm. "Besides, the best way to dissuade gossip is to confront it head on. You shall favor the prince with a dance while

I shall do the same with your charming husband." The duchess turned to Rand. "My lord?"

"Of course, Your Grace." A resigned look flitted through Rand's eyes but he smiled nonetheless and escorted the duchess onto the dance floor. Jocelyn and Alexei followed a few steps behind.

It was yet another waltz and while Jocelyn adored the dance she'd much prefer something, anything, that would keep her well away from Alexei. His intentions might well be innocent but she saw no reason to trust him.

Alexei smiled down at her but his tone was sober. "I must speak to you alone."

"Certainly not." Jocelyn's own smile belied her adamant tone.

"Meet me in the library in a quarter hour." Alexei's pleasant expression remained but his voice was firm.

"I believe we've been this route before, Your Highness, and I will not travel it again."

"You will, my lady." His smile didn't waver. "Your husband's life depends on it."

Her heart leapt to her throat and her step faltered but she recovered at once, praying no one had noticed. "I don't believe you. What do you mean?"

"I will explain later. And you would do best to believe me." There was no mistaking the look in Alexei's eye. There was no choice. She would meet him.

They continued the remainder of the dance in silence. Jocelyn had no idea how she managed to go on as if nothing had happened but somehow she made it though the steps. The music ended and Alexei escorted her back to join Rand and the duchess. They exchanged a few polite comments and Alexei took his leave.

"Charming man," the duchess murmured. "However, Thomas said he doesn't trust him and I daresay he is right. There's something about him . . ." She shrugged. "I suspect it's the natural arrogance that accompanies men of great power. Not that it matters, I suppose. I understand he's leaving tomorrow."

"I know I shall miss him," Rand said under his breath and flagged a passing waiter bearing trays of champagne-filled glasses. He passed one to each of the ladies and took a glass for himself.

"Now then, Lord Beaumont," the duchess began. "How do you feel about . . ."

Jocelyn maintained a pleasant smile but her mind was nowhere near the discussion whirling about her. *Your husband's life depends on it.* She shivered at the memory. Even if this was simply a ploy on Alexei's part to get her alone, and at this point she doubted that, she couldn't take the chance. She had to find out the meaning of the prince's cryptic comment. If there was indeed a threat to Rand's life.

". . . then we will expect you sometime later in the summer." The duchess's comment caught Jocelyn's attention.

"We look forward to it." Rand nodded and Jocelyn wondered exactly what she had missed.

"I am off then. I see a friend I have not spoken to in a very long time." The duchess lowered her voice. "A dreadful gossip but she does always have some interesting *bon mot* to share. And she will be quite useful at telling the world how very much the duke and I approve of your match."

Rand chuckled. "Thank you, Your Grace."

The duchess waved off the comment. "Not at all. It's the very least I can do and it's rather a lot of fun. And I truly am happy for you both." Once again she took Jocelyn's hands and leaned forward to touch her cheek to the younger woman's, her quiet words meant for Jocelyn's ears alone. "I don't know what's afoot, my dear, but do be careful. And try a bit harder to look like you're enjoying yourself." The duchess straightened and smiled. "Off to continue my good work." Her Grace turned and vanished into the crowd.

"I think," Rand said slowly, "I understand Thomas's nature a bit better now that I've met his mother."

"She's lovely," Jocelyn murmured, hoping Rand was not quite as observant of the change in her demeanor as the duchess.

He slanted her a curious glance. "Are you all right?"

"Of course." She forced a lighthearted laugh. "Although I fear the last few days have taken more of a toll than I suspected. I am rather weary."

"As am I. We could certainly leave now if you'd like."

"No," she said a shade more sharply than she intended and a little too quickly. "I mean it simply wouldn't be polite to leave so soon. We've scarcely been here any time at all. People would surely notice and think —"

"They'd think" — he bent his head close to hers — "I wished to be with my beautiful wife. Alone. In my home. In my bed. Or my bath."

She laughed. "You do make it sound appealing."

"In fact, we need never leave my rooms again. The servants could bring up all our meals on trays." His voice lowered suggestively. "We could disdain clothes altogether and greet callers sitting in bed wrapped in blankets or linens like some decadent —"

"Prince?" she asked with exaggerated innocence.

"I was thinking more of a desert chieftain." He grinned. "But *prince* would do as well, I suspect. Frankly, if we ever do get home, I daresay I could sleep for a week."

"As could I." It did sound wonderful. But

382

home and bed and especially peace would have to wait. There would be no finding it here.

Within moments Jocelyn and Rand were besieged by well-wishers. Now that the duchess had bestowed her public approval, even the most casual of acquaintances seemed compelled to offer their congratulations and perhaps gain a still unknown detail of the match with which to regale their friends. It would be difficult to slip away when the time came but Jocelyn was determined to meet Alexei. His charge was too terrifying to ignore.

Your husband's life depends on it.

"What do you want, Alexei?" Jocelyn closed the library door behind her, fairly confident she had managed to slip away without notice. But she could not stay long. "What is this all about?"

Alexei sipped a glass of brandy and nodded at the decanter on the table beside him. "Would you care for a brandy, Jocelyn? It's Lord Westerfield's finest."

"No. I'm here for one purpose and one purpose only." She clenched her jaw and fought to maintain a collected air even though she wanted nothing more than to scream at the arrogant prince. "What did you mean when you said Rand's life was in danger?"

"I don't believe those were my precise words," Alexei murmured.

"Nonetheless, that was the effect. I cannot stay for more than a few minutes. So if the pleasantries are over" — she narrowed her eyes — "do be so kind as to explain."

"Very well." Alexei paused and her irritation grew. "Should I start at the beginning?"

"Please do," she snapped.

"As you wish." Alexei shrugged. "You see, my dear, this peace ceremony, this gala, all of it was initiated at my request for the simple purpose of providing me with a legitimate reason to come to England."

"Why?" Suspicion sounded in her voice.

"Have you ever heard of the Heavens of Avalonia?" he said in an all too casual manner.

She shook her head. "No. What is it?"

"It is a set of precious gems. Each is priceless in its own right but together they are more important as a symbol of hereditary power of the royal family of Avalonia." His gaze flicked over her. "That's a lovely ring, by the way. I see my cousin finally came up to snuff."

She folded her arms over her chest and glared. "Thank you."

"I had hoped to find the Heavens here in England."

At once she remembered his odd questions at Worthington Castle. "You thought Rand had them?"

Alexei nodded. "Or someone in his family. Unfortunately he is as ignorant of their whereabouts as I. He said he's never heard of the Heavens."

"And you believed him," she said without thinking.

Alexei chuckled. "Naïve of me, probably, but yes I do believe him. He is an extremely honorable man. Too honorable, I suspect. I have no doubt he would return the gems if he could. I believe him when he says wants nothing to do with his royal heritage, my country, or me. It's most disconcerting but I find it oddly admirable." He took a thoughtful sip of his drink. "He is a true man of principle and they are exceedingly rare."

"What does any of this have to do with Rand's life being in danger?" she asked impatiently.

"I am getting to that." His tone was mild but intensity burned in his eyes, and fear gripped her stomach. "As I've explained, your husband represents the third branch of the royal family. I represent the first, along with my brother and sister. My cousin, the Princess Valentina, represents the second. With my father's illness, Valentina has taken the opportunity presented by the possibility of his death and my subsequent succession to encourage unrest in hopes of seizing power for herself." He grimaced. "That would not bode well for my country. She is quite ruthless and I fear what the future would hold for Avalonia under her rule." Alexei paused as if the thought of Valentina on the throne was too dreadful even to consider.

"I had hoped to use the jewels as a symbol of tradition, even" — he uttered a short, derisive laugh — "of the divine right of my family to rule. A rallying point, as it were. Something to unite the people and ease the fears Valentina has encouraged about succession."

"But you didn't find them," she said slowly.

"I did not. Someday, perhaps. Now, however" — he swirled the brandy in his glass — "I believe I may have found a far more powerful symbol of unity."

She shook her head. "I don't understand."

"Don't you?" Alexei's gaze bored into hers.

Her breath caught. "Rand?"

"You are indeed as clever as you are pretty. Pity. I am not overly fond of intelligent women."

"Then all has ended well as I don't really care what you're fond of," she said sharply.

He ignored her outburst. "With my cousin at my side, we can show the people the strength and unity of the House of Pruzinsky. Rand is a direct descendent of King Frederick and an heir to the throne. But, more than anything else, he is —"

"Your symbol," she said evenly.

"Precisely." He raised his glass to her.

"He'll never agree. Rand is vehement when it comes to Avalonia. He is a British subject and has no desire to claim the title of prince. He'll want no part of this." She shook her head firmly. "He'll never go with you."

"I have no doubt of that." He smiled in a smug manner. "But you will accompany me. And he will follow."

"Don't be absurd," she scoffed. "I would never so much as consider . . ." *Your husband's life depends on it.* Her eyes widened with realization.

"I see you do understand." Alexei chuckled.

"You're bluffing, Alexei," she said staunchly. "You would never hurt him."

"Of course I personally would never lay a hand on him. That would be most distasteful. But I would not hesitate for an instant to order his death if necessary. I would prefer not to, but" — he shrugged — "it is entirely up to you."

She stared in disbelief. "How could you do such a thing?"

"Desperate times call for desperate measures," he said offhandedly. "I would take no particular pleasure in it."

"I suppose that makes all the difference." Sarcasm dripped from her words.

"It is the difference between Valentina and

myself. She would rather enjoy it." He drained the last of his brandy and refilled the glass. "Now then, we leave at dawn. I have worked out the details. A carriage will —"

"I'm not going." She took a backward step, fighting to keep a rising sense of panic from her voice.

"Do you doubt me?" His voice was sharp. "Do not make that mistake, Jocelyn. I would regret the need to have my cousin killed but I will do it. And furthermore, I will find a way to use his death to suit my purposes. Perhaps blame it on Valentina. Yes, that would do. A dead prince. Martyred. Now that I think about it, that might very well work better than —"

"Stop it!" She thrust out her hands in front of her. "All right. I'll go. But" — she drew a deep breath — "what if he doesn't come after me?"

"Oh, he will." Alexei smiled confidently.

"What if he doesn't?" She whirled around and paced the floor. "What if he thinks I've changed my mind about the two of us? He knows you, and everything you offer, are exactly what I always wanted."

"I can certainly understand that," Alexei murmured.

"What if he decides" — she stopped and stared at Alexei with growing horror — "to let me go?"

"He won't." Alexei sipped his liquor.

"Aside from the fact that you are his wife, and I suspect he will be quite possessive about that, he loves you."

"What makes you think so?" She held her breath.

"My dear lady, it's in the man's eyes whenever he looks at you. My cousin is positively besotted. You are his weakness. Love has felled far greater men than he. Besides . . ." He considered her thoughtfully. "He said he trusts you. If he meant what he said, he'll never believe you left him voluntarily. Consider this a test of his worth. Does he trust you or does he not?"

"He does," she said firmly, brushing aside a twinge of doubt.

"Then his protective nature will assure that he will come to your rescue."

"He'll hate you for this." She fairly spit the words at him. "I hate you."

Alexei gasped and clutched at his heart. "Oh no, not that!" His tone was droll. "Do you think I care? I don't." His expression hardened. "I am trying to save my country. Salvage its future. If I can do so now, before violence erupts, it is well worth the enduring hate of my cousin and his wife. It is worth any price."

She raised her chin defiantly. "Even if he comes to Avalonia, he'll never help you."

"That is a chance I am willing to take. He, above anyone I've ever met, well understands the nature of duty and responsibility to one's country. Once he's in Avalonia, I shall endeavor to convince him of the necessity of his assistance. The need to avoid bloodshed. Damnation, Jocelyn!" He slammed the glass onto the table. "Why can't you understand? This is not a step I want to take but I can think of nothing else. My country's future is at stake and I will do whatever I have to do to secure it." A weary look crossed Alexei's face and she resisted an immediate rush of sympathy.

She stared at him for a long moment. "As I have no choice, what am I supposed to do?"

He drew a steadying breath and gestured at the table. "Paper and pens are on the table. You will write him a note simply saying you have gone with me. Nothing else. I do not wish to be overly dramatic."

"Oh, we can't have that now, can we?" She stalked to the table and scribbled the single line, then thrust the note at Alexei.

He glanced at it and nodded his approval. "Excellent. I have arranged for Rand to be called out of town. A messenger will arrive shortly after dawn. That should give us at least a two-day start. I do not want him catching up to us until we reach Avalonia. With luck the journey should take no more than a fortnight. A carriage will arrive for you shortly after his departure."

"Is there anything else?" She glared.

"I daresay I needn't tell you not to say a word to your husband. Or perhaps I do." A hard light shone in Alexei's eyes. "Should you have any thoughts of revealing my plan to my cousin I shall make certain he does not live long enough to so much as be indignant. His life is in your hands, and you will hold your tongue." He stepped closer and pinned her with an unyielding glare. "And that, my dear Lady Beaumont, is an order."

She bit back a sharp retort, knowing it would do her no good.

"Now then, we must both return to the celebration before we are missed." He raised his glass and cast her a pleasant smile. "I look forward to seeing you in the morning."

She smiled sweetly. "And I look forward to seeing you in hell."

She turned and left the library, his laugh echoing behind her. Jocelyn hurried down the long hallway and slipped into the ballroom as unobtrusively as possible. Her heart thudded in her chest, her breath was fast, and her hands shook. She twisted the ring on her finger nervously and struggled to pull herself together. No one must notice her distress.

Especially not Rand.

She had no choice in the matter. She didn't want to believe Alexei would really have Rand killed but it was a gamble she was not willing to take. He was the man she loved and she would do whatever was necessary to keep him safe. Up to and including letting him think she had left him for another man. Abandoned him. Betrayed him.

He had married her to protect her. Now it was Jocelyn's turn to protect him.

Chapter 18

"You were exceptionally quiet this evening." Rand pulled off his waistcoat and dropped it on a chair.

"Was I?" Jocelyn said brightly. She had changed to her nightclothes before he came up. It seemed altogether natural to be here in his rooms, *their rooms,* alone with him, preparing for bed.

She sat on an overstuffed chair near the hearth. In spite of the warm, early summer night, she'd been chilled all evening. A chill that had little to do with the temperature of the night air. "I hadn't noticed."

She'd tried, of course, to maintain a light-hearted air, but it was nearly impossible given her talk with Alexei and her role in his plan. How could she pretend that all was well when the specter of what she was about to do hung over her? How could she consider anything at all save what Rand would think when he discovered she'd gone?

"You seemed rather preoccupied as well," Rand said casually.

"Not at all," she murmured, mesmerized by the play of light from the fire across the jewels on her ring.

Would he think everything between them was a lie? Would he wonder if indeed she was exactly as he'd thought when they'd first met: shallow and spoiled, with questionable morals? Would he be angry when he discovered she'd left him for Alexei? Or heartbroken? Or would he care at all?

"Jocelyn?"

The diamonds sparkled and blue fire shot from the sapphire.

Would he come after her? Or would he be relieved to see her go?

The back of her throat ached and a heavy weight settled in the pit of her stomach. She wanted to tell him everything and had indeed come close to confessing a dozen times or more in the past hours, but fear had kept her still.

Would he understand? Would he ever forgive her?

The ring was heavy on her finger, at once a token and an accusation.

"Jocelyn?"

The concerned note in his voice caught her attention and she jerked her gaze to his. "Yes?"

His brow furrowed. "Are you certain there is nothing amiss?"

He stood beside the bed, clad now only in

trousers and shirt. She drank in the sight of him, wondering when, or even if, she'd see him like this again.

"No, not at all." She shook her head, then got to her feet and walked toward him, twisting the ring on her finger in what was fast becoming a comforting habit. "May I ask you a question?"

"I thought this was coming." He smiled tolerantly.

"What?" She brushed aside a stab of fear.

"My finances." He grimaced in a sheepish manner. "First I should apologize —"

"No, no." Jocelyn waved away his words. "I am curious of course, who wouldn't be? But that's of no consequence at the moment. What I was wondering . . ." She blew a long breath and stepped closer to him. She caught his dark gaze with her own and gathered her courage. "Do you . . ."

"Do I what?" His lips curved in a curious smile.

"Do you . . ." She squared her shoulders. "Do you love me?"

"Do I love you?" he said thoughtfully. He took her hands in his, turned them palms up, and brought them to his lips. "I would climb mountains for you." He kissed the center of one palm. "Swim oceans." He kissed the other palm, then turned her hands over and brushed his lips across the back of one hand. His gaze never left hers. "Slay dragons." He did the same with the other hand. "Capture the stars."

"That's all very well and good, Rand, but —"

"Yes." He laughed. "My dear Lady Beaumont, my darling wife, I do indeed love you."

She swallowed hard. "And I love you."

He wrapped his arms around her and pulled her close. Amusement twinkled in his eyes. "It's only because you know I am not as poor as you thought, isn't it?"

"That's it entirely." She was abruptly grateful for the teasing turn their talk had taken. A moment ago she had been perilously close to tears and that would never do. She was terrified at the thought of breaking down and telling him everything. "It has nothing whatsoever to do with that slaying dragon or catching stars nonsense."

"That's a relief." Rand sighed dramatically. "My sword is a bit rusty and my star-catching net has a nasty hole in it." He shook his head mournfully. "Couldn't catch so much as a firefly at the moment."

"Oh dear." She brushed her lips across his. "You shall have to find another way to prove your love then."

His arms tightened around her. "How could I possibly do that?"

"Let me think." Her lips whispered against his. "I am having a most difficult time coming up with even a vague idea. I might well be able to think better if I was not over-dressed." She stepped back, out of his arms, and shrugged off her wrapper, letting it fall to the floor.

"I was thinking the same thing." He pulled his shirt over his head and tossed it aside.

"I am getting an idea now." She stepped closer.

"As am I," he said softly. He grasped the fine fabric of her nightrail and slowly pulled it up and over her head. It joined the wrapper and his shirt. She shook her hair free and felt it drift over her shoulders. He drew her back into his arms and bent his head to trail kisses along the side of her neck and over her shoulder. His hands skimmed over the length of her arms, and she shivered with his touch. "Have you thought of any-thing yet?"

"Not a thing," she whispered. "I fear the blood has rushed from my head and my mind is not working at all."

"Perhaps you would do better lying down?"

"Indeed, I think that would be much, much better."

He swept her into his arms and carried her to the bed, laying her down as if she might break if he was not careful. As if she was cherished. She lay on the bed and watched him strip off his trousers, marveling at the unique circumstances that had brought them to this point. And praying that the fates that controlled their lives would not pull them apart forever.

The candlelight cast a warm glow over the hard planes of his body and she reached out for him. He sank onto the bed beside her and took her into his arms. Gently, as if they had all the time in the world, never knowing they had only this last night.

Their lips met with a sweetness born of love, and for a long while kissing him, tasting the faint echo of champagne, was enough. Her tongue met and mated with his in a leisurely, sensuous dance. Her body fit against his with a naturalness that defied reason and defined fate. Her breasts pressed against his chest and his body warmed hers with a heat that enveloped her, surrounded her, sank into her soul.

His hands traveled over her back, caressed her buttocks, teasing her flesh. She fought against the urgency rising within her at his touch. She wanted this night to last forever. Wanted to remain in the circle of his arms, safe and protected and loved. And wanted to love and protect him in return.

She explored his body with her fingers and her lips, memorizing every plane, every angle, every valley. She needed to remember every nuance of his touch, every subtlety of every caress. She kissed the scar on his shoulder and traced it with the tips of her fingers. She ran her hands over the muscles of his chest and tasted the pulse point at the base of his throat.

He responded in kind, his movements slow and languorous as if he too wanted this night to never end. His lips drifted over her throat and lower to the valley between her breasts. His tongue encircled one nipple, then the next. Her mind fogged with the exquisite sensations and she wanted nothing more than the plea sure of his mouth on her skin. His hand lightly trailed up between her legs to the juncture of her thighs and her legs opened for him. His fingers slipped over her, slick with desire and need. He stroked the wondrous point of passion she'd discovered only with him, and she shuddered beneath his easy, measured rhythm. And gloried in the erotic torture of his touch. Tension built within her and she fought against release.

When she thought she could take no more, he shifted to kneel over her and straddled her legs. She reached up and caressed the hard, velvet length of him with both hands. He groaned at her touch and she stroked him until he quivered beneath her fingers. She guided him downward and he slid into her.

The muscles of his back were tense beneath her hands and she knew he was as taut with need as she. Yet she refused to lose herself in surrender.

Slowly he moved within her. She matched

his movement with her own, with an ease and a joy and a touch of sorrow even the pleasure of their mating couldn't dispel. He thrust harder and faster and she moved with him, allowing sheer sensation to flood her, fill her, consume her. Until at last the tight, aching spiral within her shattered and her body arched upward and she cried aloud with the bittersweet glory of their joining. He groaned against her neck and his body trembled with his own release.

And they were one. Now and always.

And if there was a tear or two upon her cheek at the end, she dashed it away for fear he would notice.

She clung to him for a long time, not wanting as much as a breath of space between them. At last she reluctantly released him and rolled onto her side. Rand wrapped himself around her, his chest against her back, his legs curved behind hers.

"Well, that was certainly . . . certainly . . ." His sigh of contentment shivered through her as if they were still one.

"Yes indeed, it was, most definitely, *certainly*." She laughed lightly in spite of her heavy heart.

"It does strike me, though, that while I have valiantly offered proof of my love for you, you have offered none to me." His voice was teasing.

"Oh? This was not proof?"

"Mutual proof perhaps." He chuckled. "However, it does seem that if I am willing to swim oceans and climb mountains to show my love for you . . ." He nuzzled her ear. "What will you do to show your love for me?"

She paused for a long moment.

"Jocelyn?"

"Whatever I must," she said softly. "Whatever I must."

They made love again in the night until finally Rand fell into a deep, satisfied sleep. But slumber offered no escape for Jocelyn. She propped herself up on her elbow and studied his dear face by the faint light of the stars from the window. His features were relaxed and content, like an innocent, without a care in the world. She did so like watching him sleep.

She ignored the tears that slipped down her cheeks. Was it only a fortnight ago that they'd wed? Did he know her well enough to truly trust her? Their newly acknowledged love was so fragile, so untested, was it strong enough to see them through this?

She watched him for long hours, trying to fix his features forever in her mind. The sweet curve of his lips, the firm line of his jaw, his lashes dark against his cheek, until finally the gray light of dawn peeked through the window.

And she knew their time together was at an end.

Moments later a sharp rap sounded at the door. Rand was awake at once. He stumbled out of bed and strode toward the door, grabbing his dressing gown on the way. Jocelyn followed a step behind.

"Yes," he snapped. "What in the hell is it?"

"A messenger, my lord, bearing a note from Worthington." Chesney's sleepy voice sounded from the hall. "He said it was quite urgent."

"Slip it under the door." Rand cast her a quick glance, then retrieved the folded note that slid into sight. He scanned it, the lines of his face hardening.

"What is it?" She stepped closer, afraid to hear what form Alexei's ruse had taken.

"It's from your brother. He says there was a mishap with the fire they set." His gaze met hers and fear shone in his dark eyes. "Nigel was injured."

"Oh no, not that." Shock swept through her. How could Alexei be so cruel? Surely he knew how close Rand was to the elderly man.

"I have to go back." He raked his fingers through his hair and called through the door. "Chesney, are you still there?"

"Certainly, my lord." Chesney's voice came without hesitation.

"See to it my horse is saddled immediately.

I shall leave at once."

"Yes, my lord." Chesney's voice faded into faint commands in the hall.

"Rand." She stepped to him and framed his face with her hands, meeting his gaze directly. She longed to tell him this was nothing more than Alexei's scheme to lure him away but she couldn't. "Try not to worry. I know Nigel will be all right."

Rand's expression didn't falter but apprehension edged his voice. "He is an old man, Jocelyn. He seems quite healthy now but he barely survived his recent illness. I don't know if he . . ." Rand shook his head and blew a resigned breath. "I just don't know."

"I do," she said with all the conviction of truth. "He will be fine."

He pulled her into his arms and for a long moment they held each other. It wasn't nearly enough but it was the only comfort she could offer. At least he wouldn't have to worry about Nigel for long. Once he reached Worthington Castle he'd know the truth. About his uncle anyway.

He released her with a reluctance she shared. "I have to go."

"I know," she said with a catch in her throat.

In no time at all he was dressed and ready to leave. He took her in his arms and kissed her long and hard.

"I hate to leave you but —"

She quieted him with another kiss, then drew back and gazed into his eyes. "I know."

His gaze searched hers. "No matter what I find, it will be easier knowing you are here waiting for me."

She swallowed hard.

"I could take you with me."

For less than a moment she wanted to agree. Run away from Alexei's plots with Rand and never stop running. But would Alexei permit that? Would Rand ever be safe from his cousin's threats? She shook her head. "You'll travel faster alone."

He nodded and opened the door.

Panic seized her and she grabbed his hand and stared into his eyes. "No matter how far apart we may be, regardless of any distance between us, know that I will always, always love you. Promise me you will remember that."

He cast her a puzzled smile and pulled her hand to his lips, his dark, endless eyes echoing his words. "I promise."

"Now go," she whispered.

He nodded and took his leave. She sagged against the door frame and allowed tears once again to flow, but only for a moment. There was no time for sorrow. Impatiently she swiped at her cheeks, closed the door, and strode across the room to the window. She twisted her ring absently and waited. He appeared on the street beneath her almost at once, mounting his horse and riding off without a backward glance.

And why not? As far as he knew there was nothing behind him to cause concern.

She turned away from the window, washed and dressed hurriedly in one of the gowns she pulled from her bag. The dresses still in the small valise were sadly wrinkled but she didn't particularly care about her appearance at the moment. The irony of the thought struck her. Aunt Louella would love it. She placed her spectacles on her nose defiantly. If she was going to be hauled halfway across Europe she'd prefer to see where she was going.

She started to close the bag, then realized the wrapped portrait was still inside. She pulled it out and set it on the floor, leaning against the wall. Pity she couldn't use it in some way to leave Rand a message. To let him know the truth.

She hesitated to put anything in writing. Who knew what hands a note might fall into? And Alexei had been firm about exactly what to tell her husband.

She glanced out the window. Rand had said the men he had watching the house would leave at dawn. With Alexei scheduled to leave London after daybreak, her husband was confident any threat to her would leave with the prince.

There was no coach yet but she knew she

had precious few minutes to think of something. She paced the room, absently twisting the ring on her finger. If only she'd paid more attention to coming up with her own plan to counteract Alexei through the long hours of the night instead of feeling sorry for herself. Damnation, perhaps she wasn't the least bit intelligent after all. And *pretty* certainly wasn't going to do her much good now.

She looked out the window once again and her heart sank. A traveling coach pulled into sight. There was no time left. She grabbed her bag and started toward the door. She reached to open it and the sapphire caught the light and her eye.

She'd sworn she'd never take it off. What if she did?

The woman she'd been a few weeks ago would have worn it for its beauty and value alone. The woman she was now cared only for the meaning behind it. Would Rand realize the difference?

She pulled off the ring, crossed the room, and placed it on the table beside the bed, then turned to leave.

And prayed her husband would understand exactly what that meant.

Chapter 19

"Jocelyn!"

Rand slammed open the door of his town-house and strode into the entry hall. It had been three full days since he'd left and the thought of what he might find at home terrified him as much as anything in war ever had.

"Jocelyn!" Richard called, close on Rand's heels.

A heavy knot had lain in the pit of Rand's stomach since he'd arrived at Worthington Castle the day before yesterday and discovered there was nothing amiss at all. Nigel was well, Richard had sent no note, and something was very, very wrong.

Rand strode to the foot of the stairs and struggled to keep a note of panic from his voice. "Jocelyn!"

"My lord." Chesney appeared in the hall.

"Chesney," Rand barked. "Where is Lady Beaumont?"

Confusion colored Chesney's face. "She is not with you, my lord?"

"Does it look like she's with me?" Rand snapped.

Richard laid a hand on his arm. "Rand."

Rand drew a calming breath. "Forgive me, Chesney. Now." He struggled to control his voice. "Explain what you meant."

"Lady Beaumont left soon after you did. We thought" — the butler drew his brows together — "rather we assumed, given her comments, or lack of them, she was following you."

"She's been gone for three days then," Rand said slowly.

Chesney stepped to a side table and opened the drawer, pulling out a folded paper and something else Rand didn't see. The butler returned to face Rand and handed him the note. "This arrived for you shortly after her departure."

Rand stared at the paper in his hand but couldn't bring himself to open it.

"And . . ." Chesney hesitated. "The maids found this in your room after she'd gone." He held out Jocelyn's ring. "We thought she'd left it behind simply for purposes of safety in travel."

Rand took the ring numbly. It was cold and heavy in his hand. For the first time in his life he didn't know what to do. His faculties had shut down. His mind no longer functioned. His heart barely beat. Dimly, in the back of his head, he noted he'd seen cases like this before. Men too thoroughly shocked to do anything more than stare. He'd never imagined anything would produce that effect in him.

Jocelyn was gone?

"Chesney," Richard said quietly. "I daresay we could use some brandy."

"It's in here, Richard," Rand responded without thinking and walked into the parlor, sinking into the nearest chair.

Jocelyn had left him?

Richard murmured something to Chesney, and a moment later the butler placed a large glass of brandy on the table beside Rand.

"Aren't you going to read it?" Richard said gently.

"Yes, of course." Rand unfolded the note. The single line seemed to swim before his eyes.

I have gone to Avalonia with Alexei.
                                          Jocelyn

"What does it say?" Richard asked.

Rand held it out to him wordlessly.

Richard took the paper, read it, and blew a long breath. "Bloody hell. I am sorry."

Rand stared unseeing at the ring in his hand. He vaguely heard the murmur of voices in the hall and scarcely noted Richard leaving the room.

Had she decided Alexei was the man she

wanted after all? Was she going to accept his offer of annulment? Was everything between his wife and him a lie?

"I don't believe it for a moment." The new Lady Helmsley, Marianne, marched into the room, followed by her husband and her brother, Richard. She halted in front of Rand's chair and glared down at him. "How could you think such a thing?"

"Come now, Marianne." Richard blew a long breath. "As much as I hate to say this, all her life Jocelyn has been determined to marry well. A prince is what she's always wanted and —"

Marianne whirled to face him. "You, dear brother, have not been around for the past year, and can scarcely say what Jocelyn wants and doesn't want!"

"Well, she was prepared to marry that annoying prince in the first place. Wanted to, in fact," Thomas pointed out. "I knew he was not to be trusted."

Marianne turned on him. "That certainly does little good now!"

"You wouldn't listen to me before," Thomas said indignantly. He strode to the brandy decanter, poured himself a glass, and turned to Richard. "None of your sisters would listen to me about anything. Each and every one is stubborn and opinionated."

Richard snorted. "Welcome to my life."

Someone thrust the glass of brandy into

Rand's hand and he drank it absently.

"No!" Marianne glared at her brother. "If Jocelyn wanted to leave Beaumont, she would never do it like this. She would never sneak off leaving nothing more than a note. If she was going to do something so scandalous and, mind you, she, above any of us, has always been aware of the rules of proper behavior —"

The comments and accusations whirled around him and he could hardly hear the words through the roar of blood in his ears and the twisting pain in his heart.

"That's true enough," Richard muttered. "But if she was —"

"Let me finish, Richard," Marianne snapped.

"What have you done to her?" Richard said in an aside to Thomas.

Thomas shrugged. "Don't blame me. She was like this when you left her and charged me with her protection. It's those blasted books she's always reading. Damned independent heroines."

Rand stared at the ring in his hand and heard her words . . .

I shall never take it off.

"As I was saying, Thomas," Marianne said through clenched teeth. "If she were to do something like this, completely destroy her reputation and ruin her life, she would do in it a spectacular way. It would be her finest moment. A scandal London would talk about for years. Jocelyn has always delighted in being the center of attention, primarily because of her appearance —"

"She wears those spectacles now that you gave her," Rand murmured.

"Really?" she said in surprise. "I never imagined —" She shook her head and continued her tirade. "At any rate, Jocelyn would do something quite dramatic and altogether memorable. She would not slink off in secret."

"I'll give you that, Marianne," Richard said. "But still and all, you have to accept the possibility that she simply could not resist the lure of royalty and great wealth."

"She left the ring," Rand said slowly, hefting the bauble in his hand. "A woman interested in great wealth would not leave something so valuable behind."

No matter how far apart we may be, know that I will always, always love you.

"She didn't leave me," Rand said as if waking from a dream, knowing without doubt, without question, it was the truth.

"Well, she *is* gone," Thomas said apologetically.

"Marianne's right on one count." Rand got to his feet. "If she wanted to leave me for another man, this is not how she would do it. However" — he nodded at Marianne — "I don't agree with your assessment of exactly how she would. From the start she has been honest with me, and if she wanted to end our relationship, she would be honest about that as well."

He shook his head, his certainty growing with every moment. "She didn't go with Alexei because she wanted to. I have no idea how he forced her cooperation, but I'm certain he did. The note that drew me to Worthington has his hand behind it. She would never do anything so cruel."

"She has never been cruel," Marianne said loftily.

"Rand." Thomas's gaze caught his. "What if you're wrong?"

"I'm not," Rand said simply. "I trust her." It was, he realized, a great leap of faith, but somehow he knew, as surely as he knew he would never give her up, he was right. "Since the day we met, Jocelyn has done nothing to deserve anything less than my absolute trust and complete faith."

"Do you think he'll . . ." Marianne paused, unable to say the words.

"Hurt her?" Rand's stomach clenched at the thought. "No."

"However, she might hurt him," Thomas said. "If she really didn't want to go with him, she will be rather, well, peevish." Thomas took a sip of his brandy. "I've seen her peevish before and it's not overly pleasant."

"Not at all." Richard shuddered. "I don't envy the prince, traveling across the continent with a peevish Jocelyn in tow."

"I cannot believe the two of you." Rand looked from one man to the other in disbelief. "This is my wife you're talking about."

"Come now, Rand," Richard chided. "Don't tell us you've never seen her peevish."

"On occasion." Rand glared. "But usually with just cause."

"I'd call this just cause." Thomas nudged Richard with his elbow. "She's more or less been kidnapped."

"She *has* been kidnapped," Rand said.

"God save the prince," Richard said under his breath.

"Stop it at once," Marianne ordered. "There are far more important things to discuss than the state of Jocelyn's temperament."

She stepped to her husband, plucked his glass from his hand and drew a long swallow, then turned to Rand. "Now, it seems to me the real question, if indeed she is not with him of her own accord, is why the prince would want to take Jocelyn —"

"A peevish Jocelyn." Richard raised his glass.

"— with him?" Marianne studied each man in turn. "Well?"

"She's pretty?" Thomas said helpfully.

"No. That can't be it." Richard furrowed

his brow. "After all, the man's a prince. He has his own country, a significant fortune —"

"No doubt with his own portrait on the money," Thomas murmured.

"— and beautiful women probably fall at his feet. No." Richard shook his head. "He would have no need to go to this much trouble. Dragging a peevish," — he glanced at his sister — "or rather a reluctant Jocelyn across half of Europe."

Marianne took a thoughtful sip. "He'd have to realize you'd go after her."

"Of course I'd go after her. I'd never . . . That's it." Rand smacked his palm against his forehead. "He doesn't want her. He wants me."

Richard smirked. "It was the dress, wasn't it? It did complement your eyes."

"What dress?" Thomas looked from Richard to Rand. "And whatever are you talking about?"

"The dress is of no importance." Rand waved off the question. "What is significant is the current state of affairs in Avalonia. Alexei is embroiled in the type of political turmoil that has plagued his country throughout its existence, brought on primarily by fighting for power within the royal family. It's possible he thinks with me by his side, he can quell the unrest peacefully, with a symbolic show of family unity. He did mention something along those lines."

Thomas frowned skeptically. "Why would he want you?"

"Rand is a prince," Richard said in the smug manner of someone who knows a secret no one else does. "A real prince. Alexei's cousin. Jocelyn married her prince after all."

"Aunt Louella will love the irony," Marianne murmured, a stunned look on her face.

Thomas's mouth dropped open. "You never told me."

"You never asked," Rand said firmly.

"It never came up in casual conversation." Thomas glared at his friend.

"I don't consider it important, Thomas, I never have." He studied his friend. "I'm certain there are things about yourself you've never mentioned to me."

"No. Nothing," Thomas said, his manner disgruntled.

"Really." Rand raised a brow. "Until recently, I never knew you wrote poetry."

"Well, that's entirely dif—" Thomas started.

"His poetry is very bad." Richard said with a shrug. "I wouldn't mention it either if I were he."

"Well, you . . . you . . . you paint!" Thomas glared at Richard.

"Yes." Richard grinned. "But I am very good."

"You two sound like children," Marianne

said with a sigh and drained the rest of Thomas's brandy. "And I've had quite enough."

"And I do not have time for such nonsense." Rand bowed toward Marianne. "Lady Helmsley." He nodded at the men. "Gentlemen, I am off to recover my wife."

"She is my sister." Richard stepped forward. "I'm going with you."

"I'm going too," Thomas said quickly. "She was under my protection when all this began."

Richard narrowed his eyes. "You have a new wife to take care of."

"And you have a new daughter." Thomas returned his brother-in-law's stare.

"Oh go, both of you." Marianne huffed. "You obviously see it as some kind of grand adventure. If you don't go, neither of you will be of any use here whatsoever."

"I warn you, however." Rand's voice brooked no nonsense. "This is not a game."

"Of course not," Richard said indignantly. "My sister's life may well be at stake."

"I certainly didn't think it was a game." Thomas huffed. "I have already been shot at, remember?"

"We'll leave at once." Rand turned toward the door.

"You most certainly will not." Marianne shook her head firmly. "You'll leave in the morning. You and Richard are both obviously exhausted. You're bound to have some sort of mishap in your condition. My lord." She laid a hand on Rand's arm and met his gaze. "Rand. You will travel much faster if you are rested. It will do Jocelyn no good if you do not arrive safely."

"Very well then." He could scarcely argue with her. He'd been traveling in one manner or another for nearly a week now and he was, in truth, close to exhaustion.

"Besides." Thomas drew his brows together thoughtfully. "We can't just go off without due consideration. We need a plan."

Marianne rolled her eyes toward the ceiling.

"He's right." Richard nodded, obviously forgetting that Thomas's plans were notorious for being rarely successful.

"Thank you," Thomas said with satisfaction. "First of all, I think . . ."

The conversation eddied about him but aside from an occasional nod or offhand muttering, Rand paid little notice. His own thoughts demanded attention.

He was determined to trust her. Determined to disregard any semblance of doubt. He suspected he would go mad otherwise. He hadn't completely trusted anyone for a long time and he'd never loved before.

Even so, it was difficult to ignore the unanswered questions preying on his mind. Jocelyn's departure was obviously planned;

her behavior on their last night and morning together clearly indicated that. There was no struggle involved, nothing amiss, according to Chesney when Jocelyn left. How had Alexei forced her to accompany him?

No matter how far apart we may be, know that I will always, always love you.

Jocelyn's comment as well as her ring were a message to him as surely if she had written it in her own hand. A message to let him know that she did not leave willingly. That she did not betray him with another man. That she loved him. Of that he was certain.

He'd promised to slay dragons for her and climb mountains and catch stars. And he would no matter what the cost.

And she'd promised to do . . . what for him?

Whatever I must. Had she? And at what cost? He didn't know, wouldn't know, until he found her. At the moment, the answers scarcely mattered.

Still, there was one question, and one question alone, he couldn't get past.

What if he was wrong?

How long had she been cooped up in this blasted coach?

Jocelyn shifted on the leather seat and tried to find a comfortable position, which was next to impossible after four long days of confinement. At least at this point she was alone.

Until yesterday she'd shared the coach with an exceptionally nervous lady-in-waiting who Jocelyn couldn't help but think of, if only to herself, as Lady Insipid. The woman was assigned to accompany her, probably to give a semblance of propriety to what Jocelyn had decided was nothing less than kidnapping.

Hers was one of three coaches escorted by half a dozen armed men on horseback in what amounted to a royal caravan. There were a few other ladies along and several gentlemen she assumed were royal advisers although she hadn't actually met any of them. Even so, she was informed that most of the prince's party and a substantial amount of their luggage would follow later. It was a question of speed, and indeed they scarcely ever stopped for anything other than to change horses, continuing to press onward even at night. This trip was no better than the one she'd shared with Rand and Alexei and not nearly as amusing.

Thus far Alexei had left her quite alone. She suspected his absence was partially due to that pale, frightened lady she'd been trapped with in there, who undoubtedly reported back to Alexei whenever possible that Jocelyn was not being at all pleasant.

Jocelyn snorted in disdain. Pleasant was not part of the arrangement. Besides, she'd never done a thing to Lady Insipid. Not really. Oh, certainly she'd snapped at the cowering creature whenever she'd opened her mouth to attempt useless chatter. And there had been a bit of a rant on Jocelyn's part when the other woman mentioned offhandedly how kind and generous Alexei was. And there was that one moment when Jocelyn could take no more of her insistent attempts at conversation and had tried to throw her bodily out of the carriage. For goodness sakes, they weren't moving all that fast and the lady probably would have suffered no more than a few bruises if she'd rolled when she hit the ground. Still, Jocelyn did give her credit for being surprisingly strong and rather agile as well for such a weak-willed little thing.

Jocelyn blew a long breath and gazed out the window, trying, as she had so often since leaving London, to see the road behind them. To catch any sight of a lone pursuing rider silhouetted against the setting sun. So far she'd seen nothing of any significance. She refused to consider the possibility that Rand would not come after her. He loved her and trusted her and he would not fail her. Still, ignoring the doubts that plagued her when she least expected them was not easy.

What she did not ignore, what indeed she held on to, was the anger that grew with every passing mile and endless day. Anger directed at Alexei, of course, but at herself as well.

How could she have been so stupid as to

take Alexei's threats without question? She should have told Rand at once and she certainly should never have left him. Her husband could protect himself if he knew he was in danger. Surely Rand would have been able to deal with Alexei. Surely . . .

She rested her head against the seat back and heaved a heartfelt sigh. She'd been all over this a hundred times or more and in the end, it all came down to the same thing. Given the same circumstances, right or wrong, she would do exactly as she had.

The coach rumbled to a halt. She did hope the stop meant someone would bring her a food basket; she was rather hungry. There was something about being on the open road that left her famished. They'd eaten all their meals while moving thus far, and while she didn't especially mind it, she'd just as soon consume one meal without the constant lurching and rocking of the coach.

The coach door opened and a basket appeared, carried by Alexei.

"Hungry, my dear?" Alexei climbed into the coach and settled in the seat across from her.

"I was but I find I have quite lost my appetite." She pointedly turned away.

"Pity." He opened the basket and the mouth-watering scent of roasted meat and some kind of pie and who knew what other lovely things filled the air. Lady Insipid had proudly explained that the party had a horseman ride ahead to the next inn to ensure food was ready when the rest of the group arrived. Jocelyn had promptly told her what she could do with her food.

"I shall have to eat it all myself then."

"Not in here you won't," she snapped.

"Oh, but I will," Alexei said firmly.

The carriage lurched forward and they were once again on their way. Alexei obviously planned on staying for a while. She clenched her teeth and resisted the impulse to scream in frustration.

"How could I possibly pass up the opportunity to dine with such a charming companion, even if your behavior thus far has not been particularly charming?" His voice was casual and he rummaged in the basket while he talked. "Poor, dear Countess Lenosky refuses to come anywhere near you."

"Countess Lenosky?" *Lady Insipid.* Jocelyn tried and failed to ignore a sharp stab of guilt. She sighed. "Please offer her my apologies. I was inexcusably —"

"Rude? Ill-tempered?"

"I was going to say peevish," she muttered.

"Disagreeable? Ill-mannered?"

"That's enough."

"In point of fact," he continued as if she hadn't spoken, "it isn't. She is a very nice woman and you have been extremely unpleasant."

"Have I really?" She widened her eyes in feigned surprise. "And what could possibly have caused that?"

"I have no idea," he said mildly.

"No? Well, then, let me prod your memory." She crossed her arms over her chest and glared at him. "I'm here against my will and you've threatened to kill my husband. Why, you're right, Your Highness. Nothing at all has happened that would make me less than gracious."

"Here." He thrust a cloth-wrapped bundle at her.

"What is it?" she said suspiciously, knowing full well it was something delicious.

"I have no idea but it smells quite tasty. However, if you'd prefer —" He started to pull the packet away.

"I'll take it," she said quickly and grabbed the offering. After all, she did have to eat. She simply didn't want to eat with him. "Thank you."

"My pleasure."

She unfolded the cloth to find chunks of roasted meat and potatoes, with a wonderful crusty bread. They ate in silence, he apparently as hungry as she. It was just as good as it smelled and wonderfully satisfying. At last she sat back and studied him.

"I don't suppose —"

He pulled a jug of wine and two glasses from the basket at his feet. She raised a brow. Those horsemen of his certainly were efficient. He poured a glass and handed it to her.

She took a sip. It was red and rich and quite appealing. "You are prepared, aren't you?"

"Not at all." He filled a second glass for himself, then settled back in the seat. "None of this" — he swept a wave at their surroundings — "was planned."

"Why did you do it?"

"I told you. I did not locate the Heavens and my cousin is the next best thing."

She sipped at her wine and considered him. "There's more to it than that, I think."

He laughed. "Isn't saving a crown enough?"

"Perhaps." She paused thoughtfully. "You are an interesting combination, you and your cousin."

"Oh?"

"I watched the two of you together on our trip from Worthington Castle and there were moments, granted not many, but a few when you weren't sniping at one another, when I thought you actually enjoyed each other's company."

"I doubt that." Alexei drew a swallow of his wine. "He doesn't like me very much."

"And that bothers you."

"Not particularly." He shrugged.

"It does. I can see it in your eyes." She

425

leaned forward curiously. "Why is that? It strikes me that there are any number of people who dislike you, up to and including those who would prefer to see you dead. I personally am not especially fond of you."

"My cousin's like or dislike of me is of absolutely no consequence," he said loftily. "Nor is yours."

An odd idea was forming in her mind.

"I don't believe you. Furthermore, I wonder . . ."

"What?"

"Why you would truly want Rand in Avalonia."

Alexei heaved an annoyed sigh. "I have explained —"

She waved aside his words. "Yes, yes, I know. Third branch of the royal family and all that. But you have other family besides that nasty Valentina creature."

"Of course." He nodded. "I have a brother and a sister."

She couldn't possibly be right.

"But they're younger and you're the one everything falls upon. Saving your country and all that. You're the one who will someday be king unless one of those people who doesn't like you does you in first."

"I had almost forgotten that for a moment." He raised his glass to her. "I am grateful for the reminder."

She ignored his sarcasm, trying to refine

the vague thought that had occurred to her. "You and Rand are about the same age. You admire him. You've said as much yourself. You . . ." She narrowed her eyes. "You even trust him."

"He's an honorable man."

Ridiculous of course, yet . . .

"You don't just need Rand's help; you need . . . Of course." She straightened in her seat. "That's it. You need an ally. A friend —"

"That's absurd." His laugh had a bitter edge. "I have no need for friends."

She studied him for a long moment, realization dawning even as she looked at him. Her anger vanished. Her voice was soft. "It must be terribly lonely in those high, lofty places where princes live all by themselves."

"I am not lonely. I have no need for friends or allies or . . ." He clenched his jaw. Perhaps it was the intimacy of the closed coach. Or the strain of recent days. Or he might just have long needed a confidant. A friend. He met her gaze defiantly. "Very well. You win. I confess. Yes, I would like my cousin to join me permanently. To be by my side and help me rule this tiny country that is my life, my blood, my very soul. And whether he admits it or not, it is part of him as well." He shook his head. "The world is changing, Jocelyn. Empires crumble, new ones form, and kingdoms like Avalonia vanish every day, absorbed into greater powers without so much as a by-your-leave.

"A hundred years from now, even fifty years from now, I don't want my country to be nothing more than a footnote in history. I owe my family and my people more than that.

"When I conceived this idea of using you to lure Rand to Avalonia, I knew the possibility that he would choose to stay would be nonexistent. I do not expect that. I can only hope he will help me stabilize the current situation and in the process come to know the land of his ancestors and, with luck, even care about it. There now." Alexei glared. "Are you quite happy?"

"You were never going to kill him, were you?"

"You do refuse to let go of even the most insignificant of matters." Alexei heaved an irritated sigh. "Probably not."

"Probably?"

"Probably," he said firmly. "That's the best I will do. Damnation, Jocelyn, I am a prince. I wield a great deal of power. You would be wise to remember that. I can indeed have someone killed if I so wish."

"But you don't wish to have someone killed." She tried and failed to hold back a grin. "And I would wager that you never have."

He glowered.

"I am getting extremely close."

He reached up and rapped on the roof of the coach. It stopped almost at once.

"You're leaving?" She was surprised and the tiniest bit disappointed.

"I am indeed." He nodded firmly and opened the coach door. "I have had more than enough of your comprehensive assessment of my needs and my nature. If I stay a moment longer, you will no doubt wish to evaluate the rest of my life. My passion for fine art and the reasons I have not yet found a bride who would suit me."

"Well, you could have had me," she teased.

He snorted. "Then I would surely insist on someone's demise. No doubt, whoever introduced me to you."

"You don't mean that."

"Oh, but I do." His voice was resolute. "I will admit, however, that in those rare moments when your mouth is shut, you would have made a lovely queen. But . . ." He stepped down and turned back with a wicked grin. "You would have been a magnificent mistress." He slammed the door before she could so much as gasp. Or, in this case, grin.

She settled back in her seat and considered their odd meeting and the radical change in her perception of him.

It was clear that Alexei never would have had Rand killed. And while his methods were somewhat wicked, and she might never forgive him for letting Rand worry about Nigel, she now had difficulty faulting his purpose. He was as passionate about his country, and his place in it, as Rand was about his. In that the cousins were very similar. After all, Rand had been willing to do whatever he had to for his country. How could she condemn Alexei for the same devotion?

Jocelyn very much suspected Alexei was rather more noble and even good than she'd ever thought. Ruthless when necessary, perhaps, but good nonetheless.

She should still be furious with him for the terror he'd caused her if nothing else, but she wasn't anymore. It was the look in his eyes when he'd talked about Avalonia and the flash of vulnerability when he'd spoken of needing help to rule. She'd only ever thought of the pleasures of being a prince or princess and never considered the awesome responsibilities the position entails. Wouldn't anyone in that position do whatever was necessary to protect the country and the people placed in his charge? How could she fault Alexei for that? How could Rand?

When and if her husband ever arrived, any problems they might need to resolve would simply have to wait. There was the future of a country to consider. The prevention of bloodshed. The stakes involved were far greater than the relationship between a man and a woman.

There was no choice and Rand would have

to understand that. He would have to help Alexei save his country, because it was the right thing to do. And because, regardless of his attitude, it was, in a tiny way at least, his country too.

She just hoped she could convince her husband.

Chapter 20

It had been nearly three weeks, in truth closer to a lifetime, since Jocelyn had said good-bye to her husband.

She paced the long length of the opulent suite given her at the palace of the ruling House of Pruzinsky in the capital of the Kingdom of Greater Avalonia. Her rooms were decorated with the finest fabrics and the most elegant furnishings. Plush carpets lay beneath her feet and magnificent paintings hung on the walls. Alexei had even provided her with a wardrobe worthy of, well, a princess. She had, in truth, everything she'd ever dreamed of.

Except her prince.

Where was Rand? Shouldn't he have been there by now?

If indeed he was coming at all?

She'd expected him to appear every day of their more than two-week journey, and thought certainly he would arrive any minute in the three days since they'd reached the palace. It was becoming harder to ignore the terrifying thought that he might have decided she was not worth following. Or worse, that something had happened to him along the way. She would never forgive herself in either case.

She stepped to the window that overlooked the stunning vista of the mountains and valleys of Avalonia. She scarcely ever took her spectacles off now, and relished the ability to see. Under other circumstances she could quite enjoy her stay. For one thing, everyone here called her *princess,* which was ever so much fun. She'd even become friends with Countess Lenosky, who wasn't as timid as Jocelyn had thought once she got to know her.

Among those she didn't particularly warm to was Alexei's chief adviser, the Count Borloff. He'd accompanied Alexei to England and had returned with them, although Jocelyn hadn't actually been introduced until their arrival in Avalonia. His manner was polite enough, and he was certainly attractive, but time and again she'd caught him studying her when he'd thought she wasn't looking. They'd scarcely exchanged more than a few words, yet she took an instant dislike to him and suspected the feeling was mutual.

And she didn't trust the Princess Valentina one bit. Alexei's cousin was beautiful, but the look in her eye was cold and calculating.

Jocelyn could well believe this was a woman who would not hesitate to do whatever necessary to achieve her ends — including murder. And Jocelyn was certain the princess would indeed enjoy it.

Jocelyn learned Alexei's younger brother and sister had been sent out of the country for their own safety but she did have a brief audience with the king, who was still confined to bed. His physicians said he would fully recover his health and the knowledge seemed to ease Alexei's burden, although he was essentially running the country, and Jocelyn knew it was not easy.

She and Alexei had spent a great deal of time in conversation while on the journey there. Jocelyn was right: Alexei did need a friend and a confidant. Exactly what he'd found in her. He confided his ambitions for his country, his hopes, his dreams. He confessed his fears as well. About Avalonia's survival as an independent nation, the need to modernize, and his own ability to rule. They talked about politics and the world and the future. The more time she spent with Alexei, the more she thought he would one day make an excellent king. A leader his country could depend on. A man his cousin could be proud of.

She leaned against the window frame and gazed into the distance. She would give her husband until the end of the week, and if he had still not arrived, she'd return to England herself and drag him back here. Whether he wanted to come or not. Whether he wanted her or not.

A knock sounded at the door.

"Come in."

The door opened and Countess Lenosky stepped inside without so much as a moment of hesitation. "Your Highness —"

Jocelyn bit back a grin at the title.

"— we have had word from the border. Your husband —"

Jocelyn's heart leapt. *Rand!*

"— will be here any moment." The countess smiled. "I would suggest —"

Jocelyn was out the door before the other woman could finish her sentence. She headed toward the grand chamber where Alexei met with visitors and members of the court, raced through the long corridor, flew down the nearest stairway and straight into Count Borloff.

"His Highness wishes to inform you of the imminent arrival of your husband." Borloff's voice was cool but his gaze was intense. Dislike and an odd touch of apprehension washed through her. "But I see you are already aware of that."

"Yes, thank you." Jocelyn forced a pleasant smile and tried to step around him. "Now, if you don't mind —"

"His Highness also suggests you might

prefer a more private meeting place in which to greet your husband." He directed her from the main corridor into a smaller hall. "I am to escort you."

"How thoughtful." Alexei had proven to be most thoughtful even if she would have preferred he send someone other than Borloff to accompany her. "Where are we going?"

"A parlor in the prince's private apartments." He took another turn and another, then went down a flight of steps, the hallways they passed through progressively less crowded, older in appearance, and obviously far less used.

"He certainly does like his privacy," she murmured.

"Indeed he does," Borloff said curtly.

She'd never been in this part of the palace and would be hard pressed to find her way back. Of course she'd have Rand to help her. Still, the secluded nature of the hall, the fact that they hadn't seen another person for several minutes, and Borloff at her side all combined to send a shiver of unease up her spine.

Her step slowed. "Perhaps it would be best if —"

"Here we are." Borloff pushed open a door and stepped aside, allowing Jocelyn to enter first. She walked into a fair-sized room, sparsely appointed with a pair of loveseats and a handful of chairs and tables against pale silk-paneled walls, bordered with carved moldings. It was elegant enough but there was an odd, unoccupied feel to it. It was not the sort of room she'd imagined Alexei would prefer. She stepped farther in and heard the door close behind her, followed by the faint but distinct click of a key turning in a lock.

Her heart lodged in her throat with the certain knowledge that her instincts about Borloff were right. She had no idea what he was up to but it was obviously no good. She turned toward him with a calm she didn't feel and an imperious tone any princess would envy. "What are you doing? Unlock that door at once."

"I am ensuring privacy, precisely as His Highness commanded." Borloff stood before the door, blocking any possibility of escape.

"I don't believe this is what Alexei had in mind."

"Nonetheless, the door will remain secured. We will not be here for long." A cold, speculative look glittered in Borloff's eye. "I should have taken care of you myself when I had the chance. Now, however, you will prove useful."

I should have taken care of you. The comment caught in her mind.

"Will I?" she said with a calm she didn't feel.

"I find it prudent to leave Avalonia at once, and with you by my side I should have safe conduct to the border." He dropped the key into his waistcoat pocket. "I had hoped your husband would not arrive until after sunset. It would be much easier to slip away from the palace under cover of darkness, but even the best plans can go awry."

"Yes, well, these things happen." She tried to ignore the fear rising within her. Surely she misunderstood what he was saying.

"Valentina has already fled the country, leaving me to face the consequences of our little venture alone." He heaved an overly dramatic sigh. "I should have expected it of her, I suppose. Yet I did so hope she would have a modicum of loyalty within her. It is never wise to place your trust in a woman who is both ambitious and clever. One never knows precisely what game is being played. As for you . . ." He stepped toward her. "What game are you playing, Princess?"

Princess didn't sound so very nice the way he said it. "Game? I have no idea what you mean."

"You know perfectly well what I mean," he snapped.

What was he talking about? She stepped back, stifled her rising panic, and smiled. "No, in truth, I don't."

Borloff laughed. "Come now, His Highness has mentioned to me how much more clever you are than your initial appearance would indicate. You cannot play the pretty, empty-headed ninny with me."

"No?" It was probably best not to confess she wasn't playing. She laughed lightly. "I must have lost my head for a moment. I should have known I couldn't fool you."

"Yet you have." He shook his head slowly. "I have not been able to determine your purpose in not revealing all to the prince."

She's seen us. Take care of it.

Realization slammed into Jocelyn with the force of a physical blow and it took all the control she had not to react. She should have known it sooner. Should have recognized Borloff's voice the moment they met.

This was the unknown man plotting against Alexei. The one in the music room on that fateful first night. The one who'd wanted her dead!

"I confess waiting for your denunciation has been most irritating, and it is my own curiosity on that score that has brought me to the precarious spot I now find myself in."

"I do apologize." She shrugged in a casual manner, as if her heart weren't thudding in terror. "I simply did not think it was advantageous to reveal what I knew."

"Advantageous?" Suspicion sounded in his voice. "For whom?"

"Myself, of course, and . . ." Frantically she groped for an answer. "My husband." Surely Rand had arrived at the palace by now? "I thought perhaps my information about Alexei's most trusted adviser could be used to further my husband's position here."

He stared for a moment, then laughed. The wicked sound echoed in the room and chilled her blood. "Excellent, Princess. Not that I believe you."

"You should," she said in her haughtiest tone. The longer she could engage Borloff in conversation, the better the chances were of someone discovering she was missing. "I find I quite enjoy being a princess. My husband is, in truth, a prince, and would make an excellent ruler."

Borloff raised a brow. "I thought he had no interest in the throne."

"He doesn't at the moment but . . ." She lifted her shoulders dismissively. "It's impossible to predict how his attitude might change once he's here and sees for himself the possibilities. And with your help . . ."

"With my help?" He studied her thoughtfully, then chuckled. "I think not. I have already been duped by one clever, ambitious woman, and I shall not fall into that trap again." He started toward her and she backed away. Terror clogged her throat and she wanted to run, but there was no place to go.

He stalked past her and stopped before the wall panel to the right of the fireplace. Jocelyn quickly surveyed the room in hopes of finding something to use as a weapon against him, but the room was too minimally furnished to provide anything of use.

Borloff studied the molding carved with vines and flowers but directed his comments to her. "Word has reached me that your husband has uncovered my involvement in Valentina's schemes, and I suspect he will not hesitate to inform Prince Alexei the moment he arrives. Therefore it is in my best interest to follow in the princess's footsteps." He turned a carved blossom and the panel swung open into a dimly lit corridor. "This leads to a tunnel beneath the palace and ends in a secret exit in the forest. Only the royal family and a few trusted advisers know of its existence." He turned toward her. "I placed a torch in here before I realized I would never be able to escape without a guarantee of safe passage. You."

"How convenient for you." She stared at him, and abruptly anger overwhelmed her fear. "What kind of a man are you? Alexei is your prince and, I suspect, your friend. He trusts you and yet you betray him. How could you?"

"The usual reasons, Princess. Money. Power. Desire for the wrong woman." His expression hardened. "They are powerful inducements, yet not nearly as strong as my desire at the moment for my life and my freedom. Now." He nodded toward the passageway. "After you."

"No." She crossed her arms over her chest. "I'm not going anywhere. I'm going to stay right here and scream my head off until someone finds me."

"Oh dear, I must have failed to mention a rather pertinent detail." He smacked his palm against his forehead. "What was I thinking? You will accompany me, and you will do so at once" — he pulled a nasty-looking pistol from his waistcoat — "because if you don't I shall be forced to kill you."

"That would be pointless." She raised her chin in defiance. "If you kill me, what happens to your safe passage?"

"Precisely why I would prefer not to. However" — his eyes narrowed — "you have been a great irritant to me, and the pleasure I would derive from your death would provide a certain measure of satisfaction."

She had no doubt he wouldn't hesitate to shoot. There was no choice. "My husband will come after me."

"I don't think so. I have taken steps to ensure he and Prince Alexei know why I am taking you with me and what will happen to you should I become aware of pursuit."

Her stomach clenched. Borloff had planned his escape well.

"Nonetheless," she said staunchly, "he will follow."

"Perhaps." His voice was thoughtful. "Although your disappearance might be ultimately convenient."

"Convenient?"

"Indeed. If even half of that drivel you told me is true, and I really didn't believe a word of it, have you stopped to consider what might happen should your husband decide to take his rightful place as a prince of Avalonia?"

"What do you mean?" An entirely new kind of fear touched her.

"Princes have an obligation when it comes to marriage. They marry for political alliances, for the security of their country. You are quite lovely, and I daresay any man would be happy to have you in his bed, but you are not a suitable wife for a prince. Should he choose to accept his heritage, you would be rather . . . inconvenient."

"He loves me," she said without thinking.

"Love is relative." He shook his head bitterly. "As I well know." He gestured with the pistol. "Now then, if you please."

She walked slowly toward the passageway, trying to think of something, anything to keep her here. She racked her brains but her skills were limited to flirtatious banter and the fluttering of fans and other talents well-bred young ladies practiced. What did a well-bred young lady do when her life was threatened by a madman? Most probably couldn't take so much as a single step. Most would be hysterical and no doubt swoon at the very sight of a pistol.

And if nothing else, Jocelyn Shelton was well bred.

She raised her hand to her throat, widening her eyes and staring at Borloff. "I . . ." Her step faltered. "I feel so . . . so . . ."

"What?" His brows drew together in annoyance.

"I don't know. I . . ." She gasped and closed her eyes and prayed he'd believe her, then crumpled to the floor in her best imitation of a dead faint and tried not to wince when she hit the marble surface. If that thud didn't convince him, nothing would.

"Princess," he snapped.

She'd managed to fall on her side, with her arm half covering her face, shielding her eyes.

"Get up or I will shoot you where you lie." Borloff's voice rang hard and cold in the room.

She willed herself not to move a muscle. Her heart thudded in her ears. If he did shoot, she prayed death would be swift, and not too painful. With luck he'd simply leave without her.

Instead she heard his footsteps approach.

She opened her eyes the barest slit, just enough to see his black boots pause beside her. He nudged her with his foot.

"I will shoot," he warned and nudged her

again, hard. She bit her lip to restrain any response.

She braced herself for the inevitable and waited for an endless moment. At last Borloff heaved a sigh and swore under his breath.

"Get up," he ordered, punctuating his words with more of a kick than a nudge and she couldn't hold back a groan. She had to do something. Anything. If she was going to die, she'd rather meet her end with the courage befitting, well, a true princess. Without a second thought, she grabbed his ankle and pulled with all her might.

It seemed as if she were in a dream, as if time itself slowed and a heartbeat lasted forever. She looked up at Borloff's startled face. He fell backward, his arms flailing, the pistol flying free to skid across the floor and into the passageway. He hit the floor with a solid thump followed by a crack when his head smacked onto the marble tile.

She scrambled to her feet and stared down at him in horror. For a moment hoping she hadn't killed him. For a moment hoping she had.

Unrelenting panic gripped her. She had to get out of here. Now. There were only two ways of escape and she wasn't going into that dark, forbidding tunnel. The key to the door was in Borloff's waistcoat pocket.

She drew a deep breath, bent over him,

and quickly slid her hand into the pocket. She found the key and pulled it out.

His hand gripped her wrist.

Her heart stopped. Borloff's eyes opened and trapped hers. "I think not, Princess."

"Let me go!" Terror flooded through her. She struggled against an iron grip. He reached for her with his free hand. And she did what any well-bred young lady would do.

She sank her teeth into his hand.

He screamed and she wrenched away, scrambling across the room and into the passageway. She stumbled through the opening and spied a lever beside the door. She grabbed it and pulled with everything she had. Across the room Borloff got to his feet and started after her. The door swung closed and his muffled cry of outrage sounded from the other side. A large bolt was affixed to the wall and she put her full weight behind it and shoved, sliding it into place.

Jocelyn rested her forehead against the door and tried to catch her breath. She'd never, even in her darkest nightmares, been so scared. Pounding sounded from the other side and she jumped back. She could hear Borloff's outrage, barely audible behind the thick wall. At least she was safe for the moment. And Borloff was trapped. She still had the key.

She brushed her hair out of her eyes and realized she'd lost her glasses sometime during the struggle. Not that it mattered. There was no light beyond the circle of brightness cast by the wall torch.

She spotted the pistol and carefully picked it up. It was probably loaded, and she knew nothing about guns. She gingerly gripped it and pointed it away from her. She'd hate to accidentally shoot herself. Pity, Rand had chosen to teach her archery instead of shooting. Now *that* was a skill that could come in handy.

Had Rand arrived at the palace? Was he even now searching for her? Worrying about her? And would he find her in time? Before . . . She brushed away farfetched thoughts of what could happen to her. The danger was still all too real. It was entirely possible Borloff knew of another entry from the room she'd locked him in and could come after her. And who knew how long it would take Rand, or anyone else, to look in this part of the palace.

Without warning the door shook. Fear again caught at her but the bolt held. She snatched the torch from its holder and hurried down the dark, cavelike walkway, resisting the urge to run and give in to the panic that still simmered beneath raw nerves. She had a torch, she had a pistol, and she would find her way out. She would not give up.

And she brushed aside the nagging thought

that she could be every bit as trapped as Borloff.

Rand didn't like any of this at all.

Not the armed contingent that greeted them at the border claiming to be an escort provided for their "safety." Not the long, impressive palace gallery he stalked through now, flanked by Thomas on one side and Richard on the other. Not the heavy weight that had taken up permanent residence in the pit of his stomach nearly three weeks ago, a weight prompted by fear, worry, and a frustrating helplessness.

If he'd decided nothing else on their long journey, he'd decided he would do whatever he had to do to get Jocelyn back. Whatever Alexei wanted of him, he would do. Whatever Jocelyn wanted, she could have. Nothing was too much to ask.

She was in his thoughts every hour, every moment. He was certain she was safe, confident Alexei wouldn't harm her, and confident as well that she hadn't left him of her own free will.

He trusted her. He loved her. And if, in those last moments before sleep claimed him at some flea-ridden inn or, more often than not, on the hard ground, a tiny doubt nagged at him that perhaps he was wrong, he ignored it.

Footmen in powdered wigs and formal

livery flanked the ornate doors at the end of the corridor, opening them as they approached with timing so perfect, Rand and the others didn't break stride. He stalked into what appeared to be a grand receiving chamber. A large gathering of ladies and gentlemen, members of Alexei's court, no doubt, parted before them, leaving a clear path to the end of room. A quick glance confirmed Jocelyn was not among the group.

Alexei stood beside an ornate, gilded table speaking with a handful of men. He paused at Rand's approach and turned toward him with a steady, assessing gaze.

"Welcome, cousin," Alexei said mildly.

"Where is she?" Rand's voice was curt.

Alexei's manner was cool, regal. "I do hope your journey was not unpleasant?"

"It was delightful. Thank you for providing me with the opportunity to travel." Rand's eyes narrowed. "Now where is my wife?"

"She should be here momentarily." Alexei's gaze locked with Rand's. "We have a great deal to talk about, cousin."

"Indeed we do. But first —"

"Yes, yes, I know." Alexei waved away his comment. "And frankly I do not wish to begin our discussion without her. She has become an integral part of all this."

"Has she?" Rand narrowed his eyes and pushed aside thoughts of exactly what Alexei meant.

"Do not glare at me like that, cousin." Alexei huffed a short sigh. "She has come to no harm. Neither has she betrayed you in any way. And while she did not accompany me of her own accord" — an unexpected sense of relief rushed through Rand — "she well understands my reasons for luring you here."

"Does she?" Rand said slowly.

"She does indeed." Alexei shook his head. "I will confess I am not in the habit of confiding in women, nor, overall, do I especially trust them. Particularly clever women. However, I have found in your wife both a courageous spirit and a perceptive wisdom."

"Jocelyn?" Thomas said under his breath to Richard.

Richard shrugged.

"You are a lucky man, cousin." Alexei's gaze was unyielding. "And I envy you. And should you decide, for whatever reason, your marriage is not to your liking, there will always be a place for your wife here as my cousin and my friend should she so choose."

Rand clenched his fists by his side, his tone as firm as the prince's. "My wife's place is with me. Always."

"Excellent." Alexei smiled with satisfaction. "Now where is the blasted woman?" He glanced around the room. "She's been counting the minutes until your arrival. I must say, we did expect you before now. Odd

450

that she isn't here yet."

"Your Highness." A short, attractive lady approached and curtsied. "The princess met Count Borloff in the hall and went with him, I believe toward the older section of the palace. I was but a few steps behind her and I heard him say he'd been sent by you to escort her to a place where she could greet her husband" — the lady cast a shy smile at Rand — "in private."

Alexei frowned and shook his head. "I did nothing of the sort."

"Did you say Borloff?" Rand turned to the woman. She nodded. His stomach twisted and he looked at Alexei. "Borloff is your traitor. The man he was working with in London, Strizich, was caught and told us everything. That's what delayed my arrival. I was informed of his capture the morning we planned to leave and felt it imperative to talk to him myself."

"Borloff?" Disbelief and shock washed across Alexei's face.

"Strizich told us Borloff was operating under the orders of the Princess Valentina." He looked at Alexei. "Exactly as you thought."

"Valentina's involvement comes as no surprise, however, this gives me the proof I need to deal with her. But the count . . ." Alexei drew a deep breath and shook his head. "I have known him most of my life and I trusted him implicitly. Indeed, I considered him" — he uttered a short, mirthless laugh — "a friend."

"Your Highness." A page stepped forward, a worried look on his face. "Count Borloff requested I deliver this to you when your cousin arrived. I thought it unusual but . . ." He shook his head helplessly and handed the prince a sealed note.

Alexei tore it open and scanned it quickly, then glanced up to meet Rand's gaze. "Valentina has left the country and Borloff demands safe passage to the border. If he is interfered with in any way he threatens —"

"What?" Rand said sharply, already knowing the answer.

"To kill your wife," Alexei said simply.

"Kidnapped? Again?" Richard said in disbelief.

"That will make her peevish," Thomas murmured.

"If not dead," Rand snapped.

"Captain." Alexei addressed a uniformed officer of the guard. "Station some of your men outside the palace and have as many others as possible scour the north wing. Search every room, particularly those that are not in use. Keep in mind most of those chambers are connected to one another by doors hidden in the panels. We may be able to catch them before they leave the palace itself. Once they are outside, it will be impossible to approach Borloff without notice. You and the rest will come with me."

He looked at Rand. "The palace has been built and rebuilt over and over again. The rooms are not only connected to one another but the ancient part of the building is riddled with secret entrances to a passageway that leads to a tunnel and an exit into the woods. It is the only way to escape the palace undetected. Fortunately, while one can move from room to room without entering the hall, there are only a dozen or so entrances to the passageway. And only a handful of people who know where these are, including myself."

"And Borloff?" Rand asked.

Alexei nodded and blew a long breath. "I never suspected . . ."

Rand started toward the door. "Let's go then."

"Rand." Alexei caught his arm and met his gaze. "I cannot permit Borloff to reach the border. Do you understand? I cannot allow him to escape."

"Regardless of the cost?" Rand's gaze bored into his cousin's and he read resolve and genuine regret in his eyes. At once he understood he and Alexei were more alike than he'd ever suspected. Each would do what had to be done for the sake of his country. No matter the personal sacrifice or how great the price.

A price Rand would not pay without a fight.

He grasped Alexei's hand, his voice as unyielding as any prince's.

"Then we shall make certain it does not come to that."

Chapter 21

Jocelyn had lost all sense of time and place. She might have been wandering through the twisting, turning passageway for minutes, or for hours, searching for a way out. The ground beneath her feet was uneven, cobwebs caught at her hair, the walls were rough, unbroken stone on one side and, here and there, wood on the other. She suspected the way into the palace itself was behind the wooden sections and she would stop and press her ear against the wood hoping to hear voices. So far she'd heard nothing save the scurrying of tiny feet. She tried not to speculate on what kind of creatures they belonged to but the word *rats* kept coming to mind.

Jocelyn realized it would be wiser to stay in one spot, but fear would not allow her to keep still. Terror would crowd in on her if she stopped moving. Even so, she was exhausted. She held the heavy pistol in one hand and the cumbersome torch before her with the other — and she grew weary of struggling against an ever-growing desperation.

Would Rand find her? Would *anyone?*

She tried to fill her head with thoughts of her husband, the joy they'd shared, and the future they would have, but she could not escape the specter of Borloff's vile charges.

He couldn't possibly be right. No matter what Rand ultimately found in Avalonia he would not abandon her. He loved her. He'd said so.

Still, hadn't his country, hadn't England, always come first with him? Hadn't he risked his life over and over again to ensure his nation's victory? And if he decided Avalonia was indeed his country, wouldn't his sense of responsibility and honor dictate this land would be his first priority as well?

No. She pushed the thought firmly aside. Only madness and despair lay in dwelling on such things, and in this eerie passageway she needed all her wits about her if she was to survive. And she was determined to survive.

She rounded a bend and pulled up short. Her heart plummeted.

"I wondered when you would get here." Borloff leaned insolently against the wall, no more than ten feet away, barely within the range of the light from the torch and her own poor vision.

"Do forgive me for keeping you waiting." Her voice was surprisingly clear and calm, and the sound of it boosted her courage.

"You've been a great deal of trouble, Princess." Borloff straightened. "My head aches and my hand throbs and I am not at all inclined to patience at this point."

"Again, my apologies."

"Now." His tone hardened and he took a step forward. "If you would hand over the firearm we shall at last be on our way."

She stepped back. "For a clever woman that would be an exceedingly stupid thing to do."

"Come now, you won't shoot me." He took another step and again she backed up. "I can well see you can barely lift the pistol. You can't hold the torch and shoot at the same time."

"Then it seems there is only one thing to do." She tossed the torch aside and grasped the pistol with both hands, holding it out in front of her. Aiming at his heart. "You're right. This is much better."

"Very good. I should have expected as much." He chuckled and the sound echoed in the distance, mixing with the scrabble of the movement of unseen creatures. She shivered in spite of herself.

"However, as you might notice, on the ground the torch is already beginning to burn itself out. I have no doubt as to my ability to disarm you once that occurs. And I have no fear of the darkness nor of those who inhabit it." His eyes gleamed in the faint light. "Do you?"

"No," she lied and swallowed hard, vaguely noting the sounds of tiny feet seemed to be getting closer.

"We can wait until the light fails but it would be wise of you to give me the pistol now and save yourself undue pain." His voice was cold. "At the moment I am not inclined toward treating you kindly."

"I *will* shoot you." She struggled to keep her hands and her voice steady. The torch flickered and dimmed.

"I doubt that. You don't —" He paused and abruptly she realized the approaching sounds belonged to creatures much more substantial than rats.

"Rand!" she screamed.

At that moment the torch died. Unyielding darkness enveloped her. A body slammed into her, knocking her to the ground, snatching her breath. The pistol flew out of her hands and exploded. Pain ripped through her leg. Loud voices sounded.

Abruptly light from a dozen torches seemed to surround her. She was swept up by strong arms and stared into Rand's wonderful, worried face. She gazed at him and said the first thing that came into her mind.

"Where have you been?"

A scant half hour later, Jocelyn reclined on

a chaise in her rooms. A physician had proclaimed her wound not overly serious. It was cleaned and bandaged and throbbed painfully, but it scarcely mattered.

Rand was finally here and that was *all* that mattered.

She was surprised to see Richard and Thomas had arrived as well. They stood near the door with Alexei, speaking to her husband and the physician. Rand caught her gaze and crossed the room to join her.

He sat down on the edge of the chaise and took her hand. In spite of everything she wanted to say to him, everything she wanted to ask, at this moment she was oddly uncertain and couldn't find the words. Abruptly she realized they'd been apart longer than they'd been together.

"Are you all right?" Rand asked politely as if he too had no idea how to proceed.

"Quite. Thank you for asking," she said, her manner equally reserved. "Of course, I've been kidnapped, kicked —"

"He kicked you?" Anger burned in his dark eyes. "I should have killed him."

"Probably," she said primly. "However, as satisfying as that might be for us both, it's, well, wrong, and it would no doubt be best to let Alexei deal with him. Although it is entirely Borloff's fault that I've been bruised, lost, and shot."

"Actually, you weren't exactly shot." He

grinned. "Apparently the bullet hit the wall and it was a shard of stone that wounded you. Fortunately Borloff took most of the damage. He will not be sitting easily for quite some time."

"Good." She narrowed her eyes. "As you are allowing him to live, it's good to know it will be an uncomfortable existence."

"Well, there is a great deal more. He will face —"

"Rand." She struggled to sit upright and drew a deep breath, searching his eyes. "What took you so long?"

"Jocelyn, the passageway is convoluted and lengthy and we had no idea where Borloff —"

"No, not that." She shook her head impatiently. "What took you so long to get to Avalonia? I'd begun to think you weren't coming. That you didn't trust me. And you didn't love me and" — she swallowed an unexpected sob — "it was all a lie."

He looked firmly into her eyes. "I didn't lie to you."

She stared at him for a long moment and then she was in his arms, his lips crushing hers. He gripped her tightly and she wanted nothing more than to stay in his embrace forever. He smelled of horse and man and open road, and at the moment she'd never smelled anything as wonderful.

"Well, that's a good sign," Richard murmured.

At last Rand drew his head back and gazed at her. "When I arrived home and found you were gone, I feared I might never see you again. I have never been so scared in my life until, of course, we got here and discovered Borloff had taken you." He blew a long breath. "And then I knew true terror."

Her heart twisted. "I'm sorry about leaving. I couldn't say anything to you."

"I assumed as much." He shook his head. "But I knew, the moment I saw your ring —"

"Did you bring it?" she said quickly.

"Yes." He grinned and released her. She held out her hand. He pulled the ring from the pocket of his waistcoat and slipped it on her finger. "And this time do not take it off."

"Never." She beamed at him. "Unless, of course, I have the need to leave you a message as to why —"

"There will be no more such need," he said in a no-nonsense tone that sounded very much like an order. For now she'd let it pass.

"Here. We found these." He pulled her spectacles from the same pocket and passed them to her. She put them on at once. He studied her, and his forehead furrowed. "I am curious, though. How did Alexei get you to go with him anyway?"

She shrugged. "He threatened to have you killed."

"What?" Rand's voice rose.

"I say, that is bad," Thomas said under his

breath. She hadn't noticed the rest of the gathering had joined them.

"Not at all sporting of him," Richard added.

Rand gripped her shoulders and his gaze searched hers. "You should have told me. At once. I would have dealt with it."

"I couldn't tell you." She smiled weakly. "I couldn't take the chance. It was, dear husband, my turn to save your life."

Rand considered her silently for a moment, then nodded. "I should have known it was something like that."

"And I needed you to come to Avalonia," Alexei said simply.

Rand turned to him. "Now you've gone to all this trouble, do you really think my presence will make a difference?"

"I don't know." Alexei ran his hand through his hair, and for a moment Jocelyn could see beyond the prince to the man. "The public revelation of Valentina's and Borloff's treachery will have an impact of course, but whether anything else will make a difference remains to be seen."

"You have to help him," she said to Rand, pinning him with a firm look.

"Help him?" Rand blew a short breath. "Why should I help him? The man kidnaps you and threatens to kill me —"

"Not at all the way to win friends," Thomas said under his breath to Richard.

Jocelyn ignored them. "Yes, I know he did and that was wrong of him."

"Wrong?" Rand's brow lifted.

"Very wrong," she said firmly.

"Given his actions, tell me, dear wife, why I should help him in any way whatsoever."

"I knew you would ask and I have given this a great deal of thought." She met her husband's gaze directly. "I can give you any number of reasons why you should help him." She ticked them off on her fingers. "Because, first of all, whether you like it or not, he is your cousin. Your blood relation. Unless I'm mistaken, aside from your mother and Nigel you have very little family, very few relations. You can't afford to squander them aimlessly.

"Secondly, again whether you like it or not, this tiny realm you have never claimed is a part of your heritage. As much a part of who you are as anything else about you. Some Avalonian blood does indeed flow in your veins.

"Your grandfather died for this country. Your great-grandfather was king. And until today, you have never been asked to so much as acknowledge that fact. Now you are needed. If you owe nothing else to your ancestors you owe them this. In a very real sense it is, well, your duty." Even as she said the words she wondered if this was a mistake. If indeed Borloff was right, that encouraging Rand . . . No. She firmly set the thought aside. "And because" — she lifted her chin — "I think it is the right thing to do."

Rand stared at her.

"Good argument," Thomas murmured.

"I didn't know she had it in her," Richard said softly. "I am extremely proud of you, little sister."

"Thank you." She turned to her husband and held her breath. "Well?"

Rand heaved a resigned sigh and glanced at Alexei. "What exactly do you want me to do? Crush peasants? Lead troops?"

"My dear cousin." Alexei sniffed with indignation. "This is the nineteenth century. The House of Pruzinsky rules not merely by virtue of heredity but by the will of the people. And it is to the people we must appeal."

"How progressive of you," Rand muttered.

"He's very progressive." Jocelyn nodded. "However, he doesn't need you to crush peasants, which does sound rather ridiculous, but he needs you in the same way he needed those jewels he was looking for. The whole concept is really rather simple." She pulled her brows together. "I find I think better when I walk. Do you mind?"

"Not at all." A slight smile lifted Rand's lips and he helped her to her feet.

She hooked her arm through his and

started to pace. Her leg ached a bit but she had no problem walking. "As I started to say, you represent the third branch of the House of Pruzinsky. With you at Alexei's side, the people will see the royal family is truly united and because of that can be trusted to lead. People do need to have confidence in their leaders, you know. Once they see the two of you, meet you, speak with you, or whatever else Alexei has in mind, well, with luck, any dissension Valentina and Borloff might have encouraged can be laid to rest."

She waved her free hand for emphasis. "It's symbolic more than anything else and has to do, on the surface at least, with tradition and the hereditary monarchy. But it's really a matter of politics, as everything is these days. It all strikes me as being very similar to campaigns for Parliament, at least that's the way I understand —" Abruptly she realized all four men stared at her with similar expressions of surprise. She halted and looked around the group. "What?"

"It's the glasses, isn't it," Richard asked cautiously.

"Excellent analysis." Alexei smiled.

Thomas stared. "I never knew she had this in her either."

"I did," Rand said staunchly and drew her back into his arms. "Pretty, smart, and long legs. I am indeed a lucky man."

"Yes, you are." She grinned up at him.

Alexei cleared his throat. "If you are quite finished, we need to be on our way."

"Now?" She pulled away from Rand and glared at Alexei, not bothering to hide her disappointment. "This minute?"

"I am sorry to cut short your reunion but it is necessary to leave at once." Alexei's voice was curt. "We have engagements around the country that we have been forced to rearrange over and over while awaiting your husband's arrival. Additional delay would only hurt our cause."

"Doesn't he have time for . . . well" — she slanted an innocent glance at her husband — "a quick bath?"

Rand choked back a laugh.

"Our first meeting is in a town about an hour's ride from here. You may bathe and change there." Alexei flicked his gaze over Rand. "I have arranged for suitable clothing."

"You do think of everything." Rand studied him. "How did you know I would agree?"

"I didn't." Alexei smiled at Jocelyn. "She did."

Thomas nudged Richard, and her brother stepped forward. "We're coming too."

"Why?" Alexei frowned.

"We think it's in Rand's best interest that we accompany him." Thomas crossed his arms over his chest. "You did threaten to kill him."

"He threatened to have him killed," Jocelyn

pointed out. "It's not the same thing at all."

"Very well." Alexei sighed. "You may come along if you wish."

Her brother and brother-in-law traded smug grins.

"Well, if they're going" — Jocelyn looked from one man to the next — "I want to go as well."

"No," all four said in unison and varying degrees of firmness.

She planted her hands on her hips and glared. "Why not?"

"These are unsettled times. And while I do not anticipate trouble" — Alexei shook his head — "it simply would not be wise."

"Jocelyn." Rand placed two fingers under her chin and tilted her face upward toward his. "Keep in mind this is not an order, it is simply a request. I don't know what to expect. Now that Borloff is taken care of, I am certain you are safe here and I would very much appreciate it if this is where you would remain. In addition, you've been injured. You have done quite enough."

She did so hate to give in and, more than that, hated to see him leave without her, but in truth her leg did throb. And remaining behind in a luxurious palace where she was called *princess* had a certain appeal. She sighed in surrender. "As you wish."

"Besides," Alexei said casually, "if you come with us I will not be able to use your safety as leverage to assure your husband's cooperation."

Rand's eyes narrowed. Richard stepped forward. Thomas glared.

"Oh stop that, Your Highness, no one believes you anymore. Rand" — she turned to her husband — "he's not going to hurt me and he never would have hurt you. He's not that kind of prince."

Alexei's brows pulled together in annoyance. "I do wish, my dear Lady Beaumont, that just once you would take my position and the power I hold seriously."

"Come now, Alexei, you can be very annoying and very arrogant but, well, I believe your heart is in the right place." She smiled sweetly.

Rand bit back a laugh. Richard snorted. Thomas chuckled.

Alexei ignored them all. "We shouldn't be gone more than a week."

"A week? Another week?" Dismay sounded in her voice and she met her husband's gaze. "Perhaps I was wrong. Perhaps you shouldn't go after all."

Rand laughed. "I can scarcely back out of it now. Remember, my love, you have made this my duty."

"I know and I haven't changed my mind; I just didn't realize we wouldn't get a chance to even . . ." She groped for the right word. "Well . . . play billiards before you left."

"We do indeed need to have a long . . . game." The light in Rand's eyes told her he knew full well billiards was not the game she had in mind. And obviously not what he wanted either.

"Do go if you're going." She glanced around the room. With the exception of Nigel, these were the most important men in her life. "And take care of one another." She cast a firm glance at Richard and Thomas. "I am placing my husband's care in your charge." She turned to Rand. "And I expect you to watch over Alexei. His position and the power he's always going on about make him a target for any number of lunatics."

Rand studied her carefully, an odd expression on his face. "Jocelyn, you aren't . . ." Rand glanced at Alexei and back to her. "That is, you don't have . . . What I mean to say . . ."

"I like Alexei very much. As strange as it sounds, given the circumstances, we've become friends. But you, my darling husband" — she stepped closer and wrapped her arms around his neck — "are my one and only prince."

"It shall be very hard to leave." His dark eyes smoldered.

"It shall be very hard to let you leave." Her voice was low and sultry.

"I will, however, ask a promise of you before I go."

"Anything." The word was practically a sigh. She realized she would indeed do anything for this man and suspected he would do anything for her.

"Swear to me, this time" — his lips quirked upward in a wry grin — "you will stay exactly where I leave you."

A Treatise on Princes and Princesses and Other Related Matters
by Lady Jocelyn Shelton, age 10

Part Three: Other Related Matters

Now that I have written all this down, especially the part about what a real princess should be, I'm not certain that a true princess should care as much about things like castles and servants and fortunes as I do. At least I'm sure that's what my sisters would say. So I don't know if any of this will come true even if it would be ever so nice.

But this is my treatise and my wish and it is supposed to be about my dreams and what I want. And I do very much want a prince and want to be a princess. At least I think I do. But I am still a bit young and might forget all about this when I grow up although I doubt it.

Even so, I expect that I will still want to be very, very happy someday. Preferably with a prince. Or at least with a gentleman who will think I am a princess whether he is a prince or just a very nice man.

471

And if he is just an ordinary gentleman I should like him to be handsome and kind and rich. Or at least not very poor.

I do think it would also be very nice if he loved me and I loved him and if he was willing to slay just one dragon for me.

And then I will be content to live happily for all the rest of my days.

Chapter 22

The week drew to a close, and as his horse turned back toward the palace, Rand realized that his attitude about his cousin, as well as his own life, was forever changed.

Rand had accompanied Alexei, together with Thomas and Richard, a small honor guard, and various advisers, to towns and villages and hamlets. They spoke to large crowds in town squares and small groups in cafes and on street corners. Rand wondered if, indeed, they had talked to every resident of Avalonia or if it only seemed that way.

Slowly, grudgingly, Rand grew to admire his cousin. Even, perhaps, like him. Rand's role was minimal in their tour. He was a presence more than anything else and he had a great deal of time to simply observe the crown prince. He was surprised to find Alexei's behavior with ordinary people far less arrogant and much more relaxed than Rand had expected. As if Alexei was first an Avalonian and only then a prince. One of the people. And by the end of the week Rand no longer thought of the farmers and merchants and noblemen of the small kingdom as Alexei's people alone but Rand's people as well.

It was an odd realization. By birthplace and title, Rand considered himself a true Englishman. A viscount and as much, if not more, a product of his father's blood as his mother's. Still, his wife was right. He might deny it all he wished but there was a touch of Avalonia in his blood.

And more than a touch of Jocelyn in his heart.

His thoughts turned to her constantly, much as they had when he and Thomas and Richard had undertaken their long journey to rescue her. Even now the word drew a smile to his lips. She'd needed no rescue although none of them, including Jocelyn herself, fully realized it at the time. She was, in truth, the one rescuing him. Doing what she thought she had to do to save his life. And fully capture his heart in the process.

Had he ever had so remarkable a gift? So remarkable a woman?

Was anything too great to offer her in return?

"This week has passed swiftly, cousin." Alexei rode up beside him. "And it has been most successful."

"That was my impression." Rand nodded thoughtfully. "Your fears and your father's should be set to rest." He studied the other man curiously. "Your people quite like you, you know."

"For the moment, but tomorrow all may change." Alexei's voice was wry. "The world is not as it was when my grandfather ruled. When a single man held a power that commanded armies and reshaped nations. Power granted to him by birth and his own strength and determination. I daresay it will not be that way again."

"Is that bad?"

"Probably not." Alexei shrugged. "Merely different. Power, in this day and age, has to be deserved, granted if you will, and the right to rule earned." He fell silent, lost in his own thoughts, and the two men rode quietly side by side. Rand noted to himself once again how very different his cousin was than he'd first thought. At last Alexei spoke. "I owe you a great debt."

"I believe I may be the one who owes you." Rand blew a long breath. "I have learned a lot in recent days. Not merely about my lineage and history but about duty and responsibility, and, perhaps, about myself."

Alexei smiled but didn't respond.

"Regardless of the manner in which you lured me here," Rand said slowly, "I am glad that I came."

"There is to be a ball tonight upon our return. I was hoping to make an announcement. Have you given any more consideration to my offer?" Alexei's tone was offhand, as if it didn't matter, but both men knew it did. Very much.

"Indeed I have."

"And will I be able to make such an announcement?"

"I think so." Rand smiled. "I have thought of little else, save my wife."

Alexei chuckled. "She is much more than I imagined when we first met. I must admit I do envy you."

"She still has one sister as yet unwed." Rand made the offer with a straight face.

Alexei looked at him skeptically and Rand grinned. Alexei laughed and shook his head. "Thank you, but I will pass. It should take me some time to recover from the effect of one sister. I am not ready for another."

"There is no one like Jocelyn," Rand said firmly.

"And that, cousin, is at once a pity" — Alexei said with a sincere note in his voice, then chuckled — "and a blessing."

"And I, *cousin*" — Rand grinned — "am damned grateful for both."

The ball was well under way, however Rand, Alexei and the others had yet to appear. Still, Jocelyn had been told their arrival was imminent. She forced herself to at least give the appearance of patience. To behave like a proper viscountess — a proper *princess*.

There was a lighthearted gaiety in the ballroom tonight that was in stark contrast to the subtle air of tension Jocelyn had noted in the court from the time of her arrival until recent days. According to Countess Lenosky, who was a veritable font of knowledge, the prince's tour of the country had been decreed a success and peace was assured for now.

Jocelyn kept one eye on the entry but chatted and danced and smiled until she thought her face would crack. She wanted her husband here and now. Wanted to see for herself he was well and safe. Wanted to know from his own lips what he thought of the country of his ancestors. And wanted to know if everything between them had changed.

What if Borloff was right? What if after this taste of being a prince, and indeed that's what this last week had been, he decided that's what he now wished? And wished as well an appropriate wife in the bargain?

The music stopped abruptly and a trumpet sounded. All eyes turned toward the ballroom doors.

A majordomo in formal livery, from his powdered wig to his highly polished shoes, stepped forward. "His Royal Highness, heir to the throne of the Kingdom of Greater

Avalonia, Servant of the Doctrines of St. Stanislaus, Guardian of the Heavens of Avalonia, Protector of the People, Crown Prince Alexei Frederick Berthold Ruprecht Pruzinsky."

Alexei stepped into the room and paused. Elegantly clad in white and gold, a military uniform of sorts, he looked every inch a royal prince. A future king. The ladies curtsied and the gentlemen bowed in a brightly colored wave that washed outward from the door through the room.

The majordomo waited for the crowd to straighten, then continued. "His Royal Highness, Prince Randall Charles Frederick Beaumont."

Rand stepped into the room behind Alexei and once again the gathering bowed and curtsied. All except for Jocelyn, who stared in shock and struggled to keep her mouth from dropping open.

Rand wore a uniform similar to Alexei's, a dark, royal blue as opposed to white, but festooned with the same gold braids and buttons as his cousin's. A sword hung at his side. He looked magnificent. He looked like a prince. For the first time it struck her that indeed he was a prince.

He spotted her at once and started toward her. Without warning she was as nervous as if she'd never met him before. Never spoken to him, danced with him, shared his bed. Her blood roared in her ears and she scarcely noted the grand introductions of the Marquess of Helmsley or the Earl of Shelbrooke.

Fear seized her. The man walking toward her was not the viscount she'd married, but a prince of a sovereign nation. Would he still wish to be wed to the sister of a mere earl? Would he want the annulment Alexei had offered? Would he now want a real princess?

Rand stepped before her and stopped. His expression was cool, collected, his dark eyes somber without a hint as to his thoughts. She stared at him and realized if indeed he was different, so too was she. She was not the same woman she'd been the first time they met. And realized as well, whatever his intent, she could bear it. At least in public.

Without thinking she held out her hand. He drew it to his lips; his gaze caught hers; his voice was low. "I have a question to ask you."

She swallowed hard. Her voice trembled. "Yes?"

Rand's gaze bored into hers. "Count Borloff and the Princess Valentina have been stripped of their wealth, their property, and their titles. He has been imprisoned and she will never be permitted to step foot in Avalonia again. Alexei has offered me their fortunes and lands. He has asked me to remain here as a prince of the realm and his chief adviser. To help him one day rule Avalonia."

"Yes?" A lump lodged in her throat. "And?"

His eyes gleamed with an intense light. "I told him I could not accept his offer without the consent of my wife."

"Your wife?" She could barely get the words out.

"My wife." He kissed her hand and straightened.

"Then you want me to remain your wife?" She held her breath.

He frowned. "Of course. How could you possibly —"

Relief washed through her and she no longer cared about the rules of etiquette governing royal affairs. She threw herself into his arms with a cry of joy. "Oh Rand," she sobbed, "I thought, I was afraid that you didn't want . . ."

He held her tight and whispered against her hair. "What?"

"I was afraid." She pulled away and looked up at him. "The way you're dressed and what you were saying, I thought you might want . . . might need a real princess."

"My darling, Jocelyn." He grinned. "You are a real princess. My own princess, and you always shall be."

"Ahem." Alexei appeared beside them with an annoyed frown. Thomas and Richard grinned at his side. "I daresay I am getting quite tired of interrupting the two of you."

She laughed and sniffed back a tear.

"You shall have to adjust, cousin," Rand growled but released her nonetheless.

"This infuriating husband of yours says he will not accept my offer without your complete support and approval. I think it's ridiculous, of course, but there you have it. Well?" Alexei studied her. "What's it to be?"

She considered her husband thoughtfully. "If you accept, will we have a castle? A castle with a proper roof?"

Rand glanced at Alexei. The prince shrugged. "You may take your pick of castles."

She narrowed her eyes. "And a great number of servants?"

Rand nodded. "As many as you wish."

"And ladies-in-waiting?" she asked. "I've always rather wanted ladies-in-waiting."

"If you like." Rand smiled. "You may have everything you've ever wanted. It can all be yours."

"When I was a small girl, I wished for this and buried my wish beneath the light of a full moon. It was a delightful dream and I cherished it for a very long time. Still . . ." She paused for a moment, knowing full well there was really no decision to make. She drew a deep breath and turned to Alexei. "It is a wonderful offer, Your Highness, and I know what it would mean to you but" — she shook her head regretfully — "I think not."

"What?" Alexei stared.

"You owe me ten pounds," Thomas said under his breath to Richard, who simply grinned.

"Why on earth not?" Shock colored Rand's face.

"Because, my dear darling husband" — she cast him her warmest smile — "regardless of what Alexei or anyone else says you're really not an Avalonian, not in your heart; nor are you a prince."

"He most certainly is," Alexei snapped.

"I'm not?" A stunned smile curved Rand's lips.

"No indeed. You are a subject of His Majesty" — she aimed a pointed look at Alexei — "King George. You are the sixth Viscount Beaumont and an Englishman." She stepped closer and stared into his dark, wonderful eyes. "All of which makes you, well, you. If you accepted Alexei's offer you wouldn't be the man I married. The man I love."

"And you don't mind giving up all of this?" Rand said carefully.

"Perhaps a little." She flashed him a grin.

"Actually," Alexei said, "even if he does not choose to remain here, the property and the wealth and his royal title will still be his."

"That's lovely but" — she shrugged — "it's of no importance. You're what I want, Rand, all that I want, and it scarcely matters if you own all of Avalonia or nothing more than a cottage and little money —"

"Little money?" Thomas scoffed. "Don't you think it's time you told her the truth?"

"I've tried," Rand said with a laugh.

"Jocelyn," Thomas said firmly. "Rand's fortune is quite acceptable, even a bit impressive, and Beaumont Abbey is scarcely a cottage."

"His finances come as no surprise at this point but . . ." She stared at her husband, who had the good grace to look a bit sheepish. "Beaumont Abbey? You have an abbey?"

"It's a small abbey," he said weakly.

"Yet another lie of omission on your part, I suppose?" Jocelyn raised a brow.

"I simply failed to correct a few erroneous assumptions you made." His manner was lofty.

"Why?" Richard's brow furrowed. "I always thought money was rather attractive to women."

"That's part of it. At first I remained silent because she was, well, rather mercenary, and I thought it served her right. And later I didn't want her to care for me only because I had a fair amount of money. And then it was, well, too late." He smiled apologetically. "I am sorry."

"Is there anything else you haven't told me? Anything not relating to government secrets, that is," she added quickly.

He shook his head firmly. "I can't think of a thing.

"I'm not sure I believe you." She cast him a wicked smile. "But I do believe I'll have a great deal of fun finding out."

He pulled her back into his arms and she didn't care at all if they were being watched by princes and brothers and all of Avalonia as well.

"The fun, my dear wife," he said as his lips brushed hers, "will be entirely mutual."

And she knew without question, without doubt that everything she'd ever wanted, everything she'd ever dreamed of, her every wish had indeed come true. Regardless of title or position, of castle or cottage, of great fortune or nothing at all, with this man she was, for now and for always . . .

A prince's bride.

Epilogue

Six weeks later . . .

It was generally acknowledged, in the circles of polite society, that London was simply not tolerable in late summer. Never tolerable, regardless of the circumstances. Yet each and every guest who flitted through the elegant townhouse, from jaded rakes to overdressed matrons, from sweet young things in the first flower of youth to elderly lords on their last legs, from the envious to the curious to the vastly amused, had indeed made the journey to town for this overly crowded and overly warm event.

And why not? It wasn't every day London discovered one of its own was the prince of a foreign realm. That he was handsome and mysterious and had furthermore stolen the heart of the season's loveliest incomparable from beneath the nose of his equally royal cousin made this reception given by his mother an event not to be missed by anyone who was anyone. Or at least anyone who believed himself to be anyone, which was nearly as important.

The Dowager Viscountess Beaumont, Natasha Beaumont, surveyed the scene with satisfaction. She'd always believed the world was filled with intriguing possibilities and wonderful twists and turns. And didn't all this prove her point?

She watched her son and his bride, in the midst of the crowd, have eyes only for each other and smiled at the knowledge that somehow life did indeed work out as it should. And if their adventures were over and they would not be easing unrest or fleeing for their lives or uncovering conspirators, well, love was a great adventure and that was just beginning.

Still, Natasha wondered if there weren't too many questions unanswered for the adventures to be over for long. If not for Rand and Jocelyn, then for others. Perhaps even herself. Why, the possibilities were endless.

She glanced at the wall beside her and the small portrait of the father she had never known and smiled.

"Indeed, Father, the world is full of possibilities."